THE DEATH OF IVAN ILYCH
AND OTHER STORIES

T0385389

THE DEATH OF IVAN ILYCH

AND OTHER STORIES

Leo Tolstoy

Translated from the Russian by
Louise and Aylmer Maude

Selected and with a preface by
Sharon Cameron

riverrun

The translation first published in 2001 by Alfred A. Knopf
This edition published in 2022 by

riverrun

An imprint of

Quercus Editions Limited
Carmelite House
50 Victoria Embankment
London EC4Y 0DZ

An Hachette UK company

A CIP catalogue record for this book is available
from the British Library

PB ISBN 978 1 52941 057 0
EBOOK ISBN 978 152941 058 7

10 9 8 7 6 5 4 3

Typeset by CC Book Production
Printed and bound in Great Britain by Clays Ltd, Elcograf S.p.A.

Papers used by riverrun are from well-managed forests and other responsible sources.

Contents

Preface

L EO TOLSTOY (1828–1910) was born to Russian aristocrats on the family estate, Yasnaya Polyana, eight miles from
Moscow. By the end of his life he had written in many genres for
different audiences. He wrote 'God Sees the Truth but Waits'(1872)
and 'A Prisoner in the Caucasus' (1872) for children, and folk-
loric fables for all, among them 'The Three Hermits' (1886) and
'Alyosha Gorshok' (1905). He wrote ethical treatises: *What Then
Must We Do?* (1882), in which he argued against the injustices of
contemporary Russian society, urging intellectuals, aristocrats, and
artists who exploit the poor working on their behalf to see that
such a division of labour blights their own spiritual welfare; and in
Why Do Men Stupefy Themselves? (1891), he maintained that the
aim of alcohol, opium, and other drugs is to permit actions that
violate reason and conscience. *What Is Religion and of What Does
Its Essence Consist?* (1902), 'The Kingdom of Heaven Is Within
You' (1893), and 'An Appeal to the Clergy' (1902) shocked the

Russian Orthodox Church – which excommunicated him – by announcing that Church doctrine and rituals, the belief in Christ's divine origin, in such miracles as 'the turning of water into wine' and even in 'the resurrection of Jesus himself', are 'fairy-tales' extraneous to the essence of religion, which is discovered only in the love preached by the Gospels. In the didactic 'What Is Art?' (1898), Tolstoy answered: 'an infection', in which the author inflames an audience to share his feelings. Tolstoy also wrote essays on vegetarianism (1891), against capital punishment (1900), and on the education of peasant children: 'Who Should Learn Writing of Whom; Peasant Children of Us, or We of Peasant Children?' (1862) is an early essay whose counter-intuitive conclusion might give a reader pause about the periodization of Tolstoy's thinking, which is in some ways continuous. The tenets of Tolstoy's ethical, social, and religious writing are reflected in many of his post-1880s stories, and anticipated by *A Confession* (1882), in which he rejected the Orthodox Church, his own debauched way of living, and the fame that followed the titanic *War and Peace* (1865–69) and *Anna Karenina* (1875–78). In an 1878 letter to his editor, Nikolai Strakhov, Tolstoy called the energy that fuelled his famous novels 'the energy of delusion'. Yet he is celebrated for these novels. He himself could not assign *War and Peace* to any 'existing genre'. It is 'neither novel, nor tale, nor long poem, nor history'. In their unwavering gaze at the disparity between what is abstract or imaginary and what is actual, Tolstoy's stories are also *sui generis*.

As in *War and Peace*, in the sketch 'Sevastopol in May 1855'

(1855) the arc of a historical event, here the Crimean War, indiscriminately shapes destinies. In the battle scenes 'vanity, the wish to shine, the hope of rewards, of gaining a reputation' mingle with chaos and terror. Thus Adjutant Kalugin, 'who always boasted that he never even stooped', finds himself in a 'trench almost on all fours' as a bomb 'whizzed near him . . . He was surprised at himself but no longer strove to master his feelings.' Sentences that amass quantities – the fates of 'hundreds of men with curses or prayers on their parched lips' who 'crawled, writhed, and groaned'; 'a heap of corpses'; 'a million fires flashed from all sides' – shift to close-ups of individual confusion in which no one can fathom what will happen, or what *has* happened, to him. In 'What Men Live By' (1881), no man knows 'whether, when evening comes, he will need boots for his body, or slippers for his corpse'. When a bomb explodes near Captain Praskukhin, he thinks, 'Thank God, I'm only bruised,' though in fact he had been 'killed on the spot by a bomb-splinter in the middle of his chest', while Lieutenant-Captain Mikhaylov – sure he is dying: '"That's the soul passing," he thought' – is only 'slightly wounded in the head by a stone'. The technique of juxtaposing panoptic scenes of carnage with their reflection in the consciousness of multiple characters, each experiencing disorientation in his own flawed way, is amplified on the vaster canvas of *War and Peace*, but 'Sevastopol in May 1855' has an analogous feel of inclusiveness.

Throughout Tolstoy's stories, there is inclusiveness of a

different order – not the pairing of wide-angle and close-up lenses that melds communal and personal nightmares, but an array of calamities from which there seems no escape. 'Oh, my God, what is it for?' moans the invalid whose lungs are failing in 'Three Deaths' (1859), because 'the word "die" . . . frightened her'. 'This is impossible . . . There must be some remedy for it,' Eugene, in 'The Devil' (1890), says to himself, 'walking up and down in his room', tormented by an 'almost insane' lust for Stepanida, the peasant who was his mistress before his marriage to Liza, now five months pregnant. In 'The Kreutzer Sonata' (1889), Pozdnyshev is intoxicated by the fantasy of his wife's infidelity with a violinist: 'The more I gazed at those imaginary pictures, the stronger grew my belief in their reality.' Their 'vividness . . . seemed to serve as proof that what I imagined was real'. In 'Polikushka' (1863), delusion slides into hypocrisy when the mistress of a large estate laments the 'evil' of 'dreadful money' after a peasant's loss of fifteen hundred rubles leads to a hanging and a baby's drowning. Her display of empathy for the well-being of her serfs (she 'would do everything in my power . . . sacrifice everything' to keep them from 'harm') does not blind the reader to the emptiness of that hyperbole, because she will not spend 'three hundred rubles' to save her serfs from a conscription, which will almost certainly end in death. In 'Father Sergius' (1898), penance for such posturing is deluded – as when, to chastise his pride, his atheism, his coldness, his attraction to a feeble-minded girl, his seductive thought of suicide, Sergius cuts off 'the forefinger of his left hand . . . below the second joint', but cannot cut off his transgressive thoughts.

Tolstoy's antidotes to delusion, fear, jealousy, and even madness have a common ethical thread pulled through the fabric of very different narrative structures, themes, and genres, whether realist, didactic, or parabolic. In the stark form of homily that shapes Tolstoy's late stories, life considered as one's own has no rational meaning. Thus, in the fable 'Esarhaddon, King of Assyria' (1903), an old man tells the King that his enemy 'Lailie is you, and the warriors you put to death were you also. And not the warriors only, but the animals which you slew . . . Life is one in them all, and yours is but a portion of this same common life.' Narrative structure dramatizes that realization in the rival logics of violence and love that shape the two halves of 'The Forged Coupon' (1904). Stepan's indiscriminate enmity towards all leads to a series of thefts and murders, and has a domino effect in crimes perpetrated by his victims, until he encounters Mariya Semyonovna, who – before he slits her throat – admonishes: 'Have pity on yourself . . . it's your own soul you are destroying.' When her benevolence dawns on him, the domino effect of love transforms not only him but his fellow prison inmates, who 'began to understand this new world of spiritual aspirations which had formerly seemed . . . alien'.

How truth thickens and deepens when it migrates from didactic fable to the raw experience of a visceral awakening is one of the thrills of Tolstoy's stories. Insight can bypass thought and rise up mutely in an instant, as in 'Master and Man' (1895), or seem as though it will never arrive, as in 'The Death of Ivan Ilych' (1886). In 'Master and Man' the miserly Vasili Andreevich's 'sole aim' is to calculate 'how much money he had made and might still make . . . how much other people he knew had made', and 'how he, like them, might still make much more'. When he sets out with his peasant Nikita to buy land for which he plans to offer 'only a third of its real value', they get lost in dark, cold, 'drifting snow' and 'wind [that] blew in their faces'. In the blizzard, the men sink into a ravine and begin to freeze to death until, 'with the same resolution with which he used to strike hands when making a good purchase, [Vasili] began raking the snow off Nikita' and 'lay down on top of him . . . it seemed to him that he was Nikita and Nikita was he, and that his life was not in himself but in Nikita'. Comparably, in 'Memoirs of a Madman' (1884), the fear of death 'tearing asunder within me' inexplicably dissolves before a greater mystery, while in 'How Much Land Does a Man Need?' (1886), Pahom believes he can outrun fear by dint of physical prowess. Though he dreams of a man 'prostrate on the ground', and even sees that 'the man was dead, and that it was himself' lying there, he waves away the premonition that he could become such a man, and muses: 'What things one does dream.'

'The Death of Ivan Ilych' exposes the illusions of everyday existence behind such incredulity – the zeal for comfort, pleasure, money, property, and status, which is incompatible with a finality that renders acquisitions paltry. The pity of such ambitions is signalled in Tolstoy's startling sentence, 'Ivan Ilych's life had been most simple and most ordinary and therefore most terrible'. Viktor Shklovsky underscores Tolstoy's conviction that in the 'most ordinary . . . the habitual, nothing amaz[es]' or even penetrates. He writes that, in 'The Death of Ivan Ilych', when, Tolstoy 'rip[s] off the mask of all that is mundane', a flood of sensation immediately testifies to the deception of the 'ordinary', which stupefies with its abstractions, hypocrisy, and platitudes. Nowhere is there more visceral intensity than in the torment of Ivan Ilych's shock that death, an unnameable '*It*', could come to *him*, 'little Vanya', who once had 'a mamma and a papa'. Yet death's insistent presence does not exhaust itself: '*It* would come and stand before him and look at him, and he would be petrified and the light would die out of his eyes, and he would again begin asking himself whether *It* alone was true.' Above all, there is no response that could assuage what he sees: 'what was worst of all was that *It* drew his attention to itself not in order to make him take some action, but only so that he should look at *It*, look it straight in the face', and 'suffer inexpressibly'. Only unflinching, acquiescent to mental and physical pain, stripped of consolation, can Ivan Ilych see that 'all that for which he had lived . . . was not real at all, but a terrible and huge deception which had hidden both life and death'. For the critic Natalie Repin, therefore, the question is not 'whether there is life after death', but 'whether there could be life before [the lived immediacy of] death'. Ivan Ilych's dying, unmediated by screens, prompts the memory of other palpable experiences: 'the raw shrivelled French plums of his childhood', the 'flavour and the flow of saliva when he sucked their pits', and, in 'the present', the pressure of 'the button on the back of the sofa and the creases in its morocco'. The same sensory awareness prompts him suddenly to see past his own suffering to his family's misery ('Yes, I am making them wretched') and to experience a common wonder, his capacity to feel for them. The flavour of the plums Ivan Ilych sucked as a child, and the terrible *It* that is death, though antitheses, are more like each other than the damasks, plants, rugs, positions, pleasures in which he has shrouded himself. In 'The Death of Ivan Ilych' life and death converge beneath the surface of unlikeness to disclose the essential strangeness of their connection.

'There is always at the centre' of Tolstoy's writing, Virginia Woolf wrote, some character 'who gathers into himself all experience, turns the world round between his fingers, and never ceases to ask, even as he enjoys it, what is the meaning of it'. Tolstoy's stories – in which nothing but artifice seems omitted – also include experience that is meaningless, even nonsensical, as when this locution pops into the mind of a cavalry officer in 'Two Hussars' (an early story from 1856): '"I have ruined my youth!" he suddenly said to himself, not because he really thought he had ruined his youth . . . but because the phrase happened to occur to him.' Or as when, in 'The Devil', Eugene (who that morning 'rode' out to his 'fallow land which was to be sprinkled with phosphates', to revitalize the soil) returns home to Liza, his pregnant wife, and, still obsessed with his mistress, 'repeat[s] a phrase he had just uttered . . . The phrase was: "phosphates justify" – what or to whom, he neither knew nor reflected.' 'Phosphates', plant nutrients, are lodged in Eugene's mind from the visit to his fields, where they will be disseminated so seedlings can grow. Coupled with 'justify', the agricultural moves to a juridical, even a theological, context, where the phrase is intoned as a mantra. Approaching the house, Eugene sees that 'they were beating a carpet on the grass', and marvels:

'What a house cleaning Liza has undertaken! . . . Phosphates justify . . . Yes, I must change my boots, or else "phosphates justify", that is, smell of manure, and the manageress is in such a condition . . . Because a new little Irtenev is growing there inside her,' he thought. 'Yes, phosphates justify.'

The association of soil and womb is warranted by the fertilization of each. But nothing *justifies* Eugene's consuming lust for his mistress when a 'little Irtenev' is 'growing', or explains the logic of the unnerving mantra whose repetitions derange his thinking. 'Phosphates justify' is like a maxim with a meaningful sound, but a different kind of nonsense from 'I have ruined my youth'. Tolstoy's stories voice thoughts that barge unharnessed into consciousness, as in 'Two Hussars', or as in 'The Devil', whose conflict erupts in a stutter – two examples from Tolstoy's vast repertoire of surprises by which everyday sense is punctured, riddled, or broken open to arresting new associations and energies.

The majority of the stories collected here were written after 1880; after, that is, the spiritual crisis Tolstoy documented in *A Confession*. They appear in these volumes in roughly chronological order, with the exception of 'Family Happiness' (1859), which I have moved to Volume Two, where it precedes 'The Devil' (1890) and 'The Kreutzer Sonata' (1889), Tolstoy's other unhappy-marriage stories, written thirty years later.

With the exception of 'Family Happiness' (translated by J. D. Duff) and 'After the Ball', 'The Forged Coupon', 'Alyosha Gorshok', and 'What For?' (translated by Nigel J. Cooper), the stories in this edition are translated by Louise and Aylmer Maude, of whom Tolstoy wrote: 'Better translators . . . could not be invented.' The Maudes were friends of Tolstoy and translated his major works. Aylmer Maude, who also wrote a classic two-volume biography of Tolstoy, supplied the notes for the stories translated by the Maudes; Nigel Cooper annotated those which he translated.

Sharon Cameron

Sevastopol in May 1855

I

SIX MONTHS HAVE passed since the first cannon-ball went whistling from the bastions of Sevastopol and threw up the earth of the enemy's entrenchments. Since then bullets, balls, and bombs by the thousand have flown continually from the bastions to the entrenchments and from the entrenchments to the bastions, and above them the angel of death has hovered unceasingly.

Thousands of human ambitions have had time to be mortified, thousands to be gratified and extend, thousands to be lulled to rest in the arms of death. What numbers of pink coffins and linen palls! And still the same sounds from the bastions fill the air; the French still look from their camp with involuntary trepidation and fear at the yellowy earth of the bastions of Sevastopol and count the embrasures from which the iron cannon frown fiercely;

as before, through the fixed telescope on the elevation of the signal-station the pilot still watches the bright-coloured figures of the French, their batteries, their tents, their columns on the green hill, and the puffs of smoke that rise from the entrenchments; and as before, crowds of different men, with a still greater variety of desires, stream with the same ardour from many parts of the world to this fatal spot. But the question the diplomatists did not settle still remains unsettled by powder and blood.

II

A REGIMENTAL band was playing on the boulevard near the pavilion in the besieged town of Sevastopol, and crowds of women and military men strolled along the paths making holiday. The bright spring sun had risen in the morning above the English entrenchments, had reached the bastions, then the town and the Nicholas Barracks, shining with equal joy on all, and was now sinking down to the distant blue sea which, rocking with an even motion, glittered with silvery light.

A tall infantry officer with a slight stoop, drawing on a presentable though not very white glove, passed out of the gate of one of the small sailors' houses built on the left side of the Morskaya Street and gazing thoughtfully at the ground ascended the hill towards the boulevard. The expression of his plain face did not reveal much intellectual power, but rather good-nature, common sense, honesty, and an inclination to respectability. He was badly built, and seemed rather shy and awkward in his movements. His cap was nearly new, a gold watch-chain showed from under his thin cloak of a rather peculiar lilac shade, and he wore trousers with foot-straps, and clean, shiny calf-skin boots. He might have been a German (but that his features indicated his purely Russian origin), an adjutant, or a regimental quartermaster (but in that case he would have worn spurs), or an officer transferred from the cavalry or the Guards for the duration of the war. He was in fact an officer who had exchanged from the cavalry, and as he ascended the hill towards the boulevard he was thinking of a letter he had received from a former comrade now retired from the army, a landed proprietor in the government of T——, and of his great friend, the pale, blue-eyed Natasha, that comrade's wife. He recalled a part of the letter where his comrade wrote:

'When we receive the *Invalide*,* Pupka' (so the retired Uhlan called his wife) 'rushes headlong into the hall, seizes the paper, and runs with it to a seat in the arbour or the drawing-room — in which, you remember, we spent such jolly winter evenings when your regiment was stationed in our town — and reads of *your* heroic deeds with an ardour you cannot imagine. She often speaks of you. "There now," she says, "Mikhaylov is a *darling*. I am ready to cover him with kisses when I see him. He is fighting

---

* The Army and Navy Gazette.

3

on the bastions and is certain to receive a St George's Cross, and they'll write about him in the papers," &c., &c., so that I am beginning to be quite jealous of you.'

In another place he wrote: 'The papers reach us awfully late, and though there are plenty of rumours one cannot believe them all. For instance, those musical young ladies you know of, were saying yesterday that Napoleon has been captured by our Cossacks and sent to St Petersburg, but you can imagine how much of this I believe. One fresh arrival from Petersburg tells us for certain (he is a capital fellow, sent by the Minister on special business – and now there is no one in the town you can't think what a *resource* he is to us), that we have taken Eupatoria [so that the French are cut off from Balaclava], and that we lost two hundred in the affair and the French as many as fifteen thousand. My wife was in such raptures that she *caroused* all night and said that a presentiment assured her that you distinguished yourself in that affair.'

In spite of the words and expressions I have purposely italicized, and the whole tone of the letter, Lieutenant-Captain Mikhaylov thought with an inexpressibly melancholy pleasure about his pale-faced provincial friend and how he used to sit with her of an evening in the arbour, talking *sentiment*. He thought of his kind comrade the Uhlan: how the latter used to get angry and lose when they played cards in the study for kopek points and how his wife used to laugh at him. He recalled the friendship these people had for him (perhaps he thought there was something more on the side of the pale-faced friend): these people and their surroundings flitted through his memory in a wonderfully sweet, joyously rosy light and, smiling at the recollection, he put his hand to the pocket where this *dear* letter lay.

From these recollections Lieutenant-Captain Mikhaylov involuntarily passed to dreams and hopes. 'How surprised and pleased Natasha will be,' he thought as he passed along a narrow side-street, 'when she reads in the *Invalide* of my being the first to climb on the cannon, and receiving the St George! I ought to be made full captain on that former recommendation. Then I may easily become a major this year by seniority, because so many of our fellows have been killed and no doubt many more will be killed this campaign. Then there'll be more fighting and I, as a well-known man, shall be entrusted with a regiment . . . then a lieutenant-colonel, the order of St Anna . . . a colonel . . .' and he was already a general, honouring with a visit Natasha, the widow of his comrade (who would be dead by that time according to his day-dream) – when the sounds of the music on the boulevard reached his ears more distinctly, a crowd of people appeared before his eyes, and he realized that he was on the boulevard and a lieutenant-captain of infantry as before.

III

HE WENT first to the pavilion, beside which stood the band with soldiers of the same regiment acting as music-stands and holding open the music books, while around them clerks, cadets, nursemaids, and children formed a circle, looking on rather than listening. Most of the people who were standing, sitting, and sauntering round the pavilion were naval officers, adjutants, and white-gloved army officers. Along the broad avenue of the boulevard walked officers of all sorts and women of all sorts – a few of the latter in hats, but the greater part with kerchiefs on their heads, and some with neither kerchiefs nor hats – but it was remarkable that there was not a single old woman amongst them – all were young. Lower down, in the scented alleys shaded by the white acacias, isolated groups sat or strolled.

No one was particularly glad to meet Lieutenant-Captain Mikhaylov on the boulevard, except perhaps Captain Obzhogov of his regiment and Captain Suslikov who pressed his hand warmly, but the first of these wore camel-hair trousers, no gloves, and a shabby overcoat, and his face was red and perspiring, and the second shouted so loud and was so free and easy that one felt ashamed to be seen walking with him, especially by those white-gloved officers – to one of whom, an adjutant, Mikhaylov bowed, and he might have bowed to another, a Staff officer whom he had twice met at the house of a mutual acquaintance. Besides, what was the fun of walking with Obzhogov and Suslikov when as it was he met them and shook hands with them six times a day? Was this what he had come to hear *the music* for?

He would have liked to accost the adjutant whom he had bowed to and to talk with those gentlemen, not at all that he wanted Captains Obzhogov and Suslikov and Lieutenant Pashtetski and others to see him talking to them, but simply because they were pleasant people who knew all the news and might have told him something.

But why is Lieutenant-Captain Mikhaylov afraid and unable to muster courage to approach them? 'Supposing they don't return my greeting,' he thinks, 'or merely bow and go on talking among themselves as if I were not there, or simply walk away and leave me standing among the aristocrats?' The word 'aristocrats' (in the sense of the highest and most select circle of any class) has lately gained great popularity in Russia, where one would think it ought not to exist. It has made its way to every part of the country, and into every grade of society which can be reached by vanity – and to what conditions of time and circumstance does this pitiful propensity not penetrate? You find it among merchants, officials, clerks, officers – in Saratov, Mamadishi, Vinnitza, in fact wherever men are to be found. And since there are many men, and consequently much vanity, in the besieged town of Sevastopol, aristocrats are to be found here too, though death hangs over everyone, be he aristocrat or not.

To Captain Obzhogov, Lieutenant-Captain Mikhaylov was an

aristocrat, and to Lieutenant-Captain Mikhaylov, Adjutant Kalugin was an aristocrat, because he was an adjutant and intimate with another adjutant. To Adjutant Kalugin, Count Nordov was an aristocrat, because he was an aide-de-camp to the Emperor.

Vanity! vanity! vanity! everywhere, even on the brink of the grave and among men ready to die for a noble cause. Vanity! It seems to be the characteristic feature and special malady of our time. How is it that among our predecessors no mention was made of this passion, as of small-pox and cholera? How is it that in our time there are only three kinds of people: those who, considering vanity an inevitably existing fact and therefore justifiable, freely submit to it; those who regard it as a sad but unavoidable condition; and those who act unconsciously and slavishly under its influence? Why did the Homers and Shakespeares speak of love, glory, and suffering, while the literature of today is an endless story of snobbery and vanity?

Twice the lieutenant-captain passed irresolutely by the group of his aristocrats, but drawing near them for the third time he made an effort and walked up to them. The group consisted of four officers: Adjutant Kalugin, Mikhaylov's acquaintance, Adjutant Prince Galtsin who was rather an aristocrat even for Kalugin himself, Lieutenant-Colonel Neferdov, one of the so-called 'two hundred and twenty-two' society men, who being on the retired list re-entered the army for this war, and Cavalry-Captain Praskukhin, also of the 'two hundred and twenty-two'. Luckily for Mikhaylov, Kalugin was in splendid spirits (the general had just spoken to him in a very confidential manner, and Prince Galtsin who had arrived from Petersburg was staying with him), so he did not think it beneath his dignity to shake hands with Mikhaylov, which was more than Praskukhin did though he had often met Mikhaylov on the bastion, had more than once drunk his wine and vodka, and even owed him twelve and a half rubles lost at cards. Not being yet well acquainted with Prince Galtsin he did not like to appear to be acquainted with a mere lieutenant-captain of infantry. So he only bowed slightly.

'Well, Captain,' said Kalugin, 'when will you be visiting the bastion again? Do you remember our meeting at the Schwartz Redoubt? Things were hot, weren't they, eh?'

'Yes, very,' said Mikhaylov, and he recalled how when making his way along the trench to the bastion he had met Kalugin walking bravely along, his sabre clanking smartly.

'My turn's tomorrow by rights, but we have an officer ill,' continued Mikhaylov, 'so—'

He wanted to say that it was not his turn but as the Commander of the 8th Company was ill and only the ensign was left in the company, he felt it his duty to go in place of Lieutenant Nepshisetski and would therefore be at the bastion that evening. But Kalugin did not hear him out.

'I feel sure that something is going to happen in a day or two,' he said to Prince Galtsin.

'How about today? Will nothing happen today?' Mikhaylov asked shyly, looking first at Kalugin and then at Galtsin.

No one replied. Prince Galtsin only puckered up his face in a curious way and looking over Mikhaylov's cap said after a short silence:

'Fine girl that, with the red kerchief. You know her, don't you, Captain?'

'She lives near my lodgings, she's a sailor's daughter,' answered the lieutenant-captain.

'Come, let's have a good look at her.'

And Prince Galtsin gave one of his arms to Kalugin and the other to the lieutenant-captain, being sure he would confer great pleasure on the latter by so doing, which was really quite true.

The lieutenant-captain was superstitious and considered it a great sin to amuse himself with women before going into action; but on this occasion he pretended to be a *roué*, which Prince Galtsin and Kalugin evidently did not believe and which greatly surprised the girl with the red kerchief, who had more than once noticed how the lieutenant-captain blushed when he passed her window. Praskukhin walked behind them, and kept touching Prince Galtsin's arm and making various remarks in French, but as four people could not walk abreast on the path he was obliged to go alone until, on the second round, he took the arm of a well-known brave naval officer, Servyagin, who came up and spoke to him, being also anxious to join the aristocrats. And the well-known hero gladly passed his honest muscular hand under the elbow of Praskukhin, whom everybody, including Servyagin himself, knew to be no better than he should be. When, wishing to explain his acquaintance with this sailor, Praskukhin whispered to Prince Galtsin that this was the well-known hero, Prince Galtsin – who had been in the Fourth Bastion the day before and seen a shell burst at some twenty yards' distance – considering himself no less courageous than the newcomer, and believing that many reputations are obtained by luck, paid not the slightest attention to Servyagin.

Lieutenant-Captain Mikhaylov found it so pleasant to walk in this company that he forgot the nice letter from T—— and his gloomy forebodings at the thought of having to go to the bastion. He remained with them till they began talking exclusively among themselves, avoiding his eyes to show that he might go, and at last walked away from him. But all the same the lieutenant-captain was contented, and when he passed Cadet Baron Pesth – who was particularly conceited and self-satisfied since the previous night, when for the first time in his life he had been in the bomb-proof of the Fifth Bastion and had consequently become a hero in his own estimation – he was not at all hurt by the suspiciously haughty expression with which the cadet saluted him.

IV

BUT THE lieutenant-captain had hardly crossed the threshold of his lodgings before very different thoughts entered his head.

He saw his little room with its uneven earth floor, its crooked windows, the broken panes mended with paper, his old bedstead with two Tula pistols and a rug (showing a lady on horseback) nailed to the wall beside it,* as well as the dirty bed of the cadet who lived with him, with its cotton quilt. He saw his man Nikita, with his rough greasy hair, rise from the floor scratching himself, he saw his old cloak, his common boots, a little bundle tied in a handkerchief ready for him to take to the bastion, from which peeped a bit of cheese and the neck of a porter bottle containing vodka – and he suddenly remembered that he had to go with his company to spend the whole night at the lodgements.

'I shall certainly be killed tonight,' thought he, 'I feel I shall. And there was really no need for me to go – I offered to do it of my own accord. And it always happens that the one who offers himself gets killed. And what is the matter with that confounded Nepshisetski? He may not be ill at all, and they'll go and kill me because of him – they're sure to. Still, if they don't kill me I shall certainly be recommended for promotion. I saw how pleased the regimental commander was when I said: "Allow me to go if Lieutenant Nepshisetski is ill." If I'm not made a major then I'll get the Order of Vladimir for certain. Why, I am going to the bastion for the thirteenth time. Oh dear, the thirteenth! Unlucky number! I am certain to be killed. I feel I shall . . . but

---

* A common way in Russia of protecting a bed from the damp or cold of a wall, is to nail a rug or carpet to the wall by the side of the bed.

somebody had to go: the company can't go with only an ensign. Supposing something were to happen ... Why, the honour of the regiment, the honour of the army is at stake. It is my *duty* to go. Yes, my sacred duty ... But I have a presentiment.'

The lieutenant-captain forgot that it was not the first time he had felt this presentiment: that in a greater or lesser degree he had it whenever he was going to the bastion, and he did not know that before going into action everyone has such forebodings more or less strongly. Having calmed himself by appealing to his sense of duty – which was highly developed and very strong – the lieutenant-captain sat down at the table and began writing a farewell letter to his father. Ten minutes later, having finished his letter, he rose from the table his eyes wet with tears, and repeating mentally all the prayers he knew he began to dress. His rather tipsy and rude servant lazily handed him his new cloak – the old one which the lieutenant-captain usually wore at the bastion not being mended.

'Why isn't my cloak mended? You do nothing but sleep,' said Mikhaylov angrily.

'Sleep indeed!' grumbled Nikita, 'I do nothing but run about like a dog the whole day, and when I get fagged I mayn't even go to sleep!'

'I see you are drunk again.'

'It's not at your expense if I am, so you needn't complain.'

'Hold your tongue, you dolt!' shouted the lieutenant-captain, ready to strike the man.

Already upset, he now quite lost patience and felt hurt by the rudeness of Nikita, who had lived with him for the last twelve years and whom he was fond of and even spoilt.

'Dolt? Dolt?' repeated the servant. 'And why do you, sir, abuse me and call me a dolt? You know in times like these it isn't right to abuse people.'

Recalling where he was about to go, Mikhaylov felt ashamed.

'But you know, Nikita, you would try anyone's patience!' he said mildly. 'That letter to my father on the table you may leave where it is. Don't touch it,' he added reddening.

'Yes, sir,' said Nikita, becoming sentimental under the influence of the vodka he had drunk, as he said, at his own expense, and blinking with an evident inclination to weep.

But at the porch, when the lieutenant-captain said, 'Goodbye, Nikita,' Nikita burst into forced sobs and rushed to kiss his master's hand, saying, 'Goodbye, sir,' in a broken voice. A sailor's widow who was also standing in the porch could not, as a woman, help joining in this tender scene, and began wiping her eyes on her dirty sleeve, saying something about people who, though they were gentlefolk, took such sufferings upon themselves while she, poor woman, was left a widow. And she told the tipsy Nikita for the hundredth time about her sorrows; how her husband had been killed in the first *bondbarment*, and how her hut had been shattered (the one she lived in now was not her own) and so on. After his master was gone Nikita lit his pipe, asked the landlady's little girl to get some vodka, very soon left off crying, and even had a quarrel with the old woman about a pail he said she had smashed for him.

'But perhaps I shall only be wounded,' reasoned the lieutenant-captain as he drew near the bastion with his company when twilight had already begun to fall. 'But where, and how? Here or here?' he said to himself, mentally passing his chest, his stomach, and his thighs in review. 'Supposing it's here' (he thought of his thighs) 'and goes right round ... Or goes here with a piece of a bomb, then it will be all up.'

The lieutenant-captain passed along the trenches and reached the lodgements safely. In perfect darkness he and an officer of Engineers set the men to their work, after which he sat down in a pit under the breastwork. There was little firing; only now and again there was a lightning flash on our side or *his*, and the brilliant fuse of a bomb formed a fiery arc on the dark, star-speckled sky. But all the bombs fell far beyond or far to the right of the lodgement where the lieutenant-captain sat in his pit. He drank some vodka, ate some cheese, smoked a cigarette, said his prayers, and felt inclined to sleep for a while.

V

PRINCE GATSIN, Lieutenant-Colonel Neferdov, and Pras-kukhin – whom no one had invited and to whom no one spoke, but who still stuck to them – went to Kalugin's to tea.

'But you did not finish telling me about Vaska Mendel,' said Kalugin, when he had taken off his cloak and sat in a soft easy chair by the window unbuttoning the collar of his clean starched shirt. 'How did he get married?'

'It was a joke, my boy! . . . *Je vous dis, il y avait un temps, on ne parlait que de ça à Pétersbourg*,'* said Prince Galtsin, laughing as he jumped up from the piano-stool and sat down near Kalugin on the window-sill,† 'a capital joke. I know all about it.'

And he told, amusingly, cleverly, and with animation, a love story which, as it has no interest for us, we will omit.

It was noticeable that not only Prince Galtsin but each of these gentlemen who established themselves, one on the window-sill, another with his legs in the air, and a third by the piano, seemed quite different people now from what they had been on the boulevard. There was none of the absurd arrogance and haughtiness they had shown towards the infantry officers; here among themselves they were natural, and Kalugin and Prince Galtsin in particular showed themselves very pleasant, merry, and good-natured young fellows. Their conversation was about their Petersburg fellow-officers and acquaintances.

'What of Maslovski?'

---

* 'I tell you, at one time it was the only thing talked of in Petersburg.'
† The thick walls of Russian houses allow ample space to sit or lounge at the windows.

'Which one – the Leib-Uhlan, or the Horse Guard?'

'I know them both. The one in the Horse Guards I knew when he was a boy just out of school. But the eldest – is he a captain yet?'

'Oh yes, long ago.'

'Is he still fussing about with his gypsy?'

'No, he has dropped her . . .' And so on in the same strain.

Later on Prince Galtsin went to the piano and gave an excellent rendering of a gypsy song. Praskukhin, chiming in unasked, put in a second and did it so well that he was invited to continue, and this delighted him.

A servant brought tea, cream, and cracknels on a silver tray.

'Serve the prince,' said Kalugin.

'Isn't it strange to think that we're in a besieged town,' said Galtsin, taking his tea to the window, 'and here's a *pianerforty*, tea with cream, and a house such as I should really be glad to have in Petersburg?'

'Well, if we hadn't even that much,' said the old and ever-dissatisfied lieutenant-colonel, 'the constant uncertainty we are living in – seeing people killed day after day and no end to it – would be intolerable. And to have dirt and discomfort added to it—'

'But our infantry officers live at the bastions with their men in the bomb-proofs and eat the soldiers' soup', said Kalugin, 'what of them?'

'What of them? Well, though it's true they don't change

their shirts for ten days at a time, they are heroes all the same – wonderful fellows.'

Just then an infantry officer entered the room.

'I . . . I have orders . . . may I see the gen— His Excellency? I have come with a message from General N——,' he said with a timid bow.

Kalugin rose and without returning the officer's greeting asked with an offensive, affected, official smile if he would not have the goodness to wait; and without asking him to sit down or taking any further notice of him he turned to Galtsin and began talking French, so that the poor officer left alone in the middle of the room did not in the least know what to do with himself.

'It is a matter of the utmost urgency, sir,' he said after a short silence.

'Ah! Well then, please come with me,' said Kalugin, putting on his cloak and accompanying the officer to the door.

'*Eh bien, messieurs, je crois que cela chauffera cette nuit,*'* said Kalugin when he returned from the general's.

'Ah! What is it – a sortie?' asked the others.

'That I don't know. You will see for yourselves,' replied Kalugin with a mysterious smile.

'And my commander is at the bastion, so I suppose I must go too,' said Praskukhin, buckling on his sabre.

---

* 'Well, gentlemen, I think there will be warm work tonight.'

No one replied, it was his business to know whether he had to go or not.

Praskukhin and Neferdov left to go to their appointed posts.

'Goodbye, gentlemen. *Au revoir!* We'll meet again before the night is over,' shouted Kalugin from the window as Praskukhin and Neferdov, stooping on their Cossack saddles, trotted past. The tramp of their Cossack horses soon died away in the dark street.

'*Non, dites-moi, est-ce qu'il y aura véritablement quelque chose cette nuit?*'* said Galtsin as he lounged in the window-sill beside Kalugin and watched the bombs that rose above the bastions.

'I can tell *you*, you see . . . you have been to the bastions?' (Galtsin nodded, though he had only been once to the Fourth Bastion). 'You remember just in front of our lunette there is a trench –' and Kalugin, with the air of one who without being a specialist considers his military judgement very sound, began, in a rather confused way and misusing the technical terms, to explain the position of the enemy, and of our own works, and the plan of the intended action.

'But I say, they're banging away at the lodgements! O-ho! I wonder if that's ours or *his*? . . . Now it's burst,' said they as they lounged on the window-sill looking at the fiery trails of the bombs crossing one another in the air, at flashes that for a

---

* 'No, tell me, will there really be anything tonight?'

moment lit up the dark sky, at puffs of white smoke, and listened to the more and more rapid reports of the firing.

'*Quel charmant coup d'oeil! a?*'* said Kalugin, drawing his guest's attention to the really beautiful sight. 'Do you know, you sometimes can't distinguish a bomb from a star.'

'Yes, I thought that was a star just now and then saw it fall . . . there! it's burst. And that big star – what do you call it? – looks just like a bomb.'

'Do you know, I am so used to these bombs that I am sure when I'm back in Russia I shall fancy I see bombs every starlight night – one gets so used to them.'

'But hadn't I better go with this sortie?' said Prince Galtsin after a moment's pause.

'Humbug, my dear fellow! Don't think of such a thing. Besides, I won't let you,' answered Kalugin. 'You will have plenty of opportunities later on.'

'Really? You think I need not go, eh?'

At that moment, from the direction in which these gentlemen were looking, amid the boom of the cannon came the terrible rattle of musketry, and thousands of little fires flaming up in quick succession flashed all along the line.

'There! Now it's the real thing!' said Kalugin. 'I can't keep cool when I hear the noise of muskets. It seems to seize one's very soul, you know. There's an *hurrah*!' he added, listening

_____

* 'What a charming sight, eh?'

intently to the distant and prolonged roar of hundreds of voices –
'Ah – ah – ah' – which came from the bastions.

'Whose *hurrah* was it? Theirs or ours?'

'I don't know, but it's hand-to-hand fighting now, for the firing has ceased.'

At that moment an officer followed by a Cossack galloped under the window and alighted from his horse at the porch.

'Where are you from?'

'From the bastion. I want the general.'

'Come along. Well, what's happened?'

'The lodgements have been attacked – and occupied. The French brought up tremendous reserves – attacked us – we had only two battalions,' said the officer, panting. He was the same officer who had been there that evening, but though he was now out of breath he walked to the door with full self-possession.

'Well, have we retired?' asked Kalugin.

'No,' angrily replied the officer, 'another battalion came up in time – we drove them back, but the colonel is killed and many officers. I have orders to ask for reinforcements.'

And saying this he went with Kalugin to the general's, where we shall not follow him.

Five minutes later Kalugin was already on his Cossack horse (again in the semi-Cossack manner which I have noticed that all adjutants, for some reason, seem to consider the proper thing), and rode off at a trot towards the bastion to deliver some orders and await the final result of the affair. Prince Galtsin, under the influence of that oppressive excitement usually produced in a spectator by proximity to an action in which he is not engaged, went out, and began aimlessly pacing up and down the street.

VI

SOLDIERS PASSED carrying the wounded on stretchers or supporting them under their arms. It was quite dark in the streets, lights could be seen here and there, but only in the hospital windows or where some officers were sitting up. From the bastions still came the thunder of cannon and the rattle of muskets,* and flashes kept on lighting up the dark sky as before. From time to time the tramp of hoofs could be heard as an orderly galloped past, or the groans of a wounded man, the steps and voices of stretcher-bearers, or the words of some frightened women who had come out onto their porches to watch the cannonade.

Among the spectators were our friend Nikita, the old sailor's widow with whom he had again made friends, and her ten-year-old daughter.

'O Lord God! Holy Mary, Mother of God!' said the old woman, sighing as she looked at the bombs that kept flying

---

* Rifles, except some clumsy *stutzers*, had not been introduced into the Russian army, but were used by the besiegers, who had a still greater advantage in artillery. It is characteristic of Tolstoy that, occupied with men rather than mechanics, he does not in these sketches dwell on this disparity of equipment.

across from side to side like balls of fire; 'What horrors! What horrors! Ah, ah! Oh, oh! Even at the first *bondbarment* it wasn't like that. Look now where the cursed thing has burst just over our house in the suburb.'

'No, that's further, they keep tumbling into Aunt Irene's garden,' said the girl.

'And where, where, is master now?' drawled Nikita, who was not quite sober yet. 'Oh! You don't know how I love that master of mine! I love him so that if he were killed in a sinful way, which God forbid, then would you believe it, granny, after that I myself don't know what I wouldn't do to myself! I don't! . . . My master is that sort, there's only one word for it. Would I change him for such as them there, playing cards? What are they? Ugh! There's only one word for it!' concluded Nikita, pointing to the lighted window of his master's room to which, in the absence of the lieutenant-captain, Cadet Zhvadchevski had invited Sub-Lieutenants Ugrovich and Nepshisetski – the latter suffering from face-ache – and where he was having a spree in honour of a medal he had received.

'Look at the stars! Look how they're rolling!' The little girl broke the silence that followed Nikita's words as she stood gazing at the sky. 'There's another rolled down. What is it a sign of, mother?'

'They'll smash up our hut altogether,' said the old woman with a sigh, leaving her daughter unanswered.

'As we went there today with uncle, mother,' the little girl continued in a sing-song tone, becoming loquacious, 'there was such a b–i–g cannon-ball inside the room close to the cupboard. Must have smashed in through the passage and right into the room! Such a big one – you couldn't lift it.'

'Those who had husbands and money all moved away,' said the old woman, 'and there's the hut, all that was left me, and that's been smashed. Just look at *him* blazing away! The fiend! . . . O Lord! O Lord!'

'And just as we were going out, comes a bomb fly-ing, and goes and bur-sts and co-o-vers us with dust. A bit of it nearly hit me and uncle.'

VII

PRINCE GALTSIN met more and more wounded carried on stretchers or walking supported by others who were talking loudly.

'Up they sprang, friends,' said the bass voice of a tall soldier with two guns slung from his shoulder, 'up they sprang, shouting "Allah! Allah!"* and just climbing one over another. You kill one and another's there, you couldn't do anything; no end of 'em—'

But at this point in the story Galtsin interrupted him.

---

* Our soldiers fighting the Turks have become so accustomed to this cry of the enemy that they now always say that the French also shout 'Allah!' L. T.

'You are from the bastion?'

'Yes, your Honour.'

'Well, what happened? Tell me.'

'What happened? Well, your Honour, such a force of 'em poured down on us over the rampart, it was all up. They quite overpowered us, your Honour!'

'Overpowered? . . . But you repulsed them?'

'How could we repulse them when *his* whole force came on, killed all our men, and no re'forcements were given us?'

The soldier was mistaken, the trench had remained ours; but it is a curious fact which anyone may notice, that a soldier wounded in action always thinks the affair lost and imagines it to have been a very bloody fight.

'How is that? I was told they had been repulsed,' said Galtsin irritably. 'Perhaps they were driven back after you left? Is it long since you came away?'

'I am straight from there, your Honour,' answered the soldier, 'it is hardly possible. They must have kept the trench, *he* quite overpowered us.'

'And aren't you ashamed to have lost the trench? It's terrible!' said Galtsin, provoked by such indifference.

'Why, if the strength is on their side . . .' muttered the soldier.

'Ah, your Honour,' began a soldier from a stretcher which had just come up to them, 'how could we help giving it up when *he* had killed almost all our men? If we'd had the strength we wouldn't have given it up, not on any account. But as it was, what could we do? I stuck one, and then something hits me. Oh, oh-h! Steady, lads, steady! Oh, oh!' groaned the wounded man.

'Really, there seem to be too many men returning,' said Galtsin, again stopping the tall soldier with the two guns. 'Why are you retiring? You there, stop!'

The soldier stopped and took off his cap with his left hand.

'Where are you going, and why?' shouted Galtsin severely, 'you scoun—'

But having come close up to the soldier, Galtsin noticed that no hand was visible beneath the soldier's right cuff and that the sleeve was soaked in blood to the elbow.

'I am wounded, your Honour.'

'Wounded? How?'

'Here. Must have been with a bullet,' said the man, pointing to his arm, 'but I don't know what struck my head here,' and bending his head he showed the matted hair at the back stuck together with blood.

'And whose is this other gun?'

'It's a French rifle I took, your Honour. But I wouldn't have come away if it weren't to lead this fellow – he may fall,' he added, pointing to a soldier who was walking a little in front leaning on his gun and painfully dragging his left leg.

Prince Galtsin suddenly felt horribly ashamed of his unjust suspicions. He felt himself blushing, turned away, and went to the hospital without either questioning or watching the wounded men any more.

Having with difficulty pushed his way through the porch among the wounded who had come on foot and the bearers who were carrying in the wounded and bringing out the dead, Galtsin entered the first room, gave a look round, and involuntarily turned back and ran out into the street: it was too terrible.

VIII

THE LARGE, lofty, dark hall, lit up only by the four or five candles with which the doctors examined the wounded, was quite full. Yet the bearers kept bringing in more wounded – laying them side by side on the floor which was already so packed that the unfortunate patients were jostled together, staining one another with their blood – and going to fetch more wounded. The pools of blood visible in the unoccupied spaces, the feverish breathing of several hundred men, and the perspiration of the bearers with the stretchers, filled the air with a peculiar, heavy, thick, fetid mist, in which the candles burnt dimly in different parts of the hall. All sorts of groans, sighs, death-rattles, now and then interrupted by shrill screams, filled the whole room. Sisters with quiet faces, expressing no empty feminine tearful pity, but active practical sympathy, stepped here and there across the wounded with medicines, water, bandages, and lint, flitting among the blood-stained coats and shirts. The doctors, kneeling with rolled-up sleeves beside the wounded, by the light of the candles their assistants held, examined, felt, and probed their wounds, heedless of the terrible groans and entreaties of the sufferers. One doctor sat at a table near the door and at the moment Galtsin came in was already entering No. 532.

'Ivan Bogaev, Private, Company Three, S—— Regiment, *fractura femuris complicata!*' shouted another doctor from the end of the room, examining a shattered leg. 'Turn him over.'

'Oh, oh, fathers! Oh, you're our fathers!' screamed the soldier, beseeching them not to touch him.

'*Perforatio capitis!*'

'Simon Neferdov, Lieutenant-Colonel of the N—— Infantry Regiment. Have a little patience, Colonel, or it is quite impossible: I shall give it up!' said a third doctor, poking about with some kind of hook in the unfortunate colonel's skull.

'Oh, don't! Oh, for God's sake be quick! Be quick! Ah——!'

'*Perforatio pectoris* . . . Sebastian Sereda, Private . . . what regiment? But you need not write that: *moritur*. Carry him away,' said the doctor, leaving the soldier, whose eyes turned up and in whose throat the death-rattle already sounded.

About forty soldier stretcher-bearers stood at the door waiting to carry the bandaged to the wards and the dead to the chapel. They looked on at the scene before them in silence, only broken now and then by a heavy sigh.

IX

ON HIS way to the bastion Kalugin met many wounded, but knowing by experience that in action such sights have a bad effect on one's spirits, he did not stop to question them but tried on the contrary not to notice them. At the foot of the hill he met an orderly-officer galloping fast from the bastion.

'Zobkin! Zobkin! Wait a bit!'

'Well, what is it?'

'Where are you from?'

'The lodgements.'

'How are things there – hot?'

'Oh, awful!'

And the orderly galloped on.

In fact, though there was now but little small-arms firing, the cannonade had recommenced with fresh heat and persistence.

'Ah, that's bad!' thought Kalugin with an unpleasant sensation, and he too had a presentiment – a very usual thought, the thought of death. But Kalugin was ambitious and blessed with nerves of oak – in a word, he was what is called brave. He did not yield to the first feeling but began to nerve himself. He recalled how an adjutant, Napoleon's he thought, having delivered an order, galloped with bleeding head full speed to Napoleon. '*Vous êtes blessé?*' said Napoleon. '*Je vous* *demande pardon, sire, je suis mort,*'* and the adjutant fell from his horse, dead.

That seemed to him very fine, and he pictured himself for a moment in the role of that adjutant. Then he whipped his horse, assuming a still more dashing Cossack seat, looked back at the Cossack who, standing up in his stirrups, was trotting behind, and rode quite gallantly up to the spot where he had to dismount. Here he found four soldiers sitting on some stones smoking their pipes.

'What are you doing there?' he shouted at them.

'Been carrying off a wounded man and sat down to rest a bit, your Honour,' said one of them, hiding his pipe behind his back and taking off his cap.

'Resting, indeed! . . . To your places, march!'

And he went up the hill with them through the trench, meeting wounded men at every step.

After ascending the hill he turned to the left, and a few steps farther on found himself quite alone. A splinter of a bomb whizzed near him and fell into the trench. Another bomb rose in front of him and seemed flying straight at him. He suddenly felt frightened, ran a few steps at full speed, and lay down flat. When the bomb burst a considerable distance off he felt exceedingly vexed with himself and rose, looking round to see if anyone had noticed his downfall, but no one was near.

* 'You are wounded?' / 'Excuse me, sire, I am dead.'

But when fear has once entered the soul it does not easily yield to any other feeling. He, who always boasted that he never even stooped, now hurried along the trench almost on all fours. He stumbled, and thought, 'Oh, it's awful! They'll kill me for certain!' His breath came with difficulty, and perspiration broke out over his whole body. He was surprised at himself but no longer strove to master his feelings.

Suddenly he heard footsteps in front. Quickly straightening himself he raised his head, and boldly clanking his sabre went on more deliberately. He felt himself quite a different man. When he met an officer of the Engineers and a sailor, and the officer shouted to him to lie down, pointing to a bright spot which growing brighter and brighter approached more and more swiftly and came crashing down close to the trench, he only bent a little, involuntarily influenced by the frightened cry, and went on.

'That's a brave one,' said the sailor, looking quite calmly at the bomb and with experienced eye deciding at once that the splinters could not fly into the trench, 'he won't even lie down.'

It was only a few steps across open ground to the bomb-proof shelter of the commander of the bastion, when Kalugin's mind again became clouded and the same stupid terror seized him: his heart beat more violently, the blood rushed to his head, and he had to make an effort to force himself to run to the bomb-proof.

'Why are you so out of breath?' said the general, when Kalugin had reported his instructions.

'I walked very fast, your Excellency!'

'Won't you have a glass of wine?'

Kalugin drank a glass of wine and lit a cigarette. The action was over, only a fierce cannonade still continued from both sides. In the bomb-proof sat General N——, the commander of the bastion, and some six other officers among whom was Praskukhin. They were discussing various details of the action. Sitting in this comfortable room with blue wall-paper, a sofa, a bed, a table with papers on it, a wall-clock with a lamp burning before it, and an icon* – looking at these signs of habitation, at the beams more than two feet thick that formed the ceiling, and listening to the shots that sounded faint here in the shelter, Kalugin could not understand how he had twice allowed himself to be overcome by such unpardonable weakness. He was angry with himself and wished for danger in order to test his nerve once more.

'Ah! I'm glad you are here, Captain,' said he to a naval officer with big moustaches who wore a Staff officer's coat with a St George's Cross and had just entered the shelter and asked the general to give him some men to repair two embrasures of his battery which had become blocked. When the general had finished speaking to the captain, Kalugin said: 'The commander-in-chief told me to ask if your guns can fire case-shot into the trenches.'

---

* The Russian icons are paintings in Byzantine style of God, the Holy Virgin, Christ, or some saint, martyr, or angel. They are usually on wood and often covered over, except the face and hands, with an embossed gilt cover.

'Only one of them can,' said the captain sullenly.

'All the same, let us go and see.'

The captain frowned and gave an angry grunt.

'I have been standing there all night and have come in to get a bit of rest – couldn't you go alone?' he added. 'My assistant, Lieutenant Kartz, is there and can show you everything.'

The captain had already been more than six months in command of this, one of the most dangerous batteries. From the time the siege began, even before the bomb-proof shelters were constructed, he had lived continuously on the bastion and had a great reputation for courage among the sailors. That is why his refusal struck and surprised Kalugin. 'So much for reputation,' thought he.

'Well then, I will go alone if I may,' he said in a slightly sarcastic tone to the captain, who however paid no attention to his words.

Kalugin did not realize that whereas he had spent some fifty hours all in all at different times on the bastions, the captain had lived there for six months. Kalugin was still actuated by vanity, the wish to shine, the hope of rewards, of gaining a reputation, and the charm of running risks. But the captain had already lived through all that: at first he had felt vain, had shown off his courage, had been foolhardy, had hoped for rewards and reputation and had even gained them, but now all these incentives had lost their power over him and he saw things differently. He fulfilled his duty exactly, but quite understanding how much the chances of life were against him after six months at the bastion, he no longer ran risks without serious need, and so the young lieutenant who had joined the battery a week ago and was now showing it to Kalugin, with whom he vied in uselessly leaning out of the embrasures and climbing out on the banquette, seemed ten times braver than the captain.

Returning to the shelter after examining the battery, Kalugin in the dark came upon the general, who accompanied by his Staff officers was going to the watch-tower.

'Captain Praskukhin,' he heard the general say, 'please go to the right lodgement and tell the second battalion of the M—— Regiment which is at work there to cease their work, leave the place, and noiselessly rejoin their regiment which is stationed in reserve at the foot of the hill. Do you understand? Lead them yourself to the regiment.'

'Yes, sir.'

And Praskukhin started at full speed towards the lodgements.

The firing was now becoming less frequent.

X

'IS THIS the second battalion of the M—— Regiment?' asked Praskukhin, having run to his destination and coming across some soldiers carrying earth in sacks.

'It is, your Honour.'

'Where is the commander?'

Mikhaylov, thinking that the commander of the company was being asked for, got out of his pit and taking Praskukhin for a commanding officer saluted and approached him.

'The general's orders are . . . that you . . . should go . . . quickly . . . and above all quietly . . . back – no, not back, but to the reserves,' said Praskukhin, looking askance in the direction of the enemy's fire.

Having recognized Praskukhin and made out what was wanted, Mikhaylov dropped his hand and passed on the order. The battalion became alert, the men took up their muskets, put on their cloaks, and set out.

No one without experiencing it can imagine the delight a man feels when, after three hours' bombardment, he leaves so dangerous a spot as the lodgements. During those three hours Mikhaylov, who more than once and not without reason had thought his end at hand, had had time to accustom himself to the conviction that he would certainly be killed and that he no longer belonged to this world. But in spite of that he had great difficulty in keeping his legs from running away with him when, leading the company with Praskukhin at his side, he left the lodgement.

'*Au revoir!*' said a major with whom Mikhaylov had eaten bread and cheese sitting in the pit under the breastwork and who was remaining at the bastion in command of another battalion. 'I wish you a lucky journey.'

'And I wish you a lucky defence. It seems to be getting quieter now.'

But scarcely had he uttered these words before the enemy, probably observing the movement in the lodgement, began to fire more and more frequently. Our guns replied and a heavy firing recommenced.

The stars were high in the sky but shone feebly. The night was pitch dark, only the flashes of the guns and the bursting bombs made things around suddenly visible. The soldiers walked quickly and silently, involuntarily outpacing one another; only their measured footfall on the dry road was heard besides the incessant roll of the guns, the ringing of bayonets when they touched one another, a sigh, or the prayer of some poor soldier lad: 'Lord, O Lord! What does it mean?' Now and again the moaning of a man who was hit could be heard, and the cry, 'Stretchers!' (In the company Mikhaylov commanded artillery fire alone carried off twenty-six men that night.) A flash on the dark and distant horizon, the cry, 'Can-n-on!' from the sentinel on the bastion, and a ball flew buzzing above the company and plunged into the earth, making the stones fly.

'What the devil are they so slow for?' thought Praskukhin, continually looking back as he marched beside Mikhaylov. 'I'd really better run on. I've delivered the order . . . But no, they might afterwards say I'm a coward. What must be will be. I'll keep beside him.'

'Now why is he walking with me?' thought Mikhaylov on his

part. 'I have noticed over and over again that he always brings ill-luck. Here it comes, I believe, straight for us.'

After they had gone a few hundred paces they met Kalugin, who was walking briskly towards the lodgements clanking his sabre. He had been ordered by the general to find out how the works were progressing there. But when he met Mikhaylov he thought that instead of going there himself under such a terrible fire – which he was not ordered to do – he might just as well find out all about it from an officer who had been there. And having heard from Mikhaylov full details of the work and walked a little way with him, Kalugin turned off into a trench leading to the bomb-proof shelter.

'Well, what news?' asked an officer who was eating his supper there all alone.

'Nothing much. It seems that the affair is over.'

'Over? How so? On the contrary, the general has just gone again to the watch-tower and another regiment has arrived. Yes, there it is. Listen! The muskets again! Don't you go – why should you?' added the officer, noticing that Kalugin made a movement.

'I certainly ought to be there,' thought Kalugin, 'but I have already exposed myself a great deal today: the firing is awful!'

'Yes, I think I'd better wait here for him,' he said.

And really about twenty minutes later the general and the officers who were with him returned. Among them was Cadet Baron Pesth but not Praskukhin. The lodgements had been retaken and occupied by us.

After receiving a full account of the affair Kalugin, accompanied by Pesth, left the bomb-proof shelter.

XI

'THERE'S BLOOD on your coat! You don't mean to say you were in the hand-to-hand fight?' asked Kalugin.

'Oh, it was awful! Just fancy—'

And Pesth began to relate how he had led his company, how the company-commander had been killed, how he himself had stabbed a Frenchman, and how if it had not been for him we should have lost the day.

This tale was founded on fact: the company-commander had been killed and Pesth had bayoneted a Frenchman, but in recounting the details the cadet invented and bragged.

He bragged unintentionally, because during the whole of the affair he had been as it were in a fog and so bewildered that all he remembered of what had happened seemed to have happened somewhere, at some time, and to somebody. And very naturally he tried to recall the details in a light advantageous to himself. What really occurred was this:

The battalion the cadet had been ordered to join for the sortie stood under fire for two hours close to some low wall. Then the battalion-commander in front said something, the company-commanders became active, the battalion advanced from behind the breastwork, and after going about a hundred paces stopped to form into company columns. Pesth was told to take his place on the right flank of the second company.

Quite unable to realize where he was and why he was there, the cadet took his place, and involuntarily holding his breath while cold shivers ran down his back he gazed into the dark distance expecting something dreadful. He was however not so much frightened (for there was no firing) as disturbed and agitated at being in the field beyond the fortifications.

Again the battalion-commander in front said something. Again the officers spoke in whispers passing on the order, and the black wall, formed by the first company, suddenly sank out of sight. The order was to lie down. The second company also lay down and in lying down Pesth hurt his hand on a sharp prickle. Only the commander of the second company remained standing. His short figure brandishing a sword moved in front of the company and he spoke incessantly.

'Mind, lads! Show them what you're made of! Don't fire, but give it them with the bayonet – the dogs! – when I cry "Hurrah!" Altogether, mind, that's the thing! We'll let them see who we are. We won't disgrace ourselves, eh lads? For our father the Tsar!'

'What's your company-commander's name?' asked Pesth of a cadet lying near him. 'How brave he is!'

'Yes he always is, in action,' answered the cadet. 'His name is Lisinkovski.'

Just then a flame suddenly flashed up right in front of the company, who were deafened by a resounding crash. High up in the air stones and splinters clattered. (Some fifty seconds later a stone fell from above and severed a soldier's leg.) It was a bomb fired from an elevated stand, and the fact that it reached the company showed that the French had noticed the column.

'You're sending bombs, are you? Wait a bit till we get at you, then you'll taste a three-edged Russian bayonet, damn you!' said the company-commander so loud that the battalion-commander had to order him to hold his tongue and not make so much noise.

After that the first company got up, then the second. They were ordered to fix bayonets and the battalion advanced. Pesth was in such a fright that he could not in the least make out how long it lasted, where he went, or who was who. He went on as if he were drunk. But suddenly a million fires flashed from all sides, and something whistled and clattered. He shouted and ran somewhere, because everyone shouted and ran. Then he stumbled and fell over something. It was the company-commander, who had been wounded at the head of his company, and who taking the cadet for a Frenchman had seized him by the leg. Then when Pesth had freed his leg and got up, someone else ran against him from behind in the dark and nearly knocked him down again. 'Run him through!' someone else shouted. 'Why are you stopping?' Then someone seized a bayonet and stuck it into something soft. '*Ah Dieu!*' came a dreadful, piercing voice and Pesth only then understood that he had bayoneted a

Frenchman. A cold sweat covered his whole body, he trembled as in a fever and threw down his musket. But this lasted only a moment; the thought immediately entered his head that he was a hero. He again seized his musket, and shouting 'Hurrah!' ran with the crowd away from the dead Frenchman. Having run twenty paces he came to a trench. Some of our men were there with the battalion-commander.

'And I have killed one!' said Pesth to the commander.

'You're a fine fellow, Baron!'

XII

'DO YOU know Praskukhin is killed?' said Pesth, while accompanying Kalugin on his way home.

'Impossible!'

'It is true. I saw him myself.'

'Well, goodbye . . . I must be off.'

'This is capital!' thought Kalugin, as he came to his lodgings. 'It's the first time I have had such luck when on duty. It's first-rate. I am alive and well, and shall certainly get an excellent recommendation and am sure of a gold sabre. And I really have deserved it.'

After reporting what was necessary to the general he went to his room, where Prince Galtsin, long since returned, sat awaiting him, reading a book he had found on Kalugin's table.

It was with extraordinary pleasure that Kalugin found himself safe at home again, and having put on his night-shirt and got into bed he gave Galtsin all the details of the affair, telling them very naturally from a point of view where those details showed what a capable and brave officer he, Kalugin, was (which it seems to me it was hardly necessary to allude to, since everybody knew it and had no right or reason to question it, except perhaps the deceased Captain Praskukhin who, though he had considered it an honour to walk arm in arm with Kalugin, had privately told a friend only yesterday that though Kalugin was a first-rate fellow, yet, 'between you and me, he was awfully disinclined to go to the bastions').

Praskukhin, who had been walking beside Mikhaylov after Kalugin had slipped away from him, had scarcely begun to revive a little on approaching a safer place, than he suddenly saw a bright light flash up behind him and heard the sentinel shout 'Mortar!' and a soldier walking behind him say: 'That's coming straight for the bastion!'

Mikhaylov looked round. The bright spot seemed to have stopped at its zenith, in the position which makes it absolutely impossible to define its direction. But that only lasted a moment: the bomb, coming faster and faster, nearer and nearer, so that the sparks of its fuse were already visible and its fatal whistle audible, descended towards the centre of the battalion.

'Lie down!' shouted someone.

Mikhaylov and Praskukhin lay flat on the ground. Praskukhin, closing his eyes, only heard the bomb crash down on the hard earth close by. A second passed which seemed an hour: the bomb had not exploded. Praskukhin was afraid. Perhaps he had played the coward for nothing. Perhaps the bomb had fallen far away and it only seemed to him that its fuse was fizzing close by. He opened his eyes and was pleased to see Mikhaylov lying immovable at his feet. But at that moment he caught sight of the glowing fuse of the bomb which was spinning on the ground not a yard off. Terror, cold terror excluding every other thought and feeling, seized his whole being. He covered his face with his hands.

Another second passed – a second during which a whole world of feelings, thoughts, hopes, and memories flashed before his imagination.

'Whom will it hit – Mikhaylov or me? Or both of us? And if it's me, where? In the head? Then I'm done for. But if it's the leg, they'll cut it off (I'll certainly ask for chloroform) and I may survive. But perhaps only Mikhaylov will be hit. Then I will tell how we were going side by side and how he was killed and I was splashed with his blood. No, it's nearer to me ... it will be I.'

Then he remembered the twelve rubles he owed Mikhaylov, remembered also a debt in Petersburg that should have been paid long ago, and the gypsy song he had sung that evening. The woman he loved rose in his imagination wearing a cap with lilac ribbons. He remembered a man who had insulted him five years ago and whom he had not yet paid out. And yet, inseparable from all these and thousands of other recollections, the present thought, the expectation of death, did not leave him for an instant. 'Perhaps it won't explode,' and with desperate decision he resolved to open his eyes. But at that instant a red flame pierced through the still closed lids and something struck him in the middle of his chest with a terrible crash. He jumped up and began to run, but stumbling over the sabre that got between his legs he fell on his side.

'Thank God, I'm only bruised!' was his first thought, and he was about to touch his chest with his hand, but his arms seemed tied to his sides and he felt as if a vice were squeezing his head. Soldiers flitted past him and he counted them unconsciously: 'One, two, three soldiers! And there's an officer with his cloak tucked up,' he thought. Then lightning flashed before his eyes and he wondered whether the shot was fired from a mortar or a cannon. 'A cannon, probably. And there's another shot and here are more soldiers – five, six, seven soldiers . . . They all pass by!' He was suddenly seized with fear that they would crush him. He wished to shout that he was hurt, but his mouth was so dry that his tongue clove to the roof of his mouth and a terrible thirst tormented him. He felt a wetness about his chest and this sensation of being wet made him think of water, and he longed to drink even this that made him feel wet. 'I suppose I hit myself in falling and made myself bleed,' thought he, and giving way more and more to fear lest the soldiers who kept flitting past might trample on him, he gathered all his strength and tried to shout, 'Take me with you!' but instead of that he uttered such a terrible groan that the sound frightened him. Then some other red fires began dancing before his eyes and it seemed to him that the soldiers put stones on him. The fires danced less and less but the stones they put on him pressed more and more heavily. He made an effort to push off the stones, stretched himself, and saw and heard and felt nothing more. He had been killed on the spot by a bomb-splinter in the middle of his chest.

XIII

WHEN MIKHAYLOV dropped to the ground on seeing the bomb he too, like Praskukhin, lived through an infinitude of thoughts and feelings in the two seconds that elapsed before the bomb burst. He prayed mentally and repeated, 'Thy will be done.' And at the same time he thought, 'Why did I enter the army? And why did I join the infantry to take part in this campaign? Wouldn't it have been better to have remained with the Uhlan regiment at T—— and spent my time with my friend Natasha? And now here I am . . .' and he began to count, 'One, two, three, four,' deciding that if the bomb burst at an even number he would live but if at an odd number he would be killed. 'It is all over, I'm killed!' he thought when the bomb burst (he did not remember whether at an odd or even number) and he felt a blow and a cruel pain in his head. 'Lord, forgive me my trespasses!' he muttered, folding his hands. He rose, but fell on his back senseless.

When he came to, his first sensations were that of blood trickling down his nose, and the pain in his head which had become much less violent. 'That's the soul passing,' he thought. 'How will it be *there*? Lord, receive my soul in peace! . . . Only it's strange,' thought he, 'that while dying I should hear the steps of the soldiers and the sounds of the firing so distinctly.'

'Bring stretchers! Eh, the captain has been hit!' shouted a voice above his head, which he recognized as the voice of the drummer Ignatyev.

Someone took him by the shoulders. With an effort he opened his eyes and saw above him the sky, some groups of stars, and two bombs racing one another as they flew over him. He saw Ignatyev, soldiers with stretchers and guns, the embankment, the trenches, and suddenly realized that he was not yet in the other world.

He had been slightly wounded in the head by a stone. His first feeling was one almost of regret: he had prepared himself so well and so calmly to go *there* that the return to reality, with its bombs, stretchers, and blood, seemed unpleasant. The second feeling was unconscious joy at being alive, and the third a wish to get away from the bastion as quickly as possible. The drummer tied a handkerchief round his commander's head and taking his arm led him towards the ambulance station.

'But why and where am I going?' thought the lieutenant-captain when he had collected his senses. 'My duty is to remain with the company and not leave it behind – especially,' whispered a voice, 'as it will soon be out of range of the guns.'

'Don't trouble about me, my lad,' said he, drawing his hand away from the attentive drummer. 'I won't go to the ambulance station: I'll stay with the company.'

And he turned back.

'It would be better to have it properly bandaged, your Honour,' said Ignatyev. 'It's only in the heat of the moment that it seems nothing. Mind it doesn't get worse . . . And just see what warm work it is here . . . Really, your Honour—'

Mikhaylov stood for a moment undecided, and would probably have followed Ignatyev's advice had he not reflected how many severely wounded there must be at the ambulance station. 'Perhaps the doctors will smile at my scratch,' thought the lieutenant-captain, and in spite of the drummer's arguments he returned to his company.

'And where is the orderly officer Praskukhin, who was with me?' he asked when he met the ensign who was leading the company.

'I don't know. Killed, I think,' replied the ensign unwillingly.

'Killed? Or only wounded? How is it you don't know? Wasn't he going with us? And why didn't you bring him away?'

'How could we, under such a fire?'

'But how could you do such a thing, Michael Ivanych?' said Mikhaylov angrily. 'How could you leave him supposing he is alive? Even if he's dead his body ought to have been brought away.'

'Alive indeed, when I tell you I went up and saw him myself!' said the ensign. 'Excuse me . . . It's hard enough to collect our own. There, those villains are at it again!' he added. 'They're sending up cannon-balls now.'

Mikhaylov sat down and lifted his hands to his head, which ached terribly when he moved.

'No, it is absolutely necessary to go back and fetch him,' he said. 'He may still be alive. It is our *duty*, Michael Ivanych.'

Michael Ivanych did not answer.

'O Lord! Just because he didn't bring him in at the time, soldiers will have to be sent back alone now. . . and yet can I possibly send them under this terrible fire? They may be killed for nothing,' thought Mikhaylov.

'Lads! Someone will have to go back to fetch the officer who was wounded out there in the ditch,' said he, not very loudly or peremptorily, for he felt how unpleasant it would be for the soldiers to execute this order. And he was right. Since he had not named anyone in particular no one came forward to obey the order.

'And after all he may be dead already. It isn't worth exposing men uselessly to such danger. It's all my fault, I ought to have seen to it. I'll go back myself and find out whether he is alive. It is my *duty*,' said Mikhaylov to himself.

'Michael Ivanych, you lead the company, I'll catch you up,' said he, and holding up his cloak with one hand while with the other he kept touching a small icon of St Metrophanes that hung round his neck and in which he had great faith, he ran quickly along the trench.

Having convinced himself that Praskukhin was dead he dragged himself back panting, holding the bandage that had slipped on his head, which was beginning to ache very badly. When he overtook the battalion it was already at the foot of the hill and almost beyond the range of the shots. I say 'almost', for a stray bomb reached even here now and then.

'Tomorrow I had better go and be entered at the ambulance station,' thought the lieutenant-captain, while a medical assistant, who had turned up, was bandaging his head.

XIV

HUNDREDS OF bodies, which a couple of hours before had been men full of various lofty or trivial hopes and wishes, were lying with fresh bloodstains on their stiffened limbs in the dewy, flowery valley which separated the bastions from the trenches and on the smooth floor of the mortuary chapel in Sevastopol. Hundreds of men with curses or prayers on their

49

parched lips, crawled, writhed, and groaned, some among the dead in the flowery valley, some on stretchers, or beds, or on the blood-stained floor of the ambulance station. Yet the dawn broke behind the Sapun hill, the twinkling stars grew pale and the white mists spread from the dark roaring sea just as on other days, and the rosy morning glow lit up the east, long streaks of red clouds spread along the pale-blue horizon, and just as in the old days the sun rose in power and glory, promising joy, love, and happiness to all the awakening world.

XV

NEXT EVENING the Chasseurs' band was again playing on the boulevard, and officers, cadets, soldiers, and young women, again promenaded round the pavilion and along the side-walks under the acacias with their sweet-scented white blossoms.

Kalugin was walking arm in arm with Prince Galtsin and a colonel near the pavilion and talking of last night's affair. The main theme of their conversation, as usual in such cases, was not the affair itself, but the part each of the speakers had taken in it. Their faces and the tone of their voices were serious, almost sorrowful, as if the losses of the night had touched and saddened them all. But to tell the truth, as none of them had lost anyone very dear to him, this sorrowful expression was only an official one they considered it their duty to exhibit.

Kalugin and the colonel in fact, though they were first-rate fellows, were ready to see such an affair every day if they could gain a gold sword and be made major-general each time. It is all very well to call some conqueror a monster because he destroys millions to gratify his ambition, but go and ask any Ensign Petrushev or Sub-Lieutenant Antonov on their conscience, and you will find that every one of us is a little Napoleon, a petty monster ready to start a battle and kill a hundred men merely to get an extra medal or one-third additional pay.

'No, I beg your pardon,' said the colonel. 'It began first on the left side. I was there myself.'

'Well, perhaps,' said Kalugin. 'I spent more time on the right. I went there twice: first to look for the general, and then just to see the lodgements. It was hot there, I can tell you!'

'Kalugin ought to know,' said Galtsin. 'By the way, V——— told *me* today that you are a trump—'

'But the losses, the losses are terrible!' said the colonel. 'In my regiment we had four hundred casualties. It is astonishing that I'm still alive.'

Just then the figure of Mikhaylov, with his head bandaged, appeared at the end of the boulevard walking towards these gentlemen.

'What, are you wounded, Captain?' said Kalugin.

'Yes, slightly, with a stone,' answered Mikhaylov.

'*Est-ce que le pavillon est baissé déjà?*' asked Prince Galtsin, glancing at the lieutenant-captain's cap and not addressing anyone in particular.

'*Non, pas encore*,'* answered Mikhaylov, wishing to show that he understood and spoke French.

'Do you mean to say the truce still continues?' said Galtsin, politely addressing him in Russian and thereby (so it seemed to the lieutenant-captain) suggesting: 'It must no doubt be difficult for you to have to speak French, so hadn't we better simply . . .' and with that the adjutants went away. The lieutenant-captain again felt exceedingly lonely, just as he had done the day before. After bowing to various people – some of whom he did not wish and some of whom he did not venture to join – he sat down near the Kazarski monument and smoked a cigarette.

Baron Pesth also turned up on the boulevard. He mentioned that he had been at the parley and had spoken to the French officers. According to his account one of them had said to him: '*S'il n'avait pas fait clair encore pendant une demi-heure, les ambuscades auraient été reprises*,' and he replied, '*Monsieur, je ne dis pas non, pour ne pas vous donner un démenti*,'† and he told how pat it had come out, and so on.

But though he had been at the parley he had not really managed to say anything in particular, though he much wished to

_____

* 'Is the flag (of truce) lowered already?' / 'No, not yet.'

† 'Had it remained dark for another half-hour, the ambuscades would have been recaptured.' / 'Sir, I will not say no, lest I give you the lie.'

speak with the French ('for it's awfully jolly to speak to those fellows'). He had paced up and down the line for a long time asking the Frenchmen near him: '*De quel régiment êtes-vous?*' and had got his answer and nothing more. When he went too far beyond the line, the French sentry, not suspecting that 'that soldier' knew French, abused him in the third person singular: '*Il vient regarder nos travaux, ce sacré——*'* in consequence of which Cadet Baron Pesth, finding nothing more to interest him at the parley, rode home, and on his way back composed the French phrases he now repeated.

On the boulevard was Captain Zobov talking very loud, and Captain Obzhogov, the artillery captain who never curried favour with anyone, was there too, in a dishevelled condition, and also the cadet who was always fortunate in his love affairs, and all the same people as yesterday, with the same motives as always. Only Praskukhin, Neferdov, and a few more were missing, and hardly anyone now remembered or thought of them, though there had not yet been time for their bodies to be washed, laid out, and put into the ground.

---

* 'What regiment do you belong to?' ... 'He's come to look at our works, the confounded——'

XVI

WHITE FLAGS are hung out on our bastions and on the French trenches, and in the flowery valley between them lie heaps of mangled corpses without boots, some clad in blue and others in grey, which workmen are removing and piling onto carts. The air is filled with the smell of decaying flesh. Crowds of people have poured out from Sevastopol and from the French camp to see the sight, and with eager and friendly curiosity draw near to one another.

Listen to what these people are saying.

Here, in a circle of Russians and Frenchmen who have collected round him, a young officer, who speaks French badly but sufficiently to be understood, is examining a guardsman's pouch.

'*Eh sussy, poor quah se waso lié?*'

'*Parce que c'est une giberne d'un régiment de la garde, monsieur, qui porte l'aigle impérial.*'

'*Eh voo de la guard?*'

'*Pardon, monsieur, du sixième de ligne.*'

'*Eh sussy oo ashtay?*' pointing to a cigarette-holder of yellow wood, in which the Frenchman is smoking a cigarette.

'*À Balaclava, monsieur. C'est tout simple en bois de palme.*'

'*Joli,*' says the officer, guided in his remarks not so much by what he wants to say as by the French words he happens to know.

'*Si vous voulez bien garder cela comme souvenir de cette rencontre, vous m'obligerez.*'*

And the polite Frenchman puts out his cigarette and presents the holder to the officer with a slight bow. The officer gives him his, and all present, both French and Russian, smile and seem pleased.

Here is a bold infantryman in a pink shirt with his cloak thrown over his shoulders, accompanied by other soldiers standing near him with their hands folded behind their backs and with merry inquisitive faces. He has approached a Frenchman and asked for a light for his pipe. The Frenchman draws at and stirs up the tobacco in his own short pipe and shakes a light into that of the Russian.

'*Tabac boon?*' says the soldier in the pink shirt, and the spectators smile. '*Oui, bon tabac, tabac turc,*' says the Frenchman. '*Chez vous autres tabac – Russe? Bon?*'†

'*Roos boon,*' says the soldier in the pink shirt while the onlookers shake with laughter. '*Fransay* not *boon. Bongjour,*

---

* 'And what is this tied bird for?' / 'Because this is a cartridge pouch of a guard regiment, monsieur, and bears the Imperial eagle.' / 'And do you belong to the Guards?' / 'No, monsieur, to the Sixth Regiment of the Line.' / 'And where did you buy this?' / 'At Balaclava, monsieur. It's only made of palm wood.' / 'Pretty.' / 'If you will be so good as to keep it as a souvenir of this meeting you will do me a favour.'

† 'Yes, good tobacco, Turkish tobacco . . . You others have Russian tobacco. Is it good?'

mossier!', and having let off his whole stock of French at once, he slaps the Frenchman on the stomach and laughs. The French also laugh.

'*Ils ne sont pas jolis ces b—— de Russes,*' says a Zouave among the French.

'*De quoi est-ce qu'ils rient donc?*'* says another with an Italian accent, a dark man, coming up to our men.

'Coat *boon,*' says the cheeky soldier, examining the embroidery of the Zouave's coat, and everybody laughs again.

'*Ne sors pas de ta ligne, à vos places, sacré nom!*'† cries a French corporal, and the soldiers separate with evident reluctance.

And here, in the midst of a group of French officers, one of our young cavalry officers is gushing. They are talking about some Count Sazonov, '*que j'ai beaucoup connu, monsieur,*' says a French officer with only one epaulette – '*c'est un de ces vrais comtes russes, comme nous les aimons.*'

'*Il y a un Sazónoff, que j'ai connu,*' says the cavalry officer, '*mais il n'est pas comte, à moins que je sache, un petit brun de votre âge à peu près.*'

'*C'est ça, monsieur, c'est lui. Oh! que je voudrais le voir, ce cher comte. Si vous le voyez, je vous prie bien de lui faire mes compliments – Capitaine Latour,*' he said, bowing.

---

* 'They are not handsome, these d—Russians.' / 'What are they laughing about?'
† 'Don't leave your ranks. To your places, damn it!'

'*N'est-ce pas terrible la triste besogne que nous faisons? Ça chauffait cette nuit, n'est-ce pas?*' said the cavalry officer, wishing to maintain the conversation and pointing to the corpses.

'*Oh, monsieur, c'est affreux! Mais quels gaillards vos soldats, quels gaillards! C'est un plaisir que de se battre avec des gaillards comme eux.*'

'*Il faut avouer que les vôtres ne se mouchent pas du pied non plus,*'* said the cavalry officer, bowing and imagining himself very agreeable.

But enough.

Let us rather look at this ten-year-old boy in an old cap (probably his father's), with shoes on his stockingless feet and nankeen trousers held up by one brace. At the very beginning of the truce he came over the entrenchments, and has been walking about the valley ever since, looking with dull curiosity at the French and at the corpses that lie on the ground and gathering the blue flowers with which the valley is strewn. Returning home with a large bunch of flowers he holds his nose to escape the

___

* 'Whom I knew very intimately, monsieur. He is one of those real Russian counts of whom we are so fond.' / 'I am acquainted with a Sazonov, but he is not a count, as far as I know – a small dark man, of about your age.' / 'Just so, monsieur, that is he. Oh, how I should like to meet the dear count. If you should see him, please be so kind as to give him my compliments – Captain Latour.' / 'Isn't it terrible, this sad duty we are engaged in? It was warm work last night, wasn't it?' / 'Ah, monsieur, it is terrible! But what fine fellows your men are, what fine fellows! It is a pleasure to fight with such fellows!' / 'It must be admitted that yours are no fools either.' (Literally, 'don't wipe their noses with their feet'.)

smell that is borne towards him by the wind, and stopping near a heap of corpses gazes for a long time at a terrible headless body that lies nearest to him. After standing there some time he draws nearer and touches with his foot the stiff outstretched arm of the corpse. The arm trembles a little. He touches it again more boldly; it moves and falls back to its old position. The boy gives a sudden scream, hides his face in his flowers, and runs towards the fortifications as fast as his legs can carry him.

Yes, there are white flags on the bastions and the trenches but the flowery valley is covered with dead bodies. The glorious sun is sinking towards the blue sea, and the undulating blue sea glitters in the golden light. Thousands of people crowd together, look at, speak to, and smile at one another. And these people – Christians professing the one great law of love and self-sacrifice – on seeing what they have done do not at once fall repentant on their knees before Him who has given them life and laid in the soul of each a fear of death and a love of the good and the beautiful, and do not embrace like brothers with tears of joy and gladness.

The white flags are lowered, the engines of death and suffering are sounding again, innocent blood is flowing and the air is filled with moans and curses.

There, I have said what I wished to say this time. But I am seized by an oppressive doubt. Perhaps I ought to have left it unsaid. What I have said perhaps belongs to that class of evil truths that lie unconsciously hidden in the soul of each man and should not be uttered lest they become harmful, as the dregs in a bottle must not be disturbed for fear of spoiling the wine . . .

Where in this tale is the evil that should be avoided, and where the good that should be imitated? Who is the villain and who the hero of the story? All are good and all are bad.

Not Kalugin, with his brilliant courage – *bravoure de gentilhomme* – and the vanity that influences all his actions, not Praskukhin, the empty harmless fellow (though he fell in battle for faith, throne, and fatherland), not Mikhaylov with his shyness, nor Pesth, a child without firm principles or convictions, can be either the villain or the hero of the tale.

The hero of my tale – whom I love with all the power of my soul, whom I have tried to portray in all his beauty, who has been, is, and will be beautiful – is Truth.

Three Deaths

A Tale

I

IT WAS AUTUMN. Two vehicles were going along the highway at a quick trot. In the first sat two women: a lady, thin and pale, and a maidservant, plump and rosy and shining. The maid's short dry hair escaped from under her faded bonnet, and her red hand in its torn glove kept pushing it back by fits and starts; her full bosom, covered by a woollen shawl, breathed health, her quick black eyes now watched the fields as they glided past the window, now glanced timidly at her mistress, and now restlessly scanned the corners of the carriage. In front of her nose dangled her mistress's bonnet, pinned to the luggage carrier, on her lap lay a puppy, her feet were raised on the boxes standing on the floor and just audibly tapped against them to the creaking of the coach-springs and the clatter of the window-panes.

Having folded her hands on her knees and closed her eyes, the lady swayed feebly against the pillows placed at her back, and, frowning slightly, coughed inwardly. On her head she had a white nightcap, and a blue kerchief was tied round her delicate white throat. A straight line receding under the cap parted her light brown, extremely flat, pomaded hair, and there was something dry and deathly about the whiteness of the skin of that wide parting. Her features were delicate and handsome, but her skin was flabby and rather sallow, though there was a hectic flush on her cheeks. Her lips were dry and restless, her scanty eyelashes had no curl in them, and her cloth travelling coat fell in straight folds over a sunken breast. Though her eyes were closed, her face bore an expression of weariness, irritation, and habitual suffering.

A footman, leaning on the arms of his seat, was dozing on the box. The mail-coach driver, shouting lustily, urged on his four big sweating horses, occasionally turning to the other driver who called to him from the calèche behind. The broad parallel tracks of the tyres spread themselves evenly and fast on the muddy, chalky surface of the road. The sky was grey and cold, and a damp mist was settling on the fields and road. It was stuffy in the coach and there was a smell of eau-de-cologne and dust. The invalid drew back her head and slowly opened her beautiful dark eyes, which were large and brilliant.

'Again,' she said, nervously pushing away with her beautiful thin hand an end of her maid's cloak which had lightly touched her foot, and her mouth twitched painfully. Matresha gathered up her cloak with both hands, rose on her strong legs, and seated herself farther away, while her fresh face grew scarlet. The lady, leaning with both hands on the seat, also tried to raise herself so as to sit up higher, but her strength failed her. Her mouth twisted, and her whole face became distorted by a look of impotent malevolence and irony. 'You might at least help me! . . . No, don't bother! I can do it myself, only don't put your bags or anything behind me, for goodness' sake! . . . No, better not touch me since you don't know how to!' The lady closed her eyes and then, again quickly raising her eyelids, glared at the maid. Matresha, looking at her, bit her red nether lip. A deep sigh rose from the invalid's chest and turned into a cough before it was completed. She turned away, puckered her face, and clutched her chest with both hands. When the coughing fit was over she once more closed her eyes and continued to sit motionless. The carriage and calèche entered a village. Matresha stretched out her thick hand from under her shawl and crossed herself.

'What is it?' asked her mistress.

'A post-station, madam.'

'I am asking why you crossed yourself.'

'There's a church, madam.'

The invalid turned to the window and began slowly to cross herself, looking with large wide-open eyes at the big village church her carriage was passing.

The carriage and calèche both stopped at the post-station

and the invalid's husband and doctor stepped out of the calèche and went up to the coach.

'How are you feeling?' asked the doctor, taking her pulse.

'Well, my dear, how are you – not tired?' asked the husband in French. 'Wouldn't you like to get out?'

Matresha, gathering up the bundles, squeezed herself into a corner so as not to interfere with their conversation.

'Nothing much, just the same,' replied the invalid. 'I won't get out.'

Her husband after standing there a while went into the station-house, and Matresha, too, jumped out of the carriage and ran on tiptoe across the mud and in at the gate.

'If I feel ill, it's no reason for you not to have lunch,' said the sick woman with a slight smile to the doctor, who was standing at her window.

'None of them has any thought for me,' she added to herself as soon as the doctor, having slowly walked away from her, ran quickly up the steps to the station-house. 'They are well, so they don't care. Oh, my God!'

'Well, Edward Ivanovich?' said the husband, rubbing his hands as he met the doctor with a merry smile. 'I have ordered the lunch-basket to be brought in. What do you think about it?'

'A capital idea,' replied the doctor.

'Well, how is she?' asked the husband with a sigh, lowering his voice and lifting his eyebrows.

'As I told you: it is impossible for her to reach Italy – God grant that she gets even as far as Moscow, especially in this weather.'

'But what are we to do? Oh, my God, my God!' and the husband hid his eyes with his hand. 'Bring it here!' he said to the man who had brought in the lunch-basket.

'She ought to have stayed at home,' said the doctor, shrugging his shoulders.

'But what could I do?' rejoined the husband. 'You know I used every possible means to get her to stay. I spoke of the expense, of our children whom we had to leave behind, and of my business affairs, but she would not listen to anything. She is making plans for life abroad as if she were in good health. To tell her of her condition would be to kill her.'

'But she is killed already – you must know that, Vasili Dmitrich. A person can't live without lungs, and new lungs won't grow. It is sad and hard, but what is to be done? My business and yours is to see that her end is made as peaceful as possible. It's a priest who is needed for that.'

'Oh, my God! Think of my condition, having to remind her about her will. Come what may I can't tell her that, you know how good she is . . .'

'Still, try to persuade her to wait till the roads are fit for sledging,' said the doctor, shaking his head significantly, 'or something bad may happen on the journey.'

'Aksyusha, hello Aksyusha!' yelled the station-master's daughter, throwing her jacket over her head and stamping her feet on the muddy back porch. 'Come and let's have a look at the Shirkin lady: they say she is being taken abroad for a chest trouble, and I've never seen what consumptive people look like!'

She jumped onto the threshold, and seizing one another by the hand the two girls ran out of the gate. Checking their pace, they passed by the coach and looked in at the open window. The invalid turned her head towards them but, noticing their curiosity, frowned and turned away.

'De-ar-ie me!' said the station-master's daughter, quickly turning her head away. 'What a wonderful beauty she must have been, and see what she's like now! It's dreadful. Did you see, did you, Aksyusha?'

'Yes, how thin!' Aksyusha agreed. 'Let's go and look again, as if we were going to the well. See, she has turned away, and I hadn't seen her yet. What a pity, Masha!'

'Yes, and what mud!' said Masha, and they both ran through the gate.

'Evidently I look frightful,' thought the invalid. 'If only I could get abroad quicker, quicker. I should soon recover there.'

'Well, my dear, how are you?' said her husband, approaching her and still chewing.

'Always the same question,' thought the invalid, 'and he himself is eating.'

'So-so,' she murmured through her closed teeth.

'You know, my dear, I'm afraid you'll get worse travelling

65

in this weather, and Edward Ivanovich says so too. Don't you think we'd better turn back?'

She remained angrily silent.

'The weather will perhaps improve and the roads be fit for sledging; you will get better meanwhile, and we will all go together.'

'Excuse me. If I had not listened to you for so long, I should now at least have reached Berlin, and have been quite well.'

'What could be done, my angel? You know it was impossible. But now if you stayed another month you would get nicely better, I should have finished my business, and we could take the children with us.'

'The children are well, but I am not.'

'But do understand, my dear, that if in this weather you should get worse on the road . . . At least you would be at home.'

'What of being at home? . . . To die at home?' answered the invalid, flaring up. But the word 'die' evidently frightened her, and she looked imploringly and questioningly at her husband. He hung his head and was silent. The invalid's mouth suddenly widened like a child's, and tears rolled down her cheeks. Her husband hid his face in his handkerchief and stepped silently away from the carriage.

'No, I will go on,' said the invalid, and lifting her eyes to the sky she folded her hands and began whispering incoherent words: 'Oh, my God, what is it for?' she said, and her tears flowed faster. She prayed long and fervently, but her chest ached and felt as tight as before; the sky, the fields, and the road were just as grey and gloomy, and the autumnal mist fell, neither thickening nor lifting, and settled on the muddy road, the roofs, the carriage, and the sheepskin coats of the drivers, who talking in their strong merry voices were greasing the wheels and harnessing the horses.

II

THE CARRIAGE was ready but the driver still loitered. He had gone into the drivers' room at the station. It was hot, stuffy, and dark there, with an oppressive smell of baking bread, cabbage, sheepskin garments, and humanity. Several drivers were sitting in the room, and a cook was busy at the oven, on the top of which lay a sick man wrapped in sheepskins.

'Uncle Theodore! I say, Uncle Theodore!' said the young driver, entering the room in his sheepskin coat with a whip stuck in his belt, and addressing the sick man.

'What do you want Theodore for, lazybones?' asked one of the drivers. 'There's your carriage waiting for you.'

'I want to ask for his boots; mine are quite worn out,' answered the young fellow, tossing back his hair and straightening the mittens tucked in his belt. 'Is he asleep? I say, Uncle Theodore!' he repeated, walking over to the oven.

'What is it?' answered a weak voice, and a lean face with a

67

red beard looked down from the oven, while a broad, emaciated, pale, and hairy hand pulled up the coat over the dirty shirt covering his angular shoulder.

'Give me a drink, lad . . . What is it you want?'

The lad handed him up a dipper with water.

'Well, you see, Theodore,' he said, stepping from foot to foot, 'I expect you don't need your new boots now; won't you let me have them? I don't suppose you'll go about any more.'

The sick man, lowering his weary head to the shiny dipper and immersing his sparse drooping moustache in the turbid water, drank feebly but eagerly. His matted beard was dirty, and his sunken clouded eyes had difficulty in looking up at the lad's face. Having finished drinking he tried to lift his hand to wipe his wet lips, but he could not do so, and rubbed them on the sleeve of his coat instead. Silently, and breathing heavily through his nose, he looked straight into the lad's eyes, collecting his strength.

'But perhaps you have promised them to someone else?' asked the lad. 'If so, it's all right. The worst of it is, it's wet outside and I have to go about my work, so I said to myself: "Suppose I ask Theodore for his boots; I expect he doesn't need them." If you need them yourself – just say so.'

Something began to rumble and gurgle in the sick man's chest; he doubled up and began to choke with an abortive cough in his throat.

'Need them indeed!' the cook snapped out unexpectedly so

68

as to be heard by the whole room. 'He hasn't come down from the oven for more than a month! Hear how he's choking – it makes me ache inside just to hear him. What does he want with boots? They won't bury him in new boots. And it was time long ago – God forgive me the sin! See how he chokes. He ought to be taken into the other room or somewhere. They say there are hospitals in the town. Is it right that he should take up the whole corner? – there's no more to be said. I've no room at all, and yet they expect cleanliness!'

'Hullo, Sergey! Come along and take your place, the gentle-folk are waiting!' shouted the drivers' overseer, looking in at the door.

Sergey was about to go without waiting for a reply, but the sick man, while coughing, let him understand by a look that he wanted to give him an answer.

'Take my boots, Sergey,' he said when he had mastered the cough and rested a moment. 'But listen . . . Buy a stone for me when I die,' he added hoarsely.

'Thank you, uncle. Then I'll take them, and I'll buy a stone for sure.'

'There, lads, you heard that?' the sick man managed to utter, and then bent double again and began to choke.

'All right, we heard,' said one of the drivers. 'Go and take your seat, Sergey, there's the overseer running back. The Shirkin lady is ill, you know.'

Sergey quickly pulled off his unduly big, dilapidated boots

69

and threw them under a bench. Uncle Theodore's new boots just fitted him, and having put them on he went to the carriage with his eyes fixed on his feet.

'What fine boots! Let me grease them,' said a driver, who held some axle-grease in his hand, as Sergey climbed onto the box and gathered up the reins. 'Did he give them to you for nothing?'

'Why, are you envious?' Sergey replied, rising and wrapping the skirts of his coat under his legs. 'Off with you! Gee up, my beauties!' he shouted to the horses, flourishing the whip, and the carriage and calèche with their occupants, portmanteaux, and trunks rolled rapidly along the wet road and disappeared in the grey autumnal mist.

The sick driver was left on the top of the oven in the stuffy room and, unable to relieve himself by coughing, turned with an effort onto his other side and became silent.

Till late in the evening people came in and out of the room and dined there. The sick man made no sound. When night came, the cook climbed up onto the oven and stretched over his legs to get down her sheepskin coat.

'Don't be cross with me, Nastasya,' said the sick man. 'I shall soon leave your corner empty.'

'All right, all right, never mind,' muttered Nastasya. 'But what is it that hurts you? Tell me, uncle.'

'My whole inside has wasted away. God knows what it is!'

'I suppose your throat hurts when you cough?'

'Everything hurts. My death has come – that's how it is. Oh, oh, oh!' moaned the sick man.

'Cover up your feet like this,' said Nastasya, drawing his coat over him as she climbed down from the oven.

A night-light burnt dimly in the room. Nastasya and some ten drivers slept on the floor or on the benches, loudly snoring. The sick man groaned feebly, coughed, and turned about on the oven. Towards morning he grew quite quiet.

'I had a queer dream last night,' said Nastasya next morning, stretching herself in the dim light. 'I dreamt that Uncle Theodore got down from the oven and went out to chop wood. "Come, Nastasya," he says, "I'll help you!" and I say, "How can you chop wood now?", but he just seizes the axe and begins chopping quickly, quickly, so that the chips fly all about. "Why," I say, "haven't you been ill?" "No," he says, "I am well," and he swings the axe so that I was quite frightened. I gave a cry and woke up. I wonder whether he is dead! Uncle Theodore! I say, Uncle Theodore!'

Theodore did not answer.

'True enough he may have died. I'll go and see,' said one of the drivers, waking up.

The lean hand covered with reddish hair that hung down from the oven was pale and cold.

'I'll go and tell the station-master,' said the driver. 'I think he is dead.'

Theodore had no relatives: he was from some distant place.

They buried him next day in the new cemetery beyond the wood, and Nastasya went on for days telling everybody of her dream, and of having been the first to discover that Uncle Theodore was dead.

III

SPRING HAD come. Rivulets of water hurried down the wet streets of the city, gurgling between lumps of frozen manure; the colours of the people's clothes as they moved along the streets looked vivid and their voices sounded shrill. Behind the garden-fences the buds on the trees were swelling and their branches were just audibly swaying in the fresh breeze. Everywhere transparent drops were forming and falling . . . The sparrows chirped, and fluttered awkwardly with their little wings. On the sunny side of the street, on the fences, houses, and trees, everything was in motion and sparkling. There was joy and youth everywhere in the sky, on the earth, and in the hearts of men.

In one of the chief streets fresh straw had been strewn on the road before a large, important house, where the invalid who had been in a hurry to go abroad lay dying.

At the closed door of her room stood the invalid's husband and an elderly woman. On the sofa a priest sat with bowed head, holding something wrapped in his stole. In a corner of the room the sick woman's old mother lay on an invalid chair weeping bitterly: beside her stood one maidservant holding a clean handkerchief, waiting for her to ask for it; while another was rubbing her temples with something and blowing under the old lady's cap onto her grey head.

'Well, may Christ aid you, dear friend,' the husband said to the elderly woman who stood near him at the door. 'She has such confidence in you, and you know so well how to talk to her, so persuade her as well as you can, my dear – go to her.' He was about to open the door, but her cousin stopped him, pressing her handkerchief several times to her eyes and giving her head a shake.

'Well, I don't think I look as if I had been crying now,' said she and, opening the door herself, went in.

The husband was in great agitation and seemed quite distracted. He walked towards the old woman, but while still several steps from her turned back, walked about the room, and went up to the priest. The priest looked at him, raised his eyebrows to heaven, and sighed: his thick, greyish beard also rose as he sighed and then came down again.

'My God, my God!' said the husband.

'What is to be done?' said the priest with a sigh, and again his eyebrows and beard rose and fell.

'And her mother is here!' said the husband almost in despair. 'She won't be able to bear it. You see, loving her as she does . . . I don't know! If you would only try to comfort her, Father, and persuade her to go away.'

The priest got up and went to the old woman.

'It is true, no one can appreciate a mother's heart,' he said – 'but God is merciful.'

The old woman's face suddenly twitched all over, and she began to hiccup hysterically.

'God is merciful,' the priest continued when she grew a little calmer. 'Let me tell you of a patient in my parish who was much worse than Mary Dmitrievna, and a simple tradesman cured her in a short time with various herbs. That tradesman is even now in Moscow. I told Vasili Dmitrich – we might try him . . . It would at any rate comfort the invalid. To God all is possible.'

'No, she will not live,' said the old woman. 'God is taking her instead of me,' and the hysterical hiccuping grew so violent that she fainted.

The sick woman's husband hid his face in his hands and ran out of the room.

In the passage the first person he met was his six-year-old son, who was running full speed after his younger sister.

'Won't you order the children to be taken to their mamma?' asked the nurse.

'No, she doesn't want to see them – it would upset her.'

The boy stopped a moment, looked intently into his father's face, then gave a kick and ran on, shouting merrily.

'She pretends to be the black horse, Papa!' he shouted, pointing to his sister.

Meanwhile in the other room the cousin sat down beside the

invalid, and tried by skilful conversation to prepare her for the thought of death. The doctor was mixing a draught at another window.

The patient, in a white dressing-gown, sat up in bed supported all round by pillows, and looked at her cousin in silence.

'Ah, my dear friend,' she said, unexpectedly interrupting her, 'don't prepare me! Don't treat me like a child. I am a Christian. I know it all. I know I have not long to live, and know that if my husband had listened to me sooner I should now have been in Italy and perhaps – no, certainly – should have been well. Everybody told him so. But what is to be done? Evidently this is God's wish. We have all sinned heavily. I know that, but I trust in God's mercy everybody will be forgiven, probably all will be forgiven. I try to understand myself. I have many sins to answer for, dear friend, but then how much I have had to suffer! I try to bear my sufferings patiently . . .'

'Then shall I call the priest, my dear? You will feel still more comfortable after receiving Communion,' said her cousin.

The sick woman bent her head in assent.

'God forgive me, sinner that I am!' she whispered.

The cousin went out and signalled with her eyes to the priest.

'She is an angel!' she said to the husband, with tears in her eyes. The husband burst into tears; the priest went into the next room; the invalid's mother was still unconscious, and all was silent there. Five minutes later he came out again, and after taking off his stole, straightened out his hair.

'Thank God she is calmer now,' she said, 'and wishes to see you.'

The cousin and the husband went into the sick-room. The invalid was silently weeping, gazing at an icon.

'I congratulate you, my dear,'* said her husband.

'Thank you! How well I feel now, what inexpressible sweetness I feel!' said the sick woman, and a soft smile played on her thin lips. 'How merciful God is! Is He not? Merciful and all powerful!' and again she looked at the icon with eager entreaty and her eyes full of tears.

Then suddenly, as if she remembered something, she beckoned to her husband to come closer.

'You never want to do what I ask . . .' she said in a feeble and dissatisfied voice.

The husband, craning his neck, listened to her humbly.

'What is it, my dear?'

'How many times have I not said that these doctors don't know anything; there are simple women who can heal, and who do cure. The priest told me . . . there is also a tradesman . . . Send!'

'For whom, my dear?'

'O God, you don't want to understand anything! . . .' And the sick woman's face puckered and she closed her eyes.

The doctor came up and took her hand. Her pulse was beating

---

* It was customary in Russia to congratulate people who had received Communion.

76

more and more feebly. He glanced at the husband. The invalid noticed that gesture and looked round in affright. The cousin turned away and began to cry.

'Don't cry, don't torture yourself and me,' said the patient. 'Don't take from me the last of my tranquillity.'

'You are an angel,' said the cousin, kissing her hand.

'No, kiss me here! Only dead people are kissed on the hand. My God, my God!'

That same evening the patient was a corpse, and the body lay in a coffin in the music-room of the large house. A deacon sat alone in that big room reading the Psalms of David through his nose in a monotonous voice. A bright light from the wax candles in their tall silver candlesticks fell on the pale brow of the dead woman, on her heavy wax-like hands, on the stiff folds of the pall which brought out in awesome relief the knees and the toes. The deacon without understanding the words read on monotonously, and in the quiet room the words sounded strangely and died away. Now and then from a distant room came the sounds of children's voices and the patter of their feet.

'Thou hidest thy face, they are troubled,' said the Psalter. 'Thou takest away their breath, they die and return to their dust. Thou sendest forth thy spirit, they are created: and thou renewest the face of the earth. The glory of the Lord shall endure for ever.'

The dead woman's face looked stern and majestic. Neither in the clear cold brow nor in the firmly closed lips was there any movement. She seemed all attention. But had she even now understood those solemn words?

IV

A MONTH later a stone chapel was being erected over the grave of the deceased woman. Over the driver's tomb there was still no stone, and only the light green grass sprouted on the mound which served as the only token of the past existence of a man.

'It will be a sin, Sergey,' said the cook at the station-house one day, 'if you don't buy a stone for Theodore. You kept saying "It's winter, it's winter!" but why don't you keep your word now? You know I witnessed it. He has already come back once to ask you to do it; if you don't buy him one, he'll come again and choke you.'

'But why? I'm not backing out of it,' replied Sergey. 'I'll buy a stone as I said I would, and give a ruble and a half for it. I haven't forgotten it, but it has to be fetched. When I happen to be in town I'll buy one.'

'You might at least put up a cross – you ought to – else it's really wrong,' interposed an old driver. 'You know you are wearing his boots.'

'Where can I get a cross? I can't cut one out of a log.'

'What do you mean, can't cut one out of a log? You take an axe and go into the forest early, and you can cut one there. Cut down a young ash or something like that, and you can make a cross of it . . . you may have to treat the forester to vodka; but one can't afford to treat him for every trifle. There now, I broke my splinter-bar and went and cut a new one, and nobody said a word.'

Early in the morning, as soon as it was daybreak, Sergey took an axe and went into the wood.

A cold white cover of dew, which was still falling untouched by the sun, lay on everything. The east was imperceptibly growing brighter, reflecting its pale light on the vault of heaven still veiled by a covering of clouds. Not a blade of grass below, nor a leaf on the topmost branches of the trees, stirred. Only occasionally a sound of wings amid the brushwood, or a rustling on the ground, broke the silence of the forest. Suddenly a strange sound, foreign to Nature, resounded and died away at the outskirts of the forest. Again the sound was heard, and was rhythmically repeated at the foot of the trunk of one of the motionless trees. A tree-top began to tremble in an unwonted manner, its juicy leaves whispered something, and the robin who had been sitting in one of its branches fluttered twice from place to place with a whistle, and jerking its tail sat down on another tree.

The axe at the bottom gave off a more and more muffled sound, sappy white chips were scattered on the dewy grass and a slight creaking was heard above the sound of the blows. The tree, shuddering in its whole body, bent down and quickly rose again, vibrating with fear on its roots. For an instant all was still, but the tree bent again, a crashing sound came from its trunk, and with its branches breaking and its boughs hanging down it fell with its crown on the damp earth.

The sounds of the axe and of the footsteps were silenced. The robin whistled and flitted higher. A twig which it brushed with its wings shook a little and then with all its foliage grew still like the rest. The trees flaunted the beauty of their motionless branches still more joyously in the newly cleared space.

The first sunbeams, piercing the translucent cloud, shone out and spread over earth and sky. The mist began to quiver like waves in the hollows, the dew sparkled and played on the verdure, the transparent cloudlets grew whiter, and hurriedly dispersed over the deepening azure vault of the sky. The birds stirred in the thicket and, as though bewildered, twittered joyfully about something; the sappy leaves whispered gladly and peacefully on the tree-tops, and the branches of those that were living began to rustle slowly and majestically over the dead and prostrate tree.

Polikushka

I

'I T'S FOR YOU to say, ma'am! Only it would be a pity if it's the Dutlovs. They're all good men and one of them must go if we don't send at least one of the house-serfs,' said the steward. 'As it is, everyone is hinting at them ... But it's just as you please, ma'am!'

And he placed his right hand over his left in front of him, inclined his head towards his right shoulder, drew in his thin lips almost with a smack, turned up his eyes, and said no more, evidently intending to keep silent for a long time and to listen without reply to all the nonsense his mistress was sure to utter.

The steward – clean-shaven and dressed in a long coat of a peculiar steward-like cut – who had come to report to his proprietress that autumn evening, was by birth a domestic serf.

The report from the lady's point of view meant listening

to a statement of the business done on her estate and giving instructions for further business. From Egor Mikhaylovich's (the steward's) point of view, 'reporting' was a ceremony of standing straight on both feet with out-turned toes in a corner facing the sofa, and listening to all sorts of irrelevant chatter, and by various ways and means getting the mistress into a state of mind in which she would quickly and impatiently say, 'All right, all right!' to all that Egor Mikhaylovich proposed.

The business under consideration was the conscription. The Pokrovsk estate had to supply three recruits at the Feast of Pokrov.* Fate itself seemed to have selected two of them by a coincidence of domestic, moral, and economic circumstances. As far as they were concerned there could be no hesitation or dispute either on the part of the mistress, the Commune, or of public opinion. But who the third was to be was a debatable point. The steward was anxious to save the Dutlovs (in which family there were three men of military age), and to send Polikushka, a married house-serf with a very bad reputation, who had been caught more than once stealing sacks, harness, and hay; but the mistress, who had often petted Polikushka's ragged children and improved his morals by exhortations from the Bible, did not wish to give him up. At the same time she did not wish to injure the Dutlovs, whom she did not know and had never even seen. But for some reason she did not seem able to grasp

---

* The Intercession of the Virgin, the 1st of October (old style).

the fact, and the steward could not make up his mind to tell her straight out that if Polikushka did not go, one of the Dutlovs would have to. 'But I don't wish the Dutlovs any ill!' she said feelingly. 'If you don't – then pay three hundred rubles for a substitute,' should have been the steward's reply; but that would have been bad policy.

So Egor Mikhaylovich took up a comfortable position, and even leant imperceptibly against the door-post, while keeping a servile expression on his face and watching the movements of the lady's lips and the flutter of the frills of her cap and their shadow on the wall beneath a picture. But he did not consider it at all necessary to attend to the meaning of her words. The lady spoke long and said much. A desire to yawn gave him cramp behind his ears, but he adroitly turned the spasm into a cough, and holding his hand to his mouth gave a croak. Not long ago I saw Lord Palmerston sitting with his hat over his face while a member of the Opposition was storming at the Ministry, and then suddenly rise and in a three-hours' speech answer his opponent point by point. I saw it without surprise, because I had seen the same kind of thing going on between Egor Mikhaylovich and his mistress a thousand times. At last – perhaps he was afraid of falling asleep or thought she was letting herself go too far – he changed the weight of his body from his left to his right foot and began, as he always did, with an unctuous preface:

'Just as you please to order, ma'am . . . Only there is a gathering of the Commune now being held in front of my office window and we must come to some decision. The order says that the recruits are to be in town before the Feast of Pokrov. Among the peasants the Dutlovs are being suggested, and no one else. The *mir** does not trouble about your interests. What does it care if we ruin the Dutlovs? I know what a hard time they've been having! Ever since I first had the stewardship they have been living in want. The old man's youngest nephew has scarcely had time to grow up to be a help, and now they're to be ruined again! And I, as you well know, am as careful of your property as of my own . . . It's a pity, ma'am, whatever you're pleased to think! . . . After all they're neither kith nor kin to me, and I've had nothing from them . . .'

'Why, Egor, as if I ever thought of such a thing!' interrupted the lady, and at once suspected him of having been bribed by the Dutlovs.

'. . . Only theirs is the best-kept homestead in the whole of Pokrovsk. They're God-fearing, hard-working peasants. The old man has been church Elder for thirty years; he doesn't drink or swear, and he goes to church . . .' (The steward well knew with what to bait the hook.) '. . . But the chief thing that I would like to report to you is that he has only two sons – the others are nephews adopted out of charity – and so they ought to cast lots only with the two-men families. Many families have split up because of their own improvidence and their sons have

---

* The Village Commune.

separated from them, and so they are safe now – while these will have to suffer just because they have been charitable.'

Here the lady could not follow at all. She did not understand what he meant by 'two-men families' or 'charitableness'. She only heard sounds and observed the nankeen buttons on the steward's coat. The top one, which he probably did not button up so often, was firmly fixed on, the middle one was hanging loose and ought long ago to have been sewn on again. But it is a well-known fact that in a conversation, especially a business conversation, it is not at all necessary to understand what is being said, but only to remember what you yourself want to say. The lady acted accordingly.

'How is it you won't understand, Egor Mikhaylovich?' she said. 'I have not the least desire that a Dutlov should go as a soldier. One would think that knowing me as you do you might credit me with the wish to do everything in my power to help my serfs, and that I don't want any harm to come to them, and would sacrifice all I possess to escape from this sad necessity and to send neither Dutlov nor Polikushka.' (I don't know whether it occurred to the steward that to escape the sad necessity there was no need to sacrifice everything – that, in fact, three hundred rubles would suffice; but this thought might well have crossed his mind.)

'I will only tell you this: that I will not give up Polikushka on any account. When he confessed to me of his own accord after that affair with the clock, and wept, and gave his word

85

to amend, I talked to him for a long time and saw that he was touched and sincerely penitent.' ('There! She's off now!' thought Egor Mikhaylovich, and began to scrutinize the syrup she had in a glass of water: 'Is it orange or lemon? Slightly bitter, I expect,' thought he.) 'That is seven months ago now, and he has not once been tipsy, and has behaved splendidly. His wife tells me he is a different man. How can you wish me to punish him now that he has reformed? Besides it would be inhuman to make a soldier of a man who has five children, and only he to keep them . . . No, you'd better not say any more about it, Egor!'

And the lady took a sip from her glass.

Egor Mikhaylovich watched the motion of her throat as the liquid passed down it and then replied shortly and drily:

'Then Dutlov's decided on?'

The lady clasped her hands together.

'How is it you don't understand? Do I wish Dutlov ill? Have I anything against him? God is my witness I am prepared to do anything for them . . .' (She glanced at a picture in the corner, but remembered it was not an icon. 'Well, never mind . . . that's not to the point,' she thought. And again, strange to say, the idea of the three hundred rubles did not occur to her . . .) 'Well, what can I do? What do I know about it? It's impossible for me to know. Well then, I rely on you – you know my wishes . . . Act so as to satisfy everybody and according to the law . . . What's to be done?

They are not the only ones: everyone has times of trouble. Only Polikushka can't be sent. You must understand that it would be dreadful of me to do such a thing . . .'

She was roused and would have continued to speak for a long time had not one of her maidservants entered the room at that moment.

'What is it, Dunyasha?'

'A peasant has come to ask Egor Mikhaylovich if the meeting is to wait for him,' said Dunyasha, and glanced angrily at Egor Mikhaylovich. ('Oh, that steward!' she thought; 'he's upset the mistress. Now she won't let me get a wink of sleep till two in the morning!')

'Well then, Egor, go and do the best you can.'

'Yes, ma'am.' He did not say anything more about Dutlov. 'And who is to go to the market-gardener to fetch the money?'

'Has not Peter returned from town?'

'No, ma'am.'

'Could not Nicholas go?'

'Father is down with backache,' remarked Dunyasha.

'Shall I go myself tomorrow, ma'am?' asked the steward.

'No, Egor, you are wanted here.' The lady pondered. 'How much is it?'

'Four hundred and sixty-two rubles.'

'Send Polikushka,' said the lady, with a determined glance at Egor Mikhaylovich's face.

Egor Mikhaylovich stretched his lips into the semblance of

a smile but without parting his teeth, and the expression on his face did not change.

'Yes, ma'am.'

'Send him to me.'

'Yes, ma'am'; and Egor Mikhaylovich went to the counting-house.

II

Polikey (or Polikushka, as he was usually contemptuously called), as a man of little importance, of tarnished reputation, and not a native of the village, had no influence either with the housekeeper, the butler, the steward, or the lady's-maid. His *corner* was the very worst, though there were seven in his family. The late proprietor had had these *corners* built in the following manner: in the middle of a brick building, about twenty-three feet square, there was a large brick baking-oven surrounded by a passage, and the four corners of the building were separated from this 'colidor' (as the domestic serfs called it) by wooden partitions. So there was not much room in these *corners*, especially in Polikey's, which was nearest to the door. The conjugal couch, with a print quilt and pillow-cases, a cradle with a baby in it, and a small three-legged table (on which the cooking and washing were done and all sorts of domestic articles placed, and at which Polikey – who was a horse-doctor – worked), tubs, clothing, some chickens, a calf, and the seven members of the family, filled the whole *corner* – and could not have stirred in it had it not been for their quarter of the brick stove (on which both people and things could lie) and for the possibility of going out onto the steps. That, however, was hardly possible, for it is cold in October and the seven of them only possessed one sheepskin cloak between them; but on the other hand the children could keep warm by running about and the grown-ups by working, and both the one and the other could climb on the top of the stove where the temperature rose as high as 120 degrees Fahrenheit. It may seem dreadful to live in such conditions, but they did not mind – it was quite possible to live. Akulina washed and sewed her husband's and her children's clothes, spun, wove, and bleached her linen, cooked and baked in the common oven, and quarrelled and gossiped with her neighbours. The monthly rations sufficed not only for the children, but for an addition to the cow's food. Firewood was free, and so was fodder for the cattle, and a little hay from the stables sometimes came their way. They had a strip of kitchen garden. Their cow had calved, and they had their own fowls. Polikey was employed in the stables to look after two stallions; he bled horses and cattle, cleaned their hoofs, lanced their sores, administered ointments of his own invention, and for this was paid in money and in kind. Also some of the proprietress's oats used to find their way into his possession, and for two measures of it a peasant in the village gave twenty pounds of mutton regularly every month. Life would have been quite bearable had there been no trouble at heart. But the family had a great trouble. Polikey in his youth had lived at a stud-farm in another village. The groom into whose hands he happened to fall was the greatest thief in the whole district, and got exiled to Siberia. Under this man Polikey served his apprenticeship, and in his youth became so used to 'these trifles' that in later life, though he would willingly have left off, he could not rid himself of the habit. He was a young man and weak; he had neither father nor mother nor anyone else to teach him. Polikey liked drink, and did not like to see anything lying about loose. Whether it was a strap, a piece of harness, a padlock, a bolt, or a thing of greater value, Polikey found some use for everything. There were people everywhere who would take these things and pay for them in drink or in money, by agreement. Such earnings, so people say, are the easiest to get: no apprenticeship is required, no labour or anything, and he who has once tried that kind of work does not care for any other. It has only one drawback: although you get things cheap and easily and live pleasantly, yet all of a sudden – through somebody's malice – things go all wrong, the trade fails, everything has to be accounted for at once, and you rue the day you were born.

And so it happened to Polikey. Polikey had married and God had given him good luck. His wife, the herdsman's daughter, turned out to be a healthy, intelligent, hard-working woman, who bore him one fine baby after another. And though Polikey still stuck to his trade all went well till one fine day his luck forsook him and he was caught. And it was all about a trifle: he had hidden away some leather reins of a peasant's. They were found, he was beaten, the mistress was told of it, and he was watched. He was caught a second and a third time. People began to taunt him, the steward threatened to have him conscripted, the mistress gave him a scolding, and his wife wept and was broken-hearted. Everything went wrong. He was a good-natured man; not bad, but only weak. He was fond of drink and so in the habit of it that he could not leave it alone. Sometimes his wife would scold him and even beat him when he came home drunk, and he would weep, saying: 'Unfortunate man that I am, what shall I do? Blast my eyes, I'll give it up! Never again!' A month would go by, he would leave home, get drunk, and not be seen for a couple of days. And his neighbours would say: 'He must get the money somewhere to go on the spree with!' His latest trouble had been with the office clock. There was an old wall-clock there that had not been in working order for a long time. He happened to go in at the open door by himself and the clock tempted him. He took it and got rid of it in the town. As ill-luck would have it, the shopman to whom he sold the clock was related to one of the house-serfs, and coming to see her one holiday he spoke about the clock. People began making inquiries – especially the steward, who disliked Polikey – just as if it was anybody else's concern! It was all found out and reported to the mistress, and she sent for Polikey. He fell at her feet at once and pathetically confessed everything, just as his wife had told him to do. He carried out her instructions very well. The mistress began admonishing him; she talked and talked and maundered on about God and virtue and the future life and about wife and children, and at last moved him to tears. Then she said:

'I forgive you; only you must promise me never to do it again!'

'Never in all my life. May I go to perdition! May my bowels gush out!' said Polikey, and wept touchingly.

Polikey went home and for the rest of the day lay on the stove blubbering like a calf. Since then nothing more had been traced to him. But his life was no longer pleasant; he was looked on as a thief, and when the time of the conscription drew near everybody hinted at him.

As already mentioned, Polikey was a horse-doctor. How he had suddenly become one nobody knew, himself least of all. At the stud-farm, when he worked under the head-keeper who got exiled, his only duties were to clean out the dung from the stables, sometimes to groom the horses, and to carry water. He could not have learnt it there. Then he became a weaver: after that he worked in a garden, weeding the paths; then he was condemned to break bricks for some offence; then he took a place as yard-porter with a merchant, paying a yearly sum to his mistress for leave to do so. So evidently he could not have had any experience as a veterinary there either; yet somehow during his last stay at home his reputation as a wonderfully and even a rather supernaturally clever horse-doctor began gradually to spread. He bled a horse once or twice, then threw it down and prodded about in its thigh, and then demanded that it should be placed in a trave, where he began cutting its frog till it bled, though the horse struggled and even whined, and he said this meant 'letting off the sub-hoof blood'! Then he explained to a peasant that it was absolutely necessary to let the blood from both veins, 'for greater ease', and began to strike the dull lancet with a mallet; then he bandaged the inn-keeper's horse under its belly with a selvedge torn from his wife's shawl, and finally he began to sprinkle all sorts of sores with vitriol, to drench them with something out of a bottle, and sometimes to give internally whatever came into his head. And the more horses he tormented and did to death, the more he was believed in and the more of them were brought to him.

I feel that for us educated people it is hardly the thing to laugh at Polikey. The methods he employed to inspire confidence are the same that influenced our fathers, that influence us, and will influence our children. The peasant lying prone on the head of his only mare (which not only constitutes his whole wealth but is almost one of his family) and gazing with faith and horror at Polikey's frowning look of importance and thin arms with upturned sleeves, as, with the healing rag or a bottle of vitriol between his teeth, he presses upon the very spot that is sore and boldly cuts into the living flesh (with the secret thought, 'The bow-legged brute will be sure to get over it!'), at the same time pretending to know where is blood and where pus, which is a tendon and which a vein – that peasant cannot conceive that Polikey could lift his hand to cut without knowing where to do it. He himself could not do so. And once the thing is done he will not reproach himself with having given permission to cut unnecessarily. I don't know how you feel about it, but I have gone through the same experience with a doctor who, at my request, was tormenting those dear to me. The lancet, the whitish bottle of sublimate, and the words, 'the staggers – glanders – to let blood, or matter', and so on, do they not come to the same thing as 'neurosis, rheumatism, organisms', and so forth? *Wage du zu irren und zu träumen** refers not so much to poets as to doctors and veterinary surgeons.

III

ON THE evening when the village meeting, in the cold darkness of an October night, was choosing the recruits and vociferating in front of the office, Polikey sat on the edge of his bed pounding some horse medicine on the table with a bottle – but what it was he himself did not know. He had there corrosive sublimate, sulphur, Glauber's salts, and some kind of herb which he had

---

* 'Dare to err and dream.'

gathered, having suddenly imagined it to be good for broken wind and then considered it not amiss for other disorders. The children were already lying down – two on the stove, two on the bed, and one in the cradle beside which Akulina sat spinning. The candle-end – one of the proprietress's candles which had not been put away carefully enough – was burning in a wooden candlestick on the window-sill and Akulina every now and then got up to snuff it with her fingers, so that her husband should not have to break off his important occupation. There were some free-thinkers who regarded Polikey as a worthless veterinary and a worthless man. Others, the majority, considered him a worthless man but a great master of his art; but Akulina, though she often scolded and even beat her husband, thought him undoubtedly the first of horse-doctors and the best of men. Polikey sprinkled some kind of simple on the palm of his hand (he never used scales, and spoke ironically of the Germans who use them: 'This,' he used to say, 'is not an apothecary's!'). Polikey weighed the simple on his hand and tossed it up, but there did not seem enough of it and he poured in ten times more. 'I'll put in the lot,' he said to himself. 'It will pick 'em up better.' Akulina quickly turned round at the sound of her lord and master's voice, expecting some command; but seeing that the business did not concern her she shrugged her shoulders. 'What knowledge! . . . Where does he get it?' she thought, and went on spinning. The paper which had held the simple fell to the floor. Akulina did not overlook this.

'Annie,' she cried, 'look! Father has dropped something. Pick it up!'

Annie put out her thin little bare legs from under the cloak with which she was covered, slid down under the table like a kitten, and got the paper.

'Here, daddy,' she said, and darted back into bed with her chilled little feet.

'Don't puth!' squeaked her lisping younger sister sleepily.

'I'll give it you!' muttered Akulina, and both heads disappeared again under the cloak.

'He'll give me three rubles,' said Polikey, corking up the bottle. 'I'll cure the horse. It's even too cheap,' he added, 'brain-splitting work! . . . Akulina, go and ask Nikita for a little 'baccy. I'll pay him back tomorrow.'

Polikey took out of his trouser-pocket a lime-wood pipe-stem, which had once been painted, with a sealing-wax mouthpiece, and began fixing it onto the bowl.

Akulina left her spindle and went out, managing to steer clear of everything – though this was not easy. Polikey opened the cupboard and put away the medicine, then tilted a vodka bottle into his mouth, but it was empty and he made a grimace. But when his wife brought the tobacco he sat down on the edge of the bed, after filling and lighting his pipe, and his face beamed with the content and pride of a man who has completed his day's task. Whether he was thinking how on the morrow he would catch hold of the horse's tongue and pour his wonderful mixture down its throat, or reflecting that a useful person never gets a refusal – 'There, now! Hadn't Nikita sent him the tobacco?' – anyhow he felt happy. Suddenly the door, which hung on one hinge, was thrown open and a maidservant from *up there* – not the second maid but the third, the little one that was kept to run errands – entered their *corner*. (*Up there*, as everyone knows, means the master's house, even if it stands on lower ground.) Aksyutka – that was the girl's name – always flew like a bullet, and did it without bending her arms, which keeping time with the speed of her flight swung like pendulums, not at her sides but in front of her. Her cheeks were always redder than her pink dress, and her tongue moved as fast as her legs. She flew into the room, and for some reason catching hold of the stove, began to sway to and fro; then as if intent on not emitting more than two or three words at once, she suddenly addressed Akulina breathlessly as follows:

'The mistress . . . has given orders . . . that Polikey should come this minute . . . orders to come up . . .'

She stopped, drawing breath with difficulty.

'Egor Mikhaylovich has been with the mistress . . . they talked about *rickruits* . . . they mentioned Polikey . . . Avdotya Nikolaevna . . . has ordered him to come this minute . . . Avdotya Nikolaevna has ordered . . .' again a sigh, 'to come this minute . . .'

For half a minute Aksyutka looked round at Polikey and at Akulina and the children – who had put out their heads from under their coverlets – picked up a nutshell that lay on the stove and threw it at little Annie. Then she repeated: 'To come this minute! . . .' and rushed out of the room like a whirlwind, the pendulums swinging as usual across her line of flight.

Akulina again rose and got her husband his boots – abominable soldier's boots with holes in them – and took down his coat from the stove and handed it to him without looking at him.

'Won't you change your shirt, Polikey?'

'No,' he answered.

Akulina never once looked at his face while he put on his boots and coat, and she did well not to look. Polikey's face was pale, his nether jaw twitched, and in his eyes there was that tearful, meek, and deeply mournful look one only sees in the eyes of kindly, weak, and guilty people. He combed his hair and was going out; but his wife stopped him, tucked in the string of his shirt that hung down from under his coat, and put his cap on for him.

'What's that, Polikey? Has the mistress sent for you?' came the voice of the carpenter's wife from behind the partition.

Only that very morning the carpenter's wife had had high words with Akulina about her pot of lye* that Polikey's children had upset in her *corner*, and at first she was pleased to hear Polikey being summoned to the mistress – most likely for no good. She was a subtle, diplomatic lady, with a biting tongue.

---

* Made by scalding wood-ash taken from the stove, and used for washing clothes.

Nobody knew better than she how to cut one with a word: so at least she imagined.

'I expect you'll be sent to town to buy things,' she continued. 'I suppose a trusty person is wanted for that job so she is sending you! You might buy me a quarter of a pound of tea there, Polikey.'

Akulina forced back her tears, and an angry expression distorted her lips. She felt as if she could have clutched 'that vixen, the joiner's wife, by her mangy hair'. But as she looked at her children and thought that they would be left fatherless and she herself be a soldier's wife and as good as widowed, she forgot the sharp-tongued carpenter's wife, hid her face in her hands, sat down on the bed, and let her head sink in the pillows.

'Mammy, you're cwushing me!' lisped the little girl, pulling the cloak with which she was covered from under her mother's elbow.

'If only you'd die, all of you! I've brought you into the world for nothing but sorrow!' cried Akulina, and sobbed aloud, to the delight of the carpenter's wife who had not yet forgotten the lye spilt that morning.

IV

HALF AN HOUR passed. The baby began to cry. Akulina got up and gave it the breast. Weeping no longer, but resting her thin though still handsome face on her hand and fixing her eyes on the last flickerings of the candle, she sat thinking why she had married, wondering why so many soldiers were needed, and also how she could pay out the carpenter's wife.

She heard her husband's footsteps and, wiping her tears, got up to let him pass. Polikey entered like a conqueror, threw his cap on the bed, puffed, and undid his girdle.

'Well, what did she want you for?'

'H'm! Of course! Polikushka is the least of men . . . but when there's business to be done, who's wanted? Why, Polikushka . . .'

'What business?'

Polikey was in no hurry to reply. He lit his pipe and spat.

'To go and fetch money from a merchant.'

'To fetch money?' Akulina asked.

Polikey chuckled and wagged his head.

'Ah! Ain't she clever at words? . . . "You have been regarded," she says, "as an untrustworthy man, but I trust you more than another"' (Polikey spoke loud that the neighbours might hear). '"You promised me you'd reform; here", she says, "is the first proof that I believe you. Go", she says, "to the merchant, fetch the money he owes, and bring it back to me." And I say: "We are all your serfs, ma'am," I say, "and must serve you as we serve God; so I feel that I can do anything for your Honour and cannot refuse any kind of work; whatever you order I will do, because I am your slave."' (He again smiled that peculiar, weak, kindly, guilty smile.) '"Well, then," she says, "you will do it faithfully? . . . You understand," she says, "that your fate depends on it?" — "How could I fail to understand that I can do it all? If they have told tales about me — well, anyone can tell tales about another . . . but I never in any way, I believe, have even had a thought against your Honour . . ." In a word, I buttered her up till my lady was quite softened . . . "I shall think highly of you," she says.' (He kept silent a minute, then the smile again appeared on his face.) 'I know very well how to talk to the likes of them! Formerly, when I used to go out to work on my own, at times someone would come down hard on me; but only let me get in a word or two and I'd butter him up till he'd be as smooth as silk!'

'Is it much money?'

'Fifteen hundred rubles,' carelessly replied Polikey.

She shook her head.

'When are you to go?'

'"Tomorrow," she says. "Take any horse you like," she says, "call at the office, and then start and God be with you!"'

'The Lord be praised!' said Akulina, rising and crossing herself. 'May God help you, Polikey,' she added in a whisper, so that she might not be heard beyond the partition and holding him by his shirt-sleeve. 'Polikey, listen to me! I beseech you in the name of Christ our God: kiss the cross when you start, and promise that not a drop shall pass your lips.'

'A likely thing!' he ejaculated; 'drink when carrying all that money! . . . Ah! how somebody was playing the piano up there!

Fine! . . .' he said, after a pause, and smiled. 'I suppose it was the young lady. I was standing like this in front of the mistress, beside the whatnot, and the young lady was rattling away behind the door. She rattled and rattled on, fitting it together so pat! O my! Wouldn't I like to play a tune! I'd soon master it, I would. I'm awfully good at that sort of thing . . . Let me have a clean shirt tomorrow!'

And they went to bed happy.

V

MEANWHILE the meeting in front of the office had been noisy. The business before them was no trifle. Almost all the peasants were present. While the steward was with the mistress they kept their caps on, more voices were heard, and they talked more loudly. The hum of deep voices, interrupted at rare intervals by breathless, husky, and shrill tones, filled the air and, entering through the windows of the mistress's house, sounded like the noise of a distant sea, making her feel a nervous agitation like that produced by a heavy thunderstorm – a sensation between fear and discomfort. She felt as if the voices might at any moment grow yet louder and faster and then something would happen. 'As if it could not all be done quietly, peaceably, without disputing and shouting,' she thought, 'according to the Christian law of brotherly love and meekness!'

Many voices were speaking at once, but Theodore Rezun, the carpenter, shouted loudest. There were two grown-up young men in his family and he was attacking the Dutlovs. Old Dutlov was defending himself: he stepped forward from the crowd behind which he had at first been standing. Now spreading out his arms, now clutching his little beard, he sputtered and snuffled in such a way that it would have been hard for him to understand what he himself was saying. His sons and nephews – splendid fellows all of them – stood huddled behind him, and the old man resembled the mother-hen in the game of Hawk and Chickens. The hawk was Rezun; and not only Rezun, but all the men who had two grown lads in family, and the fathers of only sons, and almost the whole meeting, were attacking Dutlov. The point was that Dutlov's brother had been recruited thirty years before, and that Dutlov wished therefore to be excused from taking his turn with the families in which there were three eligible young men, and wanted his brother's service in the army to be reckoned to the credit of his family, so that it should be given the same chance as those in which there were only two young men; and that these families should all draw lots equally and the third recruit be chosen from among all of them. Besides Dutlov's family there were four others in which there were three young men, but one was the village Elder's family and the mistress had exempted him. From the second a recruit had been taken the year before, and from each of the remaining families a recruit was now being taken. One of them had not even come to this meeting, but his wife stood sorrowfully behind all the others, vaguely hoping that the wheel of fortune might somehow turn her way. The red-haired Roman, the father of the other recruit, in a tattered coat – though he was not poor – hung his head and silently leant against the porch, only now and then looking up attentively at anyone who raised his voice, and then hanging his head again. Misery seemed to breathe from his whole figure. Old Semen Dutlov was a man to whose keeping anyone who knew anything of him would have trusted hundreds and thousands of rubles. He was a steady, God-fearing, reliable man, and was the church Elder. Therefore the excitement he was now in was all the more striking.

Rezun the carpenter, a tall dark man, was, on the contrary, a riotous drunkard, very smart in a dispute and in arguing with workmen, tradespeople, peasants, or gentlefolk, at meetings and fairs. Now he was self-possessed and sarcastic, and from his superior height was crushing down the spluttering church Elder with the whole strength of his ringing voice and oratorical talent. The church Elder was exasperated out of his usual sober groove. Besides these, the youngish, round-faced, square-headed, curly-bearded, thick-set Garaska Kopylov, one of the speakers of the younger generation, followed Rezun and took part in the dispute. He had already gained some weight at village meetings, having distinguished himself by his trenchant speeches. Then there was Theodore Melnichny, a tall, thin, yellow-faced, round-shouldered man, also young, with a scanty beard and small eyes, always embittered and gloomy, seeing the dark side of everything and often bewildering the meeting by unexpected and abrupt questions and remarks. Both these speakers sided with Rezun. Besides these there were two babblers who now and then joined in: one, called Khrapkov, with a most good-humoured face and flowing brown beard, who kept repeating the words 'Oh, my dearest friend!', the other, Zhidkov, a little fellow with a birdlike face who also kept remarking at every opportunity, 'That's how it is, brothers mine!', addressing himself to everybody and speaking fluently but never to the point. Both of these sided first with one and then with the other party, but no one listened to them. There were others like them, but these two, who kept moving through the crowd and shouting louder than anybody and frightening the mistress, were listened to less than anyone else. Intoxicated by the noise and shouting, they gave themselves up entirely to the pleasure of letting their tongues wag. There were many other characters among the members of the commune, stern, respectable, indifferent, or depressed; and there were women standing behind the men with sticks in their hands, but, God willing, I'll speak of them some other time. The greater part of the crowd, however, consisted of peasants who stood as if they were in church, whispering behind each other's backs about home affairs, or of when to cut faggots in the wood, or silently awaiting the end of the jabber. There were also rich peasants whose well-being the meeting could not add to nor diminish. Such was Ermil, with his broad shiny face, whom the peasants called the 'big-bellied', because he was rich. Such too was Starostin, whose face showed a self-satisfied expression of power that seemed to say, 'You may talk away, but no one will touch me! I have four sons, but not one of them will have to go.' Now and then these two were attacked by some independent thinker such as Kopylov and Rezun, but they replied quietly and firmly and with a consciousness of their own inviolability. If Dutlov was like the mother-hen in the game of Hawk and Chickens, his lads did not much resemble the chickens. They did not flutter about and squeak, but stood quietly behind him. His eldest son, Ignat, was already thirty; the second, Vasili, also was already a married man and moreover not fit for a recruit; the third, his nephew Elijah, who had just got married — a fair, rosy young man in a smart sheepskin coat (he was a post-chaise driver) — stood looking at the crowd, sometimes scratching his head under his hat, as if the whole matter was no concern of his, though it was just on him that the hawks wished to swoop down.

'If it comes to that, my grandfather was a soldier,' said one, 'and so I might refuse to draw lots in just the same way! . . . There's no such law, friend. Last recruiting, Mikhechev was taken though his uncle had not even returned from service then.'

'Neither your father nor your uncle ever served the Tsar,' Dutlov was saying at the same time. 'Why, you don't even serve the mistress or the commune, but spend all your time in the pub.

Your sons have separated from you because it's impossible to live with you, so you go suggesting other people's sons for recruits! But I have done police duty for ten years, and served as Elder. Twice I have been burnt out, and no one helped me over it; and now, because things are peaceable and decent in my home, am I to be ruined? . . . Give me back my brother, then! He has died in service for sure . . . Judge honestly according to God's law, Christian commune, and don't listen to a drunkard's drivel.'

And at the same time Geraska was saying to Dutlov:

'You are making your brother an excuse; but he was not sent by the commune. He was sent by the master because of his evil ways, so he's no excuse for you.'

Geraska had not finished when the lank yellow-faced Theodore Melnichny stepped forward and began dismally:

'Yes, that's the way! The masters send whom they please, and then the commune has to get the muddle straight. The commune has fixed on your lad, and if you don't like it, go and ask the lady. Perhaps she will order me, the one man of our family, to leave my children and go! . . . There's law for you!' he said bitterly, and waving his hand he went back to his former place.

Red-haired Roman, whose son had been chosen as a recruit, raised his head and muttered: 'That's it, that's it!' and even sat down on the step in vexation.

But these were not the only ones who were speaking at once. Besides those at the back who were talking about their own affairs, the babblers did not forget to do their part.

'And so it is, faithful commune,' said little Zhidkov, supporting Dutlov. 'One must judge in a Christian way . . . Like Christians I mean, brothers, we must judge.'

'One must judge according to one's conscience, my dear friend,' spoke the good-humoured Khrapkov, repeating Garaska Kopylov's words and pulling Dutlov by his sheepskin coat. 'It was the master's will and not the commune's decision.'

'That's right! So it was!' said others.

'What drunkard is drivelling there?' Rezun retorted to Dutlov. 'Did you stand me any drinks? Or is your son, whom they pick up by the roadside, going to reproach me for drinking? . . . Friends, we must decide! If you want to spare the Dutlovs, choose not only out of families with two men, but even an only son, and he will have the laugh of us!'

'A Dutlov will have to go! What's the good of talking?'

'Of course the three-men families must be the first to draw lots,' began different voices.

'We must first see what the mistress will say. Egor Mikhaylovich was saying that they wished to send a house-serf,' put in a voice.

This remark checked the dispute for a while, but soon it flared up anew and again came to personalities.

Ignat, whom Rezun had accused of being picked up drunk by the roadside, began to make out that Rezun had stolen a saw from some travelling carpenters, and that he had almost beaten his wife to death when he was drunk.

Rezun replied that he beat his wife drunk or sober, and still it was not enough, and this set everybody laughing. But about the saw he became suddenly indignant, stepped closer to Ignat and asked:

'Who stole? . . .'

'You did,' replied the sturdy Ignat, drawing still closer.

'Who stole? . . . Wasn't it you?' shouted Rezun.

'No, it was you,' said Ignat.

From the saw they went on to the theft of a horse, a sack of oats, some strip of communal kitchen-garden, and to a certain dead body; and the two peasants said such terrible things of one another that if a hundredth part of them had been true they would by law at the very least have deserved exile to Siberia.

In the meantime old Dutlov had chosen another way of defending himself. He did not like his son's shouting, and tried to stop him, saying: 'It's a sin . . . Leave off, I tell you!' At the same time he argued that not only those who had three young men at home were three-men families, but also those whose sons had separated from them, and he also pointed to Starostin.

Starostin smiled slightly, cleared his throat, and stroking his beard with the air of a well-to-do peasant, answered that it all depended on the mistress, and that evidently his sons had deserved well, since the order was for them to be exempt.

Garaska smashed Dutlov's arguments about the families that had broken up, by the remark that they ought not to have been allowed to break up, as was the rule during the lifetime of the late master; but that no one went raspberry-picking when summer was over, and that one could not now conscript the only man left in a household.

'Did they break up their households for fun? Why should they now be quite ruined?' came the voices of the men whose families had separated; and the babblers joined in too.

'You'd better buy a substitute if you're not satisfied. You can afford it!' said Rezun to Dutlov.

Dutlov wrapped his coat round him with a despairing gesture and stepped back behind the others.

'It seems you've counted my money!' he muttered angrily. 'We shall see what Egor Mikhaylovich will say when he comes from the mistress.'

VI

AT THAT very moment Egor Mikhaylovich came out of the house. One cap after another was lifted, and as the steward approached all the heads – grey, grizzled, red, brown, fair, or bald in front or on top – were uncovered, and the voices were gradually silenced till at last all was quiet. Egor Mikhaylovich stepped onto the porch, evidently intending to speak. In his long coat, his hands awkwardly thrust into the front pockets, his town-made cap pulled over his forehead, he stood firmly, with feet apart, in this elevated position, towering above all these heads – mostly old, bearded, and handsome – that were turned towards him. He was now a different man from what he had been when he stood before his mistress. He was majestic.

'This is the mistress's decision, men! It is not her pleasure to give up any of the house-serfs, but from among you – whom you yourselves decide on shall go. Three are wanted this time. By rights only two and a half are wanted, but the half will be taken into account next time. It comes to the same thing: if not today it would have to be tomorrow.'

'Of course, that's quite right!' some voices said.

'In my opinion,' continued Egor Mikhaylovich, 'Kharyushkin and Vaska Mityukhin must go, that is evidently God's will.'

'Yes, that's quite right!' said the voices.

'. . . The third will have to be one of the Dutlovs, or one out of a two-men family . . . What do you say?'

'Dutlov!' cried the voices. 'There are three of them of the right age!'

And again, little by little, the shouting increased, and somehow the question of the strip of kitchen-garden and certain sacks stolen from the mistress's yard came up again. Egor Mikhaylovich had been managing the estate for the last twenty years and was a shrewd and experienced man. He stood and listened for about a quarter of an hour, then he ordered all to be silent, and the three younger Dutlovs to draw lots to see which of them was to go. The lots were prepared, shaken up in a hat, and Khrapkov drew one out. It was Elijah's. All became silent.

'Is it mine? Let me see it!' said Elijah in a faltering voice.

All remained silent. Egor Mikhaylovich ordered that everybody should bring the recruit money – seven kopeks from each household – next day, and saying that all was over, dismissed the meeting. The crowd moved off, the men covered their heads as they turned the corner, and their voices and the sound of their footsteps mingled into a hum. The steward stood on the porch watching the departing crowd, and when the young Dutlovs were round the corner he beckoned old Dutlov, who had stopped of his own accord, and they went into the office.

'I am sorry for you, old man,' said Egor Mikhaylovich, sitting down in an armchair before the table. 'It was your turn though. Will you buy a recruit to take your nephew's place, or not?'

The old man, without speaking, gave Egor Mikhaylovich a significant look.

'There's no getting out of it,' said Egor Mikhaylovich in answer to that look.

'We'd be glad enough to buy a substitute, Egor Mikhaylovich, but we haven't the means. Two horses went to the knacker's this summer, and there was my nephew's wedding . . . Evidently it's our fate . . . for living honestly. It's very well for him to talk!' (He was thinking of Rezun.)

Egor Mikhaylovich rubbed his face with his hand and yawned. He was evidently tired of the business and was ready for his tea.

'Eh, old fellow, don't be mean!' said he. 'Have a hunt under your floor, I dare say you'll turn up some four hundred old ruble notes, and I'll get you a substitute – a regular wonder! . . . The other day a fellow came offering himself.'

'In the *government*?' asked Dutlov, meaning the town.

'Well, will you buy him?'

'I'd be glad enough, God is my witness! . . . but . . .'

Egor Mikhaylovich interrupted him sternly.

'Well then, listen to me, old man! See that Elijah does himself no mischief,* and as soon as I send word – whether today or tomorrow – he is to be taken to town at once. You will take him and you will be answerable for him, but if anything should happen to him – which God forbid! – I'll send your eldest son instead! Do you hear?'

'But could not one be sent from a two-man family? . . . Egor Mikhaylovich, this is not fair!' he said. Then after a pause he went on, almost with tears: 'When my brother has died a soldier, now they are taking my son! How have I deserved such a blow?' and he was ready to fall on his knees.

'Well, well, go away!' said Egor Mikhaylovich. 'Nothing can be done. It's the law. Keep an eye on Elijah: you'll have to answer for him!'

Dutlov went home, thoughtfully tapping the ruts with his linden stick as he walked.

---

* It sometimes happened that to escape service men mutilated themselves, for instance by cutting off the finger needed to pull the trigger.

VII

EARLY NEXT morning a big-boned bay gelding (for some reason called Drum), harnessed to a small cart (the steward himself used to drive in that cart), stood at the porch of the house-serfs' quarters. Annie, Polikey's eldest daughter, barefoot in spite of the falling sleet and the cold wind, and evidently frightened, stood at the horse's head holding the bridle at arm's length, and with her other hand held a faded yellowy-green jacket that was thrown over her head, and which served the family as blanket, cloak, hood, carpet, overcoat for Polikey, and many other things besides. Polikey's *corner* was all in a bustle. The dim light of a rainy morning was just glimmering in at the window, which was broken here and there and mended with paper. Akulina had left her cooking in the oven, and left her children – of whom the younger were still in bed – shivering, because the jacket that served them as blanket had been taken away to serve as a garment and only replaced by the shawl off their mother's head. Akulina was busy getting her husband ready for his journey. His shirt was clean, but his boots, which as the saying is were 'begging for porridge', gave her much trouble. She had taken off her thick worsted stockings (her only pair) and given them to her husband, and had managed to cut out a pair of inner soles from a saddle-cloth (which had been carelessly left about in the stable and had been brought home by Polikey two days before) in such a way as to stop up the holes in his boots and keep his feet dry. Polikey sat, feet and all, on the bed, untwisting his girdle so that it should not look like a dirty cord. The cross, lisping little girl, wrapped in the sheepskin (which though it covered her head was trailing round her feet), had been dispatched to ask Nikita to lend them a cap. The bustle was increased by house-serfs coming in to ask Polikey to get different things for them in town. One wanted needles, another tea, a third some tobacco, and another some olive oil. The carpenter's wife – who to conciliate Polikey had already found time to make her samovar boil and bring him a mug full of liquid which she called tea – wanted some sugar. Though Nikita refused to lend a cap and they had to mend his own – that is, to push in the protruding bits of wadding and sew them up with a veterinary needle; though at first the boots with the saddle-cloth soles would not go on his feet; though Annie, chilled through, nearly let Drum get out of hand, and Mary in the long sheepskin had to take her place, and then Mary had to take off the sheepskin and Akulina had to hold the horse herself – it all ended by Polikey successfully getting all the warm family garments on himself, leaving only the jacket and a pair of slippers behind. When ready, he got into the little cart, wrapped the sheepskin round him, shook up the bag of hay at the bottom of the cart, again wrapped himself up, took the reins, wrapped the coat still closer round him as very important people do, and started.

His little boy Mishka, running out onto the steps, begged to have a ride; the lisping Mary also begged that she might 'have a lide', and was 'not cold even without the theepthkin'; so Polikey stopped Drum and smiled his weak smile while Akulina put the children into the cart and, bending towards him, begged him in a whisper to remember his oath and not drink anything on the way. Polikey took the children through the village as far as the smithy, put them down, wrapped himself up and put his cap straight again, and drove off at a slow, sedate trot, his cheeks quivering at every jolt and his feet knocking against the bark sides of the cart. Mary and Mishka, barefoot, rushed down the slippery hill to the house at such a rate and yelling so loudly that a stray dog from the village looked up at them and scurried home with its tail between its legs, which made Polikey's heirs yell ten times louder.

It was abominable weather: the wind was cutting, and something between rain and snow, and now and then fine hail, beat on Polikey's face and on his bare hands which held the reins – and over which he kept drawing the sleeves of his coat – and on the leather of the horse-collar, and on the head of old Drum, who set back his ears and half closed his eyes.

Then suddenly the rain stopped and it brightened up in a moment. The bluish snow clouds stood out clear and the sun began to come out, but uncertainly and cheerlessly like Polikey's own smile. Notwithstanding all this, Polikey was deep in pleasant thoughts. He whom they threatened to exile and conscript, whom only those who were too lazy did not scold and beat, who was always shoved into the worst places, *he* was driving now to fetch *a sum of money*, and a large sum too, and his mistress trusted him, and he was driving in the steward's cart behind Drum – with whom the lady herself sometimes drove out – just as if he were some proprietor with leather collar-strap and reins instead of ropes. And Polikey sat up straighter, pushed in the bits of wadding hanging out of his cap, and again wrapped his coat closer.

If Polikey, however, imagined that he looked just like a wealthy peasant proprietor he deluded himself. It is true, as everyone knows, that tradesmen worth ten thousand rubles drive in carts with leather harness, only this was not quite the same thing. A bearded man in a blue or black coat drives past sitting alone in a cart, driving a well-fed horse, and you just glance to see if the horse is sleek and he himself well fed, and at the way he sits, at the horse's harness, and the tyres on the cartwheels, and at his girdle, and you know at once whether the man does business in hundreds or in thousands of rubles. Every experienced person looking closer at Polikey, at his hands, his face, his newly grown beard, his girdle, at the hay carelessly thrown into the cart, at lean Drum, at the worn tyres, would know at once that it was only a serf driving past, and not a merchant or a cattle-dealer or even a peasant proprietor, and that he did not deal in thousands or hundreds, or even tens of rubles. But Polikey did not think so: he deceived himself, and deceived himself agreeably. He is going to carry home fifteen hundred rubles in the bosom of his coat. If he liked, he might turn Drum's head towards Odessa instead of homewards, and drive off where Fate might take him. But he will not do such a thing; he will bring the lady her money all in order, and will talk about having had larger sums than that on him. When they came to an inn Drum began pulling at the left rein, turning towards the inn and stopping; but Polikey, though he had the money given him to do the shopping with, gave Drum the whip and drove on. The same thing happened at the next inn, and about noon he got out of the cart, and opening the gate of the inn-keeper's house where all his mistress's people put up, he led the horse and cart into the yard. There he unharnessed, gave the horse some hay, dined with the inn-keeper's men, not omitting to mention what important business he had come on, and then went out with the market-gardener's bill in the crown of his cap.

The market-gardener (who knew and evidently mistrusted Polikey) having read the letter questioned him as to whether he had really been sent for the money. Polikey tried to seem offended, but could not manage it, and only smiled his peculiar smile. The market-gardener read the letter over once more and handed him the money. Having received the money, Polikey put it into his bosom and went back to the inn. Neither the beer-shop nor the tavern nor anything tempted him. He felt a pleasant agitation through his whole being, and stopped more than once in front of shops that showed tempting wares: boots, coats, caps, chintz, and foodstuffs, and went on with the pleasant feeling: 'I could buy it all, but there now, I won't do it!' He went to the bazaar for the things he had been asked to buy, got them all, and started bargaining for a lined sheepskin coat, for which he was asked twenty-five rubles. For some reason the dealer, after looking at Polikey, seemed to doubt his ability to buy it. But Polikey pointed to his bosom, saying that he could buy the whole shop if he liked, and insisted on trying the coat on; felt it, patted it, blew into the wool till he became permeated with the smell of it, and then took it off with a sigh. 'The price does not suit me. If you'll let it go for fifteen rubles, now!' he said. The dealer angrily threw the coat across the table, and Polikey went out and cheerfully returned to his inn. After supper, having watered Drum and given him some oats, he climbed up on the stove, took out the envelope with the money and examined it for a long time, and then asked a porter who knew how to read to read him the address and the inscription: 'With enclosure of one thousand, six hundred and seventeen assignation rubles.'* The envelope was made of common paper and sealed with brown sealing-wax with the impression of an anchor. There was one large seal in the middle, four at the corners, and there were some drops of sealing-wax near the edge. Polikey examined all this, and studied it. He even felt the sharp edges of the notes. It gave him a kind of childish pleasure to know that he had such a sum in his hands. He thrust the envelope into a hole in the lining of

* Equal to 462 'silver rubles', at 3½ assignations for one silver ruble.

his cap, and lay down with the cap under his head; but even in the night he kept waking and feeling the envelope. And each time he found it in its place he experienced the pleasant feeling that here was he, the disgraced, the down-trodden Polikey, carrying such a sum and delivering it up more accurately than even the steward could have done.

VIII

ABOUT MIDNIGHT the inn-keeper's men and Polikey were awakened by a knocking at the gate and the shouting of peasants. It was the party of recruits from Pokrovsk. There were about ten people: Khoryushkin, Mityukin, and Elijah (Dutlov's nephew), two substitutes in case of need, the village Elder, old Dutlov, and the men who had driven them. A night-light was burning in the room, and the cook was sleeping on a bench under the icons. She jumped up and began lighting a candle. Polikey also awoke, and leaning over from the top of the stove looked at the peasants as they came in. They came in crossing themselves, and sat down on the benches round the room. They all seemed perfectly calm, so that one could not tell which of them were the conscripts and which their escorts. They were greeting the people of the inn, talking loudly, and asking for food. It is true that some were silent and sad; but on the other hand others were unusually merry, evidently drunk. Among these was Elijah, who had never had too much to drink before.

'Well, lads, shall we go to sleep or have some supper?' asked the Elder.

'Supper!' said Elijah, throwing open his coat and setting himself on a bench. 'Send for some vodka.'

'Enough of your vodka!' answered the Elder shortly, and turning to the others he said: 'You just cut yourselves a bit of bread, lads! Why wake people up?'

'Give me vodka!' Elijah repeated, without looking at anybody, and in a voice that showed that he would not soon stop.

The peasants took the Elder's advice, fetched some bread out of their carts, ate it, asked for a little kvas, and lay down, some on the floor and some on the stove.

Elijah kept repeating at intervals: 'Let me have some vodka, I say, let me have some.' Then, noticing Polikey: 'Polikey! Hi, Polikey! You here, dear friend? Why, I am going for a soldier . . . Have said goodbye to my mother and my missus . . . How she howled! They've bundled me off for a soldier . . . Stand me some vodka!'

'I haven't got any money,' answered Polikey, and to comfort him added: 'Who knows? By God's aid you may be rejected! . . .'

'No, friend. I'm as sound as a young birch. I've never had an illness. There's no rejecting for me! What better soldier can the Tsar want?'

Polikey began telling him how a peasant gave a doctor a five-ruble note and got rejected.

Elijah drew nearer the oven, and they talked more freely.

'No, Polikey, it's all up now! I don't want to stay now myself. Uncle has done for me. As if he couldn't have bought a substitute! . . . No, he grudged his son, and grudges the money, so they send me. No! I don't myself want to stay.' (He spoke gently, confidingly, under the influence of quiet sorrow.) 'One thing only – I am sorry for mother, dear heart! . . . How she grieved! And the wife, too! . . . They've ruined the woman just for nothing; now she'll perish – in a word, she'll be a soldier's wife! Better not to have married. What did they marry me for? . . . They're coming here tomorrow.'

'But why have they brought you so soon?' asked Polikey. 'Nothing was heard about it, and then, all of a sudden . . .'

'Why, they're afraid I shall do myself some mischief,' answered Elijah, smiling. 'No fear! I'll do nothing of the kind. I shall not be lost even as a soldier; only I'm sorry for mother . . . Why did they get me married?' he said gently and sadly.

The door opened and shut with a loud slam as old Dutlov came in, shaking the wet off his cap, and as usual in bast shoes so big that they looked like boats.

'Afanasy,' he said to the porter, when he had crossed himself, 'isn't there a lantern to get some oats by?'

And without looking at Elijah he began slowly lighting a bit of candle. His mittens and whip were stuck into the girdle tied neatly round his coat, and his toil-worn face appeared as usual, simple, quiet, and full of business cares, as if he had just arrived with a train of loaded carts.

Elijah became silent when he saw his uncle, and looked dismally down at the bench again. Then, addressing the Elder, he muttered:

'Vodka, Ermil! I want some drink!' His voice sounded wrathful and dejected.

'Drink, at this time?' answered the Elder, who was eating something out of a bowl. 'Don't you see the others have had a bite and lain down? Why are you making a row?'

The word 'row' evidently suggested to Elijah the idea of violence.

'Elder, I'll do some mischief if you don't give me vodka!'

'Couldn't you bring him to reason?' the Elder said, turning to Dutlov, who had lit the lantern, but had stopped, evidently to see what would happen, and was looking pityingly at his nephew out of the corner of his eyes, as if surprised at his childishness.

Elijah, looking down, again muttered:

'Vodka! Give . . . do mischief!'

'Leave off, Elijah!' said the Elder mildly. 'Really, now, leave off! You'd better!'

But before the words were out Elijah had jumped up and hit a window-pane with his fist, and shouting at the top of his voice: 'You would not listen to me, so there you have it!' rushed to the other window to break that too.

Polikey in the twinkling of an eye rolled over twice and hid in the farthest corner of the top of the stove, so quickly that he scared all the cockroaches there. The Elder threw down his spoon and rushed towards Elijah. Dutlov slowly put down his lantern, untied his girdle, and shaking his head and making a clicking noise with his tongue, went up to Elijah, who was already struggling with the Elder and the inn-keeper's man, who were keeping him away from the window. They had caught his arms and seemed to be holding him fast; but the moment he saw his uncle with the girdle his strength increased tenfold and he tore himself away, and with rolling eyes and clenched fists stepped up to Dutlov.

'I'll kill you! Keep away, you brute! . . . You have ruined me, you and your brigands of sons, you've ruined me! . . . Why did they get me married? . . . Keep away! I'll kill you! . . .'

Elijah was terrible. His face was purple, his eyes rolled, the whole of his healthy young body trembled as in a fever. He seemed to wish and to be able to kill all the three men who were facing him.

'You're drinking your brother's blood, you blood-sucker!'

Something flashed across Dutlov's ever-serene face. He took a step forward.

'You won't take it peaceably!' said he suddenly. The wonder was where he got the energy; for with a quick motion he caught hold of his nephew, rolled to the ground with him, and with the aid of the Elder began binding his hands with the girdle. They struggled for about five minutes. At last with the help of the peasants Dutlov rose, pulling his coat out of Elijah's clutch. Then he raised Elijah, whose hands were tied behind his back, and made him sit down on a bench in a corner.

'I told you it would be the worse for you,' he said, still out of breath with the struggle, and pulling straight the narrow girdle tied over his shirt. 'Why sin? We shall all have to die! . . . Fold a coat for a pillow for him,' he said, turning to the inn-keeper's men, 'or the blood will go to his head.' And he tied the cord round his waist over his sheepskin and, taking up the lantern, went to see after the horses.

Elijah, pale, dishevelled, his shirt pulled out of place, was gazing round the room as though trying to remember where he was. The inn-keeper's men picked up the broken bits of glass and stuffed a coat into the hole in the window to keep the draught out. The Elder sat down again to his bowl.

'Ah, Elijah, Elijah! I'm sorry for you, really! What's to be done? There's Khoryushkin . . . he, too, is married. Seems it can't be helped!'

'It's all on account of that fiend, my uncle, that I'm being ruined!' Elijah repeated, drily and bitterly. 'He was chary of his own son! . . . Mother says the steward told him to buy me off. He won't: he says he can't afford it. As if what my brother and I have brought into his house were a trifle! . . . He is a fiend!'

Dutlov returned to the room, said a prayer in front of the icons, took off his outdoor things, and sat down beside the Elder. The cook brought more kvas and another spoon. Elijah grew silent, and closing his eyes lay down on the folded coat. The Elder pointed to him and shook his head silently. Dutlov waved his hand.

'As if one was not sorry! . . . My own brother's son! . . . And as if things were not bad enough it seems they also made me out a villain to him . . . Whether it's his wife – she's a cunning little woman for all she's so young – that has put it into his head that we could afford to buy a substitute! . . . Anyhow, he's reproaching me. But one does pity the lad! . . .'

'Ah! he's a fine lad,' said the Elder.

'But I'm at the end of my tether with him! Tomorrow I shall let Ignat come, and his wife wanted to come too.'

'All right – let them come,' said the Elder, rising and climbing onto the stove. 'What is money? Money is dross!'

'If one had the money, who would grudge it?' muttered one of the inn-keeper's men, lifting his head.

'Ah, money, money! It causes much sin,' replied Dutlov. 'Nothing in the world causes so much sin, and the Scriptures say so too.'

'Everything is said there,' the workman agreed. 'There was a man told me how a merchant had stored up a heap of money and did not want to leave any behind; he loved it so that he took it with him to the grave. As he was dying he asked to have a small pillow buried with him. No one suspected anything, and so it was done. Then his sons began looking for his money and nothing was to be found. At last one of them guessed that probably the notes were all in the pillow. The matter went to the Tsar, and he allowed the grave to be opened. And what do you think? They opened the coffin. There was nothing in the pillow, but the coffin was full of small snakes, and so it was buried again . . . You see what money does!'

'It's a fact, it brings much sin,' said Dutlov, and he got up and began saying his prayers.

When he had finished he looked at his nephew. The lad was asleep. Dutlov came up to him, untied the girdle with which he was bound, and then lay down. Another peasant went out to sleep with the horses.

IX

AS SOON AS all was quiet Polikey climbed down softly, like a guilty man, and began to get ready. For some reason he felt uneasy at the thought of spending the night there among the recruits. The cocks were already crowing to one another more often. Drum had eaten all his oats and was straining towards the drinking-trough. Polikey harnessed him and led him out past the peasants' carts. His cap with its contents was safe, and the wheels of the cart were soon rattling along the frosty road to Pokrovsk. Polikey felt more at ease only when he had left the town behind. Till then he kept imagining that at any moment he might hear himself being pursued, that he would be stopped, and they would tie up his arms instead of Elijah's, and he would be taken to the recruiting station next morning. It might have been the frost, or it might have been fear, but something made cold shivers run down his back, and again and again he touched Drum up. The first person he met was a priest in a tall fur cap, accompanied by a one-eyed labourer. Taking this for an evil omen Polikey grew still more alarmed, but outside the town this fear gradually passed. Drum went on at a walking pace and the road in front became more visible. Polikey took off his cap and felt the notes. 'Shall I hide it in my bosom?' he thought. 'No; I should have to undo my girdle . . . Wait a bit! When I get to the foot of the hill I'll get down and put myself to rights . . . The cap is sewn up tight at the top, and it can't fall through the lining. After all, I'd better not take the cap off till I get home.' When he had reached the foot of the incline Drum of his own accord galloped up the next hill and Polikey, who was as eager as Drum to get home, did not check him. All was well – at any rate so Polikey imagined, and he gave himself up to dreams of his mistress's gratitude, of the five rubles she would give him, and of the joy of his family. He took off his cap, felt for the envelope, and, smiling, put the cap tighter on his head. The velveteen crown of the cap was very rotten, and just because Akulina had carefully sewn up the rents in one place, it burst open in another; and the very movement by which Polikey in the dusk had thought to push the envelope with the money deeper under the wadding, tore the cap farther and pushed out a corner of the envelope through the velveteen crown.

The dawn was appearing, and Polikey, who had not slept all night, began to drowse. Pulling his cap lower down and thereby pushing the envelope still farther out, Polikey in his drowsiness let his head knock against the front of the cart. He woke up near home and was about to catch hold of his cap, but feeling that it sat firmly on his head he did not take it off, convinced that the envelope was inside. He gave Drum a touch, arranged the hay in the cart again, assumed once more the appearance of a well-to-do peasant, and proudly looking about him rattled homewards.

There was the kitchen, there the house-serfs' quarters. There was the carpenter's wife carrying some linen; there was the office, and there the mistress's house where in a few moments Polikey would show that he was a trustworthy and honest man. 'One can say anything about anybody,' he would say; and the lady would reply, 'Well, thank you, Polikey! Here are three (or perhaps five, perhaps even ten) rubles,' and she would tell them to give him some tea, or even some vodka. It would not be amiss, after being out in the cold! 'With ten rubles we would have a treat for the holiday, and buy boots, and return Nikita his four and a half rubles (it can't be helped! . . . He has begun bothering) . . .' When he was about a hundred paces from the house, Polikey wrapped his coat round him, pulled his girdle straight and his collar, took off his cap, smoothed his hair, and without haste thrust his hand under the lining. The hand began to fumble faster and faster inside the lining, then the other hand went in too, while his face grew paler and paler. One of the hands went right through the cap. Polikey fell on his knees, stopped the horse, and began searching in the cart among the hay and the things he had bought, feeling inside his coat and in his trousers. The money was nowhere to be found.

'Heavens! What does it mean? . . . What will happen? . . .' He began to roar, clutching at his hair.

But recollecting that he might be seen, he turned the horse round, pulled the cap on, and drove the surprised and disgusted Drum back along the road.

'I can't bear going out with Polikey,' Drum must have thought. 'For once in his life he has fed and watered me properly, and then only to deceive me so unpleasantly! How hard I tried, running home! I am tired, and hardly have we got within smell of our hay than he starts driving me back!'

'Now then, you devil's jade!' shouted Polikey through his tears, standing up in the cart, pulling at Drum's mouth, and beating him with the whip.

X

ALL THAT DAY no one saw Polikey in Pokrovsk. The mistress asked for him several times after dinner, and Aksyutka flew down to Akulina; but Akulina said he had not yet returned, and that evidently the market-gardener had detained him or something had happened to the horse. 'If only it has not gone lame!' she said. 'Last time, when Maxim went, he was on the road a whole day – had to walk back all the way.'

And Aksyutka turned her pendulums back to the house again, while Akulina, trying to calm her own fears, invented reasons to account for her husband's absence, but in vain! Her heart was heavy and she could not work with a will at any of the preparations for the morrow's holiday. She suffered all the more because the carpenter's wife assured her that she herself had seen 'a man just like Polikey drive up to the avenue and then turn back again'. The children, too, were anxiously and impatiently expecting 'Daddy', but for another reason. Annie and Mary, being left without the sheepskin and the coat which made it possible to take turns out of doors, could only run out in their indoor dresses with increasing rapidity in a small circle round the house. This was not a little inconvenient to all the dwellers in the serfs' quarters who wanted to go in or out. Once Mary ran against the legs of the carpenter's wife who was carrying water, and though she began to howl in anticipation as soon as she knocked against the woman's knees, she got her curls cuffed all the same, and cried still louder. When she did not knock against anyone, she flew in at the door, and immediately climbing up by means of a tub, got onto the top of the oven. Only the mistress and Akulina were really anxious about Polikey; the children were concerned only about what he had on.

Egor Mikhaylovich reporting to his mistress, in answer to her questions, 'Hasn't Polikey come back yet?' and 'Where can he be?' answered: 'I can't say,' and seemed pleased that his expectations were being fulfilled. 'He ought to have been back by noon,' he added significantly.

All that day no one heard anything of Polikey; only later on it was known that some neighbouring peasants had seen him running about on the road bareheaded, and asking everyone whether they hadn't found a letter. Another man had seen him asleep by the roadside beside a tied-up horse and cart. 'I thought he was tipsy,' the man said, 'and the horse looked as if it had not been watered or fed for two days, its sides were so fallen in.' Akulina did not sleep all night and kept listening, but Polikey did not return. Had she been alone, or had she kept a cook or a maid, she would have felt still more unhappy; but as soon as the cocks crowed and the carpenter's wife got up, Akulina was obliged to rise and light the fire. It was a holiday. The bread had to come out of the oven before daybreak, kvas had to be made, cakes baked, the cow milked, frocks and shirts ironed, the children washed, water fetched, and her neighbour prevented from taking up the whole oven. So Akulina, still listening, set to work. It had grown light and the church bells were ringing, the children were up, but still Polikey had not returned. There had been a first frost the day before, a little snow had fallen and lay in patches on the fields, on the road, and on the roofs; and now, as if in honour of the holiday, the day was fine, sunny, and frosty, so that one could see and hear a long way. But Akulina, standing by the brick oven, her head thrust into the opening, was so busy with her cakes that she did not hear Polikey drive up, and only knew from the children's cries that her husband had returned.

Annie, as the eldest, had greased her hair and dressed herself without help. She wore a new but crumpled print dress – a present from the mistress. It stuck out as stiff as if it were made of bast, and was an object of envy to the neighbours; her hair glistened; she had smeared half an inch of tallow candle onto it. Her shoes, though not new, were thin ones. Mary was still wrapped in the old jacket and was covered with mud, and Annie would not let her come near her for fear of getting soiled. Mary was outside. She saw her father drive up with a sack. 'Daddy has come!' she shrieked, and rushed headlong through the door past Annie, dirtying her. Annie, no longer fearing to be soiled, went for her at once and hit her. Akulina could not leave her work, and only shouted at the children: 'Now, then . . . I'll whip you all!' and looked round at the door. Polikey came in with a sack, and at once made his way to his own corner. It seemed to Akulina that he was pale, and his face looked as if he were either smiling or crying, but she had no time to find out which it was.

'Well, Polikey, is it all right?' she called to him from the oven.

Polikey muttered something that she did not understand.

'Eh?' she cried. 'Have you been to the mistress?'

Polikey sat down on the bed in his corner looking wildly round him and smiling his guilty, intensely miserable smile. He did not answer for a long time.

'Eh, Polikey? Why have you been so long?' came Akulina's voice.

'Yes, Akulina, I have handed the lady her money. How she thanked me!' he said suddenly, and began looking round and smiling still more uneasily. Two things attracted his feverishly staring eyes: the baby, and the cords attached to the hanging cradle. He went up to where the cradle hung, and began hastily undoing the knot of the rope with his thin fingers. Then his eyes fixed themselves on the baby; but just then Akulina entered, carrying a board of cakes, and Polikey quickly hid the rope in his bosom and sat down on the bed.

'What is it, Polikey? You are not like yourself,' said Akulina.

'Haven't slept,' he answered.

Suddenly something flitted past the window, and in a moment Aksyutka, the maid from 'up there', darted in like an arrow.

'The mistress orders Polikey to come this minute,' she said – 'this minute, Avdotya Nikolaevna's orders are . . . this minute!'

Polikey looked at Akulina, then at the girl.

'I'm coming. What can she want?' he said, so simply that Akulina grew quieter. 'Perhaps she wants to reward me. Tell her I'm coming.'

He rose and went out. Akulina took the washing-trough,

put it on a bench, filled it with water from the pails which stood by the door and from the cauldron in the oven, rolled up her sleeves, and tried the water.

'Come, Mary, I'll wash you.'

The cross, lisping little girl began howling.

'Come, you brat! I'll give you a clean smock. Now then, don't make a fuss. Come along . . . I've still got your brother to wash.'

Meanwhile Polikey had not followed the maid from 'up there', but had gone to quite a different place. In the passage by the wall was a ladder leading to the loft. Polikey, when he came out, looked round, and seeing no one, bent down and climbed that ladder almost at a run, nimbly and hurriedly.

'Why ever doesn't Polikey come?' asked the mistress impatiently of Dunyasha, who was dressing her hair. 'Where is Polikey? Why hasn't he come?'

Aksyutka again flew to the serfs' quarters, and again rushed into the entry, calling Polikey to her mistress.

'Why, he went long ago,' answered Akulina, who, having washed Mary, had just put her suckling baby boy into the wash-trough and was moistening his thin short hair, regardless of his cries. The boy screamed, puckered his face, and tried to clutch something with his helpless little hands. Akulina supported his soft, plump, dimpled little back with one large hand, while she washed him with the other.

'See if he has not fallen asleep somewhere,' said she, looking round anxiously.

Just then the carpenter's wife, unkempt and with her dress unfastened and holding up her skirts, went up into the loft to get some things she had hung there to dry. Suddenly a shriek of horror filled the loft, and the carpenter's wife, like one demented, with her eyes closed, came down the steps on all fours, backwards, sliding rather than running.

'Polikey!' she screamed.

Akulina let go the baby.

'Has hung himself!' roared the carpenter's wife.

Akulina rushed out into the passage, paying no heed to the baby, who rolled over like a ball and fell backwards with his little legs in the air and his head under water.

'On a rafter ... hanging!' the carpenter's wife ejaculated, but stopped when she saw Akulina.

Akulina darted up the ladder, and before anyone could stop her she was at the top, but from there with a terrible scream she fell back like a corpse, and would have been killed if the people who had come running from every corner had not been in time to catch her.

XI

FOR SEVERAL minutes nothing could be made out amidst the general uproar. A crowd of people had collected, everyone was shouting and talking, and the children and old women were crying. Akulina lay unconscious. At last the men, the carpenter and the steward who had run to the place, went up the ladder, and the carpenter's wife began telling for the twentieth time how she, 'suspecting nothing, went to fetch a dress, and just looked round like this – and saw . . . a man; and I looked again, and a cap is lying inside out, close by. I look . . . his legs are dangling. I went cold all over! Is it pleasant? . . . To think of a man hanging himself, and that I should be the one to see him! . . . How I came clattering down I myself don't remember . . . it's a miracle how God preserved me! Truly, the Lord has had mercy on me! . . . Is it a trifle? . . . so steep and from such a height. Why, I might have been killed!'

The men who had gone up had the same tale to tell. Polikey, in his shirt and trousers, was hanging from a rafter by the cord he had taken from the cradle. His cap, turned inside out, lay beside him, his coat and sheepskin were neatly folded and lay close by. His feet touched the ground, but he no longer showed signs of life. Akulina regained consciousness, and again made for the ladder, but was held back.

'Mamma, Semka is dwownded!' the lisping little girl suddenly cried from their *corner*. Akulina tore herself away and ran to the *corner*. The baby lay on his back in the trough and did not stir, and his little legs were not moving. Akulina snatched him out, but he did not breathe or move. She threw him on the bed, and with arms akimbo burst into such loud, piercing, terrible laughter that Mary, who at first laughed too, covered her ears with her hands, and ran out into the passage crying. The neighbours thronged into the *corner*, wailing and weeping. They carried out the little body and began rubbing it, but in vain. Akulina tossed about on the bed and laughed – laughed so that all who heard her were horror-stricken. Only now, seeing this motley crowd of men and women, old people and children, did one realize what a number of people and what sort of people lived in the serfs' quarters. All were bustling and talking, many wept, but nobody did anything. The carpenter's wife still found people who had not heard her tale of how her sensitive feelings were shocked by the unexpected sight, and how God had preserved her from falling down the ladder. An old man who had been a footman, with a woman's jacket thrown over his shoulders, was telling how in the days of the old master a woman had drowned herself in the pond. The steward sent messengers to the priest and to the constable, and appointed men to keep guard. Aksyutka, the maid from 'up there', kept gazing with staring eyes at the opening that led to the loft, and though she could not see anything was unable to tear herself away and go back to her mistress. Agatha Mikhaylovna, who had been lady's-maid to the former proprietress, was weeping and asking for some tea to soothe her nerves. Anna the midwife was laying out the little body on the table, with her plump practised hands moistened with olive oil. Other women stood round Akulina, silently looking at her. The children, huddled together in the corner, peeped at their mother and burst into howls; and then subsiding for a moment, peeped again, and huddled still closer. Boys and men thronged round the porch, looking in at the door and the windows with frightened faces unable to see or understand anything, and asking one another what was the matter. One said the carpenter had chopped off his wife's foot with an axe. Another said that the laundress had been brought to bed of triplets; a third that the cook's cat had gone mad and bitten several people. But the truth gradually spread, and at last it reached the mistress; and it seems no one understood how to break it to her. That rough Egor blurted the facts straight out to her, and so upset the lady's nerves that it was a long time before she could recover. The crowd had already begun to quiet down, the carpenter's wife set the samovar to boil and made tea, and the outsiders, not being invited, thought it improper to stay longer. Boys had begun fighting outside the porch. Everybody now knew what had happened, and crossing themselves they began to disperse, when suddenly the cry was raised: 'The mistress! The mistress!' and everybody crowded and pressed together to make way for her, but at the same time everybody wanted to see what she was going to do. The lady, with pale and tear-stained face, entered the passage, crossed the threshold, and went into Akulina's *corner*. Dozens of heads squeezed together and gazed in at the door. One pregnant woman was squeezed so that she gave a squeal, but took advantage of that very circumstance to secure a front place for herself. And how could one help wishing to see the lady in Akulina's *corner*? For the house-serfs it was just what the coloured lights are at the end of a show. It's sure to be great when they burn the coloured fires; and it must be an important occasion when the lady in her silks and lace enters Akulina's *corner*. The lady went up and took Akulina's hand, but Akulina snatched it away. The old house-serfs shook their heads reprovingly.

'Akulina!' said the lady. 'You have your children — so take care of yourself!'

Akulina burst out laughing and got up.

'My children are all silver, all silver! I don't keep paper money,' she muttered very rapidly. 'I told Polikey, "Take no notes," and there now, they've smeared him, smeared him with tar — tar and soap, madam! Any scabbiness you may have it will get rid of at once . . .' and she laughed still louder.

The mistress turned away, and gave orders that the doctor's assistant should come with mustard poultices. 'Bring some cold water!' she said, and began looking for it herself; but seeing the dead baby with Granny Anna the midwife beside it, the lady turned away, and everybody saw how she hid her face in her handkerchief and burst into tears; while Granny Anna (it was a pity the lady did not see it — she would have appreciated it, and it was all done for her benefit) covered the baby with a piece of linen, straightened his arms with her plump, deft hands, shook her head, pouted, drooped her eyelids, and sighed with so much feeling that everybody could see how excellent a heart she had. But the lady did not see it, she could not see anything. She burst out sobbing and went into hysterics. Holding her up under the arms they led her out into the porch and took her home. 'That's all there was to be seen of her!' thought many, and again began to disperse. Akulina went on laughing and talking nonsense. She was taken into another room and bled, and plastered over with mustard poultices, and ice was put on her head. Yet she did not come to her senses, and did not weep, but laughed, and kept doing and saying such things that the kind people who were looking after her could not help laughing themselves.

XII

THE HOLIDAY was not a cheerful one at Pokrovsk. Though the day was beautiful the people did not go out to amuse themselves: no girls sang songs in the street, the factory hands who had come home from town for the day did not play on their concertinas and balalaykas and did not play with the girls. Everybody sat about in corners, and if they spoke did so as softly as if an evil one were there who could hear them. It was not quite so bad in the daytime, but when the twilight fell and the dogs began to howl, and when, to make matters worse, a wind sprang up and whistled down the chimneys, such fear seized all the people of the place that those who had tapers lit them before their icons. Anyone who happened to be alone in his *corner* went to ask the neighbours' permission to stay the night with them, to be less lonely, and anyone whose business should have taken him into one of the out-houses did not go, but pitilessly left the cattle without fodder that night. And the holy water, of which everyone kept a little bottle to charm away anything evil, was all used up during the night. Many even heard something walking about with heavy steps up in the loft, and the blacksmith saw a serpent fly straight towards it. In Polikey's *corner* there was no one; the children and the mad woman had been taken elsewhere. Only the little dead body lay there, and two old women sat and watched it, while a third, a pilgrim woman, was reading the Psalms, actuated by her own zeal, not for the sake of the baby but in a vague way because of the whole calamity. The mistress had willed it so. The pilgrim woman and these old women themselves heard how, as soon as they finished reading a passage of the Psalter, the rafters above would tremble and someone would groan. Then they would say, 'Let God arise,' and all would be quiet again. The carpenter's wife invited a friend and, not sleeping all night, with her aid drank up all the tea she had laid in for the whole week. They, too, heard how the rafters creaked overhead, and a noise as if sacks were tumbling down. The presence of the peasant watchmen kept up the courage of the house-serfs somewhat, or they would have died of fear that night. The peasants lay on some hay in the passage, and afterwards declared that they too had heard wonderful things up in the loft, though at the time they were conversing very calmly together about the conscription, munching crusts of bread, scratching themselves, and above all so filling the passage with the peculiar odour characteristic of peasants that the carpenter's wife, happening to pass by, spat and called them 'peasant-brood'. However that might be, the dead man was still dangling in the loft, and it seemed as if the evil one himself had overshadowed the serfs' quarters with his huge wings that night, showing his power and coming closer to these people than he had ever done before. So at least they all felt. I do not know if they were right; I even think they were quite mistaken. I think that if some bold fellow had taken a candle or lantern that terrible night, and crossing himself, or even without crossing himself, had gone up into the loft – slowly dispelling before him the horror of the night with the candle, lighting up the rafters, the sand, the cobweb-covered flue-pipe, and the tippets left behind by the carpenter's wife – till he came to Polikey, and, conquering his fears, had raised the lantern to the level of the face, he would have beheld the familiar spare figure: the feet touching the ground (the cord had stretched), the body bending lifelessly to one side, no cross visible under the open shirt, the head drooping on the breast, the good-natured face with open sightless eyes, and the meek, guilty smile, and a solemn calmness and silence over all. Really the carpenter's wife, crouching in a corner of her bed with dishevelled hair and frightened eyes and telling how she heard the sacks falling, was far more terrible and frightful than Polikey, though his cross was off and lay on a rafter.

'Up there', that is, in the mistress's house, reigned the same horror as in the serfs' quarters. Her bedroom smelt of eau-de-cologne and medicine. Dunyasha was melting yellow wax and making a plaster. What the plaster was for I don't know, but it was always made when the lady was unwell. And now she was so upset that she was quite ill. To keep Dunyasha's courage up her aunt had come to stay the night, so there were four of them, including the girl, sitting in the maid's room, and talking in low voices.

'Who will go to get some oil?' asked Dunyasha.

'Nothing will induce me to go, Avdotya Pavlovna!' the second maid said decidedly.

'Nonsense! You and Aksyutka go together.'

'I'll run across alone. I'm not afraid of anything!' said Aksyutka, and at once became frightened.

'Well then, go, dear; ask Granny Anna to give you some in a tumbler and bring it here; don't spill any,' said Dunyasha.

Aksyutka lifted her skirt with one hand, and being thereby prevented from swinging both arms, swung one of them twice as violently across the line of her progression, and darted away. She was afraid, and felt that if she should see or hear anything, even her own living mother, she would perish with fright. She flew, with her eyes shut, along the familiar pathway.

XIII

'IS THE MISTRESS asleep or not?' suddenly asked a deep peasant-voice close to Aksyutka. She opened her eyes, which she had kept shut, and saw a figure that seemed to her taller than the house. She screeched, and flew back so fast that her skirts floated behind her. With one bound she was on the porch and with another in the maid's room, where she threw herself on her bed with a wild yell. Dunyasha, her aunt, and the second maid almost died of terror, and before they had time to recover they heard heavy, slow, hesitating steps in the passage and at their door. Dunyasha rushed to her mistress, spilling the melted wax. The second maid hid herself behind the skirts that hung on the wall; the aunt, a more determined character, was about to hold the door to the passage closed, but it opened and a peasant entered the room. It was Dutlov, with his boat-like shoes. Paying no heed to the maids' fears, he looked round for an icon, and not seeing the tiny one in the left-hand corner of the room, he crossed himself in front of a cupboard in which teacups were kept, laid his cap on the window-sill, and thrusting his arm deep into the bosom of his coat as if he were going to scratch himself under his other arm, he pulled out the letter with the five brown seals stamped with an anchor. Dunyasha's aunt held her hands to her heart and with difficulty brought out the words:

'Well, you did give me a fright, Naumych! I can't utter a wo . . . ord! I thought my last moment had come!'

'Is that the way to behave?' said the second maid, appearing from under the skirts.

'The mistress herself is upset,' said Dunyasha, coming out of her mistress's door. 'What do you mean, shoving yourself in through the maids' entrance without leave? . . . Just like a peasant lout!'

Dutlov, without excusing himself, explained that he wanted to see the lady.

'She is not well,' said Dunyasha.

At this moment Aksyutka burst into such loud and unseemly laughter that she was obliged to hide her face in the pillow on the bed, from which for a whole hour, in spite of Dunyasha's and the aunt's threats, she could not for long lift it without going off again as if something were bursting in her pink print bosom and rosy cheeks. It seemed to her so funny that everybody should have been so scared, that she again hid her head in the pillows and scraped the floor with her shoe and jerked her whole body as if in convulsions.

Dutlov stopped and looked at her attentively, as if to ascertain what was happening to her, but turned away again without having discovered what it was all about, and continued:

'You see, it's just this – it's a very important matter,' he said. 'You just go and say that a peasant has found the letter with the money.'

'What money?'

Dunyasha, before going to report, read the address and questioned Dutlov as to when and how he had found this money which Polikey was to have brought back from town. Having heard all the details and pushed the little errand-girl, who was still convulsed with laughter, out into the vestibule, Dunyasha went to her mistress; but to Dutlov's surprise the mistress would not see him and did not say anything intelligible to Dunyasha.

'I know nothing about it and don't want to know anything!' the lady said. 'What peasant? What money? . . . I can't and won't see anyone! He must leave me in peace.'

'What am I to do?' said Dutlov, turning the envelope over; 'it's not a small sum. What is written on it?' he asked Dunyasha, who again read the address to him.

Dutlov seemed in doubt. He was still hoping that perhaps the money was not the mistress's and that the address had not been read to him right, but Dunyasha confirmed it, and he put the envelope back into his bosom with a sigh, and was about to go.

'I suppose I shall have to hand it over to the police-constable,' he said.

'Wait a bit! I'll try again,' said Dunyasha, stopping him, after attentively following the disappearance of the envelope into the bosom of the peasant's coat. 'Let me have the letter.'

Dutlov took it out again, but did not at once put it into Dunyasha's outstretched hand.

'Say that Semen Dutlov found it on the road . . .'

'Well, let me have it!'

'I did think it was just nothing – only a letter; but a soldier read out to me that there was money inside . . .'

'Well then, let me have it.'

'I dared not even go home first to . . .' Dutlov continued, still not parting with the precious envelope. 'Tell the lady so.'

Dunyasha took it from him and went again to her mistress.

'O my God, Dunyasha, don't speak to me of that money!' said the lady in a reproachful tone. 'Only to think of that little baby . . .'

'The peasant does not know to whom you wish it to be given, madam,' Dunyasha again said.

The lady opened the envelope, shuddering at the sight of the money, and pondered.

'Dreadful money! How much evil it does!' she said.

'It is Dutlov, madam. Do you order him to go, or will you please come out and see him – and is the money all safe?' asked Dunyasha.

'I don't want this money. It is terrible money! What it has done! Tell him to take it himself if he likes,' said the lady suddenly, feeling for Dunyasha's hand. 'Yes, yes, yes!' she repeated to the astonished Dunyasha; 'let him take it altogether and do what he likes with it.'

'Fifteen hundred rubles,' remarked Dunyasha, smiling as if at a child.

'Let him take it all!' the lady repeated impatiently. 'How is it you don't understand me? It is unlucky money. Never speak of it to me again! Let the peasant who found it take it. Go, go along!'

Dunyasha went out into the maids' room.

'Is it all there?' asked Dutlov.

'You'd better count it yourself,' said Dunyasha, handing him the envelope. 'My orders are to give it to you.'

Dutlov put his cap under his arm, and, bending forward, began to count the money.

'Have you got a counting-frame?'*

Dutlov had an idea that the lady was stupid and could not count, and that that was why she ordered him to do so.

'You can count it at home – the money is yours . . . !' Dunyasha said crossly. '"I don't want to see it," she says; "give it to the man who brought it."'

Dutlov, without unbending his back, stared at Dunyasha.

Dunyasha's aunt flung up her hands.

'O holy Mother! What luck the Lord has sent him! O holy Mother!'

The second maid would not believe it.

'You don't mean it, Avdotya Pavlovna; you're joking!'

'Joking, indeed! She told me to give it to the peasant . . . There, take your money and go!' said Dunyasha, without hiding her vexation. 'One man's sorrow is another man's luck!'

'It's not a joke . . . fifteen hundred rubles!' said the aunt.

---

* The abacus, with wires and beads to count on, was much used in Russia.

'It's even more,' stated Dunyasha. 'Well, you'll have to give a ten-kopek candle to St Nicholas,' she added sarcastically. 'Why don't you come to your senses? If it had come to a poor man, now! . . . But this man has plenty of his own.'

Dutlov at last grasped that it was not a joke, and began gathering together the notes he had spread out to count and putting them back into the envelope. But his hands trembled, and he kept glancing at the maids to assure himself that it was not a joke.

'See! He can't come to his senses he's so pleased,' said Dunyasha, implying that she despised both the peasant and the money. 'Come, I'll put it up for you.'

She was going to take the notes, but Dutlov would not let her. He crumpled them together, pushed them in deeper, and took his cap.

'Are you glad?'

'I hardly know what to say! It's really . . .'

He did not finish, but waved his hand, smiled, and went out almost crying.

The mistress rang.

'Well, have you given it to him?'

'I have.'

'Well, was he very glad?'

'He was just like a madman.'

'Ah! call him back. I want to ask him how he found it. Call him in here; I can't come out.'

Dunyasha ran out and found the peasant in the entry. He

150

was still bareheaded, but had drawn out his purse and was stooping, untying its strings, while he held the money between his teeth. Perhaps he imagined that as long as the money was not in his purse it was not his. When Dunyasha called him he grew frightened.

'What is it, Avdotya . . . Avdotya Pavlovna? Does she want to take it back? Couldn't you say a word for me? . . . Now really, and I'd bring you some nice honey.'

'Indeed! Much you ever brought!'

Again the door was opened, and the peasant was brought in to the lady. He felt anything but cheerful. 'Oh dear, she'll want it back!' he thought on his way through the rooms, lifting his feet for some reason as if he were walking through high grass, and trying not to stamp with his bast shoes. He could make nothing of his surroundings. Passing by a mirror he saw flowers of some sort and a peasant in bast shoes lifting his feet high, a gentleman with an eyeglass painted on the wall, some kind of green tub, and something white . . . There, now! The something white began to speak. It was his mistress. He did not understand anything but only stared. He did not know where he was, and everything appeared as in a fog.

'Is that you, Dutlov?'

'Yes, lady . . . Just as it was, so I left it . . .' he said. 'I was not glad so help me God! How I've tired out my horse! . . .'

'Well, it's your luck!' she remarked contemptuously, though with a kindly smile. 'Take it, take it for yourself.'

He only rolled his eyes.

'I am glad that you got it. God grant that it may be of use. Well, are you glad?'

'How could I help being glad? I'm so glad, ma'am, so glad! I will pray for you always! . . . So glad that, thank heaven, our lady is alive! It was not my fault.'

'How did you find it?'

'Well, I mean, we can always do our best for our lady, quite honourably, and not anyhow . . .'

'He is in a regular muddle, madam,' said Dunyasha.

'I had taken my nephew, the conscript, and as I was driving back along the road I found it. Polikey must have dropped it.'

'Well, then, go – go, my good man! I am glad you found it!'

'I am so glad, lady!' said the peasant.

Then he remembered that he had not thanked her properly, and did not know how to behave. The lady and Dunyasha smiled, and then he again began stepping as if he were walking in very high grass, and could hardly refrain from running, so afraid was he that he might be stopped and the money taken from him.

XIV

WHEN HE GOT out into the fresh air Dutlov stepped aside from the road to the lindens, even undoing his belt to get at his purse more easily, and began putting away the money. His lips were twitching, stretching and drawing together again, though he uttered no sound. Having put away his money and fastened his belt, he crossed himself and went staggering along the road as though he were drunk, so full was he of the thoughts that came rushing to his mind. Suddenly he saw the figure of a man coming towards him. He called out; it was Efim, with a cudgel in his hand, on watch at the serfs' quarters.

'Ah, Daddy Semen!' said Efim cheerfully, drawing nearer (Efim felt it uncanny to be alone). 'Have you got the conscripts off, daddy?'

'We have. What are you after?'

'Why, I've been put here to watch over Polikey who's hanged himself.'

'And where is he?'

'Up there, hanging in the loft, so they say,' answered Efim, pointing with his cudgel through the darkness to the roof of the serfs' quarters.

Dutlov looked in the direction of the arm, and though he could see nothing he puckered his brows, screwed up his eyes, and shook his head.

'The police-constable has come,' said Efim, 'so the coachman said. He'll be taken down at once. Isn't it horrible at night, daddy? Nothing would make me go up at night even if they ordered me to. If Egor Mikhaylovich were to kill me outright I wouldn't go . . .'

'What a sin, oh, what a sin!' Dutlov kept repeating, evidently for propriety's sake and not even thinking what he was saying. He was about to go on his way, but the voice of Egor Mikhaylovich stopped him.

'Hi! watchman! Come here!' shouted Egor Mikhaylovich from the porch of the office.

Efim replied to him.

'Who was that other peasant standing with you?'

'Dutlov.'

'Ah! and you too, Semen! Come here!'

Having drawn near, Dutlov, by the light of a lantern the coachman was carrying, recognized Egor Mikhaylovich and a short man with a cockade on his cap, dressed in a long uniform overcoat. This was the police-constable.

'Here, this old man will come with us too,' said Egor Mikhaylovich on seeing him.

The old man felt a bit uncomfortable, but there was no getting out of it.

'And you, Efim – you're a bold lad! Run up into the loft where he's hanged himself, and set the ladder straight for his honour to mount.'

Efim, who had declared that he would not go near the loft for anything in the world, now ran towards it, clattering with his bast shoes as if they were logs.

The police-officer struck a light and lit a pipe. He lived about a mile and a half off, and having just been severely reprimanded for drunkenness by his superior, was in a zealous mood. Having arrived at ten o'clock at night, he wished to view the corpse at once. Egor Mikhaylovich asked Dutlov how he came to be there. On the way Dutlov told the steward about the money he had found and what the lady had done, and said he was coming to ask Egor Mikhaylovich's sanction. To Dutlov's horror the steward asked for the envelope and examined it. The police-constable even took the envelope in his hand and briefly and drily asked the details.

'Oh dear, the money is gone!' thought Dutlov, and began justifying himself. But the police-constable handed him back the money.

'What a piece of luck for the clodhopper!' he said.

'It comes handy for him,' said Egor Mikhaylovich. 'He's just been taking his nephew to be conscripted, and now he'll buy him out.'

'Ah!' said the policeman, and went on in front.

'Will you buy him off – Elijah, I mean?' asked Egor Mikhaylovich.

'How am I to buy him off? Will there be money enough? And perhaps it's too late . . .'

'Well, you know best,' said the steward, and they both followed the police-constable.

They approached the serfs' house, where the ill-smelling watchmen stood waiting in the passage with a lantern. Dutlov followed them. The watchmen looked guilty, perhaps because of the smell they were spreading, for they had done nothing wrong. All were silent.

'Where is he?' asked the police-constable.

'Here,' said Egor Mikhaylovich in a whisper. 'Efim,' he added, 'you're a bold lad, go on in front with the lantern.'

Efim had already put a plank straight at the top of the ladder, and seemed to have lost all fear. Taking two or three steps at a time, he clambered up with a cheerful look, only turning round to light the way for the police-constable. The constable was followed by Egor Mikhaylovich. When they had disappeared above, Dutlov, with one foot on the bottom step, sighed and stopped. Two or three minutes passed. The footsteps in the loft were no longer heard; they had no doubt reached the body.

'Daddy, they want you,' Efim called down through the opening.

Dutlov began going up. The light of the lantern showed only the upper part of the bodies of the police-constable and of Egor Mikhaylovich beyond the rafters. Beyond them again someone else was standing with his back turned. It was Polikey. Dutlov climbed over a rafter and stopped, crossing himself.

'Turn him round, lads!' said the police-constable.

No one stirred.

'Efim, you're a bold lad,' said Egor Mikhaylovich.

The 'bold lad' stepped across a rafter, turned Polikey round, and stood beside him, looking with a most cheerful face now at Polikey now at the constable, as a showman exhibiting an albino or Julia Pastrana* looks now at the public and now at what he is exhibiting, ready to do anything the spectators may wish.

'Turn him round again.'

Polikey was turned round, his arms slightly swaying and his feet dragging in the sand on the floor.

'Catch hold, and take him down.'

'Shall we cut the rope through, your Honour?' asked Egor Mikhaylovich. 'Hand us an axe, lads!'

The watchmen and Dutlov had to be told twice before they set to, but the 'bold lad' handled Polikey as he would have handled a sheep's carcass. At last the rope was cut through and the body taken down and covered up. The police-constable said that the doctor would come next day, and dismissed them all.

XV

DUTLOV WENT homeward, still moving his lips. At first he had an uncanny feeling, but it passed as he drew nearer home, and a feeling of gladness gradually penetrated his heart. In the village he heard songs and drunken voices. Dutlov never drank, and this time too he went straight home. It was late when he entered his hut. His old wife was asleep. His eldest son and grandsons

---

* Julia Pastrana was exhibited as being half-woman, half-monkey, and created a considerable sensation.

were asleep on the stove, and his second son in the store-room. Elijah's wife alone was awake, and sat on the bench bareheaded, in a dirty, working-day smock, wailing. She did not come out to meet her uncle, but only sobbed louder, lamenting her fate, when he entered. According to the old woman, she 'lamented' very fluently and well, taking into consideration the fact that at her age she could not have had much practice.

The old woman rose and got supper for her husband. Dutlov turned Elijah's wife away from the table, saying: 'That's enough, that's enough!' Aksinya went away, and lying down on a bench continued to lament. The old woman put the supper on the table and afterwards silently cleared it away again. The old man did not speak either. When he had said grace he hiccuped, washed his hands, took the counting-frame from a nail in the wall, and went into the store-room. There he and the old woman spoke in whispers for a little while, and then, after she had gone away, he began counting on the frame, making the beads click. Finally he banged the lid of the chest standing there, and clambered into the space under the floor. For a long time he went on bustling about in the room and in the space below. When he came back to the living-room it was dark in the hut. The wooden splint that served for a candle had gone out. His old woman, quiet and silent in the daytime, had rolled herself up on the sleeping-bunk and filled the hut with her snoring. Elijah's noisy young wife was also asleep, breathing quietly. She lay on the bench dressed just as she had been, and with nothing under her head for a pillow.

Dutlov began to pray, then looked at Elijah's wife, shook his head, put out the light, hiccuped again, and climbed up on the stove, where he lay down beside his little grandson. He threw down his plaited bast shoes from the stove in the dark, and lay on his back looking up at the rafter which was hardly discernible just over his head above the stove, and listening to the sounds of the cockroaches swarming along the walls, and to the sighs, the snoring, the rubbing of one foot against another, and the noise made by the cattle outside. It was a long time before he could sleep. The moon rose. It grew lighter in the hut. He could see Aksinya in her corner and something he could not make out: was it a coat his son had forgotten, or a tub the women had put there, or a man standing there? Perhaps he was drowsing, perhaps not: anyhow he began to peer into the darkness. Evidently that evil spirit who had led Polikey to commit his awful deed and whose presence was felt that night by all the house-serfs, had stretched out his wing and reached across the village to the house in which lay the money that *he* had used to ruin Polikey. At least, Dutlov felt *his* presence and was ill at ease. He could neither sleep nor get up. After noticing the something he could not make out, he remembered Elijah with his arms bound, and Aksinya's face and her eloquent lamentations; and he recalled Polikey with his swaying hands. Suddenly it seemed to the old man that someone passed by the window. 'Who was that? Could it be the village Elder coming so early with a notice?' thought he. 'How did he open the door?' thought the old man, hearing a step in the passage. 'Had the old woman not put up the bar when she went out into the passage?' The dog began to howl in the yard and *he* came stepping along the passage, so the old man related afterwards, as though he were trying to find the door, then passed on and began groping along the wall, stumbled over a tub and made it clatter, and again began groping as if feeling for the latch. Now *he* had hold of the latch. A shiver ran down the old man's body. Now *he* pulled the latch and entered in the shape of a man. Dutlov knew it was *he*. He wished to cross himself, but could not. *He* went up to the table which was covered with a cloth, and, pulling it off, threw it on the floor and began climbing onto the stove. The old man knew that *he* had taken the shape of Polikey. *He* was showing his teeth and his hands were swinging about. *He* climbed up, fell on the old man's chest, and began to strangle him.

'The money's mine!' muttered Polikey.

'Let me go! I won't do it!' Semen tried to say, but could not.

Polikey was pressing down on him with the weight of a mountain of stone. Dutlov knew that if he said a prayer *he* would let him go, and he knew which prayer he ought to recite, but could not utter it. His grandson sleeping beside him uttered a shrill scream and began to cry. His grandfather had pressed him against the wall. The child's cry loosened the old man's lips. 'Let God arise! . . .' he said. *He* pressed less hard. 'And let his enemies be scattered . . .' spluttered Dutlov. *He* got off the stove. Dutlov heard his two feet strike the floor. Dutlov went on repeating in turn all the prayers he knew. *He* went towards the door, passed the table, and slammed the door so that the whole hut shook. Everybody but the grandfather and grandson continued to sleep however. The grandfather, trembling all over, muttered prayers, while the grandson was crying himself to sleep and pressing close to his grandfather. All became quiet once more. The old man lay still. A cock crowed behind the wall close to Dutlov's ear. He heard the hens stirring, and a cockerel unsuccessfully trying to crow in answer to the old cock. Something moved over the old man's legs. It was the cat; she jumped on her soft pads from the stove to the floor, and stood mewing by the door. The old man got up and opened the window. It was dark and muddy in the street. The front of the cart was standing there close to the window. Crossing himself he went out barefoot into the yard to the horses. One could see that *he* had been there too. The mare, standing under the lean-to beside a tub of chaff, had got her foot into the cord of her halter and had spilt the chaff, and now, lifting her foot, turned her head and waited for her master. Her foal had tumbled over a heap of manure. The old man raised him to his feet, disentangled the mare's foot and fed her, and went back to the hut. The old woman got up and lit the splint. 'Wake the lads, I'm going to the town!' And taking a wax taper from before the icon Dutlov lit it and went down with it into the opening under the floor. When he came up again lights were burning not only in his hut but in all the neighbouring houses. The young fellows were up and preparing to start. The women were coming in and out with pails of milk. Ignat was harnessing the horse to one cart and the second son was greasing the wheels of another. The young wife was no longer wailing. She had made herself neat and had bound a shawl over her head, and now sat waiting till it would be time to go to town to say goodbye to her husband.

The old man seemed particularly stern. He did not say a word to anyone, put on his best coat, tied his belt round him, and with all Polikey's money in the bosom of his coat, went to Egor Mikhaylovich.

'Don't dawdle,' he called to his son, who was turning the wheels round on the raised and newly greased axle. 'I'll be back in a minute; see that everything is ready.'

The steward had only just got up and was drinking tea. He himself was preparing to go to town to deliver up the recruits.

'What is it?' he asked.

'Egor Mikhaylovich, I want to buy the lad off. Do be so good! You said t'other day that you knew one in the town that was willing . . . Explain to me how to do it; we are ignorant people.'

'Why, have you reconsidered it?'

'I have, Egor Mikhaylovich. I'm sorry for him. My brother's child after all, whatever he may be. I'm sorry for him! It's the cause of much sin, money is. Do be good enough to explain it to me!' he said, bowing to his waist.

Egor Mikhaylovich, as was his wont on such occasions, stood for a long time thoughtfully smacking his lips. Then, having considered the matter, he wrote two notes and told him what to do in town and how to do it.

When Dutlov got home, the young wife had already set off with Ignat. The fat roan mare stood ready harnessed at the gate. Dutlov broke a stick out of the hedge and, lapping his coat over, got into the cart and whipped up the horse. He made the mare run so fast that her fat sides quickly shrank, and Dutlov did not look at her so as not to feel sorry for her. He was tormented by the thought that he might come too late for the recruiting, that Elijah would go as a soldier and the devil's money would be left on his hands.

I will not describe all Dutlov's proceedings that morning. I will only say that he was specially lucky. The man to whom Egor Mikhaylovich had given him a note had a volunteer quite ready who was already twenty-three silver rubles in debt and had been passed by the recruiting-board. His master wanted four hundred silver rubles for him and a buyer in the town had for the last three weeks been offering him three hundred. Dutlov settled the matter in a couple of words. 'Will you take three twenty-five?' he said, holding out his hand, but with a look that showed that he was prepared to give more. The master held back his hand and went on asking four hundred. 'You won't take three and a quarter?' Dutlov said, catching hold with his left hand of the man's right and preparing to slap his own right hand down on it. 'You won't take it? Well, God be with you!' he said suddenly, smacking the master's hand with the full swing of his other hand

and turning away with his whole body. 'It seems it has to be so . . . take three and a half hundred! Get out the discharge and bring the fellow along. And now here are two ten-ruble notes on account. Is it enough?'

And Dutlov unfastened his girdle and got out the money.

The man, though he did not withdraw his hand, yet did not seem quite to agree and, not accepting the deposit money, went on stipulating that Dutlov should wet the bargain and stand treat to the volunteer.

'Don't commit a sin,' Dutlov kept repeating as he held out the money. 'We shall all have to die some day,' he went on, in such a mild, persuasive and assured tone that the master said:

'So be it, then!' and again clapped Dutlov's hand and began praying for God's blessing. 'God grant you luck,' he said.

They woke the volunteer, who was still sleeping after yesterday's carouse, examined him for some reason, and went with him to the offices of the Administration. The recruit was merry. He demanded rum as a refresher, for which Dutlov gave him some money, and only when they came into the vestibule of the recruiting-board did his courage fail him. For a long time they stood in the entrance-hall, the old master in his full blue cloak and the recruit in a short sheepskin, his eyebrows raised and his eyes staring. For a long time they whispered, tried to get somewhere, looked for somebody, and for some reason took off their caps and bowed to every copying-clerk they met, and meditatively listened to the decision which a scribe whom the master knew brought out to them. All hope of getting the business done that day began to vanish, and the recruit was growing more cheerful and unconstrained again, when Dutlov saw Egor Mikhaylovich, seized on him at once, and began to beg and bow to him. Egor Mikhaylovich helped him so efficiently that by about three o'clock the recruit, to his great dissatisfaction and surprise, was taken into the hall and placed for examination, and amid general merriment (in which for some reason everybody joined, from the watchmen to the President), he was undressed, dressed again, shaved, and led out at the door; and five minutes later Dutlov counted out the money, received the discharge and, having taken leave of the volunteer and his master, went to the lodging-house where the Pokrovsk recruits were staying. Elijah and his young wife were sitting in a corner of the kitchen, and as soon as the old man came in they stopped talking and looked at him with a resigned expression, but not with goodwill. As was his wont the old man said a prayer, and he then unfastened his belt, got out a paper, and called into the room his eldest son Ignat and Elijah's mother, who were in the yard.

'Don't sin, Elijah,' he said, coming up to his nephew. 'Last night you said a word to me . . . Don't I pity you? I remember how my brother left you to me. If it had been in my power would I have let you go? God has sent me luck, and I am not grudging it you. Here it is, the paper'; and he put the discharge on the table and carefully smoothed it out with his stiff, unbending fingers.

All the Pokrovsk peasants, the inn-keeper's men, and even

some outsiders, came in from the yard. All guessed what was happening, but no one interrupted the old man's solemn discourse.

'Here it is, the paper! Four hundred silver rubles I've given for it. Don't reproach your uncle.'

Elijah rose, but remained silent not knowing what to say. His lips quivered with emotion. His old mother came up and would have thrown herself sobbing on his neck; but the old man motioned her away slowly and authoritatively and continued speaking.

'You said a word to me yesterday,' the old man again repeated. 'You stabbed me to the heart with that word as with a knife! Your dying father left you to me and you have been as my own son to me, and if I have wronged you in any way, well, we all live in sin! Is it not so, good Christian folk?' he said, turning to the peasants who stood round. 'Here is your own mother and your young wife, and here is the discharge for you. I don't regret the money, but forgive me for Christ's sake!'

And, turning up the skirts of his coat, he deliberately sank to his knees and bowed down to the ground before Elijah and his wife. The young people tried in vain to restrain him, but not till his forehead had touched the floor did he get up. Then, after giving his skirts a shake, he sat down on a bench. Elijah's mother and wife howled with joy, and words of approval were heard among the crowd. 'That is just, that's the godly way,' said one. 'What's money? You can't buy a fellow for money,' said another. 'What happiness!' said a third; 'no two ways about it, he's a just man!' Only the peasants who were to go as recruits said nothing, and went quietly out into the yard.

Two hours later Dutlov's two carts were driving through the outskirts of the town. In the first, to which was harnessed the roan mare, her sides fallen in and her neck moist with sweat, sat the old man and Ignat. Behind them jerked strings of ring-shaped fancy-bread. In the second cart, in which nobody held the reins, the young wife and her mother-in-law, with shawls over their heads, were sitting, sedate and happy. The former held a bottle of vodka under her apron. Elijah, very red in the face, sat all in a heap with his back to the horse, jolting against the front of the cart, biting into a roll and talking incessantly. The voices, the rumbling of the cart-wheels on the stony road, and the snorting of the horses, blent into one note of merriment. The horses, swishing their tails, increased their speed more and more, feeling themselves on the homeward road. The passers-by, whether driving or on foot, involuntarily turned round to look at the happy family party.

Just as they left the town the Dutlovs overtook a party of recruits. A group of them were standing in a ring outside a tavern. One of the recruits, with that unnatural expression on his face which comes of having the front of the head shaved,* his grey cap pushed back, was vigorously strumming a balalayka;

---

* On being conscripted, a man's head was partially shaved to make desertion more difficult.

another, bareheaded and with a bottle of vodka in his hand, was dancing in the middle of the ring. Ignat stopped his horse and got down to tighten the traces. All the Dutlovs looked with curiosity, approval, and amusement at the dancer. The recruit seemed not to see anyone, but felt that the public admiring him had grown larger, and this added to his strength and agility. He danced briskly. His brows were knitted, his flushed face was set, and his lips were fixed in a grin that had long since lost all meaning. It seemed as if all the strength of his soul was concentrated on placing one foot as quickly as possible after the other, now on the heel and now on the toe. Sometimes he stopped suddenly and winked to the balalayka-player, who began playing still more briskly, strumming on all the strings and even striking the case with his knuckles. The recruit would stop, but even when he stood still he still seemed to be dancing all over. Then he began slowly jerking his shoulders, and suddenly twirling round, leapt in the air with a wild cry, and descending, crouched down, throwing out first one leg and then the other. The little boys laughed, the women shook their heads, the men smiled approvingly. An old sergeant stood quietly by, with a look that seemed to say: 'You think it wonderful, but we have long been familiar with it.' The balalayka-player seemed tired; he looked lazily round, struck a false chord, and suddenly knocked on the case with his knuckles, and the dance came to an end.

'Eh, Alekha,' he said to the dancer, pointing at Dutlov, 'there's your sponsor!'

'Where? You, my dearest friend!' shouted Alekha, the very recruit whom Dutlov had bought; and staggering forward on his weary legs and holding the bottle of vodka above his head he moved towards the cart. 'Mishka, a glass!' he cried to the player. 'Master! My dearest friend! What a pleasure, really!' he shouted, drooping his tipsy head over the cart, and he began to treat the men and women to vodka. The men drank, but the women refused. 'My dear friends, what can I offer you?' exclaimed Alekha, embracing the old women.

A woman selling eatables was standing among the crowd. Alekha noticed her, seized her tray, and poured its contents into the cart.

'I'll pay, no fear, you devil!' he howled tearfully, pulling a purse from his pocket and throwing it to Mishka.

He stood leaning with his elbows on the cart and looking with moist eyes at those who sat in it.

'Which is the mother . . . you?' he asked. 'I must treat you too.'

He stood thinking for a moment, then he put his hand in his pocket and drew out a new folded handkerchief, hurriedly took off a sash which was tied round his waist under his coat, and also a red scarf he was wearing round his neck, and, crumpling them all together, thrust them into the old woman's lap.

'There! I'm sacrificing them for you,' he said in a voice that was growing more and more subdued.

'What for? Thank you, sonny! Just see what a simple lad it

is!' said the old woman, addressing Dutlov, who had come up to their cart.

Alekha was now quite quiet, quite stupefied, and looked as if he were falling asleep. He drooped his head lower and lower.

'It's for you I am going, for you I am perishing!' he muttered; 'that's why I am giving you gifts.'

'I dare say he, too, has a mother,' said someone in the crowd. 'What a simple fellow! What a pity!'

Alekha lifted his head.

'I have a mother,' said he; 'I have a father too. All have given me up. Listen to me, old woman,' he went on, taking Elijah's mother by the hand. 'I have given you presents. Listen to me for Christ's sake! Go to Vodnoe village, ask for the old woman Nikonovna – she's my own mother, see? Say to this same old woman, Nikonovna, the third hut from the end, by the new well. Tell her that Alekha – her son, you see . . . Eh! musician! strike up!' he shouted.

And muttering something he immediately began dancing again, and hurled the bottle with the remaining vodka to the ground.

Ignat got into the cart and was about to start.

'Goodbye! May God bless you!' said the old woman, wrapping her cloak closer round her.

Alekha suddenly stopped.

'Go to the devil!' he shouted, clenching his fists threateningly. 'May your mother be . . .'

'O Lord!' exclaimed Elijah's mother, crossing herself.

Ignat touched the reins, and the carts rattled on again. Alekha, the recruit, stood in the middle of the road with clenched fists and with a look of fury on his face, and abused the peasants with all his might.

'What are you stopping for? Go on, devils! cannibals!' he cried. 'You won't escape me! . . . Devil's clodhoppers!'

At these words his voice broke, and he fell full length to the ground just where he stood.

Soon the Dutlovs reached the open fields, and looking back could no longer see the crowd of recruits. Having gone some four miles at a walking pace Ignat got down from his father's cart, in which the old man lay asleep, and walked beside Elijah's cart.

Between them they emptied the bottle they had brought from town. After a while Elijah began a song, the women joined in, and Ignat shouted merrily in time with the song. A post-chaise drove merrily towards them. The driver called lustily to his horses as he passed the two festive carts, and the post-boy turned round and winked at the men and women who with flushed faces sat jolting inside singing their jovial song.

God Sees the Truth, but Waits

IN THE TOWN of Vladimir lived a young merchant named Ivan Dmitritch Aksyonof. He had two shops and a house of his own.

Aksyonof was a handsome, fair-haired, curly-headed fellow, full of fun, and very fond of singing. When quite a young man he had been given to drink, and was riotous when he had had too much; but after he married he gave up drinking, except now and then.

One summer Aksyonof was going to the Nizhny Fair, and as he bade goodbye to his family his wife said to him, 'Ivan Dmitritch, do not start today; I have had a bad dream about you.'

Aksyonof laughed, and said, 'You are afraid that when I get to the fair I shall go on the spree.'

His wife replied: 'I do not know what I am afraid of; all I know is that I had a bad dream. I dreamt you returned from the town, and when you took off your cap I saw that your hair was quite grey.'

Aksyonof laughed. 'That's a lucky sign,' said he. 'See if I don't sell out all my goods, and bring you some presents from the fair.'

So he said goodbye to his family, and drove away.

When he had travelled halfway, he met a merchant whom he knew, and they put up at the same inn for the night. They had some tea together, and then went to bed in adjoining rooms.

It was not Aksyonof's habit to sleep late, and, wishing to travel while it was still cool, he aroused his driver before dawn, and told him to put in the horses.

Then he made his way across to the landlord of the inn (who lived in a cottage at the back), paid his bill, and continued his journey.

When he had gone about twenty-five miles, he stopped for the horses to be fed. Aksyonof rested a while in the passage of the inn, then he stepped out into the porch, and, ordering a samovar to be heated, got out his guitar and began to play.

Suddenly a troyka drove up with tinkling bells, and an official alighted, followed by two soldiers. He came to Aksyonof and began to question him, asking him who he was and whence he came. Aksyonof answered him fully, and said, 'Won't you have some tea with me?' But the official went on cross-questioning him and asking him, 'Where did you spend last night? Were you alone, or with a fellow-merchant? Did you see the other merchant this morning? Why did you leave the inn before dawn?'

Aksyonof wondered why he was asked all these questions, but he described all that had happened, and then added, 'Why do you cross-question me as if I were a thief or a robber? I am travelling on business of my own, and there is no need to question me.'

Then the official, calling the soldiers, said, 'I am the police-officer of this district, and I question you because the merchant with whom you spent last night has been found with his throat cut. We must search your things.'

They entered the house. The soldiers and the police-officer unstrapped Aksyonof's luggage and searched it. Suddenly the officer drew a knife out of a bag, crying, 'Whose knife is this?'

Aksyonof looked, and seeing a blood-stained knife taken from his bag, he was frightened.

'How is it there is blood on this knife?'

Aksyonof tried to answer, but could hardly utter a word, and only stammered: 'I – I don't know – not mine.'

Then the police-officer said, 'This morning the merchant was found in bed with his throat cut. You are the only person who could have done it. The house was locked from inside, and no one else was there. Here is this blood-stained knife in your bag, and your face and manner betray you! Tell me how you killed him, and how much money you stole?'

Aksyonof swore he had not done it; that he had not seen the

merchant after they had had tea together; that he had no money except eight thousand rubles of his own, and that the knife was not his. But his voice was broken, his face pale, and he trembled with fear as though he were guilty.

The police-officer ordered the soldiers to bind Aksyonof and to put him in the cart. As they tied his feet together and flung him into the cart, Aksyonof crossed himself and wept. His money and goods were taken from him, and he was sent to the nearest town and imprisoned there. Inquiries as to his character were made in Vladimir. The merchants and other inhabitants of that town said that in former days he used to drink and waste his time, but that he was a good man. Then the trial came on: he was charged with murdering a merchant from Ryazan, and robbing him of twenty thousand rubles.

His wife was in despair, and did not know what to believe. Her children were all quite small; one was a baby at her breast. Taking them all with her, she went to the town where her husband was in gaol. At first she was not allowed to see him; but, after much begging, she obtained permission from the officials, and was taken to him. When she saw her husband in prison-dress and in chains, shut up with thieves and criminals, she fell down, and did not come to her senses for a long time. Then she drew her children to her, and sat down near him. She told him of things at home, and asked about what had happened to him. He told her all, and she asked, 'What can we do now?'

'We must petition the Tsar not to let an innocent man perish.'

His wife told him that she had sent a petition to the Tsar, but that it had not been accepted.

Aksyonof did not reply, but only looked downcast.

Then his wife said, 'It was not for nothing I dreamt your hair had turned grey. You remember? You should not have started that day.' And passing her fingers through his hair, she said: 'Vanya dearest, tell your wife the truth; was it not you who did it?'

'So you, too, suspect me!' said Aksyonof, and, hiding his face in his hands, he began to weep. Then a soldier came to say that the wife and children must go away; and Aksyonof said goodbye to his family for the last time.

When they were gone, Aksyonof recalled what had been said, and when he remembered that his wife also had suspected him, he said to himself, 'It seems that only God can know the truth; it is to Him alone we must appeal, and from Him alone expect mercy.'

And Aksyonof wrote no more petitions; gave up all hope, and only prayed to God.

Aksyonof was condemned to be flogged and sent to the mines. So he was flogged with a knout, and when the wounds made by the knout were healed, he was driven to Siberia with other convicts.

For twenty-six years Aksyonof lived as a convict in Siberia. His hair turned white as snow, and his beard grew long, thin, and grey. All his mirth went; he stooped; he walked slowly, spoke little, and never laughed, but he often prayed.

In prison Aksyonof learnt to make boots, and earned a little money, with which he bought *The Lives of the Saints*. He read this book when there was light enough in the prison; and on Sundays in the prison-church he read the lessons and sang in the choir; for his voice was still good.

The prison authorities liked Aksyonof for his meekness, and his fellow-prisoners respected him: they called him 'Grand-father', and 'The Saint'. When they wanted to petition the prison authorities about anything, they always made Aksyonof their spokesman, and when there were quarrels among the prisoners they came to him to put things right, and to judge the matter.

No news reached Aksyonof from his home, and he did not even know if his wife and children were still alive.

One day a fresh gang of convicts came to the prison. In the evening the old prisoners collected round the new ones and asked them what towns or villages they came from, and what they were sentenced for. Among the rest Aksyonof sat down near the newcomers, and listened with downcast air to what was said.

One of the new convicts, a tall, strong man of sixty, with a closely cropped grey beard, was telling the others what he had been arrested for.

'Well, friends,' he said, 'I only took a horse that was tied to a sledge, and I was arrested and accused of stealing. I said I had only taken it to get home quicker, and had then let it go; besides, the driver was a personal friend of mine. So I said, "It's all right." "No," said they, "you stole it." But how or where I stole it they could not say. I once really did something wrong, and ought by rights to have come here long ago, but that time I was not found out. Now I have been sent here for nothing at all . . . Eh, but it's lies I'm telling you; I've been to Siberia before, but I did not stay long.'

'Where are you from?' asked someone.

'From Vladimir. My family are of that town. My name is Makar, and they also call me Semyonitch.'

Aksyonof raised his head and said: 'Tell me, Semyonitch, do you know anything of the merchants Aksyonof, of Vladimir? Are they still alive?'

'Know them? Of course I do. The Aksyonofs are rich, though their father is in Siberia: a sinner like ourselves, it seems! As for you, Gran'dad, how did you come here?'

Aksyonof did not like to speak of his misfortune. He only sighed, and said, 'For my sins I have been in prison these twenty-six years.'

'What sins?' asked Makar Semyonitch.

But Aksyonof only said, 'Well, well – I must have deserved it!' He would have said no more, but his companions told the new-comer how Aksyonof came to be in Siberia: how someone had killed a merchant, and had put a knife among Aksyonof's things, and Aksyonof had been unjustly condemned.

When Makar Semyonitch heard this, he looked at Aksyonof, slapped his own knee, and exclaimed, 'Well, this is wonderful! Really wonderful! But how old you've grown, Gran'dad!'

The others asked him why he was so surprised, and where he had seen Aksyonof before; but Makar Semyonitch did not reply. He only said: 'It's wonderful that we should meet here, lads!'

These words made Aksyonof wonder whether this man knew who had killed the merchant; so he said, 'Perhaps, Semyonitch, you have heard of that affair, or maybe you've seen me before?'

'How could I help hearing? The world's full of rumours. But it's long ago, and I've forgotten what I heard.'

'Perhaps you heard who killed the merchant?' asked Aksyonof.

Makar Semyonitch laughed, and replied, 'It must have been him in whose bag the knife was found! If someone else hid the knife there, "He's not a thief till he's caught," as the saying is. How could anyone put a knife into your bag while it was under your head? It would surely have woke you up?'

When Aksyonof heard these words, he felt sure this was the man who had killed the merchant. He rose and went away. All that night Aksyonof lay awake. He felt terribly unhappy, and all sorts of images rose in his mind. There was the image of his wife as she was when he parted from her to go to the fair. He saw her as if she were present; her face and her eyes rose before him; he heard her speak and laugh. Then he saw his children, quite little, as they were at that time: one with a little cloak on, another at his mother's breast. And then he remembered himself as he used to be – young and merry. He remembered how he sat playing the guitar in the porch of the inn where he was arrested, and how free from care he had been. He saw, in his mind, the place where he was flogged, the executioner, and the people standing around; the chains, the convicts, all the twenty-six years of his prison life, and his premature old age. The thought of it all made him so wretched that he was ready to kill himself.

'And it's all that villain's doing!' thought Aksyonof. And his anger was so great against Makar Semyonitch that he longed for vengeance, even if he himself should perish for it. He kept repeating prayers all night, but could get no peace. During the day he did not go near Makar Semyonitch, nor even look at him.

A fortnight passed in this way. Aksyonof could not sleep at nights, and was so miserable that he did not know what to do.

One night as he was walking about the prison he noticed some earth that came rolling out from under one of the shelves on which the prisoners slept. He stopped to see what it was. Suddenly Makar Semyonitch crept out from under the shelf, and looked up at Aksyonof with frightened face. Aksyonof tried to pass without looking at him, but Makar seized his hand and told him that he had dug a hole under the wall, getting rid of the earth by putting it into his high-boots, and emptying it out every day on the road when the prisoners were driven to their work.

'Just you keep quiet, old man, and you shall get out too. If you blab they'll flog the life out of me, but I will kill you first.'

Aksyonof trembled with anger as he looked at his enemy. He drew his hand away, saying, 'I have no wish to escape, and you have no need to kill me; you killed me long ago! As to telling of you — I may do so or not, as God shall direct.'

Next day, when the convicts were led out to work, the convoy soldiers noticed that one or other of the prisoners emptied some earth out of his boots. The prison was searched, and the tunnel found. The Governor came and questioned all the prisoners to find out who had dug the hole. They all denied any knowledge of it. Those who knew, would not betray Makar Semyonitch, knowing he would be flogged almost to death. At last the Governor turned to Aksyonof, whom he knew to be a just man, and said:

'You are a truthful old man; tell me, before God, who dug the hole?'

Makar Semyonitch stood as if he were quite unconcerned, looking at the Governor and not so much as glancing at Aksyonof. Aksyonof's lips and hands trembled, and for a long time he could not utter a word. He thought, 'Why should I screen him who ruined my life? Let him pay for what I have suffered. But if I tell, they will probably flog the life out of him, and maybe I suspect him wrongly. And, after all, what good would it be to me?'

'Well, old man,' repeated the Governor, 'tell us the truth: who has been digging under the wall?'

Aksyonof glanced at Makar Semyonitch, and said, 'I cannot say, your Honour. It is not God's will that I should tell! Do what you like with me; I am in your hands.'

However much the Governor tried, Aksyonof would say no more, and so the matter had to be left.

That night, when Aksyonof was lying on his bed and just

beginning to doze, someone came quietly and sat down on his bed. He peered through the darkness and recognized Makar.

'What more do you want of me?' asked Aksyonof. 'Why have you come here?'

Makar Semyonitch was silent. So Aksyonof sat up and said, 'What do you want? Go away, or I will call the guard!'

Makar Semyonitch bent close over Aksyonof, and whispered, 'Ivan Dmitritch, forgive me!'

'What for?' asked Aksyonof.

'It was I who killed the merchant and hid the knife among your things. I meant to kill you too, but I heard a noise outside; so I hid the knife in your bag and escaped out of the window.'

Aksyonof was silent, and did not know what to say. Makar Semyonitch slid off the bed-shelf and knelt upon the ground. 'Ivan Dmitritch,' said he, 'forgive me! For the love of God, forgive me! I will confess that it was I who killed the merchant, and you will be released and can go to your home.'

'It is easy for you to talk,' said Aksyonof, 'but I have suffered for you these twenty-six years. Where could I go to now? . . . My wife is dead, and my children have forgotten me. I have nowhere to go . . .'

Makar Semyonitch did not rise, but beat his head on the floor. 'Ivan Dmitritch, forgive me!' he cried. 'When they flogged me with the knout it was not so hard to bear as it is to see you now . . . yet you had pity on me, and did not tell. For Christ's sake forgive me, wretch that I am!' And he began to sob.

When Aksyonof heard him sobbing he, too, began to weep.

'God will forgive you!' said he. 'Maybe I am a hundred times worse than you.' And at these words his heart grew light, and the longing for home left him. He no longer had any desire to leave the prison, but only hoped for his last hour to come.

In spite of what Aksyonof had said, Makar Semyonitch confessed his guilt. But when the order for his release came, Aksyonof was already dead.

A Prisoner in the Caucasus

I

AN OFFICER named Zhilin was serving in the army in the Caucasus.

One day he received a letter from home. It was from his mother, who wrote: 'I am getting old, and should like to see my dear son once more before I die. Come and say goodbye to me and bury me, and then, if God pleases, return to service again with my blessing. But I have found a girl for you, who is sensible and good and has some property. If you can love her, you might marry her and remain at home.'

Zhilin thought it over. It was quite true, the old lady was failing fast and he might not have another chance to see her alive. He had better go, and, if the girl was nice, why not marry her?

So he went to his colonel, obtained leave of absence, said

goodbye to his comrades, stood the soldiers four pailfuls of vodka as a farewell treat, and got ready to go.

It was a time of war in the Caucasus. The roads were not safe by night or day. If ever a Russian ventured to ride or walk any distance away from his fort, the Tartars killed him or carried him off to the hills. So it had been arranged that twice every week a body of soldiers should march from one fortress to the next to convey travellers from point to point.

It was summer. At daybreak the baggage-train got ready under shelter of the fortress; the soldiers marched out; and all started along the road. Zhilin was on horseback, and a cart with his things went with the baggage-train. They had sixteen miles to go. The baggage-train moved slowly; sometimes the soldiers stopped, or perhaps a wheel would come off one of the carts, or a horse refuse to go on, and then everybody had to wait.

When by the sun it was already past noon, they had not gone half the way. It was dusty and hot, the sun was scorching, and there was no shelter anywhere: a bare plain all round – not a tree, not a bush, by the road.

Zhilin rode on in front, and stopped, waiting for the baggage to overtake him. Then he heard the signal-horn sounded behind him: the company had again stopped. So he began to think: 'Hadn't I better ride on by myself? My horse is a good one: if the Tartars do attack me, I can gallop away. Perhaps, however, it would be wiser to wait.'

As he sat considering, Kostilin, an officer carrying a gun, rode up to him and said:

'Come along, Zhilin, let's go on by ourselves. It's dreadful; I am famished, and the heat is terrible. My shirt is wringing wet.'

Kostilin was a stout, heavy man, and the perspiration was running down his red face. Zhilin thought awhile, and then asked: 'Is your gun loaded?'

'Yes, it is.'

'Well, then, let's go, but on condition that we keep together.'

So they rode forward along the road across the plain, talking, but keeping a look-out on both sides. They could see afar all round. But after crossing the plain the road ran through a valley between two hills, and Zhilin said: 'We had better climb that hill and have a look round, or the Tartars may be on us before we know it.'

But Kostilin answered: 'What's the use? Let us go on.'

Zhilin, however, would not agree.

'No,' he said; 'you can wait here if you like, but I'll go and look round.' And he turned his horse to the left, up the hill. Zhilin's horse was a hunter, and carried him up the hillside as if it had wings. (He had bought it for a hundred rubles as a colt out of a herd, and had broken it in himself.) Hardly had he reached the top of the hill, when he saw some thirty Tartars not much more than a hundred yards ahead of him. As soon as he caught sight of them he turned round, but the Tartars had also seen him, and rushed after him at full gallop, getting their guns out as they went. Down galloped Zhilin as fast as the horse's legs could go, shouting to Kostilin: 'Get your gun ready!'

And, in thought, he said to his horse: 'Get me well out of this, my pet; don't stumble, for if you do it's all up. Once I reach the gun, they shan't take me prisoner.'

But, instead of waiting, Kostilin, as soon as he caught sight of the Tartars, turned back towards the fortress at full speed, whipping his horse now on one side now on the other, and its switching tail was all that could be seen of him in the dust.

Zhilin saw it was a bad look-out; the gun was gone, and what could he do with nothing but his sword? He turned his horse towards the escort, thinking to escape, but there were six Tartars rushing to cut him off. His horse was a good one, but theirs were still better; and besides, they were across his path. He tried to rein in his horse and to turn another way, but it was going so fast it could not stop, and dashed on straight towards the Tartars. He saw a red-bearded Tartar on a grey horse, with his gun raised, come at him, yelling and showing his teeth.

'Ah,' thought Zhilin, 'I know you, devils that you are. If you take me alive, you'll put me in a pit and flog me. I will not be taken alive!'

Zhilin, though not a big fellow, was brave. He drew his sword and dashed at the red-bearded Tartar, thinking: 'Either I'll ride him down, or disable him with my sword.'

He was still a horse's length away from him, when he was

fired at from behind, and his horse was hit. It fell to the ground with all its weight, pinning Zhilin to the earth.

He tried to rise, but two ill-savoured Tartars were already sitting on him and binding his hands behind his back. He made an effort and flung them off, but three others jumped from their horses and began beating his head with the butts of their guns. His eyes grew dim, and he fell back. The Tartars seized him, and, taking spare girths from their saddles, twisted his hands behind him and tied them with a Tartar knot. They knocked his cap off, pulled off his boots, searched him all over, tore his clothes, and took his money and his watch.

Zhilin looked round at his horse. There it lay on its side, poor thing, just as it had fallen; struggling, its legs in the air, unable to touch the ground. There was a hole in its head, and black blood was pouring out, turning the dust to mud for a couple of feet around.

One of the Tartars went up to the horse and began taking the saddle off; it still kicked, so he drew a dagger and cut its windpipe. A whistling sound came from its throat, the horse gave one plunge, and all was over.

The Tartars took the saddle and trappings. The red-bearded Tartar mounted his horse, and the others lifted Zhilin into the saddle behind him. To prevent his falling off, they strapped him to the Tartar's girdle; and then they all rode away to the hills.

So there sat Zhilin, swaying from side to side, his head striking against the Tartar's stinking back. He could see nothing but that muscular back and sinewy neck, with its closely shaven, bluish nape. Zhilin's head was wounded: the blood had dried over his eyes, and he could neither shift his position on the saddle nor wipe the blood off. His arms were bound so tightly that his collar-bones ached.

They rode up and down hills for a long way. Then they reached a river which they forded, and came to a hard road leading across a valley.

Zhilin tried to see where they were going, but his eyelids were stuck together with blood, and he could not turn.

Twilight began to fall; they crossed another river, and rode up a stony hillside. There was a smell of smoke here, and dogs were barking. They had reached an *aoul* (a Tartar village). The Tartars got off their horses; Tartar children came and stood round Zhilin, shrieking with pleasure and throwing stones at him.

The Tartar drove the children away, took Zhilin off the horse, and called his man. A Nogay* with high cheek-bones, and nothing on but a shirt (and that so torn that his breast was all bare), answered the call. The Tartar gave him an order. He went and fetched shackles: two blocks of oak with iron rings attached, and a clasp and lock fixed to one of the rings.

They untied Zhilin's arms, fastened the shackles on his leg, and dragged him to a barn, where they pushed him in and locked the door.

---

* One of a certain Tartar tribe.

Zhilin fell on a heap of manure. He lay still awhile, then groped about to find a soft place, and settled down.

II

THAT NIGHT Zhilin hardly slept at all. It was the time of year when the nights are short, and daylight soon showed itself through a chink in the wall. He rose, scratched to make the chink bigger, and peeped out.

Through the hole he saw a road leading downhill; to the right was a Tartar hut with two trees near it, a black dog lay on the threshold, and a goat and kids were moving about wagging their tails. Then he saw a young Tartar woman in a long, loose, bright-coloured gown, with trousers and high boots showing from under it. She had a coat thrown over her head, on which she carried a large metal jug filled with water. She was leading by the hand a small, closely shaven Tartar boy, who wore nothing but a shirt; and as she went along balancing herself, the muscles of her back quivered. This woman carried the water into the hut, and, soon after, the red-bearded Tartar of yesterday came out dressed in a silk tunic, with a silver-hilted dagger hanging by his side, shoes on his bare feet, and a tall black sheepskin cap set far back on his head. He came out, stretched himself, and stroked his red beard. He stood awhile, gave an order to his servant, and went away.

Then two lads rode past from watering their horses. The

horses' noses were wet. Some other closely shaven boys ran out, without any trousers, and wearing nothing but their shirts. They crowded together, came to the barn, picked up a twig, and began pushing it in at the chink. Zhilin gave a shout, and the boys shrieked and scampered off, their little bare knees gleaming as they ran.

Zhilin was very thirsty: his throat was parched, and he thought: 'If only they would come and so much as look at me!'

Then he heard someone unlocking the barn. The red-bearded Tartar entered, and with him was another, a smaller man, dark, with bright black eyes, red cheeks, and a short beard. He had a merry face, and was always laughing. This man was even more richly dressed than the other. He wore a blue silk tunic trimmed with gold, a large silver dagger in his belt, red morocco slippers worked with silver, and over these a pair of thick shoes, and he had a white sheepskin cap on his head.

The red-bearded Tartar entered, muttered something as if he were annoyed, and stood leaning against the door-post, playing with his dagger, and glaring askance at Zhilin, like a wolf. The dark one, quick and lively, and moving as if on springs, came straight up to Zhilin, squatted down in front of him, slapped him on the shoulder, and began to talk very fast in his own language. His teeth showed, and he kept winking, clicking his tongue, and repeating, 'Good Russ, good Russ.'

Zhilin could not understand a word, but said, 'Drink! give me water to drink!'

The dark man only laughed. 'Good Russ,' he said, and went on talking in his own tongue.

Zhilin made signs with lips and hands that he wanted something to drink.

The dark man understood, and laughed. Then he looked out of the door, and called to someone: 'Dina!'

A little girl came running in: she was about thirteen, slight, thin, and like the dark Tartar in face. Evidently she was his daughter. She, too, had clear black eyes, and her face was good-looking. She had on a long blue gown with wide sleeves, and no girdle. The hem of her gown, the front, and the sleeves, were trimmed with red. She wore trousers and slippers, and over the slippers stouter shoes with high heels. Round her neck she had a necklace made of Russian silver coins. She was bareheaded, and her black hair was plaited with a ribbon and ornamented with gilt braid and silver coins.

Her father gave an order, and she ran away and returned with a metal jug. She handed the water to Zhilin and sat down, crouching so that her knees were as high as her head; and there she sat with wide open eyes watching Zhilin drink, as though he were a wild animal.

When Zhilin handed the empty jug back to her, she gave such a sudden jump back, like a wild goat, that it made her father laugh. He sent her away for something else. She took the jug, ran out, and brought back some unleavened bread on a round board, and once more sat down, crouching, and looking on with staring eyes.

Then the Tartars went away and again locked the door.

After a while the Nogay came and said: '*Ayda*, the master, *Ayda!*'

He, too, knew no Russian. All Zhilin could make out was that he was told to go somewhere.

Zhilin followed the Nogay, but limped, for the shackles dragged his feet so that he could hardly step at all. On getting out of the barn he saw a Tartar village of about ten houses, and a Tartar church with a small tower. Three horses stood saddled before one of the houses; little boys were holding them by the reins. The dark Tartar came out of this house, beckoning with his hand for Zhilin to follow him. Then he laughed, said something in his own language, and returned into the house.

Zhilin entered. The room was a good one: the walls smoothly plastered with clay. Near the front wall lay a pile of bright-coloured feather beds; the side walls were covered with rich carpets used as hangings, and on these were fastened guns, pistols and swords, all inlaid with silver. Close to one of the walls was a small stove on a level with the earthen floor. The floor itself was as clean as a threshing-ground. A large space in one corner was spread over with felt, on which were rugs, and on these rugs were cushions stuffed with down. And on these cushions sat five Tartars, the dark one, the red-haired one, and three guests. They were wearing their indoor slippers, and each had a cushion behind his back. Before them were standing millet cakes on a round board, melted butter in a bowl, and a jug of *buza*, or Tartar beer. They ate both cakes and butter with their hands.

The dark man jumped up and ordered Zhilin to be placed on one side, not on the carpet but on the bare ground, then he sat down on the carpet again, and offered millet cakes and *buza* to his guests. The servant made Zhilin sit down, after which he took off his own overshoes, put them by the door where the other shoes were standing, and sat down nearer to his masters on the felt, watching them as they ate, and licking his lips.

The Tartars ate as much as they wanted, and a woman dressed in the same way as the girl – in a long gown and trousers, with a kerchief on her head – came and took away what was left, and brought a handsome basin, and a ewer with a narrow spout. The Tartars washed their hands, folded them, went down on their knees, blew to the four quarters, and said their prayers. After they had talked for a while, one of the guests turned to Zhilin and began to speak in Russian.

'You were captured by Kazi-Mohammed,' he said, and pointed at the red-bearded Tartar. 'And Kazi-Mohammed has given you to Abdul Murat,' pointing at the dark one. 'Abdul Murat is now your master.'

Zhilin was silent. Then Abdul Murat began to talk, laughing, pointing to Zhilin, and repeating, 'Soldier Russ, good Russ.'

The interpreter said, 'He orders you to write home and tell them to send a ransom, and as soon as the money comes he will set you free.'

Zhilin thought for a moment, and said, 'How much ransom does he want?'

The Tartars talked awhile, and then the interpreter said, 'Three thousand rubles.'

'No,' said Zhilin, 'I can't pay so much.'

Abdul jumped up and, waving his arms, talked to Zhilin, thinking, as before, that he would understand. The interpreter translated: 'How much will you give?'

Zhilin considered, and said, 'Five hundred rubles.' At this the Tartars began speaking very quickly, all together. Abdul began to shout at the red-bearded one, and jabbered so fast that the spittle spurted out of his mouth. The red-bearded one only screwed up his eyes and clicked his tongue.

They quietened down after a while, and the interpreter said, 'Five hundred rubles is not enough for the master. He paid two hundred for you himself. Kazi-Mohammed was in debt to him, and he took you in payment. Three thousand rubles! Less than that won't do. If you refuse to write, you will be put into a pit and flogged with a whip!'

'Eh!' thought Zhilin, 'the more one fears them the worse it will be.'

So he sprang to his feet, and said, 'You tell that dog that if he tries to frighten me I will not write at all, and he will get nothing. I never was afraid of you dogs, and never will be!'

The interpreter translated, and again they all began to talk at once.

They jabbered for a long time, and then the dark man jumped up, came to Zhilin, and said: '*Dzhigit Russ, dzhigit Russ!*' (*Dzhigit* in their language means 'brave'.) And he laughed, and said something to the interpreter, who translated: 'One thousand rubles will satisfy him.'

Zhilin stuck to it: 'I will not give more than five hundred. And if you kill me you'll get nothing at all.'

The Tartars talked awhile, then sent the servant out to fetch something, and kept looking, now at Zhilin, now at the door. The servant returned, followed by a stout, barefooted, tattered man, who also had his leg shackled.

Zhilin gasped with surprise: it was Kostilin. He, too, had been taken. They were put side by side, and began to tell each other what had occurred. While they talked, the Tartars looked on in silence. Zhilin related what had happened to him; and Kostilin told how his horse had stopped, his gun missed fire, and this same Abdul had overtaken and captured him.

Abdul jumped up, pointed to Kostilin, and said something. The interpreter translated that they both now belonged to one master, and the one who first paid the ransom would be set free first.

'There now,' he said to Zhilin, 'you get angry, but your comrade here is gentle; he has written home, and they will send five thousand rubles. So he will be well fed and well treated.'

Zhilin replied: 'My comrade can do as he likes; maybe he is rich, I am not. It must be as I said. Kill me, if you like – you will gain nothing by it; but I will not write for more than five hundred rubles.'

They were silent. Suddenly up sprang Abdul, brought a little box, took out a pen, ink, and a bit of paper, gave them to Zhilin, slapped him on the shoulder, and made a sign that he should write. He had agreed to take five hundred rubles.

'Wait a bit!' said Zhilin to the interpreter; 'tell him that he must feed us properly, give us proper clothes and boots, and let us be together. It will be more cheerful for us. And he must have these shackles taken off our feet,' and Zhilin looked at his master and laughed.

The master also laughed, heard the interpreter, and said: 'I will give them the best of clothes: a cloak and boots fit to be married in. I will feed them like princes; and if they like they can live together in the barn. But I can't take off the shackles, or they will run away. They shall be taken off, however, at night.' And he jumped up and slapped Zhilin on the shoulder, exclaiming: 'You good, I good!'

Zhilin wrote the letter, but addressed it wrongly, so that it should not reach its destination, thinking to himself: 'I'll run away!'

Zhilin and Kostilin were taken back to the barn and given some maize straw, a jug of water, some bread, two old cloaks, and some worn-out military boots – evidently taken from the corpses of Russian soldiers. At night their shackles were taken off their feet, and they were locked up in the barn.

III

ZHILIN AND HIS friend lived in this way for a whole month. The master always laughed and said: 'You, Ivan, good! I, Abdul, good!' But he fed them badly, giving them nothing but unleavened bread of millet-flour baked into flat cakes, or sometimes only unbaked dough.

Kostilin wrote home a second time, and did nothing but mope and wait for the money to arrive. He would sit for days together in the barn sleeping, or counting the days till a letter could come.

Zhilin knew his letter would reach no one, and he did not write another. He thought: 'Where could my mother get enough money to ransom me? As it is she lived chiefly on what I sent her. If she had to raise five hundred rubles, she would be quite ruined. With God's help I'll manage to escape!'

So he kept on the look-out, planning how to run away.

He would walk about the *aoul* whistling; or would sit working, modelling dolls of clay, or weaving baskets out of twigs: for Zhilin was clever with his hands.

Once he modelled a doll with a nose and hands and feet and with a Tartar gown on, and put it up on the roof. When the Tartar women came out to fetch water, the master's daughter, Dina, saw the doll and called the women, who put down their jugs and stood looking and laughing. Zhilin took down the doll and held it out to them. They laughed, but dared not take it. He put down the doll and went into the barn, waiting to see what would happen.

Dina ran up to the doll, looked round, seized it, and ran away.

In the morning, at daybreak, he looked out. Dina came out of the house and sat down on the threshold with the doll, which she had dressed up in bits of red stuff, and she rocked it like a baby, singing a Tartar lullaby. An old woman came out and scolded her, and snatching the doll away she broke it to bits, and sent Dina about her business.

But Zhilin made another doll, better than the first, and gave it to Dina. Once Dina brought a little jug, put it on the ground, sat down gazing at him, and laughed, pointing to the jug.

'What pleases her so?' wondered Zhilin. He took the jug thinking it was water, but it turned out to be milk. He drank the milk and said: 'That's good!'

How pleased Dina was! 'Good, Ivan, good!' said she, and she jumped up and clapped her hands. Then, seizing the jug, she ran away. After that, she stealthily brought him some milk every day.

The Tartars make a kind of cheese out of goat's milk, which they dry on the roofs of their houses; and sometimes, on the sly, she brought him some of this cheese. And once, when Abdul had killed a sheep, she brought Zhilin a bit of mutton in her sleeve. She would just throw the things down and run away.

One day there was a heavy storm, and the rain fell in

torrents for a whole hour. All the streams became turbid. At the ford, the water rose till it was seven feet high, and the current was so strong that it rolled the stones about. Rivulets flowed everywhere, and the rumbling in the hills never ceased. When the storm was over, the water ran in streams down the village street. Zhilin got his master to lend him a knife, and with it he shaped a small cylinder, and cutting some little boards, he made a wheel to which he fixed two dolls, one on each side. The little girls brought him some bits of stuff, and he dressed the dolls, one as a peasant, the other as a peasant-woman. Then he fastened them in their places, and set the wheel so that the stream should work it. The wheel began to turn and the dolls danced.

The whole village collected round. Little boys and girls, Tartar men and women, all came and clicked their tongues.

'Ah, Russ! Ah, Ivan!'

Abdul had a Russian clock, which was broken. He called Zhilin and showed it to him, clicking his tongue.

'Give it me; I'll mend it for you,' said Zhilin.

He took it to pieces with the knife, sorted the pieces, and put them together again, so that the clock went all right.

The master was delighted, and made him a present of one of his old tunics which was all in holes. Zhilin had to accept it. He could, at any rate, use it as a coverlet at night.

After that Zhilin's fame spread; and Tartars came from distant villages, bringing him now the lock of a gun or of a pistol, now a watch, to mend. His master gave him some tools – pincers, gimlets, and a file.

One day a Tartar fell ill, and they came to Zhilin, saying, 'Come and heal him!' Zhilin knew nothing about doctoring, but he went to look, and thought to himself, 'Perhaps he will get well anyway.'

He returned to the barn, mixed some water with sand, and then in the presence of the Tartars whispered some words over it and gave it to the sick man to drink. Luckily for him, the Tartar recovered.

Zhilin began to pick up their language a little, and some of the Tartars grew familiar with him. When they wanted him, they would call: 'Ivan! Ivan!' Others, however, still looked at him askance, as at a wild beast.

The red-bearded Tartar disliked Zhilin. Whenever he saw him he frowned and turned away, or swore at him. There was also an old man there who did not live in the *aoul*, but used to come up from the foot of the hill. Zhilin only saw him when he passed on his way to the mosque. He was short, and had a white cloth wound round his hat. His beard and moustaches were clipped, and white as snow; and his face was wrinkled and brick-red. His nose was hooked like a hawk's, his grey eyes looked cruel, and he had no teeth except two tusks. He would pass, with his turban on his head, leaning on his staff, and glaring round him like a wolf. If he saw Zhilin he would snort with anger and turn away.

Once Zhilin descended the hill to see where the old man lived.

He went down along the pathway and came to a little garden surrounded by a stone wall; and behind the wall he saw cherry and apricot trees, and a hut with a flat roof. He came closer, and saw hives made of plaited straw, and bees flying about and humming. The old man was kneeling, busy doing something with a hive. Zhilin stretched to look, and his shackles rattled. The old man turned round, and, giving a yell, snatched a pistol from his belt and shot at Zhilin, who just managed to shelter himself behind the stone wall.

The old man went to Zhilin's master to complain. The master called Zhilin, and said with a laugh, 'Why did you go to the old man's house?'

'I did him no harm,' replied Zhilin. 'I only wanted to see how he lived.'

The master repeated what Zhilin said.

But the old man was in a rage; he hissed and jabbered, showing his tusks, and shaking his fists at Zhilin.

Zhilin could not understand all, but he gathered that the old man was telling Abdul he ought not to keep Russians in the *aoul*, but ought to kill them. At last the old man went away.

Zhilin asked the master who the old man was.

'He is a great man!' said the master. 'He was the bravest of our fellows; he killed many Russians, and was at one time very rich. He had three wives and eight sons, and they all lived in one village. Then the Russians came and destroyed the village, and killed seven of his sons. Only one son was left, and he gave himself up to the Russians. The old man also went and gave himself up, and lived among the Russians for three months. At the end of that time he found his son, killed him with his own hands, and then escaped. After that he left off fighting, and went to Mecca to pray to God; that is why he wears a turban. One who has been to Mecca is called "Hadji", and wears a turban. He does not like you fellows. He tells me to kill you. But I can't kill you. I have paid money for you and, besides, I have grown fond of you, Ivan. Far from killing you, I would not even let you go if I had not promised.' And he laughed, saying in Russian, 'You, Ivan, good; I, Abdul, good!'

IV

ZHILIN LIVED in this way for a month. During the day he sauntered about the *aoul* or busied himself with some handicraft, but at night, when all was silent in the *aoul*, he dug at the floor of the barn. It was no easy task digging, because of the stones; but he worked away at them with his file, and at last had made a hole under the wall large enough to get through.

'If only I could get to know the lay of the land,' thought he, 'and which way to go! But none of the Tartars will tell me.'

So he chose a day when the master was away from home, and set off after dinner to climb the hill beyond the village, and to look around. But before leaving home the master always gave orders to his son to watch Zhilin, and not to lose sight of him. So the lad ran after Zhilin, shouting: 'Don't go! Father does not allow it. I'll call the neighbours if you won't come back.'

Zhilin tried to persuade him, and said: 'I'm not going far; I only want to climb that hill. I want to find a herb – to cure sick people with. You come with me if you like. How can I run away with these shackles on? Tomorrow I'll make a bow and arrows for you.'

So he persuaded the lad, and they went. To look at the hill, it did not seem far to the top; but it was hard walking with shackles on his leg. Zhilin went on and on, but it was all he could do to reach the top. There he sat down and noted how the land lay. To the south, beyond the barn, was a valley in which a herd of horses was pasturing and at the bottom of the valley one could see another *aoul*. Beyond that was a still steeper hill, and another hill beyond that. Between the hills, in the blue distance, were forests, and still further off were mountains, rising higher and higher. The highest of them were covered with snow, white as sugar; and one snowy peak towered above all the rest. To the east and to the west were other such hills, and here and there smoke rose from *aouls* in the ravines. 'Ah,' thought he, 'all that is Tartar country.' And he turned towards the Russian side. At his feet he saw a river, and the *aoul* he lived in, surrounded by little gardens. He could see women, like tiny dolls, sitting by the river rinsing clothes. Beyond the *aoul* was a hill, lower than the one to the south, and beyond it two other hills well wooded;

and between these, a smooth bluish plain, and far, far across the plain something that looked like a cloud of smoke. Zhilin tried to remember where the sun used to rise and set when he was living in the fort, and he saw that there was no mistake: the Russian fort must be in that plain. Between those two hills he would have to make his way when he escaped.

The sun was beginning to set. The white, snowy mountains turned red, and the dark hills turned darker; mists rose from the ravine, and the valley, where he supposed the Russian fort to be, seemed on fire with the sunset glow. Zhilin looked carefully. Something seemed to be quivering in the valley like smoke from a chimney, and he felt sure the Russian fortress was there.

It had grown late. The Mullah's cry was heard. The herds were being driven home, the cows were lowing, and the lad kept saying, 'Come home!' But Zhilin did not feel inclined to go away.

At last, however, they went back. 'Well,' thought Zhilin, 'now that I know the way, it is time to escape.' He thought of running away that night. The nights were dark – the moon had waned. But as ill-luck would have it, the Tartars returned home that evening. They generally came back driving cattle before them and in good spirits. But this time they had no cattle. All they brought home was the dead body of a Tartar – the red one's brother – who had been killed. They came back looking sullen, and they all gathered together for the burial. Zhilin also came out to see it.

They wrapped the body in a piece of linen, without any

coffin, and carried it out of the village, and laid it on the grass under some plane-trees. The Mullah and the old men came. They wound clothes round their caps, took off their shoes, and squatted on their heels, side by side, near the corpse.

The Mullah was in front: behind him in a row were three old men in turbans, and behind them again the other Tartars. All cast down their eyes and sat in silence. This continued a long time, until the Mullah raised his head and said: 'Allah!' (which means 'God'). He said that one word, and they all cast down their eyes again, and were again silent for a long time. They sat quite still, not moving or making any sound.

Again the Mullah lifted his head and said, 'Allah!' and they all repeated: 'Allah! Allah!' and were again silent.

The dead body lay immovable on the grass, and they sat as still as if they too were dead. Not one of them moved. There was no sound but that of the leaves of the plane-trees stirring in the breeze. Then the Mullah repeated a prayer, and they all rose. They lifted the body and carried it in their arms to a hole in the ground. It was not an ordinary hole, but was hollowed out under the ground like a vault. They took the body under the arms and by the legs, bent it, and let it gently down, pushing it under the earth in a sitting posture, with the hands folded in front.

The Nogay brought some green rushes, which they stuffed into the hole, and, quickly covering it with earth, they smoothed the ground, and set an upright stone at the head of the grave.

Then they trod the earth down, and again sat in a row before the grave, keeping silence for a long time.

At last they rose, said, 'Allah! Allah! Allah!' and sighed.

The red-bearded Tartar gave money to the old men; then he too rose, took a whip, struck himself with it three times on the forehead, and went home.

The next morning Zhilin saw the red Tartar, followed by three others, leading a mare out of the village. When they were beyond the village, the red-bearded Tartar took off his tunic and turned up his sleeves, showing his stout arms. Then he drew a dagger and sharpened it on a whetstone. The other Tartars raised the mare's head, and he cut her throat, threw her down, and began skinning her, loosening the hide with his big hands. Women and girls came and began to wash the entrails and the innards. The mare was cut up, the pieces taken into the hut, and the whole village collected at the red Tartar's hut for a funeral feast.

For three days they went on eating the flesh of the mare, drinking *buza*, and praying for the dead man. All the Tartars were at home. On the fourth day at dinner-time Zhilin saw them preparing to go away. Horses were brought out, they got ready, and some ten of them (the red one among them) rode away; but Abdul stayed at home. It was new moon, and the nights were still dark.

'Ah!' thought Zhilin, 'tonight is the time to escape.' And he told Kostilin; but Kostilin's heart failed him.

'How can we escape?' he said. 'We don't even know the way.'

'I know the way,' said Zhilin.

'Even if you do,' said Kostilin, 'we can't reach the fort in one night.'

'If we can't,' said Zhilin, 'we'll sleep in the forest. See here, I have saved some cheeses. What's the good of sitting and moping here? If they send your ransom – well and good; but suppose they don't manage to collect it? The Tartars are angry now, because the Russians have killed one of their men. They are talking of killing us.'

Kostilin thought it over.

'Well, let's go,' said he.

V

ZHILIN CREPT into the hole, widened it so that Kostilin might also get through, and then they both sat waiting till all should be quiet in the *aoul*.

As soon as all was quiet, Zhilin crept under the wall, got out, and whispered to Kostilin, 'Come!' Kostilin crept out, but in so doing he caught a stone with his foot and made a noise. The master had a very vicious watch-dog, a spotted one called Oulyashin. Zhilin had been careful to feed him for some time before. Oulyashin heard the noise and began to bark and jump, and the other dogs did the same. Zhilin gave a slight whistle, and threw him a bit of cheese. Oulyashin knew Zhilin, wagged his tail, and stopped barking.

But the master had heard the dog, and shouted to him from his hut, 'Hayt, hayt, Oulyashin!'

Zhilin, however, scratched Oulyashin behind the ears, and the dog was quiet, and rubbed against his legs, wagging his tail.

They sat hidden behind a corner for a while. All became silent again, only a sheep coughed inside a shed, and the water rippled over the stones in the hollow. It was dark, the stars were high overhead, and the new moon showed red as it set, horns upward, behind the hill. In the valleys the fog was white as milk.

Zhilin rose and said to his companion, 'Well, friend, come along!'

They started; but they had only gone a few steps when they heard the Mullah crying from the roof, 'Allah, Beshmillah! Ilrahman!' That meant that the people would be going to the mosque. So they sat down again, hiding behind a wall, and waited a long time till the people had passed. At last all was quiet again.

'Now then! May God be with us!' They crossed themselves, and started once more. They passed through a yard and went down the hillside to the river, crossed the river, and went along the valley.

The mist was thick, but only near the ground; overhead the stars shone quite brightly. Zhilin directed their course by the stars. It was cool in the mist, and easy walking; only their boots were uncomfortable, being worn out and trodden down. Zhilin took his off, threw them away, and went barefoot, jumping from stone to stone, and guiding his course by the stars. Kostilin began to lag behind.

'Walk slower,' he said, 'these confounded boots have quite blistered my feet.'

'Take them off!' said Zhilin. 'It will be easier walking without them.'

Kostilin went barefoot, but got on still worse. The stones cut his feet, and he kept lagging behind. Zhilin said: 'If your feet get cut, they'll heal again; but if the Tartars catch us and kill us, it will be worse!'

Kostilin did not reply, but went on, groaning all the time.

Their way lay through the valley for a long time. Then, to the right, they heard dogs barking. Zhilin stopped, looked about, and began climbing the hill, feeling with his hands.

'Ah!' said he, 'we have gone wrong, and have come too far to the right. Here is another *aoul*, one I saw from the hill. We must turn back and go up that hill to the left. There must be a wood there.'

But Kostilin said: 'Wait a minute! Let me get breath. My feet are all cut and bleeding.'

'Never mind, friend! They'll heal again. You should spring more lightly. Like this!'

And Zhilin ran back and turned to the left up the hill towards the wood.

Kostilin still lagged behind, and groaned. Zhilin only said 'Hush!' and went on and on.

They went up the hill and found a wood as Zhilin had said. They entered the wood and forced their way through the brambles, which tore their clothes. At last they came to a path and followed it.

'Stop!' They heard the tramp of hoofs on the path, and waited, listening. It sounded like the tramping of a horse's feet, but then ceased. They moved on, and again they heard the tramping. When they paused, it also stopped. Zhilin crept nearer to it, and saw something standing on the path where it was not quite so dark. It looked like a horse, and yet not quite like one, and on it was something queer, not like a man. He heard it snorting. 'What can it be?' Zhilin gave a low whistle, and off it dashed from the path into the thicket, and the woods were filled with the noise of crackling, as if a hurricane were sweeping through, breaking the branches.

Kostilin was so frightened that he sank to the ground. But Zhilin laughed and said: 'It's a stag. Don't you hear him breaking the branches with his antlers? We were afraid of him, and he is afraid of us.'

They went on. The Great Bear was already setting. It was near morning, and they did not know whether they were going the right way or not. Zhilin thought it was the way he had been brought by the Tartars, and that they were still some seven miles from the Russian fort; but he had nothing certain to go by, and at night one easily mistakes the way. After a time they came to a clearing. Kostilin sat down and said: 'Do as you like, I can go no farther! My feet won't carry me.'

Zhilin tried to persuade him.

'No, I shall never get there; I can't!'

Zhilin grew angry, and spoke roughly to him.

'Well, then, I shall go on alone. Goodbye!'

Kostilin jumped up and followed. They went another three miles. The mist in the wood had settled down still more densely; they could not see a yard before them, and the stars had grown dim.

Suddenly they heard the sound of a horse's hoofs in front of them. They heard its shoes strike the stones. Zhilin lay down flat, and listened with his ear to the ground.

'Yes, so it is! A horseman is coming towards us.'

They ran off the path, crouched among the bushes, and waited. Zhilin crept to the road, looked, and saw a Tartar on horseback driving a cow and humming to himself. The Tartar rode past. Zhilin returned to Kostilin.

'God has led him past us; get up and let's go on!'

Kostilin tried to rise, but fell back again.

'I can't; on my word I can't! I have no strength left.'

He was heavy and stout, and had been perspiring freely. Chilled by the mist, and with his feet all bleeding, he had grown quite limp.

Zhilin tried to lift him, when suddenly Kostilin screamed out: 'Oh, how it hurts!'

Zhilin's heart sank.

'What are you shouting for? The Tartar is still near; he'll have heard you!' And he thought to himself, 'He is really quite done up. What am I to do with him? It won't do to desert a comrade.'

'Well, then, get up, and climb up on my back. I'll carry you if you really can't walk.'

He helped Kostilin up, and put his arms under his thighs. Then he went out onto the path, carrying him.

'Only, for the love of heaven,' said Zhilin, 'don't throttle me with your hands! Hold on to my shoulders.'

Zhilin found his load heavy; his feet, too, were bleeding, and he was tired out. Now and then he stooped to balance Kostilin better, jerking him up so that he should sit higher, and then went on again.

The Tartar must, however, really have heard Kostilin scream. Zhilin suddenly heard someone galloping behind and shouting in the Tartar tongue. He darted in among the bushes. The Tartar seized his gun and fired, but did not hit them, shouted in his own language, and galloped off along the road.

'Well, now we are lost, friend!' said Zhilin. 'That dog will gather the Tartars together to hunt us down. Unless we can get a couple of miles away from here we are lost!' And he thought to himself, 'Why the devil did I saddle myself with this block? I should have got away long ago had I been alone.'

'Go on alone,' said Kostilin. 'Why should you perish because of me?'

'No, I won't go. It won't do to desert a comrade.'

Again he took Kostilin on his shoulders and staggered on. They went on in that way for another half-mile or more. They were still in the forest, and could not see the end of it. But the mist was already dispersing, and clouds seemed to be gathering; the stars were no longer to be seen. Zhilin was quite done up. They came to a spring walled in with stones by the side of the path. Zhilin stopped and set Kostilin down.

'Let me have a rest and a drink,' said he, 'and let us eat some of the cheese. It can't be much farther now.'

But hardly had he lain down to get a drink, when he heard the sound of horses' feet behind him. Again they darted to the right among the bushes, and lay down under a steep slope.

They heard Tartar voices. The Tartars stopped at the very spot where they had turned off the path. The Tartars talked a bit, and then seemed to be setting a dog on the scent. There was a sound of crackling twigs, and a strange dog appeared from behind the bushes. It stopped, and began to bark.

Then the Tartars, also strangers, came climbing down, seized Zhilin and Kostilin, bound them, put them on horses, and rode away with them.

When they had ridden about two miles, they met Abdul, their owner, with two other Tartars following him. After talking with the strangers, he put Zhilin and Kostilin on two of his own horses and took them back to the *aoul*.

Abdul did not laugh now, and did not say a word to them.

They were back at the *aoul* by daybreak, and were set down in the street. The children came crowding round, throwing stones, shrieking, and beating them with whips.

The Tartars gathered together in a circle, and the old man from the foot of the hill was also there. They began discussing; and Zhilin heard them considering what should be done with him and Kostilin. Some said they ought to be sent farther into the mountains; but the old man said: 'They must be killed!'

Abdul disputed with him, saying: 'I gave money for them, and I must get ransom for them.' But the old man said: 'They will pay you nothing, but will only bring misfortune. It is a sin to feed Russians. Kill them, and have done with it!'

They dispersed. When they had gone, the master came up to Zhilin and said: 'If the money for your ransom is not sent within a fortnight, I will flog you; and if you try to run away again, I'll kill you like a dog! Write a letter, and write properly!'

Paper was brought to them, and they wrote the letters. Shackles were put on their feet, and they were taken behind the mosque to a deep pit about twelve feet square, into which they were let down.

VI

LIFE WAS NOW very hard for them. Their shackles were never taken off, and they were not let out into the fresh air. Unbaked dough was thrown to them as if they were dogs, and water was let down in a can.

It was wet and close in the pit, and there was a horrible stench. Kostilin grew quite ill, his body became swollen and he ached all over, and moaned or slept all the time. Zhilin, too, grew downcast; he saw it was a bad look-out, and could think of no way of escape.

He tried to make a tunnel, but there was nowhere to put the earth. His master noticed it, and threatened to kill him.

He was sitting on the floor of the pit one day, thinking of freedom and feeling very downhearted, when suddenly a cake fell into his lap, then another, and then a shower of cherries. He looked up, and there was Dina. She looked at him, laughed, and ran away. And Zhilin thought: 'Might not Dina help me?'

He cleared out a little place in the pit, scraped up some clay, and began modelling toys. He made men, horses, and dogs, thinking, 'When Dina comes I'll throw them up to her.'

But Dina did not come next day. Zhilin heard the tramp of horses; some men rode past, and the Tartars gathered in council near the mosque. They shouted and argued; the word 'Russians' was repeated several times. He could hear the voice of the old man. Though he could not distinguish what was said, he guessed that Russian troops were somewhere near, and that the Tartars, afraid they might come into the *aoul*, did not know what to do with their prisoners.

After talking awhile, they went away. Suddenly he heard a

rustling overhead, and saw Dina crouching at the edge of the pit, her knees higher than her head, and bending over so that the coins of her plait dangled above the pit. Her eyes gleamed like stars. She drew two cheeses out of her sleeve and threw them to him. Zhilin took them and said, 'Why did you not come before? I have made some toys for you. Here, catch!' And he began throwing the toys up, one by one.

But she shook her head and would not look at them.

'I don't want any,' she said. She sat silent for a while, and then went on, 'Ivan, they want to kill you!' And she pointed to her own throat.

'Who wants to kill me?'

'Father; the old men say he must. But I am sorry for you!'

Zhilin answered: 'Well, if you are sorry for me, bring me a long pole.'

She shook her head, as much as to say, 'I can't!'

He clasped his hands and prayed her: 'Dina, please do! Dear Dina, I beg of you!'

'I can't!' she said, 'they would see me bringing it. They're all at home.' And she went away.

So when evening came Zhilin still sat looking up now and then, and wondering what would happen. The stars were there, but the moon had not yet risen. The Mullah's voice was heard; then all was silent. Zhilin was beginning to doze, thinking: 'The girl will be afraid to do it!'

Suddenly he felt clay falling on his head. He looked up, and saw a long pole poking into the opposite wall of the pit. It kept poking about for a time, and then it came down, sliding into the pit. Zhilin was glad indeed. He took hold of it and lowered it. It was a strong pole, one that he had seen before on the roof of his master's hut.

He looked up. The stars were shining high in the sky, and just above the pit Dina's eyes gleamed in the dark like a cat's. She stooped with her face close to the edge of the pit, and whispered, 'Ivan! Ivan!' waving her hand in front of her face to show that he should speak low.

'What?' said Zhilin.

'All but two have gone away.'

Then Zhilin said, 'Well, Kostilin, come; let us have one last try; I'll help you up.'

But Kostilin would not hear of it.

'No,' said he, 'it's clear I can't get away from here. How can I go, when I have hardly strength to turn round?'

'Well, goodbye, then! Don't think ill of me!' and they kissed each other. Zhilin seized the pole, told Dina to hold on, and began to climb. He slipped once or twice; the shackles hindered him. Kostilin helped him, and he managed to get to the top. Dina, with her little hands, pulled with all her might at his shirt, laughing.

Zhilin drew out the pole, and said, 'Put it back in its place, Dina, or they'll notice, and you will be beaten.'

She dragged the pole away, and Zhilin went down the hill.

When he had gone down the steep incline, he took a sharp stone and tried to wrench the lock off the shackles. But it was a strong lock and he could not manage to break it, and besides, it was difficult to get at. Then he heard someone running down the hill, springing lightly. He thought: 'Surely, that's Dina again.'

Dina came, took a stone, and said, 'Let me try.'

She knelt down and tried to wrench the lock off, but her little hands were as slender as little twigs, and she had not the strength. She threw the stone away and began to cry. Then Zhilin set to work again at the lock, and Dina squatted beside him with her hand on his shoulder.

Zhilin looked round and saw a red light to the left behind the hill. The moon was just rising. 'Ah!' he thought, 'before the moon has risen I must have passed the valley and be in the forest.' So he rose and threw away the stone. Shackles or no, he must go on.

'Goodbye, Dina dear!' he said. 'I shall never forget you!'

Dina seized hold of him and felt about with her hands for a place to put some cheeses she had brought. He took them from her.

'Thank you, my little one. Who will make dolls for you when I am gone?' And he stroked her head.

Dina burst into tears, hiding her face in her hands. Then she ran up the hill like a young goat, the coins in her plait clinking against her back.

Zhilin crossed himself, took the lock of his shackles in his hand to prevent its clattering, and went along the road, dragging his shackled leg, and looking towards the place where the moon was about to rise. He now knew the way. If he went straight he would have to walk nearly six miles. If only he could reach the wood before the moon had quite risen! He crossed the river; the light behind the hill was growing whiter. Still looking at it, he went along the valley. The moon was not yet visible. The light became brighter, and one side of the valley was growing lighter and lighter, and shadows were drawing in towards the foot of the hill, creeping nearer and nearer to him.

Zhilin went on, keeping in the shade. He was hurrying, but the moon was moving still faster; the tops of the hills on the right were already lit up. As he got near the wood the white moon appeared from behind the hills, and it became light as day. One could see all the leaves on the trees. It was light on the hill, but silent, as if nothing were alive; no sound could be heard but the gurgling of the river below.

Zhilin reached the wood without meeting anyone, chose a dark spot, and sat down to rest.

He rested, and ate one of the cheeses. Then he found a stone and set to work again to knock off the shackles. He knocked his hands sore, but could not break the lock. He rose and went along the road. After walking the greater part of a mile he was quite done up, and his feet were aching. He had to stop every ten steps. 'There is nothing else for it,' thought he. 'I must drag on as long as I have any strength left. If I sit down, I shan't be able to rise again. I can't reach the fortress; but when day breaks I'll lie down in the forest, remain there all day, and go on again at night.'

He went on all night. Two Tartars on horseback passed him; but he heard them a long way off, and hid behind a tree.

The moon began to grow paler, the dew to fall. It was getting near dawn, and Zhilin had not reached the end of the forest. 'Well,' thought he, 'I'll walk another thirty steps, and then turn in among the trees and sit down.'

He walked another thirty steps, and saw that he was at the end of the forest. He went to the edge; it was now quite light, and straight before him was the plain and the fortress. To the left, quite close at the foot of the slope, a fire was dying out, and the smoke from it spread round. There were men gathered about the fire.

He looked intently, and saw guns glistening. They were soldiers – Cossacks!

Zhilin was filled with joy. He collected his remaining strength and set off down the hill, saying to himself: 'God forbid that any mounted Tartar should see me now, in the open field! Near as I am, I could not get there in time.'

Hardly had he said this when, a couple of hundred yards off, on a hillock to the left, he saw three Tartars.

They saw him also and made a rush. His heart sank. He waved his hands, and shouted with all his might, 'Brothers, brothers! Help!'

The Cossacks heard him, and a party of them on horseback darted to cut across the Tartars' path. The Cossacks were far and the Tartars were near; but Zhilin, too, made a last effort. Lifting the shackles with his hand, he ran towards the Cossacks, hardly knowing what he was doing, crossing himself and shouting, 'Brothers! Brothers! Brothers!'

There were some fifteen Cossacks. The Tartars were frightened, and stopped before reaching him. Zhilin staggered up to the Cossacks.

They surrounded him and began questioning him. 'Who are you? What are you? Where from?'

But Zhilin was quite beside himself, and could only weep and repeat, 'Brothers! Brothers!'

Then the soldiers came running up and crowded round Zhilin – one giving him bread, another buckwheat, a third vodka: one wrapping a cloak round him, another breaking his shackles.

The officers recognized him, and rode with him to the fortress. The soldiers were glad to see him back, and his comrades all gathered round him.

Zhilin told them all that had happened to him.

'That's the way I went home and got married!' said he. 'No. It seems plain that fate was against it!'

So he went on serving in the Caucasus. A month passed before Kostilin was released, after paying five thousand rubles ransom. He was almost dead when they brought him back.

What Men Live By

We know that we have passed out of death into life, because
we love the brethren. He that loveth not abideth in death.

Whoso hath the world's goods, and beholdeth his brother
in need, and shutteth up his compassion from him, how
doth the love of God abide in him? My little children,
let us not love in word,, neither with the tongue; but in
deed and truth.

Love is of God; and every one that loveth is begotten of
God, and knoweth God. He that loveth not knoweth not
God; for God is love.

No man hath beheld God at any time; if we love one
another, God abideth in us.

God is love; and he that abideth in love abideth in God, and
God abideth in him.

If a man say, I love God, and hateth his brother, he is a liar;
for he that loveth not his brother whom he hath seen,
how can he love God whom he hath not seen?

(1 John iii, 14; iii, 17–18; iv, 7–8; iv, 12; iv, 16; iv, 20)

I

A SHOEMAKER NAMED Simon, who had neither house nor land of his own, lived with his wife and children in a peasant's hut, and earned his living by his work. Work was cheap but bread was dear, and what he earned he spent for food. The man and his wife had but one sheepskin coat between them for winter wear, and even that was worn to tatters, and this was the second year he had been wanting to buy sheepskins for a new coat. Before winter Simon saved up a little money: a three-ruble note lay hidden in his wife's box, and five rubles and twenty kopeks were owed him by customers in the village.

So one morning he prepared to go to the village to buy the sheepskins. He put on over his shirt his wife's wadded nankeen jacket, and over that he put his own cloth coat. He took the three-ruble note in his pocket, cut himself a stick to serve as a staff, and started off after breakfast. 'I'll collect the five rubles that are due to me,' thought he, 'add the three I have got, and that will be enough to buy sheepskins for the winter coat.'

He came to the village and called at a peasant's hut, but the man was not at home. The peasant's wife promised that the money should be paid next week, but she would not pay it herself. Then Simon called on another peasant, but this one swore he had no money, and would only pay twenty kopeks which he owed for a pair of boots Simon had mended. Simon then tried to buy the sheepskins on credit, but the dealer would not trust him.

'Bring your money,' said he, 'then you may have your pick of the skins. We know what debt-collecting is like.'

So all the business the shoemaker did was to get the twenty kopeks for boots he had mended, and to take a pair of felt boots a peasant gave him to sole with leather.

Simon felt downhearted. He spent the twenty kopeks on vodka, and started homewards without having bought any skins. In the morning he had felt the frost; but now, after drinking the vodka, he felt warm even without a sheepskin coat. He trudged along, striking his stick on the frozen earth with one hand, swinging the felt boots with the other, and talking to himself.

'I'm quite warm,' said he, 'though I have no sheepskin coat. I've had a drop, and it runs through all my veins. I need no sheepskins. I go along and don't worry about anything. That's the sort of man I am! What do I care? I can live without sheep-skins. I don't need them. My wife will fret, to be sure. And, true enough, it *is* a shame; one works all day long, and then does not get paid. Stop a bit! If you don't bring that money along, sure enough I'll skin you, blessed if I don't. How's that? He pays twenty kopeks at a time! What can I do with twenty kopeks? Drink it – that's all one can do! Hard up, he says he is! So he may be – but what about me? You have house, and cattle, and everything; I've only what I stand up in! You have corn of your own growing; I have to buy every grain. Do what

I will, I must spend three rubles every week for bread alone. I come home and find the bread all used up, and I have to fork out another ruble and a half. So just you pay up what you owe, and no nonsense about it!'

By this time he had nearly reached the shrine at the bend of the road. Looking up, he saw something whitish behind the shrine. The daylight was fading, and the shoemaker peered at the thing without being able to make out what it was. 'There was no white stone here before. Can it be an ox? It's not like an ox. It has a head like a man, but it's too white; and what could a man be doing there?'

He came closer, so that it was clearly visible. To his surprise it really was a man, alive or dead, sitting naked, leaning motionless against the shrine. Terror seized the shoemaker, and he thought, 'Someone has killed him, stripped him, and left him here. If I meddle I shall surely get into trouble.'

So the shoemaker went on. He passed in front of the shrine so that he could not see the man. When he had gone some way, he looked back, and saw that the man was no longer leaning against the shrine, but was moving as if looking towards him. The shoemaker felt more frightened than before, and thought, 'Shall I go back to him, or shall I go on? If I go near him something dreadful may happen. Who knows who the fellow is? He has not come here for any good. If I go near him he may jump up and throttle me, and there will be no getting away. Or if not, he'd still be a burden on one's hands. What could I do with a naked man? I couldn't give him my last clothes. Heaven only help me to get away!'

So the shoemaker hurried on, leaving the shrine behind him – when suddenly his conscience smote him, and he stopped in the road.

'What are you doing, Simon?' said he to himself. 'The man may be dying of want, and you slip past afraid. Have you grown so rich as to be afraid of robbers? Ah, Simon, shame on you!'

So he turned back and went up to the man.

II

SIMON APPROACHED the stranger, looked at him, and saw that he was a young man, fit, with no bruises on his body, only evidently freezing and frightened, and he sat there leaning back without looking up at Simon, as if too faint to lift his eyes. Simon went close to him, and then the man seemed to wake up. Turning his head, he opened his eyes and looked into Simon's face. That one look was enough to make Simon fond of the man. He threw the felt boots on the ground, undid his sash, laid it on the boots, and took off his cloth coat.

'It's not a time for talking,' said he. 'Come, put this coat on at once!' And Simon took the man by the elbows and helped him to rise. As he stood there, Simon saw that his body was clean and in good condition, his hands and feet shapely, and his face good and kind. He threw his coat over the man's shoulders, but the latter could not find the sleeves. Simon guided his arms into them, and drawing the coat well on, wrapped it closely about him, tying the sash round the man's waist.

Simon even took off his torn cap to put it on the man's head, but then his own head felt cold, and he thought: 'I'm quite bald, while he has long curly hair.' So he put his cap on his own head again. 'It will be better to give him something for his feet,' thought he; and he made the man sit down, and helped him to put on the felt boots, saying, 'There, friend, now move about and warm yourself. Other matters can be settled later on. Can you walk?'

The man stood up and looked kindly at Simon, but could not say a word.

'Why don't you speak?' said Simon. 'It's too cold to stay here, we must be getting home. There now, take my stick, and if you're feeling weak, lean on that. Now step out!'

The man started walking, and moved easily, not lagging behind.

As they went along, Simon asked him, 'And where do you belong to?'

'I'm not from these parts.'

'I thought as much. I know the folks hereabouts. But how did you come to be there by the shrine?'

'I cannot tell.'

'Has someone been ill-treating you?'

'No one has ill-treated me. God has punished me.'

'Of course God rules all. Still, you'll have to find food and shelter somewhere. Where do you want to go to?'

'It is all the same to me.'

Simon was amazed. The man did not look like a rogue, and he spoke gently, but yet he gave no account of himself. Still Simon thought, 'Who knows what may have happened?' And he said to the stranger: 'Well then, come home with me, and at least warm yourself awhile.'

So Simon walked towards his home, and the stranger kept up with him, walking at his side. The wind had risen and Simon felt it cold under his shirt. He was getting over his tipsiness by now, and began to feel the frost. He went along sniffling and wrapping his wife's coat round him, and he thought to himself: 'There now – talk about sheepskins! I went out for sheepskins and come home without even a coat to my back, and what is more, I'm bringing a naked man along with me. Matryona won't be pleased!' And when he thought of his wife he felt sad; but when he looked at the stranger and remembered how he had looked up at him at the shrine, his heart was glad.

III

SIMON'S WIFE had everything ready early that day. She had cut wood, brought water, fed the children, eaten her own meal, and now she sat thinking. She wondered when she ought to make bread: now or tomorrow? There was still a large piece left.

'If Simon has had some dinner in town,' thought she, 'and does not eat much for supper, the bread will last out another day.'

She weighed the piece of bread in her hand again and again, and thought: 'I won't make any more today. We have only enough flour left to bake one batch. We can manage to make this last out till Friday.'

So Matryona put away the bread, and sat down at the table to patch her husband's shirt. While she worked she thought how her husband was buying skins for a winter coat.

'If only the dealer does not cheat him. My good man is much too simple; he cheats nobody, but any child can take him in. Eight rubles is a lot of money – he should get a good coat at that price. Not tanned skins, but still a proper winter coat. How difficult it was last winter to get on without a warm coat. I could neither get down to the river, nor go out anywhere. When he went out he put on all we had, and there was nothing left for me. He did not start very early today, but still it's time he was back. I only hope he has not gone on the spree!'

Hardly had Matryona thought this, when steps were heard on the threshold, and someone entered. Matryona stuck her needle into her work and went out into the passage. There she saw two men: Simon, and with him a man without a hat, and wearing felt boots.

Matryona noticed at once that her husband smelt of spirits.

'There now, he has been drinking,' thought she. And when she saw that he was coatless, had only her jacket on, brought no parcel, stood there silent, and seemed ashamed, her heart was ready to break with disappointment. 'He has drunk the money,' thought she, 'and has been on the spree with some good-for-nothing fellow whom he has brought home with him.'

Matryona let them pass into the hut, followed them in, and saw that the stranger was a young, slight man, wearing her husband's coat. There was no shirt to be seen under it, and he had no hat. Having entered, he stood neither moving, nor raising his eyes, and Matryona thought: 'He must be a bad man – he's afraid.'

Matryona frowned, and stood beside the oven looking to see what they would do.

Simon took off his cap and sat down on the bench as if things were all right.

'Come, Matryona; if supper is ready, let us have some.'

Matryona muttered something to herself and did not move, but stayed where she was, by the oven. She looked first at the one and then at the other of them, and only shook her head. Simon saw that his wife was annoyed, but tried to pass it off. Pretending not to notice anything, he took the stranger by the arm.

'Sit down, friend,' said he, 'and let us have some supper.'

The stranger sat down on the bench.

'Haven't you cooked anything for us?' said Simon.

Matryona's anger boiled over. 'I've cooked, but not for you.

It seems to me you have drunk your wits away. You went to buy a sheepskin coat, but come home without so much as the coat you had on, and bring a naked vagabond home with you. I have no supper for drunkards like you.'

'That's enough, Matryona. Don't wag your tongue without reason! You had better ask what sort of man—'

'And you tell me what you've done with the money?'

Simon found the pocket of the jacket, drew out the three-ruble note, and unfolded it.

'Here is the money. Trifonof did not pay, but promises to pay soon.'

Matryona got still more angry; he had bought no sheepskins, but had put his only coat on some naked fellow and had even brought him to their house.

She snatched up the note from the table, took it to put away in safety, and said: 'I have no supper for you. We can't feed all the naked drunkards in the world.'

'There now, Matryona, hold your tongue a bit. First hear what a man has to say—!'

'Much wisdom I shall hear from a drunken fool. I was right in not wanting to marry you – a drunkard. The linen my mother gave me you drank; and now you've been to buy a coat – and have drunk it too!'

Simon tried to explain to his wife that he had only spent twenty kopeks; tried to tell how he had found the man – but Matryona would not let him get a word in. She talked nineteen to the dozen, and dragged in things that had happened ten years before.

Matryona talked and talked, and at last she flew at Simon and seized him by the sleeve.

Give me my jacket. It is the only one I have, and you must needs take it from me and wear it yourself. Give it here, you mangy dog, and may the devil take you.'

Simon began to pull off the jacket, and turned a sleeve of it inside out; Matryona seized the jacket and it burst its seams. She snatched it up, threw it over her head and went to the door. She meant to go out, but stopped undecided – she wanted to work off her anger, but she also wanted to learn what sort of a man the stranger was.

IV

MATRYONA STOPPED and said: 'If he were a good man he would not be naked. Why, he hasn't even a shirt on him. If he were all right, you would say where you came across the fellow.'

'That's just what I am trying to tell you,' said Simon. 'As I came to the shrine I saw him sitting all naked and frozen. It isn't quite the weather to sit about naked! God sent me to him, or he would have perished. What was I to do? How do we know what may have happened to him? So I took him, clothed him, and brought him along. Don't be so angry, Matryona. It is a sin. Remember, we all must die one day.'

Angry words rose to Matryona's lips, but she looked at the stranger and was silent. He sat on the edge of the bench, motionless, his hands folded on his knees, his head drooping on his breast, his eyes closed, and his brows knit as if in pain. Matryona was silent, and Simon said: 'Matryona, have you no love of God?'

Matryona heard these words, and as she looked at the stranger, suddenly her heart softened towards him. She came back from the door, and going to the oven she got out the supper. Setting a cup on the table, she poured out some kvas. Then she brought out the last piece of bread, and set out a knife and spoons.

'Eat, if you want to,' said she.

Simon drew the stranger to the table.

'Take your place, young man,' said he.

Simon cut the bread, crumbled it into the broth, and they began to eat. Matryona sat at the corner of the table, resting her head on her hand and looking at the stranger.

And Matryona was touched with pity for the stranger, and began to feel fond of him. And at once the stranger's face lit up; his brows were no longer bent, he raised his eyes and smiled at Matryona.

When they had finished supper, the woman cleared away the things and began questioning the stranger. 'Where are you from?' said she.

'I am not from these parts.'

'But how did you come to be on the road?'

'I may not tell.'

'Did someone rob you?'

'God punished me.'

'And you were lying there naked?'

'Yes, naked and freezing. Simon saw me and had pity on me. He took off his coat, put it on me and brought me here. And you have fed me, given me drink, and shown pity on me. God will reward you!'

Matryona rose, took from the window Simon's old shirt she had been patching, and gave it to the stranger. She also brought out a pair of trousers for him.

'There,' said she, 'I see you have no shirt. Put this on, and lie down where you please, in the loft or on the oven.'

The stranger took off the coat, put on the shirt, and lay down in the loft. Matryona put out the candle, took the coat, and climbed to where her husband lay.

Matryona drew the skirts of the coat over her and lay down, but could not sleep; she could not get the stranger out of her mind.

When she remembered that he had eaten their last piece of bread and that there was none for tomorrow, and thought of the shirt and trousers she had given away, she felt grieved; but when she remembered how he had smiled, her heart was glad.

Long did Matryona lie awake, and she noticed that Simon also was awake – he drew the coat towards him.

'Simon!'

'Well?'

'You have had the last of the bread, and I have not put any to rise. I don't know what we shall do tomorrow. Perhaps I can borrow some off neighbour Martha.'

'If we're alive we shall find something to eat.'

The woman lay still awhile, and then said, 'He seems a good man, but why does he not tell us who he is?'

'I suppose he has his reasons.'

'Simon!'

'Well?'

'We give; but why does nobody give us anything?'

Simon did not know what to say; so he only said, 'Let us stop talking,' and turned over and went to sleep.

V

IN THE MORNING Simon awoke. The children were still asleep; his wife had gone to the neighbour's to borrow some bread. The stranger alone was sitting on the bench, dressed in the old shirt and trousers, and looking upwards. His face was brighter than it had been the day before.

Simon said to him, 'Well, friend; the belly wants bread, and the naked body clothes. One has to work for a living. What work do you know?'

236

'I do not know any.'

This surprised Simon, but he said, 'Men who want to learn can learn anything.'

'Men work, and I will work also.'

'What is your name?'

'Michael.'

'Well, Michael, if you don't wish to talk about yourself, that is your own affair; but you'll have to earn a living for yourself. If you will work as I tell you, I will give you food and shelter.'

'May God reward you! I will learn. Show me what to do.'

Simon took yarn, put it round his thumb and began to twist it.

'It is easy enough – see!'

Michael watched him, put some yarn round his own thumb in the same way, caught the knack, and twisted the yarn also.

Then Simon showed him how to wax the thread. This also Michael mastered. Next Simon showed him how to twist the bristle in, and how to sew, and this, too, Michael learnt at once.

Whatever Simon showed him he understood at once, and after three days he worked as if he had sewn boots all his life. He worked without stopping, and ate little. When work was over he sat silently, looking upwards. He hardly went into the street, spoke only when necessary, and neither joked nor laughed. They never saw him smile, except that first evening when Matryona gave them supper.

VI

DAY BY DAY and week by week the year went round. Michael lived and worked with Simon. His fame spread till people said that no one sewed boots so neatly and strongly as Simon's workman, Michael; and from all the district round people came to Simon for their boots, and he began to be well off.

One winter day, as Simon and Michael sat working, a carriage on sledge-runners, with three horses and with bells, drove up to the hut. They looked out of the window; the carriage stopped at their door, a fine servant jumped down from the box and opened the door. A gentleman in a fur coat got out and walked up to Simon's hut. Up jumped Matryona and opened the door wide. The gentleman stooped to enter the hut, and when he drew himself up again his head nearly reached the ceiling, and he seemed quite to fill his end of the room.

Simon rose, bowed, and looked at the gentleman with astonishment. He had never seen anyone like him. Simon himself was lean, Michael was thin, and Matryona was dry as a bone, but this man was like someone from another world: red-faced, burly, with a neck like a bull's, and looking altogether as if he were cast in iron.

The gentleman puffed, threw off his fur coat, sat down on the bench, and said, 'Which of you is the master bootmaker?'

'I am, your Excellency,' said Simon, coming forward.

Then the gentleman shouted to his lad, 'Hey, Fedka, bring the leather!'

The servant ran in, bringing a parcel. The gentleman took the parcel and put it on the table.

'Untie it,' said he. The lad untied it.

The gentleman pointed to the leather.

'Look here, shoemaker,' said he, 'do you see this leather?'

'Yes, your Honour.'

'But do you know what sort of leather it is?'

Simon felt the leather and said, 'It is good leather.'

'Good, indeed! Why, you fool, you never saw such leather before in your life. It's German, and cost twenty rubles.'

Simon was frightened, and said, 'Where should I ever see leather like that?'

'Just so! Now, can you make it into boots for me?'

'Yes, your Excellency, I can.'

Then the gentleman shouted at him: 'You *can*, can you? Well, remember whom you are to make them for, and what the leather is. You must make me boots that will wear for a year, neither losing shape nor coming unsewn. If you can do it, take the leather and cut it up; but if you can't, say so. I warn you now, if your boots come unsewn or lose shape within a year, I will have you put in prison. If they don't burst or lose shape for a year, I will pay you ten rubles for your work.'

Simon was frightened, and did not know what to say. He

glanced at Michael and nudging him with his elbow, whispered: 'Shall I take the work?'

Michael nodded his head as if to say, 'Yes, take it.'

Simon did as Michael advised, and undertook to make boots that would not lose shape or split for a whole year.

Calling his servant, the gentleman told him to pull the boot off his left leg, which he stretched out.

'Take my measure!' said he.

Simon stitched a paper measure seventeen inches long, smoothed it out, knelt down, wiped his hands well on his apron so as not to soil the gentleman's sock, and began to measure. He measured the sole, and round the instep, and began to measure the calf of the leg, but the paper was too short. The calf of the leg was as thick as a beam.

'Mind you don't make it too tight in the leg.'

Simon stitched on another strip of paper. The gentleman twitched his toes about in his sock, looking round at those in the hut, and as he did so he noticed Michael.

'Whom have you there?' asked he.

'That is my workman. He will sew the boots.'

'Mind,' said the gentleman to Michael, 'remember to make them so that they will last me a year.'

Simon also looked at Michael, and saw that Michael was not looking at the gentleman, but was gazing into the corner behind the gentleman, as if he saw someone there. Michael looked and looked, and suddenly he smiled, and his face became brighter.

'What are you grinning at, you fool?' thundered the gentleman. 'You had better look to it that the boots are ready in time.'

'They shall be ready in good time,' said Michael.

'Mind it is so,' said the gentleman, and he put on his boots and his fur coat, wrapped the latter round him, and went to the door. But he forgot to stoop, and struck his head against the lintel.

He swore and rubbed his head. Then he took his seat in the carriage and drove away.

When he had gone, Simon said: 'There's a figure of a man for you! You could not kill him with a mallet. He almost knocked out the lintel, but little harm it did him.'

And Matryona said: 'Living as he does, how should he not grow strong? Death itself can't touch such a rock as that.'

VII

THEN SIMON said to Michael: 'Well, we have taken the work, but we must see we don't get into trouble over it. The leather is dear, and the gentleman hot-tempered. We must make no mistakes. Come, your eye is truer and your hands have become nimbler than mine, so you take this measure and cut out the boots. I will finish off the sewing of the vamps.'

Michael did as he was told. He took the leather, spread it out on the table, folded it in two, took a knife and began to cut out.

Matryona came and watched him cutting, and was surprised

to see how he was doing it. Matryona was accustomed to seeing boots made, and she looked and saw that Michael was not cutting the leather for boots, but was cutting it round.

She wished to say something, but she thought to herself: 'Perhaps I do not understand how gentlemen's boots should be made. I suppose Michael knows more about it – and I won't interfere.'

When Michael had cut up the leather, he took a thread and began to sew not with two ends, as boots are sewn, but with a single end, as for soft slippers.

Again Matryona wondered, but again she did not interfere. Michael sewed on steadily till noon. Then Simon rose for dinner, looked around, and saw that Michael had made slippers out of the gentleman's leather.

'Ah!' groaned Simon, and he thought, 'How is it that Michael, who has been with me a whole year and never made a mistake before, should do such a dreadful thing? The gentleman ordered high boots, welted, with whole fronts, and Michael has made soft slippers with single soles, and has wasted the leather. What am I to say to the gentleman? I can never replace leather such as this.'

And he said to Michael, 'What are you doing, friend? You have ruined me! You know the gentleman ordered high boots, but see what you have made!'

Hardly had he begun to rebuke Michael, when 'rat-tat' went the iron ring that hung at the door. Someone was knocking. They looked out of the window; a man had come on horseback, and was fastening his horse. They opened the door, and the servant who had been with the gentleman came in.

'Good day,' said he.

'Good day,' replied Simon. 'What can we do for you?'

'My mistress has sent me about the boots.'

'What about the boots?'

'Why, my master no longer needs them. He is dead.'

'Is it possible?'

'He did not live to get home after leaving you, but died in the carriage. When we reached home and the servants came to help him alight, he rolled over like a sack. He was dead already, and so stiff that he could hardly be got out of the carriage. My mistress sent me here, saying: "Tell the bootmaker that the gentleman who ordered boots of him and left the leather for them no longer needs the boots, but that he must quickly make soft slippers for the corpse. Wait till they are ready, and bring them back with you." That is why I have come.'

Michael gathered up the remnants of the leather; rolled them up, took the soft slippers he had made, slapped them together, wiped them down with his apron, and handed them and the roll of leather to the servant, who took them and said: 'Goodbye, masters, and good day to you!'

VIII

ANOTHER YEAR passed, and another, and Michael was now living his sixth year with Simon. He lived as before. He went nowhere, only spoke when necessary, and had only smiled twice in all those years – once when Matryona gave him food, and a second time when the gentleman was in their hut. Simon was more than pleased with his workman. He never now asked him where he came from, and only feared lest Michael should go away.

They were all at home one day. Matryona was putting iron pots in the oven; the children were running along the benches and looking out of the window; Simon was sewing at one window, and Michael was fastening on a heel at the other.

One of the boys ran along the bench to Michael, leant on his shoulder, and looked out of the window.

'Look, Uncle Michael! There is a lady with little girls! She seems to be coming here. And one of the girls is lame.'

When the boy said that, Michael dropped his work, turned to the window, and looked out into the street.

Simon was surprised. Michael never used to look out into the street, but now he pressed against the window, staring at something. Simon also looked out, and saw that a well-dressed woman was really coming to his hut, leading by the hand two little girls in fur coats and woollen shawls. The girls could hardly be told one from the other, except that one of them was crippled in her left leg and walked with a limp.

The woman stepped into the porch and entered the passage. Feeling about for the entrance she found the latch, which she lifted, and opened the door. She let the two girls go in first, and followed them into the hut.

'Good day, good folk!'

'Pray come in,' said Simon. 'What can we do for you?'

The woman sat down by the table. The two little girls pressed close to her knees, afraid of the people in the hut.

'I want leather shoes made for these two little girls, for spring.'

'We can do that. We never have made such small shoes, but we can make them; either welted or turnover shoes, linen lined. My man, Michael, is a master at the work.'

Simon glanced at Michael and saw that he had left his work and was sitting with his eyes fixed on the little girls. Simon was surprised. It was true the girls were pretty, with black eyes, plump, and rosy-cheeked, and they wore nice kerchiefs and fur coats, but still Simon could not understand why Michael should look at them like that – just as if he had known them before. He was puzzled, but went on talking with the woman, and arranging the price. Having fixed it, he prepared the measure. The woman lifted the lame girl onto her lap and said: 'Take two measures from this little girl. Make one shoe for the lame foot and three for the sound one. They both have the same sized feet. They are twins.'

Simon took the measure and, speaking of the lame girl, said: 'How did it happen to her? She is such a pretty girl. Was she born so?'

'No, her mother crushed her leg.'

Then Matryona joined in. She wondered who this woman was, and whose the children were, so she said: 'Are not you their mother, then?'

'No, my good woman; I am neither their mother nor any relation to them. They were quite strangers to me, but I adopted them.'

'They are not your children and yet you are so fond of them?'

'How can I help being fond of them? I fed them both at my own breasts. I had a child of my own, but God took him. I was not so fond of him as I now am of them.'

'Then whose children are they?'

IX

THE WOMAN, having begun talking, told them the whole story.

'It is about six years since their parents died, both in one week: their father was buried on the Tuesday, and their mother died on the Friday. These orphans were born three days after their father's death, and their mother did not live another day. My husband and I were then living as peasants in the village. We were neighbours of theirs, our yard being next to theirs. Their father was a lonely man; a wood-cutter in the forest. When felling trees one day, they let one fall on him. It fell across his body and crushed his bowels out. They hardly got him home before his soul went to God; and that same week his wife gave birth to twins – these little girls. She was poor and alone; she had no one, young or old, with her. Alone she gave them birth, and alone she met her death.

'The next morning I went to see her, but when I entered the hut, she, poor thing, was already stark and cold. In dying she had rolled onto this child and crushed her leg. The village folk came to the hut, washed the body, laid her out, made a coffin, and buried her. They were good folk. The babies were left alone. What was to be done with them? I was the only woman there who had a baby at the time. I was nursing my first-born – eight weeks old. So I took them for a time. The peasants came together, and thought and thought what to do with them; and at last they said to me: "For the present, Mary, you had better keep the girls, and later on we will arrange what to do for them." So I nursed the sound one at my breast, but at first I did not feed this crippled one. I did not suppose she would live. But then I thought to myself, why should the poor innocent suffer? I pitied her, and began to feed her. And so I fed my own boy and these two – the three of them – at my own breast. I was young and strong, and had good food, and God gave me so much milk that at times it even overflowed. I used sometimes to feed two at a time, while the third was waiting. When one had had enough

I nursed the third. And God so ordered it that these grew up, while my own was buried before he was two years old. And I had no more children, though we prospered. Now my husband is working for the corn merchant at the mill. The pay is good, and we are well off. But I have no children of my own, and how lonely I should be without these little girls! How can I help loving them! They are the joy of my life!'

She pressed the lame little girl to her with one hand, while with the other she wiped the tears from her cheeks.

And Matryona sighed, and said: 'The proverb is true that says, "One may live without father or mother, but one cannot live without God."'

So they talked together, when suddenly the whole hut was lighted up as though by summer lightning from the corner where Michael sat. They all looked towards him and saw him sitting, his hands folded on his knees, gazing upwards and smiling.

X

THE WOMAN went away with the girls. Michael rose from the bench, put down his work, and took off his apron. Then, bowing low to Simon and his wife, he said: 'Farewell, masters. God has forgiven me. I ask your forgiveness, too, for anything done amiss.'

And they saw that a light shone from Michael. And Simon

rose, bowed down to Michael, and said: 'I see, Michael, that you are no common man, and I can neither keep you nor question you. Only tell me this: how is it that when I found you and brought you home, you were gloomy, and when my wife gave you food you smiled at her and became brighter? Then when the gentleman came to order the boots, you smiled again and became brighter still? And now, when this woman brought the little girls, you smiled a third time, and have become as bright as day? Tell me, Michael, why does your face shine so, and why did you smile those three times?'

And Michael answered: 'Light shines from me because I have been punished, but now God has pardoned me. And I smiled three times, because God sent me to learn three truths, and I have learnt them. One I learnt when your wife pitied me, and that is why I smiled the first time. The second I learnt when the rich man ordered the boots, and then I smiled again. And now, when I saw those little girls, I learnt the third and last truth, and I smiled the third time.'

And Simon said, 'Tell me, Michael, what did God punish you for? and what were the three truths? that I, too, may know them.'

And Michael answered: 'God punished me for disobeying Him. I was an angel in heaven and disobeyed God. God sent me to fetch a woman's soul. I flew to earth, and saw a sick woman lying alone, who had just given birth to twin girls. They moved feebly at their mother's side, but she could not lift them to her breast. When she saw me, she understood that God had sent me for her soul, and she wept and said: "Angel of God! My husband has just been buried, killed by a falling tree. I have neither sister, nor aunt, nor mother: no one to care for my orphans. Do not take my soul! Let me nurse my babes, feed them, and set them on their feet before I die. Children cannot live without father or mother." And I hearkened to her. I placed one child at her breast and gave the other into her arms, and returned to the Lord in heaven. I flew to the Lord, and said: "I could not take the soul of the mother. Her husband was killed by a tree; the woman has twins, and prays that her soul may not be taken. She says: 'Let me nurse and feed my children, and set them on their feet. Children cannot live without father or mother.' I have not taken her soul." And God said: "Go – take the mother's soul, and learn three truths: Learn *What dwells in man*, *What is not given to man*, and *What men live by*. When thou hast learnt these things, thou shalt return to heaven." So I flew again to earth and took the mother's soul. The babes dropped from her breasts. Her body rolled over on the bed and crushed one babe, twisting its leg. I rose above the village, wishing to take her soul to God; but a wind seized me, and my wings drooped and dropped off. Her soul rose alone to God, while I fell to earth by the roadside.'

AND SIMON and Matryona understood who it was that had lived with them, and whom they had clothed and fed. And they wept with awe and with joy. And the angel said: 'I was alone in the field, naked. I had never known human needs, cold and hunger, till I became a man. I was famished, frozen, and did not know what to do. I saw, near the field I was in, a shrine built for God, and I went to it hoping to find shelter. But the shrine was locked, and I could not enter. So I sat down behind the shrine to shelter myself at least from the wind. Evening drew on. I was hungry, frozen, and in pain. Suddenly I heard a man coming along the road. He carried a pair of boots, and was talking to himself. For the first time since I became a man I saw the mortal face of a man, and his face seemed terrible to me and I turned from it. And I heard the man talking to himself of how to cover his body from the cold in winter, and how to feed wife and children. And I thought: "I am perishing of cold and hunger, and here is a man thinking only of how to clothe himself and his wife, and how to get bread for themselves. He cannot help me." When the man saw me he frowned and became still more terrible, and passed me by on the other side. I despaired; but suddenly I heard him coming back. I looked up, and did not recognize the same man: before, I had seen death in his face; but now he was alive, and I recognized in him the presence of God. He came up to me, clothed me, took me with him, and brought me to his home. I entered the house; a woman came to meet us and began to speak. The woman was still more terrible than the man had been; the spirit of death came from her mouth; I could not breathe for the stench of death that spread around her. She wished to drive me out into the cold, and I knew that if she did so she would die. Suddenly her husband spoke to her of God, and the woman changed at once. And when she brought me food and looked at me, I glanced at her and saw that death no longer dwelt in her; she had become alive, and in her too I saw God.

'Then I remembered the first lesson God had set me: "*Learn what dwells in man.*" And I understood that in man dwells Love! I was glad that God had already begun to show me what He had promised, and I smiled for the first time. But I had not yet learnt all. I did not yet know *What is not given to man*, and *What men live by*.

'I lived with you, and a year passed. A man came to order boots that should wear for a year without losing shape or cracking. I looked at him, and suddenly, behind his shoulder, I saw my comrade – the angel of death. None but me saw that angel; but I knew him, and knew that before the sun set he would take that rich man's soul. And I thought to myself, "The man is making preparations for a year, and does not know that he will die before evening." And I remembered God's second saying, "*Learn what is not given to man.*"

'What dwells in man I already knew. Now I learnt what is not given him. It is not given to man to know his own needs. And I smiled for the second time. I was glad to have seen my comrade angel – glad also that God had revealed to me the second saying.

'But I still did not know all. I did not know *What men live by*. And I lived on, waiting till God should reveal to me the last lesson. In the sixth year came the girl-twins with the woman; and I recognized the girls, and heard how they had been kept alive. Having heard the story, I thought, "Their mother besought me for the children's sake, and I believed her when she said that children cannot live without father or mother; but a stranger has nursed them, and has brought them up." And when the woman showed her love for the children that were not her own, and wept over them, I saw in her the living God, and understood *What men live by*. And I knew that God had revealed to me the last lesson, and had forgiven my sin. And then I smiled for the third time.'

XII

AND THE angel's body was bared, and he was clothed in light so that eye could not look on him; and his voice grew louder, as though it came not from him but from heaven above. And the angel said:

'I have learnt that all men live not by care for themselves, but by love.

'It was not given to the mother to know what her children needed for their life. Nor was it given to the rich man to know

253

what he himself needed. Nor is it given to any man to know whether, when evening comes, he will need boots for his body, or slippers for his corpse.

'I remained alive when I was a man, not by care of myself, but because love was present in a passer-by, and because he and his wife pitied and loved me. The orphans remained alive, not because of their mother's care, but because there was love in the heart of a woman a stranger to them, who pitied and loved them. And all men live not by the thought they spend on their own welfare, but because love exists in man.

'I knew before that God gave life to men, and desires that they should live; now I understood more than that.

'I understood that God does not wish men to live apart, and therefore he does not reveal to them what each one needs for himself; but he wishes them to live united, and therefore reveals to each of them what is necessary for all.

'I have now understood that though it seems to men that they live by care for themselves, in truth it is love alone by which they live. He who has love, is in God, and God is in him, for God is love.'

And the angel sang praise to God, so that the hut trembled at his voice. The roof opened, and a column of fire rose from earth to heaven. Simon and his wife and children fell to the ground. Wings appeared upon the angel's shoulders, and he rose into the heavens.

And when Simon came to himself the hut stood as before, and there was no one in it but his own family.

Memoirs of a Madman

20 October 1883

TODAY I WAS taken to the Provincial Government Board to be certified. Opinions differed. They disputed, and finally decided that I was not insane – but they arrived at this decision only because during the examination I did my utmost to restrain myself and not give myself away. I did not speak out, because I am afraid of the madhouse, where they would prevent me from doing my mad work. So they came to the conclusion that I am subject to hallucinations and something else, but am of sound mind.

They came to that conclusion, but I myself know that I am mad. A doctor prescribed a treatment for me, and assured me that if I would follow his instructions exactly all would be right – all that troubled me would pass. Ah, what would I not give that it might pass! The torment is too great. I will tell in due order how and from what this medical certification came about – how I went mad and how I betrayed myself.

Up to the age of thirty-five I lived just as everybody else does and nothing strange was noticed about me. Perhaps in early childhood, before the age of ten, there was at times something resembling my present condition, but only by fits, and not continually as now. Moreover in childhood it used to affect me rather differently. For instance I remember that once when going to bed, at the age of five or six, my nurse Eupraxia, a tall thin woman who wore a brown dress and a cap and had flabby skin under her chin, was undressing me and lifting me up to put me into my cot. 'I will get into bed by myself – myself!' I said, and stepped over the side of the cot.

'Well, lie down then. Lie down, Fedya! Look at Mitya. He's a good boy and is lying down already,' she said, indicating my brother with a jerk of her head.

I jumped into the bed still holding her hand, and then let it go, kicked about under my bed-clothes, and wrapped myself up. And I had such a pleasant feeling. I grew quiet and thought: 'I love Nurse; Nurse loves me and Mitya; and I love Mitya, and Mitya loves me and Nurse. Nurse loves Taras, and I love Taras, and Mitya loves him. And Taras loves me and Nurse. And Mamma loves me and Nurse, and Nurse loves Mamma and me and Papa – and everybody loves everybody and everybody is happy!'

Then suddenly I heard the housekeeper run in and angrily

shout something about a sugar-basin, and Nurse answering indignantly that she had not taken it. And I felt pained, frightened, and bewildered, and horror, cold horror, seized me, and I hid my head under the bed-clothes but felt no better in the dark.

I also remembered how a serf-boy was once beaten in my presence, how he screamed, and how dreadful Foka's face looked when he was beating the boy. 'Then you won't do it any more, you won't?' he kept repeating as he went on beating. The boy cried, 'I won't!' but Foka still repeated, 'You won't!' and went on beating him.

And then it came upon me! I began to sob, and went on so that they could not quiet me for a long time. That sobbing and despair were the first attacks of my present madness.

I remember another attack when my aunt told us about Christ. She told the story and was about to go away, but we said: 'Tell us some more about Jesus Christ!'

'No, I have no time now,' she said.

'Yes, do tell us!'

Mitya also asked her to, and my aunt began to repeat what she had told us. She told us how they crucified, beat, and tortured him, and how he went on praying and did not reproach them.

'Why did they torment him, Auntie?'

'They were cruel people.'

'But why, when he was good?'

'There, that's enough. It's past eight! Do you hear?'

'Why did they beat him? He forgave them, then why did they hit him? Did it hurt him, Auntie? Did it hurt?'

'That will do! I'm going to have tea now.'

'But perhaps it isn't true and they didn't beat him?'

'Now, now, that will do!'

'No, no! Don't go away!'

And again I was overcome by it. I sobbed and sobbed, and began knocking my head against the wall.

That was how it befell me in my childhood. But by the time I was fourteen, and from the time the instincts of sex were aroused and I yielded to vice, all that passed away and I became a boy like other boys, like all the rest of us reared on rich, over-abundant food, effeminate, doing no physical work, surrounded by all possible temptations that inflamed sensuality, and among other equally spoilt children. Boys of my own age taught me vice, and I indulged in it. Later on that vice was replaced by another, and I began to know women. And so, seeking enjoyments and finding them, I lived till the age of thirty-five. I was perfectly well and there were no signs of my madness.

Those twenty years of my healthy life passed for me so that I can hardly remember anything of them, and now recall them with difficulty and disgust. Like all mentally healthy boys of our circle I entered the high school and afterwards the university, where I completed the course of law-studies. Then I was in the Civil Service for a short time, and then I met my present wife, married, had a post in the country and, as it is called, 'brought up' our children, managed the estates, and was Justice of the Peace.

In the tenth year of my married life I again had an attack – the first since my childhood.

My wife and I had saved money – some inherited by her and some from the bonds I, like other landowners, received from the Government at the time of the emancipation of the serfs – and we decided to buy an estate. I was much interested, as was proper, in the growth of our property and in increasing it in the shrewdest way – better than other people. At that time I inquired everywhere where there were estates for sale, and read all the advertisements in the papers. I wanted to buy an estate so that the income from it, or the timber on it, should cover the whole purchase price and I should get it for nothing. I looked out for some fool who did not understand business, and thought I had found such a man.

An estate with large forests was being sold in Penza province. From all I could learn about it, it seemed that its owner was just such a fool as I wanted and the timber would cover the whole cost of the estate. So I got ready and set out.

We (my servant and I) travelled at first by rail and then by road in a post-chaise. The journey was a very pleasant one for me. My servant, a young good-natured fellow, was in just as good spirits as I. We saw new places and met new people and enjoyed ourselves. To reach our destination we had to go about a hundred and forty miles, and decided to go without stopping except to change horses. Night came and we still went on. We grew drowsy. I fell asleep, but suddenly awoke feeling that there was something terrifying. As often happens, I woke up thoroughly alert and feeling as if sleep had gone for ever. 'Why am I going? Where am I going to?' I suddenly asked myself. It was not that I did not like the idea of buying an estate cheaply, but it suddenly occurred to me that there was no need for me to travel all that distance, that I should die here in this strange place, and I was filled with dread. Sergey, my servant, woke up, and I availed myself of the opportunity to talk to him. I spoke about that part of the country, he replied and joked, but I felt depressed. I spoke about our folks at home, and of the business before us, and I was surprised that his answers were so cheerful. Everything seemed pleasant and amusing to him while it nauseated me. But for all that while we were talking I felt easier. But besides everything seeming wearisome and uncanny, I began to feel tired and wished to stop. It seemed to me that I should feel better if I could enter a house, see people, drink tea, and above all have some sleep.

We were nearing the town of Arzamas.

'Shall we put up here and rest a bit?'

'Why not? Splendid!'

'Are we still far from the town?'

'About five miles from the last mile-post.'

The driver was a respectable man, careful and taciturn, and he drove rather slowly and wearily.

We drove on. I remained silent and felt better because I was looking forward to a rest and hoped that the discomfort would pass. We went on and on in the darkness for a terribly long time as it seemed to me. We reached the town. Everybody was already in bed. Mean little houses showed up through the darkness, and the sound of our jingling bells and the clatter of the horses' feet re-echoed, especially near the houses, and all this was far from cheerful. We passed large white houses here and there. I was impatient to get to the post-station and a samovar, and to lie down and rest.

At last we came up to a small house with a post beside it. The house was white, but appeared terribly melancholy to me, so much so that it seemed uncanny and I got out of the carriage slowly.

Sergey briskly took out all that would be wanted, running clattering up the porch, and the sound of his steps depressed me. I entered a little corridor. A sleepy man with a spot on his cheek (which seemed to me terrifying) showed us into a room. It was gloomy. I entered, and the uncanny feeling grew worse.

'Haven't you got a bedroom? I should like to rest.'

'Yes, we have. This is it.'

It was a small square room, with whitewashed walls. I remember that it tormented me that it should be square. It had one window with a red curtain, a birchwood table, and a sofa with bent-wood arms. We went in. Sergey prepared the samovar and made tea, while I took a pillow and lay down on the sofa. I was not asleep and heard how Sergey was busy with the tea and called me to have some. But I was afraid of getting up and arousing myself completely, and I thought how frightful it would be to sit up in that room. I did not get up but began to doze. I must have fallen asleep, for when I awoke I found myself alone in the room and it was dark. I was again as wide awake as I had been in the chaise. I felt that to sleep would be quite impossible. 'Why have I come here? Where am I betaking myself? Why and whither am I escaping? I am running away from something dreadful and cannot escape it. I am always with myself, and it is I who am my tormentor. Here I am, the whole of me. Neither the Penza nor any other property will add anything to or take anything from me. And it is myself I am weary of and find intolerable and a torment. I want to fall asleep and forget myself and cannot. I cannot get away from myself!'

I went out into the passage. Sergey was sleeping on a narrow bench with one arm hanging down, but he was sleeping peacefully and the man with the spot was also asleep. I had gone out into the corridor thinking to escape from what tormented me. But *it* had come out with me and cast a gloom over everything. I felt just as filled with horror or even more so.

'But what folly this is!' I said to myself. 'Why am I depressed? What am I afraid of?'

'Me!' answered the voice of Death, inaudibly. 'I am here!'

A cold shudder ran down my back. Yes! Death! It will come – here it is – and it ought not to be. Had I been actually facing death I could not have suffered as much as I did then. Then I should have been frightened. But now I was not frightened. I saw and felt the approach of death, and at the same time I felt that such a thing ought not to exist.

My whole being was conscious of the necessity and the right to live, and yet I felt that Death was being accomplished. And this inward conflict was terrible. I tried to throw off the horror. I found a brass candlestick, the candle in which had a long wick, and lighted it. The red glow of the candle and its size – little less than the candlestick itself – told me the same thing. Everything told me the same: 'There is nothing in life. Death is the only real thing, and death ought not to exist.'

I tried to turn my thoughts to things that had interested me – to the estate I was to buy, and to my wife – but found nothing to cheer me. It had all become nothing. Everything was hidden by the terrible consciousness that my life was ebbing away. I needed sleep. I lay down, but the next instant I jumped up again in terror. A fit of the spleen seized me – spleen such as the feeling before one is sick, but spiritual spleen. It was uncanny and dreadful. It seems that death is terrible, but when remembering and thinking of life it is one's dying life that is terrible. Life and death somehow merged into one another. Something was tearing my soul apart and could not complete the severance. Again I went to look at the sleepers, and again I tried to go to sleep. Always the same horror: red, white, and square. Something tearing within that yet could not be torn apart. A painful, painfully dry and spiteful feeling, no atom of kindliness, but just a dull and steady spitefulness towards myself and towards that which had made me.

What created me? God, they say. God . . . what about prayer? I remembered. For some twenty years I had not prayed, and I did not believe in anything, though as a matter of propriety I fasted and went to Communion every year. Now I began to pray. 'Lord have mercy!' 'Our Father'. 'Holy Virgin'. I began to compose new prayers, crossing myself, bowing down to the ground and glancing around me for fear that I might be seen. This seemed to divert me – the fear of being seen distracted my terror – and I lay down. But I had only to lie down and close my eyes for the same feeling of terror to knock and rouse me. I could bear it no longer. I woke the hotel servant and Sergey, gave orders to harness, and we drove off again.

The fresh air and the drive made me feel better. But I realized that something new had come into my soul and poisoned my former life.

By nightfall we reached our destination. The whole day I had been fighting my depression and had mastered it, but it had left its terrible dregs in my soul as if some misfortune had befallen me, and I could forget it only for a time. There it remained at the bottom of my soul and had me in its power.

The old steward of the estate received me well, though without any pleasure. He was sorry the estate was to be sold.

The furniture in the little rooms was upholstered. There was a new, brightly polished samovar, a large-sized tea-service, and honey for tea. Everything was good. But I questioned him about the estate unwillingly, as if it were some old forgotten lesson. However, I fell asleep without any depression, and this I attributed to my having prayed again before going to bed.

After that I went on living as before, but the fear of that spleen always hung over me. I had to live without stopping to think, and above all to live in my accustomed surroundings. As a schoolboy repeats a lesson learnt by heart without thinking, so I had to live to avoid falling a prey to that awful depression I had first experienced at Arzamas.

I returned home safely. I did not buy the estate – I had not enough money – and I continued to live as before, only with this difference, that I began to pray and went to church. As before – it seemed to me, but I now remember that it was not as before – I lived on what had been previously begun. I continued to go along the rails already laid by my former strength, but I did not undertake anything new. And I took less part in those things I had previously begun. Everything seemed dull to me and I became pious. My wife noticed this, and scolded and nagged me on account of it. But my spleen did not recur at home.

But once I had unexpectedly to go to Moscow. I got ready in the afternoon and left in the evening. It was in connection with a lawsuit. I arrived in Moscow cheerful. On the way I had talked with a landowner from Kharkov about estate-management and banks, and about where to put up, and about the theatre. We both decided to stop at the Moscow Hotel on the Myasnitsky Street, and to go to see *Faust* that same evening.

When we arrived I was shown into a small room. The oppressive air of the corridor filled my nostrils. A porter brought in my portmanteau and a chambermaid lighted a candle. The wick was lighted and then as usual the flame went down. In the next room someone coughed, probably an old man. The maid went out, but the porter remained and asked if he should uncord my luggage. The flame of the candle burnt up, revealing the blue wall-paper with yellow stripes on the partition, a shabby table, a small sofa, a looking-glass, a window, and the narrow dimensions of the room. And suddenly I was seized with an attack of the same horror as in Arzamas. 'My God! How can I stay here all night?' I thought.

'Yes, uncord, my good fellow,' I told the porter to keep him longer in the room. 'I'll dress quickly and go to the theatre.' When the porter had uncorded, I said: 'Please go to Number Eight and tell the gentleman who came here with me that I shall be ready immediately and will come to him.'

The porter went out and I dressed hurriedly, afraid to look at the walls. 'What nonsense!' I thought. 'What am I afraid of? Just like a child! I am not afraid of ghosts. Ghosts! Ghosts would be better than what I am afraid of. Why, what is it? Nothing. Myself . . . Oh, nonsense!'

However, I put on a hard, cold, starched shirt, inserted the studs, donned my evening coat and new boots, and went to find the Kharkov landowner, who was ready. We started for the opera. He stopped on the way at a hairdresser's to have his hair curled, and I had mine cut by a French assistant and had a chat with him, and bought a pair of gloves. All was well, and I quite forgot my oblong room with its partition. In the theatre, too, it was pleasant. After the opera the Kharkov landowner suggested that we should have supper. That was contrary to my habit, but just then I again remembered the partition in my room and accepted his suggestion.

We got back after one. I had had two glasses of wine, to which I was unaccustomed, but in spite of that I felt cheerful. But no sooner had we entered the corridor in which the lamp was turned low and I was surrounded by the hotel smell, than a shiver of horror ran down my spine. There was nothing to be done however, and I pressed my companion's hand and went into my room.

I spent a terrible night – worse than at Arzamas. Not till dawn, when the old man at the other side of the door was coughing again, did I fall asleep, and then not in the bed, in which I had lain down several times during the night, but on the sofa. I had suffered all night unbearably. Again my soul and body were being painfully torn asunder. 'I am living, have lived, and ought to live, and suddenly – here is death to destroy everything. Then what is life for? To die? To kill myself at once? No, I am afraid. To wait for death till it comes? I fear that even more. Then I must live. But what for? In order to die?' And I could not escape from that circle. I took up a book, read, and forgot myself for a moment, but then again the same question and the same horror. I lay down in bed and closed my eyes. It was worse still!

God has so arranged it. Why? They say: 'Don't ask, but pray!'

Very well. I prayed, and prayed as I had done at Arzamas. Then and afterwards I prayed simply, like a child. But now my prayers had a meaning. 'If Thou dost exist, reveal to me why and what I am!' I bowed down, repeated all the prayers I knew, composed my own, and added: 'Then reveal it!' and became silent, awaiting an answer. But no answer came. It was just as if there were no one who could give an answer. And I remained alone with myself. And in place of Him who would not reply I answered my own questions. 'Why? In order to live in a future life,' I said to myself. 'Then why this obscurity, this torment? I cannot believe in a future life. I believed when I did not ask with my whole soul, but now I cannot, I cannot. If Thou didst exist Thou wouldst speak to me and to all men. And if Thou dost not exist there is nothing but despair. And I do not want that. I do not want that!'

I became indignant. I asked Him to reveal the truth to me, to reveal Himself to me. I did all that everybody does, but He did not reveal Himself. 'Ask and it shall be given you,' I remembered, and I had asked and in that asking had found not consolation but relaxation. Perhaps I did not pray to Him but repudiated Him. 'You recede a span and He recedes a mile,' as the proverb has it. I did not believe in Him but I asked, and He did not reveal anything to me. I was balancing accounts with Him and blaming Him. I simply did not believe.

The next day I did all in my power to get through my ordinary affairs so as to avoid another night in the hotel. Although I did not finish everything, I left for home that evening. I did not feel any spleen. That night in Moscow still further changed my life which had begun to change from the time I was at Arzamas. I now attended still less to my affairs and became apathetic. I also grew weaker in health. My wife insisted that I should undergo a treatment. She said that my talks about faith and God arose from ill health. But I knew that my weakness and ill health were the effect of the unsolved question within me. I tried not to let that question dominate me, and tried to fill my life amid my customary surroundings. I went to church on Sundays and feast days, prepared to receive Communion, and even fasted, as I had begun to do since my visit to Penza, and I prayed, though more as a custom. I did not expect any result from this, but as it were kept the demand-note and presented it at the due date, though I knew it was impossible to secure payment. I only did it on the chance. I did not fill my life by estate-management – it repelled me by the struggle it involved (I had no energy) – but by reading magazines, newspapers, and novels, and playing cards for small stakes. I only showed energy by hunting, which I did from habit. I had been fond of hunting all my life.

One winter day a neighbouring huntsman came with his wolf-hounds. I rode out with him. When we reached the place we put on snow-shoes and went to the spot where the wolf might be found. The hunt was unsuccessful, the wolves broke through the ring of beaters. I became aware of this from a distance and went through the forest following the fresh tracks of a hare. These led me far into a glade, where I spied the hare, but it jumped out so that I lost it. I went back through the thick forest. The snow was deep, my snow-shoes sank in, and branches of the trees entangled me. The trees grew ever more and more dense. I began to ask myself: 'Where am I?' The snow had altered the look of everything.

Suddenly I realized that I had lost my way. I was far from the house and from the hunters too, and could hear nothing. I was tired and bathed in perspiration. If I stopped I should freeze. If I went on my strength would fail me. I shouted. All was still. No one answered. I turned back, but it was the same again. I looked around – nothing but trees, impossible to tell which was east or west. Again I turned back. My legs were tired. I grew frightened, stopped, and was seized with the same horror as in Arzamas and Moscow, but a hundred times worse. My heart palpitated, my arms and legs trembled. 'Is this death? I won't have it! Why death? What is death?' Once again I wanted to question and reproach God, but here I suddenly felt that I dare not and must not do so, that it is impossible to present one's account to God, that He had said what is needful and I alone was to blame. I began to implore His forgiveness, and felt disgusted with myself.

The horror did not last long. I stood there for a while, came to myself, went on in one direction and soon emerged from the forest. I had not been far from its edge, and came out onto the road. My arms and legs still trembled and my heart was beating, but I felt happy. I found the hunting party and we returned home. I was cheerful, but I knew there was something joyful which I would make out when alone. And so it was. I remained by myself in my study and began to pray, asking forgiveness and remembering my sins. There seemed to me to be but few, but when I recalled them they became hateful to me.

After that I began to read the scriptures. The Old Testament I found unintelligible though enchanting, but the Gospels moved me profoundly. But most of all I read the Lives of the Saints, and that reading consoled me, presenting examples that it seemed more and more possible to follow. From that time forth farming and family matters occupied me less and less. They even repelled me. They all seemed to me wrong. What it was that was 'right' I did not know, but what had formerly constituted my life had now ceased to do so. This became plain to me when I was going to buy another estate.

Not far from us an estate was for sale on very advantageous terms. I went to see it. Everything was excellent and advantageous; especially so was the fact that the peasants there had no land of their own except their kitchen-gardens. I saw that they would have to work on the landlord's land merely for permission to use his pastures. And so it was. I grasped all this, and by old habit felt pleased about it. But on my way home I met an old woman who asked her way. I had a talk with her, during which she told me about her poverty. I got home, and when telling my wife of the advantages that estate offered, I suddenly felt ashamed and disgusted. I told her I could not buy it because the advantages we should get would be based on the peasants' destitution and sorrow. As I said this I suddenly realized the truth of what I was saying – the chief truth, that the peasants, like ourselves, want to live, that they are human beings, our brothers, and sons of the Father as the Gospels say. Suddenly something that had long troubled me seemed to have broken away, as though it had come to birth. My wife was vexed and scolded me, but I felt glad.

That was the beginning of my madness. But my utter madness began later – about a month after that.

It began by my going to church. I stood there through the liturgy and prayed well, and listened and was touched. Then suddenly they brought me some consecrated bread: after that we went up to the Cross, and people began pushing one another. Then at the exit there were beggars. And it suddenly became clear to me that this ought not to be, and not only ought not to be but in reality was not. And if this was not, then neither was there either death or fear, and there was no longer the former tearing asunder within me and I no longer feared anything.

Then the light fully illumined me and I became what I now am. If there is nothing of all that – then it certainly does not exist within me. And there at the church door I gave away to the beggars all I had with me – some thirty-five rubles – and went home on foot talking with the peasants.

The Death of Ivan Ilych

I

DURING AN INTERVAL in the Melvinski trial in the large building of the Law Courts the members and public prosecutor met in Ivan Egorovich Shebek's private room, where the conversation turned on the celebrated Krasóvski case. Fedor Vasilievich warmly maintained that it was not subject to their jurisdiction, Ivan Egorovich maintained the contrary, while Peter Ivanovich, not having entered into the discussion at the start, took no part in it but looked through the *Gazette* which had just been handed in.

'Gentlemen,' he said, 'Ivan Ilych has died!'

'You don't say so!'

'Here, read it yourself,' replied Peter Ivanovich, handing Fedor Vasilievich the paper still damp from the press. Surrounded by a black border were the words: 'Praskovya Fedorovna

Golovina, with profound sorrow, informs relatives and friends of the demise of her beloved husband Ivan Ilych Golovin, Member of the Court of Justice, which occurred on February the 4th of this year 1882. The funeral will take place on Friday at one o'clock in the afternoon.'

Ivan Ilych had been a colleague of the gentlemen present and was liked by them all. He had been ill for some weeks with an illness said to be incurable. His post had been kept open for him, but there had been conjectures that in case of his death Alexeev might receive his appointment, and that either Vinnikov or Shtabel would succeed Alexeev. So on receiving the news of Ivan Ilych's death the first thought of each of the gentlemen in that private room was of the changes and promotions it might occasion among themselves or their acquaintances.

'I shall be sure to get Shtabel's place or Vinnikov's,' thought Fedor Vasilievich. 'I was promised that long ago, and the promotion means an extra eight hundred rubles a year for me besides the allowance.'

'Now I must apply for my brother-in-law's transfer from Kaluga,' thought Peter Ivanovich. 'My wife will be very glad, and then she won't be able to say that I never do anything for her relations.'

'I thought he would never leave his bed again,' said Peter Ivanovich aloud. 'It's very sad.'

'But what really was the matter with him?'

'The doctors couldn't say – at least they could, but each of them said something different. When last I saw him I thought he was getting better.'

'And I haven't been to see him since the holidays. I always meant to go.'

'Had he any property?'

'I think his wife had a little – but something quite trifling.'

'We shall have to go to see her, but they live so terribly far away.'

'Far away from you, you mean. Everything's far away from your place.'

'You see, he never can forgive my living on the other side of the river,' said Peter Ivanovich, smiling at Shebek. Then, still talking of the distances between different parts of the city, they returned to the Court.

Besides considerations as to the possible transfers and promotions likely to result from Ivan Ilych's death, the mere fact of the death of a near acquaintance aroused, as usual, in all who heard of it the complacent feeling that 'it is he who is dead and not I'.

Each one thought or felt, 'Well, he's dead but I'm alive!' But the more intimate of Ivan Ilych's acquaintances, his so-called friends, could not help thinking also that they would now have to fulfil the very tiresome demands of propriety by attending the funeral service and paying a visit of condolence to the widow.

Fedor Vasilievich and Peter Ivanovich had been his nearest acquaintances. Peter Ivanovich had studied law with Ivan Ilych and had considered himself to be under obligations to him.

Having told his wife at dinner-time of Ivan Ilych's death, and of his conjecture that it might be possible to get her brother transferred to their circuit, Peter Ivanovich sacrificed his usual nap, put on his evening clothes, and drove to Ivan Ilych's house.

At the entrance stood a carriage and two cabs. Leaning against the wall in the hall downstairs near the cloak-stand was a coffin-lid covered with cloth of gold, ornamented with gold cord and tassels, that had been polished up with metal powder. Two ladies in black were taking off their fur cloaks. Peter Ivanovich recognized one of them as Ivan Ilych's sister, but the other was a stranger to him. His colleague Schwartz was just coming downstairs, but on seeing Peter Ivanovich enter he stopped and winked at him, as if to say: 'Ivan Ilych has made a mess of things – not like you and me.'

Schwartz's face with his Piccadilly whiskers, and his slim figure in evening dress, had as usual an air of elegant solemnity which contrasted with the playfulness of his character and had a special piquancy here, or so it seemed to Peter Ivanovich.

Peter Ivanovich allowed the ladies to precede him and slowly followed them upstairs. Schwartz did not come down but remained where he was, and Peter Ivanovich understood that he wanted to arrange where they should play bridge that evening. The ladies went upstairs to the widow's room, and Schwartz with seriously compressed lips but a playful look in his eyes, indicated by a twist of his eyebrows the room to the right where the body lay.

Peter Ivanovich, like everyone else on such occasions, entered feeling uncertain what he would have to do. All he knew was that at such times it is always safe to cross oneself. But he was not quite sure whether one should make obeisances while doing so. He therefore adopted a middle course. On entering the room he began crossing himself and made a slight movement resembling a bow. At the same time, as far as the motion of his head and arm allowed, he surveyed the room. Two young men – apparently nephews, one of whom was a high-school pupil – were leaving the room, crossing themselves as they did so. An old woman was standing motionless, and a lady with strangely arched eyebrows was saying something to her in a whisper. A vigorous, resolute Church Reader, in a frock-coat, was reading something in a loud voice with an expression that precluded any contradiction. The butler's assistant, Gerasim, stepping lightly in front of Peter Ivanovich, was strewing something on the floor. Noticing this, Peter Ivanovich was immediately aware of a faint odour of a decomposing body.

The last time he had called on Ivan Ilych, Peter Ivanovich had seen Gerasim in the study. Ivan Ilych had been particularly fond of him and he was performing the duty of a sick-nurse.

Peter Ivanovich continued to make the sign of the cross slightly inclining his head in an intermediate direction between the coffin, the Reader, and the icons on the table in a corner of the room. Afterwards, when it seemed to him that this movement of his arm in crossing himself had gone on too long, he stopped and began to look at the corpse.

The dead man lay, as dead men always lie, in a specially heavy way, his rigid limbs sunk in the soft cushions of the coffin, with the head for ever bowed on the pillow. His yellow waxen brow with bald patches over his sunken temples was thrust up in the way peculiar to the dead, the protruding nose seeming to press on the upper lip. He was much changed and had grown even thinner since Peter Ivanovich had last seen him, but, as is always the case with the dead, his face was handsomer and above all more dignified than when he was alive. The expression on the face said that what was necessary had been accomplished, and accomplished rightly. Besides this there was in that expression a reproach and a warning to the living. This warning seemed to Peter Ivanovich out of place, or at least not applicable to him. He felt a certain discomfort and so he hurriedly crossed himself once more and turned and went out of the door – too hurriedly and too regardless of propriety, as he himself was aware.

Schwartz was waiting for him in the adjoining room with legs spread wide apart and both hands toying with his top-hat behind his back. The mere sight of that playful, well-groomed, and elegant figure refreshed Peter Ivanovich. He felt that Schwartz was above all these happenings and would not surrender to any depressing influences. His very look said that this incident of a church service for Ivan Ilych could not be a sufficient reason for infringing the order of the session – in other words, that it would certainly not prevent his unwrapping a new pack of cards and shuffling them that evening while a footman placed four fresh candles on the table: in fact, that there was no reason for supposing that this incident would hinder their spending the evening agreeably. Indeed he said this in a whisper as Peter Ivanovich passed him, proposing that they should meet for a game at Fedor Vasilievich's. But apparently Peter Ivanovich was not destined to play bridge that evening. Praskovya Fedorovna (a short, fat woman who despite all efforts to the contrary had continued to broaden steadily from her shoulders downwards and who had the same extraordinarily arched eyebrows as the lady who had been standing by the coffin), dressed all in black, her head covered with lace, came out of her own room with some other ladies, conducted them to the room where the dead body lay, and said: 'The service will begin immediately. Please go in.'

Schwartz, making an indefinite bow, stood still, evidently neither accepting nor declining this invitation. Praskovya Fedorovna recognizing Peter Ivanovich, sighed, went close up to him, took his hand, and said: 'I know you were a true friend to Ivan Ilych . . .' and looked at him awaiting some suitable response. And Peter Ivanovich knew that, just as it had been the right thing to cross himself in that room, so what he had to do here was to press her hand, sigh, and say, 'Believe me . . .'. So he did all this and as he did it he felt that the desired result had been achieved: that both he and she were touched.

'Come with me. I want to speak to you before it begins,' said the widow. 'Give me your arm.'

Peter Ivanovich gave her his arm and they went to the

inner rooms, passing Schwartz who winked at Peter Ivanovich compassionately.

'That does for our bridge! Don't object if we find another player. Perhaps you can cut in when you do escape,' said his playful look.

Peter Ivanovich sighed still more deeply and despondently, and Praskovya Fedorovna pressed his arm gratefully. When they reached the drawing-room, upholstered in pink cretonne and lighted by a dim lamp, they sat down at the table – she on a sofa and Peter Ivanovich on a low pouffe, the springs of which yielded spasmodically under his weight. Praskovya Fedorovna had been on the point of warning him to take another seat, but felt that such a warning was out of keeping with her present condition and so changed her mind. As he sat down on the pouffe Peter Ivanovich recalled how Ivan Ilych had arranged this room and had consulted him regarding this pink cretonne with green leaves. The whole room was full of furniture and knick-knacks, and on her way to the sofa the lace of the widow's black shawl caught on the carved edge of the table. Peter Ivanovich rose to detach it, and the springs of the pouffe, relieved of his weight, rose also and gave him a push. The widow began detaching her shawl herself, and Peter Ivanovich again sat down, suppressing the rebellious springs of the pouffe under him. But the widow had not quite freed herself and Peter Ivanovich got up again, and again the pouffe rebelled and even creaked. When this was all over she took out a clean cambric handkerchief and began to weep. The episode with the shawl and the struggle with the pouffe had cooled Peter Ivanovich's emotions and he sat there with a sullen look on his face. This awkward situation was interrupted by Sokolov, Ivan Ilych's butler, who came to report that the plot in the cemetery that Praskovya Fedorovna had chosen would cost two hundred rubles. She stopped weeping and, looking at Peter Ivanovich with the air of a victim, remarked in French that it was very hard for her. Peter Ivanovich made a silent gesture signifying his full conviction that it must indeed be so.

'Please smoke,' she said in a magnanimous yet crushed voice, and turned to discuss with Sokolov the price of the plot for the grave.

Peter Ivanovich while lighting his cigarette heard her inquiring very circumstantially into the prices of different plots in the cemetery and finally decide which she would take. When that was done she gave instructions about engaging the choir. Sokolov then left the room.

'I look after everything myself,' she told Peter Ivanovich, shifting the albums that lay on the table; and noticing that the table was endangered by his cigarette-ash, she immediately passed him an ashtray, saying as she did so: 'I consider it an affectation to say that my grief prevents my attending to practical affairs. On the contrary, if anything can – I won't say console me, but – distract me, it is seeing to everything concerning him.' She again took out her handkerchief as if preparing to cry, but suddenly, as if mastering her feeling, she shook herself and began to speak calmly. 'But there is something I want to talk to you about.'

Peter Ivanovich bowed, keeping control of the springs of the pouffe, which immediately began quivering under him.

'He suffered terribly the last few days.'

'Did he?' said Peter Ivanovich.

'Oh, terribly! He screamed unceasingly, not for minutes but for hours. For the last three days he screamed incessantly. It was unendurable. I cannot understand how I bore it; you could hear him three rooms off. Oh, what I have suffered!'

'Is it possible that he was conscious all that time?' asked Peter Ivanovich.

'Yes,' she whispered. 'To the last moment. He took leave of us a quarter of an hour before he died, and asked us to take Volodya away.'

The thought of the sufferings of this man he had known so intimately, first as a merry little boy, then as a school-mate, and later as a grown-up colleague, suddenly struck Peter Ivanovich with horror, despite an unpleasant consciousness of his own and this woman's dissimulation. He again saw that brow, and that nose pressing down on the lip, and felt afraid for himself.

'Three days of frightful suffering and then death! Why, that might suddenly, at any time, happen to me,' he thought, and for a moment felt terrified. But — he did not himself know how — the customary reflection at once occurred to him that this had happened to Ivan Ilych and not to him, and that it should not and could not happen to him, and that to think that it could would be yielding to depression which he ought not to do, as Schwartz's expression plainly showed. After which reflection Peter Ivanovich felt reassured, and began to ask with interest about the details of Ivan Ilych's death, as though death was an accident natural to Ivan Ilych but certainly not to himself.

After many details of the really dreadful physical sufferings Ivan Ilych had endured (which details he learnt only from the effect those sufferings had produced on Praskovya Fedorovna's nerves) the widow apparently found it necessary to get to business.

'Oh, Peter Ivanovich, how hard it is! How terribly, terribly hard!' and she again began to weep.

Peter Ivanovich sighed and waited for her to finish blowing her nose. When she had done so he said, 'Believe me . . . ', and she again began talking and brought out what was evidently her chief concern with him – namely, to question him as to how she could obtain a grant of money from the Government on the occasion of her husband's death. She made it appear that she was asking Peter Ivanovich's advice about her pension, but he soon saw that she already knew about that to the minutest detail, more even than he did himself. She knew how much could be got out of the Government in consequence of her husband's death, but wanted to find out whether she could not possibly extract something more. Peter Ivanovich tried to think of some means of doing so, but after reflecting for a while and, out of propriety, condemning the Government for its niggardliness, he said he thought that nothing more could be got. Then she sighed and evidently began to devise means of getting rid of her visitor. Noticing this, he put out his cigarette, rose, pressed her hand, and went out into the ante-room.

In the dining-room where the clock stood that Ivan Ilych had liked so much and had bought at an antique shop, Peter Ivanovich met a priest and a few acquaintances who had come to attend the service, and he recognized Ivan Ilych's daughter, a handsome young woman. She was in black and her slim figure appeared slimmer than ever. She had a gloomy, determined, almost angry expression, and bowed to Peter Ivanovich as though he were in some way to blame. Behind her, with the same offended look, stood a wealthy young man, an examining magistrate, whom Peter Ivanovich also knew and who was her fiancé, as he had heard. He bowed mournfully to them and was about to pass into the death-chamber, when from under the stairs appeared the figure of Ivan Ilych's schoolboy son, who was extremely like his father. He seemed a little Ivan Ilych, such as Peter Ivanovich remembered when they studied law together. His tear-stained eyes had in them the look that is seen in the eyes of boys of thirteen or fourteen who are not pure-minded. When he saw Peter Ivanovich he scowled morosely and shamefacedly. Peter Ivanovich nodded to him and entered the death-chamber. The service began: candles, groans, incense, tears, and sobs. Peter

Ivanovich stood looking gloomily down at his feet. He did not look once at the dead man, did not yield to any depressing influence, and was one of the first to leave the room. There was no one in the ante-room, but Gerasim darted out of the dead man's room, rummaged with his strong hands among the fur coats to find Peter Ivanovich's and helped him on with it.

'Well, friend Gerasim,' said Peter Ivanovich, so as to say something. 'It's a sad affair, isn't it?'

'It's God's will. We shall all come to it some day,' said Gerasim, displaying his teeth – the even, white teeth of a healthy peasant – and, like a man in the thick of urgent work, he briskly opened the front door, called the coachman, helped Peter Ivanovich into the sledge, and sprang back to the porch as if in readiness for what he had to do next.

Peter Ivanovich found the fresh air particularly pleasant after the smell of incense, the dead body, and carbolic acid.

'Where to, sir?' asked the coachman.

'It's not too late even now ... I'll call round on Fedor Vasilievich.'

He accordingly drove there and found them just finishing the first rubber, so that it was quite convenient for him to cut in.

II

IVAN ILYCH'S life had been most simple and most ordinary and therefore most terrible.

He had been a member of the Court of Justice, and died at the age of forty-five. His father had been an official who after serving in various ministries and departments in Petersburg had made the sort of career which brings men to positions from which by reason of their long service they cannot be dismissed, though they are obviously unfit to hold any responsible position, and for whom therefore posts are specially created, which though fictitious carry salaries of from six to ten thousand rubles that are not fictitious, and in receipt of which they live on to a great age.

Such was the Privy Councillor and superfluous member of various superfluous institutions, Ilya Epimovich Golovin.

He had three sons, of whom Ivan Ilych was the second. The eldest son was following in his father's footsteps only in another department, and was already approaching that stage in the service at which a similar sinecure would be reached. The third son was a failure. He had ruined his prospects in a number of positions and was now serving in the railway department. His father and brothers, and still more their wives, not merely disliked meeting him, but avoided remembering his existence unless compelled to do so. His sister had married Baron Greff, a Petersburg official of her father's type. Ivan Ilych was *le phénix de la famille* as people said. He was neither as cold and formal as his elder brother nor as wild as the younger, but was a happy mean between them – an intelligent, polished, lively and agreeable man. He had studied with his younger brother at the School of Law, but the latter had failed to complete the course and was expelled when he was in the fifth class. Ivan Ilych finished the course well. Even when he was at the School of Law he was just what he remained for the rest of his life: a capable, cheerful, good-natured, and sociable man, though strict in the fulfilment of what he considered to be his duty: and he considered his duty to be what was so considered by those in authority. Neither as a boy nor as a man was he a toady, but from early youth was by nature attracted to people of high station as a fly is drawn to the light, assimilating their ways and views of life and establishing friendly relations with them. All the enthusiasms of childhood and youth passed without leaving much trace on him; he succumbed to sensuality, to vanity, and latterly among the highest classes to liberalism, but always within limits which his instinct unfailingly indicated to him as correct.

At school he had done things which had formerly seemed to him very horrid and made him feel disgusted with himself when he did them; but when later on he saw that such actions were done by people of good position and that they did not regard them as wrong, he was able not exactly to regard them as right, but to forget about them entirely or not be at all troubled at remembering them.

Having graduated from the School of Law and qualified for the tenth rank of the civil service, and having received money from his father for his equipment, Ivan Ilych ordered himself clothes at Scharmer's, the fashionable tailor, hung a medallion inscribed *respice finem* on his watch-chain, took leave of his professor and the prince who was patron of the school, had a farewell dinner with his comrades at Donon's first-class restaurant, and with his new and fashionable portmanteau, linen, clothes, shaving and other toilet appliances, and a travelling rug, all purchased at the best shops, he set off for one of the provinces where, through his father's influence, he had been attached to the Governor as an official for special service.

In the province Ivan Ilych soon arranged as easy and agreeable a position for himself as he had had at the School of Law. He performed his official tasks, made his career, and at the same time amused himself pleasantly and decorously. Occasionally he paid official visits to country districts, where he behaved with dignity both to his superiors and inferiors, and performed the duties entrusted to him, which related chiefly to the sectarians, with an exactness and incorruptible honesty of which he could not but feel proud.

In official matters, despite his youth and taste for frivolous gaiety, he was exceedingly reserved, punctilious, and even severe; but in society he was often amusing and witty, and always good-natured, correct in his manner, and *bon enfant*, as the Governor and his wife – with whom he was like one of the family – used to say of him.

In the province he had an affair with a lady who made advances to the elegant young lawyer, and there was also a milliner; and there were carousals with aides-de-camp who visited the district, and after-supper visits to a certain outlying street of doubtful reputation; and there was too some obsequiousness to his chief and even to his chief's wife, but all this was done with such a tone of good breeding that no hard names could be applied to it. It all came under the heading of the French saying: '*Il faut que jeunesse se passe.*'* It was all done with clean hands, in clean linen, with French phrases, and above all among people of the best society and consequently with the approval of people of rank.

So Ivan Ilych served for five years and then came a change in his official life. The new and reformed judicial institutions were introduced, and new men were needed. Ivan Ilych became such a new man. He was offered the post of examining magistrate, and he accepted it though the post was in another province and obliged him to give up the connections he had formed and to make new ones. His friends met to give him a send-off; they had a group-photograph taken and presented him with a silver cigarette-case, and he set off to his new post.

---

* 'Youth must have its fling.'

As examining magistrate Ivan Ilych was just as *comme il faut* and decorous a man, inspiring general respect and capable of separating his official duties from his private life, as he had been when acting as an official on special service. His duties now as examining magistrate were far more interesting and attractive than before. In his former position it had been pleasant to wear an undress uniform made by Scharmer, and to pass through the crowd of petitioners and officials who were timorously awaiting an audience with the Governor, and who envied him as with free and easy gait he went straight into his chief's private room to have a cup of tea and a cigarette with him. But not many people had then been directly dependent on him – only police officials and the sectarians when he went on special missions – and he liked to treat them politely, almost as comrades, as if he were letting them feel that he who had the power to crush them was treating them in this simple, friendly way. There were then but few such people. But now, as an examining magistrate, Ivan Ilych felt that everyone without exception, even the most important and self-satisfied, was in his power, and that he need only write a few words on a sheet of paper with a certain heading, and this or that important, self-satisfied person would be brought before him in the role of an accused person or a witness, and if he did not choose to allow him to sit down, would have to stand before him and answer his questions. Ivan Ilych never abused his power; he tried on the contrary to soften its expression, but the consciousness of it and of the possibility of softening its effect, supplied the chief interest and attraction of his office. In his work itself, especially in his examinations, he very soon acquired a method of eliminating all considerations irrelevant to the legal aspect of the case, and reducing even the most complicated case to a form in which it would be presented on paper only in its externals, completely excluding his personal opinion of the matter, while above all observing every prescribed formality. The work was new and Ivan Ilych was one of the first men to apply the new Code of 1864.*

On taking up the post of examining magistrate in a new town, he made new acquaintances and connections, placed himself on a new footing, and assumed a somewhat different tone. He took up an attitude of rather dignified aloofness towards the provincial authorities, but picked out the best circle of legal gentlemen and wealthy gentry living in the town and assumed a tone of slight dissatisfaction with the Government, of moderate liberalism, and of enlightened citizenship. At the same time, without at all altering the elegance of his toilet, he ceased shaving his chin and allowed his beard to grow as it pleased.

Ivan Ilych settled down very pleasantly in this new town. The society there, which inclined towards opposition to the Governor, was friendly, his salary was larger, and he began to

---

* The emancipation of the serfs in 1861 was followed by a thorough all-round reform of judicial proceedings.

play *vint*,* which he found added not a little to the pleasure of life, for he had a capacity for cards, played good-humouredly, and calculated rapidly and astutely, so that he usually won.

After living there for two years he met his future wife, Praskovya Fedorovna Mikhel, who was the most attractive, clever, and brilliant girl of the set in which he moved, and among other amusements and relaxations from his labours as examining magistrate, Ivan Ilych established light and playful relations with her.

While he had been an official on special service he had been accustomed to dance, but now as an examining magistrate it was exceptional for him to do so. If he danced now, he did it as if to show that though he served under the reformed order of things, and had reached the fifth official rank, yet when it came to dancing he could do it better than most people. So at the end of an evening he sometimes danced with Praskovya Fedorovna, and it was chiefly during these dances that he captivated her. She fell in love with him. Ivan Ilych had at first no definite intention of marrying, but when the girl fell in love with him he said to himself: 'Really, why shouldn't I marry?'

Praskovya Fedorovna came of a good family, was not bad looking, and had some little property. Ivan Ilych might have aspired to a more brilliant match, but even this was good. He had his salary, and she, he hoped, would have an equal income. She was well connected, and was a sweet, pretty, and thoroughly

---

* A card-game resembling bridge.

correct young woman. To say that Ivan Ilych married because he fell in love with Praskovya Fedorovna and found that she sympathized with his views of life would be as incorrect as to say that he married because his social circle approved of the match. He was swayed by both these considerations: the marriage gave him personal satisfaction, and at the same time it was considered the right thing by the most highly placed of his associates.

So Ivan Ilych got married.

The preparations for marriage and the beginning of married life, with its conjugal caresses, the new furniture, new crockery, and new linen, were very pleasant until his wife became pregnant – so that Ivan Ilych had begun to think that marriage would not impair the easy, agreeable, gay and always decorous character of his life, approved of by society and regarded by himself as natural, but would even improve it. But from the first months of his wife's pregnancy, something new, unpleasant, depressing, and unseemly, and from which there was no way of escape, unexpectedly showed itself.

His wife, without any reason – *de gaieté de coeur* as Ivan Ilych expressed it to himself – began to disturb the pleasure and propriety of their life. She began to be jealous without any cause, expected him to devote his whole attention to her, found fault with everything, and made coarse and ill-mannered scenes.

At first Ivan Ilych hoped to escape from the unpleasantness of this state of affairs by the same easy and decorous relation to life that had served him heretofore: he tried to ignore his wife's disagreeable moods, continued to live in his usual easy and pleasant way, invited friends to his house for a game of cards, and also tried going out to his club or spending his evenings with friends. But one day his wife began upbraiding him so vigorously, using such coarse words, and continued to abuse him every time he did not fulfil her demands, so resolutely and with such evident determination not to give way till he submitted – that is, till he stayed at home and was bored just as she was – that he became alarmed. He now realized that matrimony – at any rate with Praskovya Fedorovna – was not always conducive to the pleasures and amenities of life, but on the contrary often infringed both comfort and propriety, and that he must therefore entrench himself against such infringe- ment. And Ivan Ilych began to seek for means of doing so. His official duties were the one thing that imposed upon Praskovya Fedorovna, and by means of his official work and the duties attached to it he began struggling with his wife to secure his own independence.

With the birth of their child, the attempts to feed it and the various failures in doing so, and with the real and imaginary illnesses of mother and child, in which Ivan Ilych's sympathy was demanded but about which he understood nothing, the need of securing for himself an existence outside his family life became still more imperative.

As his wife grew more irritable and exacting and Ivan Ilych transferred the centre of gravity of his life more and more to his official work, so did he grow to like his work better and became more ambitious than before.

Very soon, within a year of his wedding, Ivan Ilych had realized that marriage, though it may add some comforts to life, is in fact a very intricate and difficult affair towards which in order to perform one's duty, that is, to lead a decorous life approved of by society, one must adopt a definite attitude just as towards one's official duties.

And Ivan Ilych evolved such an attitude towards married life. He only required of it those conveniences – dinner at home, housewife, and bed – which it could give him, and above all that propriety of external forms required by public opinion. For the rest he looked for light-hearted pleasure and propriety, and was very thankful when he found them, but if he met with antagonism and querulousness he at once retired into his separate fenced-off world of official duties, where he found satisfaction.

Ivan Ilych was esteemed a good official, and after three years was made Assistant Public Prosecutor. His new duties, their importance, the possibility of indicting and imprisoning anyone he chose, the publicity his speeches received, and the success he had in all these things, made his work still more attractive.

More children came. His wife became more and more querulous and ill-tempered, but the attitude Ivan Ilych had adopted towards his home life rendered him almost impervious to her grumbling.

After seven years' service in that town he was transferred to another province as Public Prosecutor. They moved, but were short of money and his wife did not like the place they moved to. Though the salary was higher the cost of living was greater, besides which two of their children died and family life became still more unpleasant for him.

Praskovya Fedorovna blamed her husband for every inconvenience they encountered in their new home. Most of the conversations between husband and wife, especially as to the children's education, led to topics which recalled former disputes, and those disputes were apt to flare up again at any moment. There remained only those rare periods of amorousness which still came to them at times but did not last long. These were islets at which they anchored for a while and then again set out upon that ocean of veiled hostility which showed itself in their aloofness from one another. This aloofness might have grieved Ivan Ilych had he considered that it ought not to exist, but he now regarded the position as normal, and even made it the goal at which he aimed in family life. His aim was to free himself more and more from those unpleasantnesses and to give them a semblance of harmlessness and propriety. He attained this by spending less and less time with his family, and when obliged to be at home he tried to safeguard his position by the presence of outsiders. The chief thing however was that he had his official duties. The whole interest of his life now centred in the official world and that interest absorbed him. The consciousness of his power, being able to ruin anybody he wished to ruin, the importance, even the external dignity of his entry into court, or meetings with his subordinates, his success with superiors and inferiors, and above all his masterly handling of cases, of which he was conscious – all this gave him pleasure and filled his life, together with chats with his colleagues, dinners, and bridge. So that on the whole Ivan Ilych's life continued to flow as he considered it should do – pleasantly and properly.

So things continued for another seven years. His eldest daughter was already sixteen, another child had died, and only one son was left, a schoolboy and a subject of dissension. Ivan Ilych wanted to put him in the School of Law, but to spite him Praskovya Fedorovna entered him at the High School. The daughter had been educated at home and had turned out well: the boy did not learn badly either.

III

SO IVAN ILYCH lived for seventeen years after his marriage. He was already a Public Prosecutor of long standing, and had declined several proposed transfers while awaiting a more desirable post, when an unanticipated and unpleasant occurrence quite upset the peaceful course of his life. He was expecting to be offered the post of presiding judge in a university town, but Happe somehow came to the front and obtained the appointment instead. Ivan Ilych became irritable, reproached Happe, and quarrelled both with him and with his immediate superiors – who became colder to him and again passed him over when other appointments were made.

This was in 1880, the hardest year of Ivan Ilych's life. It was then that it became evident on the one hand that his salary was insufficient for them to live on, and on the other that he had been forgotten, and not only this, but that what was for him the greatest and most cruel injustice appeared to others a quite ordinary occurrence. Even his father did not consider it his duty to help him. Ivan Ilych felt himself abandoned by everyone, and that they regarded his position with a salary of three thousand, five hundred rubles as quite normal and even fortunate. He alone knew that with the consciousness of the injustices done him, with his wife's incessant nagging, and with the debts he had contracted by living beyond his means, his position was far from normal.

In order to save money that summer he obtained leave of absence and went with his wife to live in the country at her brother's place.

In the country, without his work, he experienced *ennui* for the first time in his life, and not only *ennui* but intolerable depression, and he decided that it was impossible to go on living like that, and that it was necessary to take energetic measures.

Having passed a sleepless night pacing up and down the verandah, he decided to go to Petersburg and bestir himself, in order to punish those who had failed to appreciate him and to get transferred to another ministry.

Next day, despite many protests from his wife and her brother, he started for Petersburg with the sole object of obtaining a post with a salary of five thousand rubles a year. He was no longer bent on any particular department, or tendency, or kind of activity. All he now wanted was an appointment to another post with a salary of five thousand rubles, either in the administration, in the banks, with the railways, in one of the Empress Marya's Institutions, or even in the customs – but it had to carry with it a salary of five thousand rubles and be in a ministry other than that in which they had failed to appreciate him.

And this quest of Ivan Ilych's was crowned with remarkable and unexpected success. At Kursk an acquaintance of his, F. I. Ilyin, got into the first-class carriage, sat down beside Ivan Ilych, and told him of a telegram just received by the Governor of Kursk announcing that a change was about to take place in the ministry: Peter Ivanovich was to be superseded by Ivan Semenovich.

The proposed change, apart from its significance for Russia, had a special significance for Ivan Ilych, because by bringing forward a new man, Peter Petrovich, and consequently his friend Zachar Ivanovich, it was highly favourable for Ivan Ilych, since Zachar Ivanovich was a friend and colleague of his.

In Moscow this news was confirmed, and on reaching Petersburg Ivan Ilych found Zachar Ivanovich and received a definite promise of an appointment in his former department of Justice.

A week later he telegraphed to his wife: 'Zachar in Miller's place. I shall receive appointment on presentation of report.'

Thanks to this change of personnel, Ivan Ilych had unexpectedly obtained an appointment in his former ministry which placed him two stages above his former colleagues besides giving him five thousand rubles salary and three thousand five hundred rubles for expenses connected with his removal. All his ill humour towards his former enemies and the whole department vanished, and Ivan Ilych was completely happy.

He returned to the country more cheerful and contented than he had been for a long time. Praskovya Fedorovna also cheered up and a truce was arranged between them. Ivan Ilych told of how he had been feted by everybody in Petersburg, how all those who had been his enemies were put to shame and now fawned on him, how envious they were of his appointment, and how much everybody in Petersburg had liked him.

Praskovya Fedorovna listened to all this and appeared to believe it. She did not contradict anything, but only made plans for their life in the town to which they were going. Ivan Ilych saw with delight that these plans were his plans, that he and his wife agreed, and that, after a stumble, his life was regaining its due and natural character of pleasant light-heartedness and decorum.

Ivan Ilych had come back for a short time only, for he had to take up his new duties on the 10th of September. Moreover, he needed time to settle into the new place, to move all his belongings from the province, and to buy and order many additional things: in a word, to make such arrangements as he had resolved on, which were almost exactly what Praskovya Fedorovna too had decided on.

Now that everything had happened so fortunately, and that he and his wife were at one in their aims and moreover saw so little of one another, they got on together better than they had done since the first years of marriage. Ivan Ilych had thought of taking his family away with him at once, but the insistence of his wife's brother and her sister-in-law, who had suddenly become particularly amiable and friendly to him and his family, induced him to depart alone.

So he departed, and the cheerful state of mind induced by his success and by the harmony between his wife and himself, the one intensifying the other, did not leave him. He found a delightful house, just the thing both he and his wife had dreamt of. Spacious, lofty reception-rooms in the old style, a convenient and dignified study, rooms for his wife and daughter, a study for his son – it might have been specially built for them. Ivan Ilych himself superintended the arrangements, chose the wall-papers, supplemented the furniture (preferably with antiques which he considered particularly *comme il faut*), and supervised the upholstering. Everything progressed and progressed and approached the ideal he had set himself: even when things were only half completed they exceeded his expectations. He saw what a refined and elegant character, free from vulgarity, it would all have when it was ready. On falling asleep he pictured to himself how the reception-room would look. Looking at the yet unfinished drawing-room he could see the fireplace, the screen, the whatnot, the little chairs dotted here and there, the dishes and plates on the walls, and the bronzes, as they would be when everything was in place. He was pleased by the thought of how his wife and daughter, who shared his taste in this matter, would be impressed by it. They were certainly not expecting as much. He had been particularly successful in finding, and buying cheaply, antiques which gave a particularly aristocratic character to the whole place. But in his letters he intentionally understated everything in order to be able to surprise them. All this so absorbed him that his new duties – though he liked his official work – interested him less than he had expected. Sometimes he even had moments of absent-mindedness during the Court Sessions, and would consider whether he should have straight or curved cornices for his curtains. He was so interested in it all that he often did things himself, rearranging the furniture, or rehanging the curtains. Once when mounting a step-ladder to show the upholsterer, who did not understand, how he wanted the hangings draped, he made a false step and slipped, but being a strong and agile man he clung on and only knocked his side against the knob of the window-frame. The bruised place was painful but the pain soon passed, and he felt particularly bright and well just then. He wrote: 'I feel fifteen years younger.' He thought he would have everything ready by September, but it dragged on till mid-October. But the result was charming not only in his eyes but to everyone who saw it.

In reality it was just what is usually seen in the houses of people of moderate means who want to appear rich, and therefore succeed only in resembling others like themselves: there were damasks, dark wood, plants, rugs, and dull and polished bronzes – all the things people of a certain class have in order to resemble other people of that class. His house was so like the others that it would never have been noticed, but to him it all seemed to be quite exceptional. He was very happy when he met his family at the station and brought them to the newly furnished house all lit up, where a footman in a white tie opened the door into the hall decorated with plants, and when they went on into the drawing-room and the study uttering exclamations of delight. He conducted them everywhere, drank in their praises eagerly, and beamed with pleasure. At tea that evening, when Praskovya Fedorovna among other things asked him about his fall, he laughed, and showed them how he had gone flying and had frightened the upholsterer.

'It's a good thing I'm a bit of an athlete. Another man might have been killed, but I merely knocked myself, just here; it hurts when it's touched, but it's passing off already – it's only a bruise.'

So they began living in their new home – in which, as always happens, when they got thoroughly settled in they found they were just one room short – and with the increased income, which as always was just a little (some five hundred rubles) too little, but it was all very nice.

Things went particularly well at first, before everything was finally arranged and while something had still to be done: this thing bought, that thing ordered, another thing moved, and something else adjusted. Though there were some disputes between husband and wife, they were both so well satisfied and had so much to do that it all passed off without any serious quarrels. When nothing was left to arrange it became rather dull and something seemed to be lacking, but they were then making acquaintances, forming habits, and life was growing fuller.

Ivan Ilych spent his mornings at the law court and came home to dinner, and at first he was generally in a good humour, though he occasionally became irritable just on account of his house. (Every spot on the table-cloth or the upholstery, and every broken window-blind string, irritated him. He had devoted so much trouble to arranging it all that every disturbance of it distressed him.) But on the whole his life ran its course as he believed life should do: easily, pleasantly, and decorously.

He got up at nine, drank his coffee, read the paper, and then put on his undress uniform and went to the law courts. There the harness in which he worked had already been stretched to fit him and he donned it without a hitch: petitioners, inquiries at the chancery, the chancery itself, and the sittings public and administrative. In all this the thing was to exclude everything fresh and vital, which always disturbs the regular course of official business, and to admit only official relations with people, and then only on official grounds. A man would come, for instance, wanting some information. Ivan Ilych, as one in whose sphere the matter did not lie, would have nothing to do with him: but if the man had some business with him in his official capacity, something that could be expressed on officially stamped paper, he would do everything, positively everything he could within the limits of such relations, and in doing so would maintain the semblance of friendly human relations, that is, would observe the courtesies of life. As soon as the official relations ended, so did everything else. Ivan Ilych possessed this capacity to separate his real life from the official side of affairs and not mix the two, in the highest degree, and by long practice and natural aptitude had brought it to such a pitch that sometimes, in the manner of a virtuoso, he would even allow himself to let the human and official relations mingle. He let himself do this just because he felt that he could at any time he chose resume the strictly official attitude again and drop the human relation. And he did it all easily, pleasantly, correctly, and even artistically. In the intervals between the sessions he smoked, drank tea, chatted a little about politics, a little about general topics, a little about cards, but most of all about official appointments. Tired, but with the feelings of a virtuoso – one of the first violins who has played his part in an orchestra with precision – he would return home to find that his wife and daughter had been out paying calls, or had a visitor, and that his son had been to school, had done his homework with his tutor, and was duly learning what is taught at High Schools. Everything was as it should be. After dinner, if they had no visitors, Ivan Ilych sometimes read a book that was being much discussed at the time, and in the evening settled down to work, that is, read official papers, compared the depositions of witnesses, and noted paragraphs of the Code applying to them. This was neither dull nor amusing. It was dull when he might have been playing bridge, but if no bridge was available it was at any rate better than doing nothing or sitting with his wife. Ivan Ilych's chief pleasure was giving little dinners to which he invited men and women of good social position, and just as his drawing-room resembled all other drawing-rooms so did his enjoyable little parties resemble all other such parties.

Once they even gave a dance. Ivan Ilych enjoyed it and everything went off well, except that it led to a violent quarrel with his wife about the cakes and sweets. Praskovya Fedorovna had made her own plans, but Ivan Ilych insisted on getting everything from an expensive confectioner and ordered too many cakes, and the quarrel occurred because some of those cakes were left over and the confectioner's bill came to forty-five rubles. It was a great and disagreeable quarrel. Praskovya Fedorovna called him 'a fool and an imbecile', and he clutched at his head and made angry allusions to divorce.

But the dance itself had been enjoyable. The best people were there, and Ivan Ilych had danced with Princess Trufonova, a sister of the distinguished founder of the Society 'Bear my Burden'.

The pleasures connected with his work were pleasures of ambition; his social pleasures were those of vanity; but Ivan Ilych's greatest pleasure was playing bridge. He acknowledged that whatever disagreeable incident happened in his life, the pleasure that beamed like a ray of light above everything else was to sit down to bridge with good players, not noisy partners, and of course to four-handed bridge (with five players it was annoying to have to stand out, though one pretended not to mind), to play a clever and serious game (when the cards allowed it), and then to have supper and drink a glass of wine. After a game of bridge, especially if he had won a little (to win a large sum was unpleasant), Ivan Ilych went to bed in specially good humour.

So they lived. They formed a circle of acquaintances among the best people and were visited by people of importance and by young folk. In their views as to their acquaintances, husband, wife and daughter were entirely agreed, and tacitly and unanimously kept at arm's length and shook off the various shabby friends and relations who, with much show of affection, gushed into the drawing-room with its Japanese plates on the walls. Soon these shabby friends ceased to obtrude themselves and only the best people remained in the Golovins' set.

Young men made up to Lisa, and Petrishchev, an examining magistrate and Dmitri Ivanovich Petrishchev's son and sole heir, began to be so attentive to her that Ivan Ilych had already spoken to Praskovya Fedorovna about it, and considered whether they should not arrange a party for them, or get up some private theatricals.

So they lived, and all went well, without change, and life flowed pleasantly.

IV

THEY WERE all in good health. It could not be called ill health if Ivan Ilych sometimes said that he had a queer taste in his mouth and felt some discomfort in his left side.

But this discomfort increased and, though not exactly painful, grew into a sense of pressure in his side accompanied by ill humour. And his irritability became worse and worse and began to mar the agreeable, easy, and correct life that had established itself in the Golovin family. Quarrels between husband and wife became more and more frequent, and soon the ease and amenity disappeared and even the decorum was barely maintained. Scenes again became frequent, and very few of those islets remained on which husband and wife could meet without an explosion. Praskovya Fedorovna now had good reason to say that her husband's temper was trying. With characteristic exaggeration she said he had always had a dreadful temper, and that it had needed all her good nature to put up with it for twenty years. It was true that now the quarrels were started by him. His bursts of temper always came just before dinner, often just as he began to eat his soup. Sometimes he noticed that a plate or dish was chipped, or the food was not right, or his son put his elbow on the table, or his daughter's hair was not done as he liked it, and for all this he blamed Praskovya Fedorovna. At first she retorted and said disagreeable things to him, but once or twice he fell into such a rage at the beginning of dinner that she realized it was due to some physical derangement brought on by taking food, and so she restrained herself and did not answer, but only hurried to get the dinner over. She regarded this self-restraint as highly praiseworthy. Having come to the conclusion that her husband had a dreadful temper and made her life miserable, she began to feel sorry for herself, and the more she pitied herself the more she hated her husband. She began to wish he would die; yet she did not want him to die because then his salary would cease. And this irritated her against him still more. She considered herself dreadfully unhappy just because not even his death could save her, and though she concealed her exasperation, that hidden exasperation of hers increased his irritation also.

After one scene in which Ivan Ilych had been particularly unfair and after which he had said in explanation that he certainly was irritable but that it was due to his not being well, she said that if he was ill it should be attended to, and insisted on his going to see a celebrated doctor.

He went. Everything took place as he had expected and as it

always does. There was the usual waiting and the important air assumed by the doctor, with which he was so familiar (resembling that which he himself assumed in court), and the sounding and listening, and the questions which called for answers that were foregone conclusions and were evidently unnecessary, and the look of importance which implied that 'if only you put yourself in our hands we will arrange everything – we know indubitably how it has to be done, always in the same way for everybody alike'. It was all just as it was in the law courts. The doctor put on just the same air towards him as he himself put on towards an accused person.

The doctor said that so-and-so indicated that there was so-and-so inside the patient, but if the investigation of so-and-so did not confirm this, then he must assume that and that. If he assumed that and that, then . . . and so on. To Ivan Ilych only one question was important: was his case serious or not? But the doctor ignored that inappropriate question. From his point of view it was not the one under consideration, the real question was to decide between a floating kidney, chronic catarrh, or appendicitis. It was not a question of Ivan Ilych's life or death, but one between a floating kidney and appendicitis. And that question the doctor solved brilliantly, as it seemed to Ivan Ilych, in favour of the appendix, with the reservation that should an examination of the urine give fresh indications the matter would be reconsidered. All this was just what Ivan Ilych had himself brilliantly accomplished a thousand times in dealing with men on trial. The doctor summed up just as brilliantly, looking over his spectacles triumphantly and even gaily at the accused. From the doctor's summing up Ivan Ilych concluded that things were bad, but that for the doctor, and perhaps for everybody else, it was a matter of indifference, though for him it was bad. And this conclusion struck him painfully, arousing in him a great feeling of pity for himself and of bitterness towards the doctor's indifference to a matter of such importance.

He said nothing of this, but rose, placed the doctor's fee on the table, and remarked with a sigh: 'We sick people probably often put inappropriate questions. But tell me, in general, is this complaint dangerous, or not? . . .'

The doctor looked at him sternly over his spectacles with one eye, as if to say: 'Prisoner, if you will not keep to the questions put to you, I shall be obliged to have you removed from the court.'

'I have already told you what I consider necessary and proper. The analysis may show something more.' And the doctor bowed.

Ivan Ilych went out slowly, seated himself disconsolately in his sledge, and drove home. All the way home he was going over what the doctor had said, trying to translate those complicated, obscure, scientific phrases into plain language and find in them an answer to the question: 'Is my condition bad? Is it very bad? Or is there as yet nothing much wrong?' And it seemed to him that the meaning of what the doctor had said was that it was very bad. Everything in the streets seemed depressing. The cabmen, the houses, the passers-by, and the shops, were dismal. His ache, this dull gnawing ache that never ceased for a moment, seemed to have acquired a new and more serious significance from the doctor's dubious remarks. Ivan Ilych now watched it with a new and oppressive feeling.

He reached home and began to tell his wife about it. She listened, but in the middle of his account his daughter came in with her hat on, ready to go out with her mother. She sat down reluctantly to listen to this tedious story, but could not stand it long, and her mother too did not hear him to the end.

'Well, I am very glad,' she said. 'Mind now to take your medicine regularly. Give me the prescription and I'll send Gerasim to the chemist's.' And she went to get ready to go out.

While she was in the room Ivan Ilych had hardly taken time to breathe, but he sighed deeply when she left it.

'Well,' he thought, 'perhaps it isn't so bad after all.'

He began taking his medicine and following the doctor's directions, which had been altered after the examination of the urine. But then it happened that there was a contradiction between the indications drawn from the examination of the urine and the symptoms that showed themselves. It turned out that what was happening differed from what the doctor had told him, and that he had either forgotten, or blundered, or hidden something from him. He could not, however, be blamed for that, and Ivan Ilych still obeyed his orders implicitly and at first derived some comfort from doing so.

From the time of his visit to the doctor, Ivan Ilych's chief occupation was the exact fulfilment of the doctor's instructions regarding hygiene and the taking of medicine, and the observation of his pain and his excretions. His chief interests came to be people's ailments and people's health. When sickness, deaths, or recoveries were mentioned in his presence, especially when the illness resembled his own, he listened with agitation which he tried to hide, asked questions, and applied what he heard to his own case.

The pain did not grow less, but Ivan Ilych made efforts to force himself to think that he was better. And he could do this so long as nothing agitated him. But as soon as he had any unpleasantness with his wife, any lack of success in his official work, or held bad cards at bridge, he was at once acutely sensible of his disease. He had formerly borne such mischances, hoping soon to adjust what was wrong, to master it and attain success, or make a grand slam. But now every mischance upset him and plunged him into despair. He would say to himself: 'There now, just as I was beginning to get better and the medicine had begun to take effect, comes this accursed misfortune, or unpleasantness . . .' And he was furious with the mishap, or with the people who were causing the unpleasantness and killing him, for he felt that this fury was killing him but could not restrain it. One would have thought that it should have been clear to him that this exasperation with circumstances and people aggravated his illness, and that he ought therefore to ignore unpleasant occurrences. But he drew the very opposite conclusion: he said that he needed peace, and he watched for everything that might disturb it and became irritable at the slightest infringement of it. His condition was rendered worse by the fact that he read medical books and consulted doctors. The progress of his disease was so gradual that he could deceive himself when comparing one day with another – the difference was so slight. But when he consulted the doctors it seemed to him that he was getting worse, and even very rapidly. Yet despite this he was continually consulting them.

That month he went to see another celebrity, who told him almost the same as the first had done but put his questions rather differently, and the interview with this celebrity only increased Ivan Ilych's doubts and fears. A friend of a friend of his, a very good doctor, diagnosed his illness again quite differently from the others, and though he predicted recovery, his questions and suppositions bewildered Ivan Ilych still more and increased his doubts. A homoeopathist diagnosed the disease in yet another way, and prescribed medicine which Ivan Ilych took secretly for a week. But after a week, not feeling any improvement and having lost confidence both in the former doctor's treatment and in this one's, he became still more despondent. One day a lady acquaintance mentioned a cure effected by a wonder-working icon. Ivan Ilych caught himself listening attentively and beginning to believe that it had occurred. This incident alarmed him. 'Has my mind really weakened to such an extent?' he asked himself. 'Nonsense! It's all rubbish. I mustn't give way to nervous fears but having chosen a doctor must keep strictly to his treatment. That is what I will do. Now it's all settled. I won't think about it, but will follow the treatment seriously till summer, and then we shall see. From now there must be no more of this wavering!' This was easy to say but impossible to carry out. The pain in his side oppressed him and seemed to grow worse and more incessant, while the taste in his mouth grew stranger and stranger. It seemed to him that his breath had a disgusting smell, and he was conscious of a loss of appetite and strength. There was no deceiving himself: something terrible, new, and more important than anything before in his life, was taking place within him of which he alone was aware. Those about him did not understand or would not understand it, but thought everything in the world was going on as usual. That tormented Ivan Ilych more than anything. He saw that his household, especially his wife and daughter who were in a perfect whirl of visiting, did not understand anything of it and were annoyed that he was so depressed and so exacting, as if he were to blame for it. Though they tried to disguise it he saw that he was an obstacle in their path, and that his wife had adopted a definite line in regard to his illness and kept to it regardless of anything he said or did. Her attitude was this: 'You know,' she would say to her friends, 'Ivan Ilych can't do as other people do, and keep to the treatment prescribed for him. One day he'll take his drops and keep strictly to his diet and go to bed in good time, but the next day unless I watch him he'll suddenly forget his medicine, eat sturgeon – which is forbidden – and sit up playing cards till one o'clock in the morning.'

'Oh, come, when was that?' Ivan Ilych would ask in vexation. 'Only once at Peter Ivanovich's.'

'And yesterday with Shebek.'

'Well, even if I hadn't stayed up, this pain would have kept me awake.'

'Be that as it may you'll never get well like that, but will always make us wretched.'

Praskovya Fedorovna's attitude to Ivan Ilych's illness, as she expressed it both to others and to him, was that it was his own fault and was another of the annoyances he caused her. Ivan Ilych felt that this opinion escaped her involuntarily – but that did not make it easier for him.

At the law courts too, Ivan Ilych noticed, or thought he noticed, a strange attitude towards himself. It sometimes seemed to him that people were watching him inquisitively as a man whose place might soon be vacant. Then again, his friends would suddenly begin to chaff him in a friendly way about his low spirits, as if the awful, horrible, and unheard-of thing that was going on within him, incessantly gnawing at him and irresistibly drawing him away, was a very agreeable subject for jests. Schwartz in particular irritated him by his jocularity, vivacity, and *savoir-faire*, which reminded him of what he himself had been ten years ago.

Friends came to make up a set and they sat down to cards.

They dealt, bending the new cards to soften them, and he sorted the diamonds in his hand and found he had seven. His partner said 'No trumps' and supported him with two diamonds. What more could be wished for? It ought to be jolly and lively. They would make a grand slam. But suddenly Ivan Ilych was conscious of that gnawing pain, that taste in his mouth, and it seemed ridiculous that in such circumstances he should be pleased to make a grand slam.

He looked at his partner Mikhail Mikhaylovich, who rapped the table with his strong hand and instead of snatching up the tricks pushed the cards courteously and indulgently towards Ivan Ilych that he might have the pleasure of gathering them up without the trouble of stretching out his hand for them. 'Does he think I am too weak to stretch out my arm?' thought Ivan Ilych, and forgetting what he was doing he overtrumped his partner, missing the grand slam by three tricks. And what was most awful of all was that he saw how upset Mikhail Mikhaylovich was about it but did not himself care. And it was dreadful to realize why he did not care.

They all saw that he was suffering, and said: 'We can stop if you are tired. Take a rest.' Lie down? No, he was not at all tired, and he finished the rubber. All were gloomy and silent. Ivan Ilych felt that he had diffused this gloom over them and could not dispel it. They had supper and went away, and Ivan Ilych was left alone with the consciousness that his life was poisoned and was poisoning the lives of others, and that this poison did not weaken but penetrated more and more deeply into his whole being.

With this consciousness, and with physical pain besides the terror, he must go to bed, often to lie awake the greater part of the night. Next morning he had to get up again, dress, go to the law courts, speak, and write; or if he did not go out, spend at home those twenty-four hours a day each of which was a torture. And he had to live thus all alone on the brink of an abyss, with no one who understood or pitied him.

V

SO ONE month passed and then another. Just before the New Year his brother-in-law came to town and stayed at their house. Ivan Ilych was at the law courts and Praskovya Fedorovna had gone shopping. When Ivan Ilych came home and entered his study he found his brother-in-law there – a healthy, florid man – unpacking his portmanteau himself. He raised his head on hearing Ivan Ilych's footsteps and looked up at him for a moment without a word. That stare told Ivan Ilych everything. His brother-in-law opened his mouth to utter an exclamation of surprise but checked himself, and that action confirmed it all.

'I have changed, eh?'

'Yes, there is a change.'

And after that, try as he would to get his brother-in-law to return to the subject of his looks, the latter would say nothing about it. Praskovya Fedorovna came home and her brother went out to her. Ivan Ilych locked the door and began to examine himself in the glass, first full face, then in profile. He took up a portrait of himself taken with his wife, and compared it with what he saw in the glass. The change in him was immense. Then he bared his arms to the elbow, looked at them, drew the sleeves down again, sat down on an ottoman, and grew blacker than night.

'No, no, this won't do!' he said to himself, and jumped up, went to the table, took up some law papers and began to read them, but could not continue. He unlocked the door and went into the reception-room. The door leading to the drawing-room was shut. He approached it on tiptoe and listened.

'No, you are exaggerating!' Praskovya Fedorovna was saying.

'Exaggerating! Don't you see it? Why, he's a dead man! Look at his eyes – there's no light in them. But what is it that is wrong with him?'

'No one knows. Nikolaevich' (that was another doctor) 'said something, but I don't know what. And Leshchetitsky' (this was the celebrated specialist) 'said quite the contrary . . .'

Ivan Ilych walked away, went to his own room, lay down, and began musing: 'The kidney, a floating kidney.' He recalled all the doctors had told him of how it detached itself and swayed about. And by an effort of imagination he tried to catch that kidney and arrest it and support it. So little was needed for this, it seemed to him. 'No, I'll go to see Peter Ivanovich again.' (That was the friend whose friend was a doctor.) He rang, ordered the carriage, and got ready to go.

'Where are you going, Jean?' asked his wife, with a specially sad and exceptionally kind look.

This exceptionally kind look irritated him. He looked morosely at her.

'I must go to see Peter Ivanovich.'

He went to see Peter Ivanovich, and together they went to see his friend, the doctor. He was in, and Ivan Ilych had a long talk with him.

Reviewing the anatomical and physiological details of what in the doctor's opinion was going on inside him, he understood it all.

There was something, a small thing, in the vermiform appendix. It might all come right. Only stimulate the energy of one organ and check the activity of another, then absorption would take place and everything would come right. He got home rather late for dinner, ate his dinner, and conversed cheerfully, but could not for a long time bring himself to go back to work in his room. At last, however, he went to his study and did what was necessary, but the consciousness that he had put something aside – an important, intimate matter which he would revert to when his work was done – never left him. When he had finished his work he remembered that this intimate matter was the thought of his vermiform appendix. But he did not give himself up to it, and went to the drawing-room for tea. There were callers there, including the examining magistrate who was a desirable match for his daughter, and they were conversing, playing the piano, and singing. Ivan Ilych, as Praskovya Fedorovna remarked, spent that evening more cheerfully than usual, but he never for a moment forgot that he had postponed the important matter of the appendix. At eleven o'clock he said goodnight and went to his bedroom. Since his illness he had slept alone in a small room next to his study. He undressed and took up a novel by Zola, but instead of reading it he fell into thought, and in his imagination that desired improvement in the vermiform appendix occurred. There was the absorption and evacuation and the re-establishment of normal activity. 'Yes, that's it!' he said to himself. 'One need only assist nature, that's all.' He remembered his medicine, rose, took it, and lay down on his back watching for the beneficent action of the medicine and for it to lessen the pain. 'I need only take it regularly and avoid all injurious influences. I am already feeling better, much better.' He began touching his side: it was not painful to the touch. 'There, I really don't feel it. It's much better already.' He put out the light and turned on his side . . . 'The appendix is getting better, absorption is occurring.' Suddenly he felt the old, familiar, dull, gnawing pain, stubborn and serious. There was the same familiar loathsome taste in his mouth. His heart sank and he felt dazed. 'My God! My God!' he muttered. 'Again, again! And it will never cease.' And suddenly the matter presented itself in a quite different aspect. 'Vermiform appendix! Kidney!' he said to himself. 'It's not a question of appendix or kidney, but of life and . . . death. Yes, life was there and now it is going, going and I cannot stop it. Yes. Why deceive myself? Isn't it obvious to everyone but me that I'm dying, and that it's only a question of weeks, days . . . it may happen this moment. There was light and now there is darkness. I was here and now I'm going there! Where?' A chill came over him, his breathing ceased, and he felt only the throbbing of his heart.

'When I am not, what will there be? There will be nothing. Then where shall I be when I am no more? Can this be dying? No, I don't want to!' He jumped up and tried to light the candle, felt for it with trembling hands, dropped candle and candlestick on the floor, and fell back on his pillow.

'What's the use? It makes no difference,' he said to himself, staring with wide-open eyes into the darkness. 'Death. Yes, death. And none of them know or wish to know it, and they have no pity for me. Now they are playing.' (He heard through the door the distant sound of a song and its accompaniment.) 'It's all the same to them, but they will die too! Fools! I first, and they later, but it will be the same for them. And now they are merry . . . the beasts!'

Anger choked him and he was agonizingly, unbearably miserable. 'It is impossible that all men have been doomed to suffer this awful horror!' He raised himself.

'Something must be wrong. I must calm myself – must think

it all over from the beginning.' And he again began thinking. 'Yes, the beginning of my illness: I knocked my side, but I was still quite well that day and the next. It hurt a little, then rather more. I saw the doctors, then followed despondency and anguish, more doctors, and I drew nearer to the abyss. My strength grew less and I kept coming nearer and nearer, and now I have wasted away and there is no light in my eyes. I think of the appendix – but this is death! I think of mending the appendix, and all the while here is death! Can it really be death?' Again terror seized him and he gasped for breath. He leant down and began feeling for the matches, pressing with his elbow on the stand beside the bed. It was in his way and hurt him, he grew furious with it, pressed on it still harder, and upset it. Breathless and in despair he fell on his back, expecting death to come immediately.

Meanwhile the visitors were leaving. Praskovya Fedorovna was seeing them off. She heard something fall and came in.

'What has happened?'

'Nothing. I knocked it over accidentally.'

She went out and returned with a candle. He lay there panting heavily, like a man who has run a thousand yards, and stared upwards at her with a fixed look.

'What is it, Jean?'

'No . . . o . . . thing. I upset it.' ('Why speak of it? She won't understand,' he thought.)

And in truth she did not understand. She picked up the stand, lit his candle, and hurried away to see another visitor off. When she came back he still lay on his back, looking upwards.

'What is it? Do you feel worse?'

'Yes.'

She shook her head and sat down.

'Do you know, Jean, I think we must ask Leshchetitsky to come and see you here.'

This meant calling in the famous specialist, regardless of expense. He smiled malignantly and said 'No'. She remained a little longer and then went up to him and kissed his forehead.

While she was kissing him he hated her from the bottom of his soul and with difficulty refrained from pushing her away.

'Goodnight. Please God you'll sleep.'

'Yes.'

VI

IVAN ILÝCH saw that he was dying, and he was in continual despair.

In the depth of his heart he knew he was dying, but not only was he not accustomed to the thought, he simply did not and could not grasp it.

The syllogism he had learnt from Kiezewetter's Logic, 'Caius is a man, men are mortal, therefore Caius is mortal', had always seemed to him correct as applied to Caius, but certainly not as applied to himself. That Caius – man in the abstract – was mortal, was perfectly correct, but he was not Caius, not an abstract man, but a creature quite, quite separate from all others. He had been little Vanya, with a mamma and a papa, with Mitya and Volodya, with the toys, a coachman and a nurse, afterwards with Katenka and with all the joys, griefs, and delights of childhood, boyhood, and youth. What did Caius know of the smell of that striped leather ball Vanya had been so fond of? Had Caius kissed his mother's hand like that, and did the silk of her dress rustle so for Caius? Had he rioted like that at school when the pastry was bad? Had Caius been in love like that? Could Caius preside at a session as he did? 'Caius really was mortal, and it was right for him to die; but for me, little Vanya, Ivan Ilych, with all my thoughts and emotions, it's altogether a different matter. It cannot be that I ought to die. That would be too terrible.'

Such was his feeling.

'If I had to die like Caius I should have known it was so. An inner voice would have told me so, but there was nothing of the sort in me and I and all my friends felt that our case was quite different from that of Caius. And now here it is!' he said to himself. 'It can't be. It's impossible! But here it is. How is this? How is one to understand it?'

He could not understand it, and tried to drive this false, incorrect, morbid thought away and to replace it by other proper and healthy thoughts. But that thought, and not the thought only but the reality itself, seemed to come and confront him.

And to replace that thought he called up a succession of others, hoping to find in them some support. He tried to get back into the former current of thoughts that had once screened the thought of death from him. But strange to say, all that had formerly shut off, hidden, and destroyed, his consciousness of death, no longer had that effect. Ivan Ilych now spent most of his time in attempting to re-establish that old current. He would say to himself: 'I will take up my duties again – after all I used to live by them.' And banishing all doubts he would go to the law courts, enter into conversation with his colleagues, and sit carelessly as was his wont, scanning the crowd with a thoughtful look and leaning both his emaciated arms on the arms of his oak chair; bending over as usual to a colleague and drawing his papers nearer he would interchange whispers with him, and then suddenly raising his eyes and sitting erect would pronounce certain words and open the proceedings. But suddenly in the midst of those proceedings the pain in his side, regardless of the stage the proceedings had reached, would begin its own gnawing work. Ivan Ilych would turn his attention to it and try to drive the thought of it away, but without success. *It* would come and stand before him and look at him, and he would be petrified and the light would die out of his eyes, and he would again begin asking himself whether *It* alone was true. And his colleagues and subordinates would see with surprise and distress that he, the brilliant and subtle judge, was becoming confused and making mistakes. He would shake himself, try to pull himself together, manage somehow to bring the sitting to a close, and return home with the sorrowful consciousness that his judicial labours could not as formerly hide from him what he wanted them to hide, and could not deliver him from *It*. And what was worst of all was that *It* drew his attention to itself not in order to make him take some action, but only that he should look at *It*, look it straight in the face: look at it and without doing anything, suffer inexpressibly.

And to save himself from this condition Ivan Ilych looked for consolations – new screens – and new screens were found and for a while seemed to save him, but then they immediately fell to pieces or rather became transparent, as if *It* penetrated them and nothing could veil *It*.

In these latter days he would go into the drawing-room he had arranged – that drawing-room where he had fallen and for the sake of which (how bitterly ridiculous it seemed) he had sacrificed his life – for he knew that his illness originated with that knock. He would enter and see that something had scratched the polished table. He would look for the cause of this and find that it was the bronze ornamentation of an album, that had got bent. He would take up the expensive album which he had lovingly arranged, and feel vexed with his daughter and her friends for their untidiness – for the album was torn here and there and some of the photographs turned upside down. He would put it carefully in order and bend the ornamentation back into position. Then it would occur to him to place all those

327

things in another corner of the room, near the plants. He would call the footman, but his daughter or wife would come to help him. They would not agree, and his wife would contradict him, and he would dispute and grow angry. But that was all right, for then he did not think about *It*. *It* was invisible.

But then, when he was moving something himself, his wife would say: 'Let the servants do it. You will hurt yourself again.' And suddenly *It* would flash through the screen and he would see it. It was just a flash, and he hoped it would disappear, but he would involuntarily pay attention to his side. 'It sits there as before, gnawing just the same!' And he could no longer forget *It*, but could distinctly see it looking at him from behind the flowers. 'What is it all for?'

'It really is so! I lost my life over that curtain as I might have done when storming a fort. Is that possible? How terrible and how stupid. It can't be true! It can't, but it is.'

He would go to his study, lie down, and again be alone with *It*: face to face with *It*. And nothing could be done with *It* except to look at it and shudder.

VII

HOW IT happened it is impossible to say because it came about step by step, unnoticed, but in the third month of Ivan Ilych's illness, his wife, his daughter, his son, his acquaintances, the doctors, the servants, and above all he himself, were aware that the whole interest he had for other people was whether he would soon vacate his place, and at last release the living from the discomfort caused by his presence and be himself released from his sufferings.

He slept less and less. He was given opium and hypodermic injections of morphine, but this did not relieve him. The dull depression he experienced in a somnolent condition at first gave him a little relief, but only as something new, afterwards it became as distressing as the pain itself or even more so.

Special foods were prepared for him by the doctors' orders, but all those foods became increasingly distasteful and disgusting to him.

For his excretions also special arrangements had to be made, and this was a torment to him every time – a torment from the uncleanliness, the unseemliness, and the smell, and from knowing that another person had to take part in it.

But just through this most unpleasant matter, Ivan Ilych obtained comfort. Gerasim, the butler's young assistant, always came in to carry the things out. Gerasim was a clean, fresh peasant lad, grown stout on town food and always cheerful and bright. At first the sight of him, in his clean Russian peasant costume, engaged on that disgusting task embarrassed Ivan Ilych.

Once when he got up from the commode too weak to draw up his trousers, he dropped into a soft armchair and looked with horror at his bare, enfeebled thighs with the muscles so sharply marked on them.

Gerasim with a firm light tread, his heavy boots emitting a pleasant smell of tar and fresh winter air, came in wearing a clean hessian apron, the sleeves of his print shirt tucked up over his strong bare young arms; and refraining from looking at his sick master out of consideration for his feelings, and restraining the joy of life that beamed from his face, he went up to the commode.

'Gerasim!' said Ivan Ilych in a weak voice.

Gerasim started, evidently afraid he might have committed some blunder, and with a rapid movement turned his fresh, kind, simple young face which just showed the first downy signs of a beard.

'Yes, sir?'

'That must be very unpleasant for you. You must forgive me. I am helpless.'

'Oh, why, sir,' and Gerasim's eyes beamed and he showed his glistening white teeth, 'what's a little trouble? It's a case of illness with you, sir.'

And his deft strong hands did their accustomed task, and he went out of the room stepping lightly. Five minutes later he as lightly returned.

Ivan Ilych was still sitting in the same position in the armchair.

'Gerasim,' he said when the latter had replaced the freshly washed utensil. 'Please come here and help me.' Gerasim went up to him. 'Lift me up. It is hard for me to get up, and I have sent Dmitri away.'

Gerasim went up to him, grasped his master with his strong arms deftly but gently, in the same way that he stepped – lifted him, supported him with one hand, and with the other drew up his trousers and would have set him down again, but Ivan Ilych asked to be led to the sofa. Gerasim, without an effort and without apparent pressure, led him, almost lifting him, to the sofa and placed him on it.

'Thank you. How easily and well you do it all!'

Gerasim smiled again and turned to leave the room. But Ivan Ilych felt his presence such a comfort that he did not want to let him go.

'One thing more, please move up that chair. No, the other one – under my feet. It is easier for me when my feet are raised.'

Gerasim brought the chair, set it down gently in place, and raised Ivan Ilych's legs onto it. It seemed to Ivan Ilych that he felt better while Gerasim was holding up his legs.

'It's better when my legs are higher,' he said. 'Place that cushion under them.'

Gerasim did so. He again lifted the legs and placed them, and again Ivan Ilych felt better while Gerasim held his legs. When he set them down Ivan Ilych fancied he felt worse.

'Gerasim,' he said. 'Are you busy now?'

'Not at all, sir,' said Gerasim, who had learnt from the townsfolk how to speak to gentlefolk.

'What have you still to do?'

'What have I to do? I've done everything except chopping the logs for tomorrow.'

'Then hold my legs up a bit higher, can you?'

'Of course I can. Why not?' And Gerasim raised his master's legs higher and Ivan Ilych thought that in that position he did not feel any pain at all.

'And how about the logs?'

'Don't trouble about that, sir. There's plenty of time.'

Ivan Ilych told Gerasim to sit down and hold his legs, and began to talk to him. And strange to say it seemed to him that he felt better while Gerasim held his legs up.

After that Ivan Ilych would sometimes call Gerasim and get him to hold his legs on his shoulders, and he liked talking to him. Gerasim did it all easily, willingly, simply, and with a good nature that touched Ivan Ilych. Health, strength, and vitality in other people were offensive to him, but Gerasim's strength and vitality did not mortify but soothed him.

What tormented Ivan Ilych most was the deception, the lie, which for some reason they all accepted, that he was not dying but was simply ill, and that he only need keep quiet and undergo a treatment and then something very good would result. He however knew that do what they would nothing would come of it, only still more agonizing suffering and death. This deception tortured him – their not wishing to admit what they all knew and what he knew, but wanting to lie to him concerning his terrible condition, and wishing and forcing him to participate in that lie.

Those lies – lies enacted over him on the eve of his death and destined to degrade this awful, solemn act to the level of their visitings, their curtains, their sturgeon for dinner – were a terrible agony for Ivan Ilych. And strangely enough, many times when they were going through their antics over him he had been within a hairbreadth of calling out to them: 'Stop lying! You know and I know that I am dying. Then at least stop lying about it!' But he had never had the spirit to do it. The awful, terrible act of his dying was, he could see, reduced by those about him to the level of a casual, unpleasant, and almost indecorous incident (as if someone entered a drawing-room diffusing an unpleasant odour) and this was done by that very decorum which he had served all his life long. He saw that no one felt for him, because no one even wished to grasp his position. Only Gerasim recognized it and pitied him. And so Ivan Ilych felt at ease only with him. He felt comforted when Gerasim supported his legs (sometimes all night long) and refused to go to bed, saying: 'Don't you worry, Ivan Ilych. I'll get sleep enough later on,' or when he suddenly became familiar and exclaimed: 'If you weren't sick it would be another matter, but as it is, why should I grudge a little trouble?' Gerasim alone did not lie; everything showed that he alone understood the facts of the case and did not consider it necessary to disguise them, but simply felt sorry for his emaciated and enfeebled master. Once when Ivan Ilych was sending him away he even said straight out: 'We shall all of us die, so why should I grudge a little trouble?' – expressing the fact that he did not think his work burdensome, because he was doing it for a dying man and hoped someone would do the same for him when his time came.

Apart from this lying, or because of it, what most tormented Ivan Ilych was that no one pitied him as he wished to be pitied. At certain moments after prolonged suffering he wished most of all (though he would have been ashamed to confess it) for someone to pity him as a sick child is pitied. He longed to be petted and comforted. He knew he was an important functionary, that he had a beard turning grey, and that therefore what he longed for was impossible, but still he longed for it. And in Gerasim's attitude towards him there was something akin to what he wished for, and so that attitude comforted him. Ivan Ilych wanted to weep, wanted to be petted and cried over, and then his colleague Shebek would come, and instead of weeping and being petted, Ivan Ilych would assume a serious, severe, and profound air, and by force of habit would express his opinion on a decision of the Court of Cassation and would stubbornly insist on that view. This falsity around him and within him did more than anything else to poison his last days.

VIII

IT WAS morning. He knew it was morning because Gerasim had gone, and Peter the footman had come and put out the candles, drawn back one of the curtains, and begun quietly to tidy up. Whether it was morning or evening, Friday or Sunday, made no difference, it was all just the same: the gnawing, unmitigated, agonizing pain, never ceasing for an instant, the consciousness of life inexorably waning but not yet extinguished, the approach of that ever dreaded and hateful Death which was the only reality, and always the same falsity. What were days, weeks, hours, in such a case?

'Will you have some tea, sir?'

'He wants things to be regular, and wishes the gentlefolk to drink tea in the morning,' thought Ivan Ilych, and only said 'No'.

'Wouldn't you like to move onto the sofa, sir?'

'He wants to tidy up the room, and I'm in the way. I am uncleanliness and disorder,' he thought, and said only:

'No, leave me alone.'

The man went on bustling about. Ivan Ilych stretched out his hand. Peter came up, ready to help.

'What is it, sir?'

'My watch.'

Peter took the watch which was close at hand and gave it to his master.

'Half-past eight. Are they up?'

'No sir, except Vladimir Ivanich' (the son) 'who has gone to school. Praskovya Fedorovna ordered me to wake her if you asked for her. Shall I do so?'

'No, there's no need to.' 'Perhaps I'd better have some tea,' he thought, and added aloud: 'Yes, bring me some tea.'

Peter went to the door, but Ivan Ilych dreaded being left alone. 'How can I keep him here? Oh yes, my medicine.' 'Peter, give me my medicine.' 'Why not? Perhaps it may still do me some good.' He took a spoonful and swallowed it. 'No, it won't help. It's all tomfoolery, all deception,' he decided as soon as he became aware of the familiar, sickly, hopeless taste. 'No, I can't believe in it any longer. But the pain, why this pain? If it would only cease just for a moment!' And he moaned. Peter turned towards him. 'It's all right. Go and fetch me some tea.'

Peter went out. Left alone, Ivan Ilych groaned not so much with pain, terrible though that was, as from mental anguish. Always and for ever the same, always these endless days and nights. If only it would come quicker! If only *what* would come quicker? Death, darkness? . . . No, no! Anything rather than death!

When Peter returned with the tea on a tray, Ivan Ilych stared at him for a time in perplexity, not realizing who and what he was. Peter was disconcerted by that look and his embarrassment brought Ivan Ilych to himself.

'Oh, tea! All right, put it down. Only help me to wash and put on a clean shirt.'

And Ivan Ilych began to wash. With pauses for rest, he washed his hands and then his face, cleaned his teeth, brushed his hair, and looked in the glass. He was terrified by what he saw, especially by the limp way in which his hair clung to his pallid forehead.

While his shirt was being changed he knew that he would be still more frightened at the sight of his body, so he avoided looking at it. Finally he was ready. He drew on a dressing-gown, wrapped himself in a plaid, and sat down in the armchair to take his tea. For a moment he felt refreshed, but as soon as he began to drink the tea he was again aware of the same taste, and the pain also returned. He finished it with an effort, and then lay down stretching out his legs, and dismissed Peter.

Always the same. Now a spark of hope flashes up, then a sea of despair rages, and always pain; always pain, always despair, and always the same. When alone he had a dreadful and distressing desire to call someone, but he knew beforehand that with others present it would be still worse. 'Another dose of morphine – to lose consciousness. I will tell him, the doctor, that he must think of something else. It's impossible, impossible, to go on like this.'

An hour and another pass like that. But now there is a ring at the door bell. Perhaps it's the doctor? It is. He comes in fresh, hearty, plump, and cheerful, with that look on his face that seems to say: 'There now, you're in a panic about something, but we'll arrange it all for you directly!' The doctor knows this expression is out of place here, but he has put it on once for all and can't take it off – like a man who has put on a frock-coat in the morning to pay a round of calls.

The doctor rubs his hands vigorously and reassuringly.

'Brr! How cold it is! There's such a sharp frost; just let me warm myself!' he says, as if it were only a matter of waiting till he was warm, and then he would put everything right.

'Well now, how are you?'

Ivan Ilych feels that the doctor would like to say: 'Well, how are our affairs?' but that even he feels that this would not do, and says instead: 'What sort of a night have you had?'

Ivan Ilych looks at him as much as to say: 'Are you really never ashamed of lying?' But the doctor does not wish to understand this question, and Ivan Ilych says: 'Just as terrible as ever. The pain never leaves me and never subsides. If only something . . .'

'Yes, you sick people are always like that . . . There, now I think I am warm enough. Even Praskovya Fedorovna, who is so particular, could find no fault with my temperature. Well, now I can say good morning,' and the doctor presses his patient's hand.

Then, dropping his former playfulness, he begins with a most serious face to examine the patient, feeling his pulse and taking his temperature, and then begins the sounding and auscultation.

Ivan Ilych knows quite well and definitely that all this is

nonsense and pure deception, but when the doctor, getting down on his knee, leans over him, putting his ear first higher then lower, and performs various gymnastic movements over him with a significant expression on his face, Ivan Ilych submits to it all as he used to submit to the speeches of the lawyers, though he knew very well that they were all lying and why they were lying.

The doctor, kneeling on the sofa, is still sounding him when Praskovya Fedorovna's silk dress rustles at the door and she is heard scolding Peter for not having let her know of the doctor's arrival.

She comes in, kisses her husband, and at once proceeds to prove that she has been up a long time already, and only owing to a misunderstanding failed to be there when the doctor arrived.

Ivan Ilych looks at her, scans her all over, sets against her the whiteness and plumpness and cleanness of her hands and neck, the gloss of her hair, and the sparkle of her vivacious eyes. He hates her with his whole soul. And the thrill of hatred he feels for her makes him suffer from her touch.

Her attitude towards him and his disease is still the same. Just as the doctor had adopted a certain relation to his patient which he could not abandon, so had she formed one towards him – that he was not doing something he ought to do and was himself to blame, and that she reproached him lovingly for this – and she could not now change that attitude.

'You see he doesn't listen to me and doesn't take his medicine at the proper time. And above all he lies in a position that is no doubt bad for him – with his legs up.'

She described how he made Gerasim hold his legs up.

The doctor smiled with a contemptuous affability that said: 'What's to be done? These sick people do have foolish fancies of that kind, but we must forgive them.'

When the examination was over the doctor looked at his watch, and then Praskovya Fedorovna announced to Ivan Ilych that it was of course as he pleased, but she had sent today for a celebrated specialist who would examine him and have a consultation with Michael Danilovich (their regular doctor).

'Please don't raise any objections. I am doing this for my own sake,' she said ironically, letting it be felt that she was doing it all for his sake and only said this to leave him no right to refuse. He remained silent, knitting his brows. He felt that he was so surrounded and involved in a mesh of falsity that it was hard to unravel anything.

Everything she did for him was entirely for her own sake, and she told him she was doing for herself what she actually was doing for herself, as if that was so incredible that he must understand the opposite.

At half-past eleven the celebrated specialist arrived. Again the sounding began and the significant conversations in his presence and in another room, about the kidneys and the appendix, and the questions and answers, with such an air of importance that again, instead of the real question of life and death which now alone confronted him, the question arose of the kidney and appendix which were not behaving as they ought to and would now be attacked by Michael Danilovich and the specialist and forced to amend their ways.

The celebrated specialist took leave of him with a serious though not hopeless look, and in reply to the timid question Ivan Ilych, with eyes glistening with fear and hope, put to him as to whether there was a chance of recovery, said that he could not vouch for it but there was a possibility. The look of hope with which Ivan Ilych watched the doctor out was so pathetic that Praskovya Fedorovna, seeing it, even wept as she left the room to hand the doctor his fee.

The gleam of hope kindled by the doctor's encouragement did not last long. The same room, the same pictures, curtains, wall-paper, medicine bottles, were all there, and the same aching suffering body, and Ivan Ilych began to moan. They gave him a subcutaneous injection and he sank into oblivion.

It was twilight when he came to. They brought him his dinner and he swallowed some beef tea with difficulty, and then everything was the same again and night was coming on.

After dinner, at seven o'clock, Praskovya Fedorovna came into the room in evening dress, her full bosom pushed up by her corset, and with traces of powder on her face. She had reminded him in the morning that they were going to the theatre. Sarah Bernhardt was visiting the town and they had a box, which he had insisted on their taking. Now he had forgotten about it and her toilet offended him, but he concealed his vexation when he remembered that he had himself insisted on their securing a box and going because it would be an instructive and aesthetic pleasure for the children.

Praskovya Fedorovna came in, self-satisfied but yet with a rather guilty air. She sat down and asked how he was, but, as he saw, only for the sake of asking and not in order to learn about it, knowing that there was nothing to learn – and then went on to what she really wanted to say: that she would not on any account have gone but that the box had been taken and Helen and their daughter were going, as well as Petrishchev (the examining magistrate, their daughter's fiancé) and that it was out of the question to let them go alone; but that she would have much preferred to sit with him for a while; and he must be sure to follow the doctor's orders while she was away.

'Oh, and Fedor Petrovich' (the fiancé) 'would like to come in. May he? And Lisa?'

'All right.'

Their daughter came in in full evening dress, her fresh young flesh exposed (making a show of that very flesh which in his own case caused so much suffering), strong, healthy, evidently in love, and impatient with illness, suffering, and death, because they interfered with her happiness.

Fedor Petrovich came in too, in evening dress, his hair curled *à la Capoul*, a tight stiff collar round his long sinewy neck, an enormous white shirt-front and narrow black trousers tightly stretched over his strong thighs. He had one white glove tightly drawn on, and was holding his opera hat in his hand.

Following him the schoolboy crept in unnoticed, in a new uniform, poor little fellow, and wearing gloves. Terribly dark shadows showed under his eyes, the meaning of which Ivan Ilych knew well.

His son had always seemed pathetic to him, and now it was dreadful to see the boy's frightened look of pity. It seemed to Ivan Ilych that Vasya was the only one besides Gerasim who understood and pitied him.

They all sat down and again asked how he was. A silence followed. Lisa asked her mother about the opera-glasses, and there was an altercation between mother and daughter as to who had taken them and where they had been put. This occasioned some unpleasantness.

Fedor Petrovich inquired of Ivan Ilych whether he had ever seen Sarah Bernhardt. Ivan Ilych did not at first catch the question, but then replied: 'No, have you seen her before?'

'Yes, in *Adrienne Lecouvreur*.'

Praskovya Fedorovna mentioned some rôles in which Sarah Bernhardt was particularly good. Her daughter disagreed. Conversation sprang up as to the elegance and realism of her acting – the sort of conversation that is always repeated and is always the same.

In the midst of the conversation Fedor Petrovich glanced at Ivan Ilych and became silent. The others also looked at him and grew silent. Ivan Ilych was staring with glittering eyes straight before him, evidently indignant with them. This had to be rectified, but it was impossible to do so. The silence had to be broken, but for a time no one dared to break it and they all became afraid that the conventional deception would suddenly become obvious and the truth become plain to all. Lisa was the first to pluck up courage and break that silence, but by trying to hide what everybody was feeling, she betrayed it.

'Well, if we are going it's time to start,' she said, looking at her watch, a present from her father, and with a faint and significant smile at Fedor Petrovich relating to something known only to them. She got up with a rustle of her dress.

They all rose, said goodnight, and went away.

When they had gone it seemed to Ivan Ilych that he felt better; the falsity had gone with them. But the pain remained — that same pain and that same fear that made everything monotonously alike, nothing harder and nothing easier. Everything was worse.

Again minute followed minute and hour followed hour. Everything remained the same and there was no cessation. And the inevitable end of it all became more and more terrible.

'Yes, send Gerasim here,' he replied to a question Peter asked.

IX

HIS WIFE returned late at night. She came in on tiptoe, but he heard her, opened his eyes, and made haste to close them again. She wished to send Gerasim away and to sit with him herself, but he opened his eyes and said: 'No, go away.'

'Are you in great pain?'

'Always the same.'

'Take some opium.'

He agreed and took some. She went away.

Till about three in the morning he was in a state of stupefied misery. It seemed to him that he and his pain were being thrust into a narrow, deep black sack, but though they were pushed further and further in they could not be pushed to the bottom. And this, terrible enough in itself, was accompanied by suffering. He was frightened yet wanted to fall through the sack, he struggled but yet co-operated. And suddenly he broke through, fell, and regained consciousness. Gerasim was sitting at the foot of the bed dozing quietly and patiently, while he himself lay with his emaciated stockinged legs resting on Gerasim's shoulders; the same shaded candle was there and the same unceasing pain.

'Go away, Gerasim,' he whispered.

'It's all right, sir. I'll stay a while.'

'No. Go away.'

He removed his legs from Gerasim's shoulders, turned

sideways onto his arm, and felt sorry for himself. He only waited till Gerasim had gone into the next room and then restrained himself no longer but wept like a child. He wept on account of his helplessness, his terrible loneliness, the cruelty of man, the cruelty of God, and the absence of God.

'Why hast Thou done all this? Why hast Thou brought me here? Why, why dost Thou torment me so terribly?'

He did not expect an answer and yet wept because there was no answer and could be none. The pain again grew more acute, but he did not stir and did not call. He said to himself: 'Go on! Strike me! But what is it for? What have I done to Thee? What is it for?'

Then he grew quiet and not only ceased weeping but even held his breath and became all attention. It was as though he were listening not to an audible voice but to the voice of his soul, to the current of thoughts arising within him.

'What is it you want?' was the first clear conception capable of expression in words, that he heard.

'What do you want? What do you want?' he repeated to himself.

'What do I want? To live and not to suffer,' he answered.

And again he listened with such concentrated attention that even his pain did not distract him.

'To live? How?' asked his inner voice.

'Why, to live as I used to – well and pleasantly.'

'As you lived before, well and pleasantly?' the voice repeated.

And in imagination he began to recall the best moments of his pleasant life. But strange to say none of those best moments of his pleasant life now seemed at all what they had then seemed — none of them except the first recollections of childhood. There, in childhood, there had been something really pleasant with which it would be possible to live if it could return. But the child who had experienced that happiness existed no longer, it was like a reminiscence of somebody else.

As soon as the period began which had produced the present Ivan Ilych, all that had then seemed joys now melted before his sight and turned into something trivial and often nasty.

And the further he departed from childhood and the nearer he came to the present, the more worthless and doubtful were the joys. This began with the School of Law. A little that was really good was still found there — there was light-heartedness, friendship, and hope. But in the upper classes there had already been fewer of such good moments. Then during the first years of his official career, when he was in the service of the Governor, some pleasant moments again occurred: they were the memories of love for a woman. Then all became confused and there was still less of what was good; later on again there was still less that was good, and the further he went the less there was. His marriage, a mere accident, then the disenchantment that followed it, his wife's bad breath and the sensuality and hypocrisy: then that deadly official life and those preoccupations about money, a year of it, and two, and ten, and twenty, and always the same thing. And the longer it lasted the more deadly it became. 'It is as if I had been going downhill while I imagined I was going up. And that is really what it was. I was going up in public opinion, but to the same extent life was ebbing away from me. And now it is all done and there is only death.'

'Then what does it mean? Why? It can't be that life is so senseless and horrible. But if it really has been so horrible and senseless, why must I die and die in agony? There is something wrong!'

'Maybe I did not live as I ought to have done,' it suddenly occurred to him. 'But how could that be, when I did everything properly?' he replied, and immediately dismissed from his mind this, the sole solution of all the riddles of life and death, as something quite impossible.

'Then what do you want now? To live? Live how? Live as you lived in the law courts when the usher proclaimed "The judge is coming!" The judge is coming, the judge!' he repeated to himself. 'Here he is, the judge. But I am not guilty!' he exclaimed angrily. 'What is it for?' And he ceased crying, but turning his face to the wall continued to ponder on the same question: Why, and for what purpose, is there all this horror? But however much he pondered he found no answer. And whenever the thought occurred to him, as it often did, that it all resulted from his not having lived as he ought to have done, he at once recalled the correctness of his whole life and dismissed so strange an idea.

X

ANOTHER FORTNIGHT passed. Ivan Ilych now no longer left his sofa. He would not lie in bed but lay on the sofa, facing the wall nearly all the time. He suffered ever the same unceasing agonies and in his loneliness pondered always on the same insoluble question: 'What is this? Can it be that it is Death?' And the inner voice answered: 'Yes, it is Death.'

'Why these sufferings?' And the voice answered, 'For no reason – they just are so.' Beyond and besides this there was nothing.

From the very beginning of his illness, ever since he had first been to see the doctor, Ivan Ilych's life had been divided between two contrary and alternating moods: now it was despair and the expectation of this uncomprehended and terrible death, and now hope and an intently interested observation of the functioning of his organs. Now before his eyes there was only a kidney or an intestine that temporarily evaded its duty, and now only that incomprehensible and dreadful death from which it was impossible to escape.

These two states of mind had alternated from the very beginning of his illness, but the further it progressed the more doubtful and fantastic became the conception of the kidney, and the more real the sense of impending death.

He had but to call to mind what he had been three months

before and what he was now, to call to mind with what regularity he had been going downhill, for every possibility of hope to be shattered.

Latterly during that loneliness in which he found himself as he lay facing the back of the sofa, a loneliness in the midst of a populous town and surrounded by numerous acquaintances and relations but that yet could not have been more complete anywhere – either at the bottom of the sea or under the earth – during that terrible loneliness Ivan Ilych had lived only in memories of the past. Pictures of his past rose before him one after another. They always began with what was nearest in time and then went back to what was most remote – to his childhood – and rested there. If he thought of the stewed prunes that had been offered him that day, his mind went back to the raw shrivelled French plums of his childhood, their peculiar flavour and the flow of saliva when he sucked their stones, and along with the memory of that taste came a whole series of memories of those days: his nurse, his brother, and their toys. 'No, I mustn't think of that . . . It is too painful,' Ivan Ilych said to himself, and brought himself back to the present – to the button on the back of the sofa and the creases in its morocco. 'Morocco is expensive, but it does not wear well: there had been a quarrel about it. It was a different kind of quarrel and a different kind of morocco that time when we tore father's portfolio and were punished, and mamma brought us some tarts . . .' And again his thoughts dwelt on his childhood, and again it was painful and he tried to banish them and fix his mind on something else.

Then again together with that chain of memories another series passed through his mind – of how his illness had progressed and grown worse. There also the further back he looked the more life there had been. There had been more of what was good in life and more of life itself. The two merged together. 'Just as the pain went on getting worse and worse, so my life grew worse and worse,' he thought. 'There is one bright spot there at the back, at the beginning of life, and afterwards all becomes blacker and blacker and proceeds more and more rapidly – in inverse ratio to the square of the distance from death,' thought Ivan Ilych. And the example of a stone falling downwards with increasing velocity entered his mind. Life, a series of increasing sufferings, flies further and further towards its end – the most terrible suffering. 'I am flying . . .' He shuddered, shifted himself, and tried to resist, but was already aware that resistance was impossible, and again with eyes weary of gazing but unable to cease seeing what was before them, he stared at the back of the sofa and waited – awaiting that dreadful fall and shock and destruction.

'Resistance is impossible!' he said to himself. 'If I could only understand what it is all for! But that too is impossible. An explanation would be possible if it could be said that I have not lived as I ought to. But it is impossible to say that,' and he remembered all the legality, correctitude, and propriety of his life. 'That at any rate can certainly not be admitted,' he thought, and his lips smiled ironically as if someone could see that smile and be taken in by it. 'There is no explanation! Agony, death . . . What for?'

XI

ANOTHER TWO weeks went by in this way and during that fortnight an event occurred that Ivan Ilych and his wife had desired. Petrishchev formally proposed. It happened in the evening. The next day Praskovya Fedorovna came into her husband's room considering how best to inform him of it, but that very night there had been a fresh change for the worse in his condition. She found him still lying on the sofa but in a different position. He lay on his back, groaning and staring fixedly straight in front of him.

She began to remind him of his medicines, but he turned his eyes towards her with such a look that she did not finish what she was saying; so great an animosity, to her in particular, did that look express.

'For Christ's sake let me die in peace!' he said.

She would have gone away, but just then their daughter came in and went up to say good morning. He looked at her as he had done at his wife, and in reply to her inquiry about his health said drily that he would soon free them all of himself. They were both silent and after sitting with him for a while went away.

'Is it our fault?' Lisa said to her mother. 'It's as if we were to blame! I am sorry for papa, but why should we be tortured?'

The doctor came at his usual time. Ivan Ilych answered 'Yes' and 'No', never taking his angry eyes from him, and at last said: 'You know you can do nothing for me, so leave me alone.'

'We can ease your sufferings.'

'You can't even do that. Let me be.'

The doctor went into the drawing-room and told Praskovya Fedorovna that the case was very serious and that the only resource left was opium to allay her husband's sufferings, which must be terrible.

It was true, as the doctor said, that Ivan Ilych's physical sufferings were terrible, but worse than the physical sufferings were his mental sufferings which were his chief torture.

His mental sufferings were due to the fact that that night, as he looked at Gerasim's sleepy, good-natured face with its prominent cheek-bones, the question suddenly occurred to him: 'What if my whole life has really been wrong?'

It occurred to him that what had appeared perfectly impossible before, namely that he had not spent his life as he should have done, might after all be true. It occurred to him that his scarcely perceptible attempts to struggle against what was considered good by the most highly placed people, those scarcely noticeable impulses which he had immediately suppressed, might have been the real thing, and all the rest false. And his professional duties and the whole arrangement of his life and of his family, and all his social and official interests, might all have been false. He tried to defend all those things to himself and suddenly felt the weakness of what he was defending. There was nothing to defend.

'But if that is so,' he said to himself, 'and I am leaving this life with the consciousness that I have lost all that was given me and it is impossible to rectify it – what then?'

He lay on his back and began to pass his life in review in quite a new way. In the morning when he saw first his footman, then his wife, then his daughter, and then the doctor, their every word and movement confirmed to him the awful truth that had been revealed to him during the night. In them he saw himself – all that for which he had lived – and saw clearly that it was not real at all, but a terrible and huge deception which had hidden both life and death. This consciousness intensified his physical suffering tenfold. He groaned and tossed about, and pulled at his clothing which choked and stifled him. And he hated them on that account.

He was given a large dose of opium and became unconscious, but at noon his sufferings began again. He drove everybody away and tossed from side to side.

His wife came to him and said:

'Jean, my dear, do this for me. It can't do any harm and often helps. Healthy people often do it.'

He opened his eyes wide.

'What? Take Communion? Why? It's unnecessary! However . . .'

She began to cry.

'Yes, do, my dear. I'll send for our priest. He is such a nice man.'

'All right. Very well,' he muttered.

When the priest came and heard his confession, Ivan Ilych was softened and seemed to feel a relief from his doubts and consequently from his sufferings, and for a moment there came a ray of hope. He again began to think of the vermiform appendix and the possibility of correcting it. He received the sacrament with tears in his eyes.

When they laid him down again afterwards he felt a moment's ease, and the hope that he might live awoke in him again. He began to think of the operation that had been suggested to him. 'To live! I want to live!' he said to himself.

His wife came in to congratulate him after his Communion, and when uttering the usual conventional words she added:

'You feel better, don't you?'

Without looking at her he said, 'Yes.'

Her dress, her figure, the expression of her face, the tone of her voice, all revealed the same thing. 'This is wrong, it is not as it should be. All you have lived for and still live for is falsehood and deception, hiding life and death from you.' And as soon as he admitted that thought, his hatred and his agonizing physical suffering again sprang up, and with that suffering a consciousness of the unavoidable, approaching end. And to this was added a new sensation of grinding shooting pain and a feeling of suffocation.

The expression of his face when he uttered that 'yes' was dreadful. Having uttered it, he looked her straight in the eyes, turned on his face with a rapidity extraordinary in his weak state and shouted:

'Go away! Go away and leave me alone!'

XII

FROM THAT moment the screaming began that continued for three days, and was so terrible that one could not hear it through two closed doors without horror. At the moment he answered his wife he realized that he was lost, that there was no return, that the end had come, the very end, and his doubts were still unsolved and remained doubts.

'Oh! Oh! Oh!' he cried in various intonations. He had begun by screaming 'I won't!' and continued screaming on the letter 'o'.

For three whole days, during which time did not exist for him, he struggled in that black sack into which he was being thrust by an invisible, resistless force. He struggled as a man condemned to death struggles in the hands of the executioner, knowing that he cannot save himself. And every moment he felt that despite all his efforts he was drawing nearer and nearer to what terrified him. He felt that his agony was due to his being thrust into that black hole and still more to his not being able to get right into it. He was hindered from getting into it by his conviction that his life had been a good one. That very justification of his life held him fast and prevented his moving forward, and it caused him most torment of all.

Suddenly some force struck him in the chest and side, making it still harder to breathe, and he fell through the hole and there at the bottom was a light. What had happened to him was like the sensation one sometimes experiences in a railway carriage when one thinks one is going backwards while one is really going forwards and suddenly becomes aware of the real direction.

'Yes, it was all not the right thing,' he said to himself, 'but that's no matter. It can be done. But what *is* the right thing?' he asked himself, and suddenly grew quiet.

This occurred at the end of the third day, two hours before his death. Just then his schoolboy son had crept softly in and gone up to the bedside. The dying man was still screaming desperately and waving his arms. His hand fell on the boy's head, and the boy caught it, pressed it to his lips, and began to cry.

At that very moment Ivan Ilych fell through and caught sight of the light, and it was revealed to him that though his life had not been what it should have been, this could still be rectified. He asked himself, 'What *is* the right thing?' and grew still, listening. Then he felt that someone was kissing his hand. He opened his eyes, looked at his son, and felt sorry for him. His wife came up to him and he glanced at her. She was gazing at him open-mouthed, with undried tears on her nose and cheek and a despairing look on her face. He felt sorry for her too.

'Yes, I am making them wretched,' he thought. 'They are sorry, but it will be better for them when I die.' He wished to say this but had not the strength to utter it. 'Besides, why speak? I must act,' he thought. With a look at his wife he indicated his son and said: 'Take him away . . . sorry for him . . . sorry for you too . . .' He tried to add, 'Forgive me,' but said 'Forego' and waved his hand, knowing that He whose understanding mattered would understand.

And suddenly it grew clear to him that what had been oppressing him and would not leave him was all dropping away at once from two sides, from ten sides, and from all sides. He was sorry for them, he must act so as not to hurt them: release them and free himself from these sufferings. 'How good and how simple!' he thought. 'And the pain?' he asked himself. 'What has become of it? Where are you, pain?'

He turned his attention to it.

'Yes, here it is. Well, what of it? Let the pain be.'

'And death . . . where is it?'

He sought his former accustomed fear of death and did not find it. 'Where is it? What death?' There was no fear because there was no death.

In place of death there was light.

'So that's what it is!' he suddenly exclaimed aloud. 'What joy!'

To him all this happened in a single instant, and the meaning of that instant did not change. For those present his agony continued for another two hours. Something rattled in his throat, his emaciated body twitched, then the gasping and rattle became less and less frequent.

'It is finished!' said someone near him.

He heard these words and repeated them in his soul.

'Death is finished,' he said to himself. 'It is no more!'

He drew in a breath, stopped in the midst of a sigh, stretched out, and died.

How Much Land Does a Man Need?

I

A N ELDER SISTER came to visit her younger sister in the country. The elder was married to a tradesman in town, the younger to a peasant in the village. As the sisters sat over their tea talking, the elder began to boast of the advantages of town life: saying how comfortably they lived there, how well they dressed, what fine clothes her children wore, what good things they ate and drank, and how she went to the theatre, promenades, and entertainments.

The younger sister was piqued, and in turn disparaged the life of a tradesman, and stood up for that of a peasant.

'I would not change my way of life for yours,' said she. 'We may live roughly, but at least we are free from anxiety. You live in better style than we do, but though you often earn more than you need, you are very likely to lose all you have. You know the proverb, "Loss and gain are brothers twain". It often happens that people who are wealthy one day are begging their bread the next. Our way is safer. Though a peasant's life is not a fat one, it is a long one. We shall never grow rich, but we shall always have enough to eat.'

The elder sister said sneeringly:

'Enough? Yes, if you like to share with the pigs and the calves! What do you know of elegance or manners! However much your goodman may slave, you will die as you are living – on a dung heap – and your children the same.'

'Well, what of that?' replied the younger. 'Of course our work is rough and coarse. But, on the other hand, it is sure; and we need not bow to anyone. But you, in your towns, are surrounded by temptations; today all may be right, but tomorrow the Evil One may tempt your husband with cards, wine, or women, and all will go to ruin. Don't such things happen often enough?'

Pahom, the master of the house, was lying on the top of the oven, and he listened to the women's chatter.

'It is perfectly true,' thought he. 'Busy as we are from childhood tilling mother earth, we peasants have no time to let any nonsense settle in our heads. Our only trouble is that we haven't land enough. If I had plenty of land, I shouldn't fear the Devil himself!'

The women finished their tea, chatted a while about dress, and then cleared away the tea-things and lay down to sleep.

But the Devil had been sitting behind the oven, and had heard all that was said. He was pleased that the peasant's wife had led her husband into boasting, and that he had said that if he had plenty of land he would not fear the Devil himself.

'All right,' thought the Devil. 'We will have a tussle. I'll give you land enough; and by means of that land I will get you into my power.'

II

CLOSE TO the village there lived a lady, a small landowner, who had an estate of about three hundred acres.* She had always lived on good terms with the peasants, until she engaged as her steward an old soldier, who took to burdening the people with fines. However careful Pahom tried to be, it happened again and again that now a horse of his got among the lady's oats, now a cow strayed into her garden, now his calves found their way into her meadows – and he always had to pay a fine.

Pahom paid up, but grumbled, and, going home in a temper, was rough with his family. All through that summer, Pahom had much trouble because of this steward; and he was even glad when winter came and the cattle had to be stabled. Though he grudged the fodder when they could no longer

---

* 120 *desyatins*. The *desyatina* is properly 2.7 acres; but in this story round numbers are used.

graze on the pastureland, at least he was free from anxiety about them.

In the winter the news got about that the lady was going to sell her land, and that the keeper of the inn on the high road was bargaining for it. When the peasants heard this they were very much alarmed.

'Well,' thought they, 'if the inn-keeper gets the land, he will worry us with fines worse than the lady's steward. We all depend on that estate.'

So the peasants went on behalf of their Commune, and asked the lady not to sell the land to the inn-keeper; offering her a better price for it themselves. The lady agreed to let them have it. Then the peasants tried to arrange for the Commune to buy the whole estate, so that it might be held by them all in common. They met twice to discuss it, but could not settle the matter; the Evil One sowed discord among them, and they could not agree. So they decided to buy the land individually, each according to his means; and the lady agreed to this plan as she had to the other.

Presently Pahom heard that a neighbour of his was buying fifty acres, and that the lady had consented to accept one-half in cash and to wait a year for the other half. Pahom felt envious.

'Look at that,' thought he, 'the land is all being sold, and I shall get none of it.' So he spoke to his wife.

'Other people are buying,' said he, 'and we must also buy twenty acres or so. Life is becoming impossible. That steward is simply crushing us with his fines.'

So they put their heads together and considered how they could manage to buy it. They had one hundred rubles laid by. They sold a colt, and one-half of their bees; hired out one of their sons as a labourer, and took his wages in advance; borrowed the rest from a brother-in-law, and so scraped together half the purchase money.

Having done this, Pahom chose out a farm of forty acres, some of it wooded, and went to the lady to bargain for it. They came to an agreement, and he shook hands with her upon it, and paid her a deposit in advance. Then they went to town and signed the deeds; he paying half the price down, and undertaking to pay the remainder within two years.

So now Pahom had land of his own. He borrowed seed, and sowed it on the land he had bought. The harvest was a good one, and within a year he had managed to pay off his debts both to the lady and to his brother-in-law. So he became a landowner, ploughing and sowing his own land, making hay on his own land, cutting his own trees, and feeding his cattle on his own pasture. When he went out to plough his fields, or to look at his growing corn, or at his grass-meadows, his heart would fill with joy. The grass that grew and the flowers that bloomed there, seemed to him unlike any that grew elsewhere. Formerly, when he had passed by that land, it had appeared the same as any other land, but now it seemed quite different.

III

SO PAHOM was well-contented, and everything would have been right if the neighbouring peasants would only not have trespassed on his corn-fields and meadows. He appealed to them most civilly, but they still went on: now the Communal herdsmen would let the village cows stray into his meadows; then horses from the night pasture would get among his corn. Pahom turned them out again and again, and forgave their owners, and for a long time he forbore from prosecuting anyone. But at last he lost patience and complained to the District Court. He knew it was the peasants' want of land, and no evil intent on their part, that caused the trouble; but he thought:

'I cannot go on overlooking it, or they will destroy all I have. They must be taught a lesson.'

So he had them up, gave them one lesson, and then another, and two or three of the peasants were fined. After a time Pahom's neighbours began to bear him a grudge for this, and would now and then let their cattle onto his land on purpose. One peasant even got into Pahom's wood at night and cut down five young lime trees for their bark. Pahom passing through the wood one day noticed something white. He came nearer, and saw the stripped trunks lying on the ground, and close by stood the stumps, where the trees had been. Pahom was furious.

'If he had only cut one here and there it would have been bad enough,' thought Pahom, 'but the rascal has actually cut down a whole clump. If I could only find out who did this, I would pay him out.'

He racked his brains as to who it could be. Finally he decided: 'It must be Simon – no one else could have done it.' So he went to Simon's homestead to have a look round, but he found nothing, and only had an angry scene. However, he now felt more certain than ever that Simon had done it, and he lodged a complaint. Simon was summoned. The case was tried, and re-tried, and at the end of it all Simon was acquitted, there being no evidence against him. Pahom felt still more aggrieved, and let his anger loose upon the Elder and the Judges.

'You let thieves grease your palms,' said he. 'If you were honest folk yourselves, you would not let a thief go free.'

So Pahom quarrelled with the Judges and with his neighbours. Threats to burn his building began to be uttered. So though Pahom had more land, his place in the Commune was much worse than before.

About this time a rumour got about that many people were moving to new parts.

'There's no need for me to leave my land,' thought Pahom. 'But some of the others might leave our village, and then there would be more room for us. I would take over their land myself, and make my estate a bit bigger. I could then live more at ease. As it is, I am still too cramped to be comfortable.'

One day Pahom was sitting at home, when a peasant, passing through the village, happened to call in. He was allowed to stay the night, and supper was given him. Pahom had a talk with this peasant and asked him where he came from. The stranger answered that he came from beyond the Volga, where he had been working. One word led to another, and the man went on to say that many people were settling in those parts. He told how some people from his village had settled there. They had joined the Commune, and had had twenty-five acres per man granted them. The land was so good, he said, that the rye sown on it grew as high as a horse, and so thick that five cuts of a sickle made a sheaf. One peasant, he said, had brought nothing with him but his bare hands, and now he had six horses and two cows of his own.

Pahom's heart kindled with desire. He thought:

'Why should I suffer in this narrow hole, if one can live so well elsewhere? I will sell my land and my homestead here, and with the money I will start afresh over there and get everything new. In this crowded place one is always having trouble. But I must first go and find out all about it myself.'

Towards summer he got ready and started. He went down the Volga on a steamer to Samara, then walked another three hundred miles on foot, and at last reached the place. It was just as the stranger had said. The peasants had plenty of land: every man had twenty-five acres of Communal land given him for his use, and anyone who had money could buy, besides, at two shillings an acre* as much good freehold land as he wanted.

Having found out all he wished to know, Pahom returned home as autumn came on, and began selling off his belongings. He sold his land at a profit, sold his homestead and all his cattle, and withdrew from membership of the Commune. He only waited till the spring, and then started with his family for the new settlement.

IV

AS SOON AS Pahom and his family arrived at their new abode, he applied for admission into the Commune of a large village. He stood treat to the Elders, and obtained the necessary documents. Five shares of Communal land were given him for his own and his sons' use: that is to say – 125 acres (not all together, but in different fields) besides the use of the Communal pasture. Pahom put up the buildings he needed, and bought cattle. Of the Communal land alone he had three times as much as at his former home, and the land was good corn-land. He was ten times better off than he had been. He had plenty of arable land and pasturage, and could keep as many head of cattle as he liked.

At first, in the bustle of building and settling down, Pahom was pleased with it all, but when he got used to it he began to

* Three rubles per *desyatina*.

think that even here he had not enough land. The first year, he sowed wheat on his share of the Communal land, and had a good crop. He wanted to go on sowing wheat, but had not enough Communal land for the purpose, and what he had already used was not available; for in those parts wheat is only sown on virgin soil or on fallow land. It is sown for one or two years, and then the land lies fallow till it is again overgrown with prairie grass. There were many who wanted such land, and there was not enough for all; so that people quarrelled about it. Those who were better off wanted it for growing wheat, and those who were poor wanted it to let to dealers, so that they might raise money to pay their taxes. Pahom wanted to sow more wheat; so he rented land from a dealer for a year. He sowed much wheat and had a fine crop, but the land was too far from the village – the wheat had to be carted more than ten miles. After a time Pahom noticed that some peasant-dealers were living on separate farms, and were growing wealthy; and he thought:

'If I were to buy some freehold land, and have a homestead on it, it would be a different thing altogether. Then it would all be nice and compact.'

The question of buying freehold land recurred to him again and again.

He went on in the same way for three years: renting land and sowing wheat. The seasons turned out well and the crops were good, so that he began to lay money by. He might have gone on living contentedly, but he grew tired of having to rent other people's land every year, and having to scramble for it. Wherever there was good land to be had, the peasants would rush for it and it was taken up at once, so that unless you were sharp about it you got none. It happened in the third year that he and a dealer together rented a piece of pasture-land from some peasants; and they had already ploughed it up, when there was some dispute, and the peasants went to law about it, and things fell out so that the labour was all lost.

'If it were my own land,' thought Pahom, 'I should be independent, and there would not be all this unpleasantness.'

So Pahom began looking out for land which he could buy; and he came across a peasant who had bought thirteen hundred acres, but having got into difficulties was willing to sell again cheap. Pahom bargained and haggled with him, and at last they settled the price at fifteen hundred rubles, part in cash and part to be paid later. They had all but clinched the matter, when a passing dealer happened to stop at Pahom's one day to get a feed for his horses. He drank tea with Pahom, and they had a talk. The dealer said that he was just returning from the land of the Bashkirs, far away, where he had bought thirteen thousand acres of land, all for a thousand rubles. Pahom questioned him further, and the tradesman said:

'All one need do is to make friends with the chiefs. I gave away about one hundred rubles' worth of dressing-gowns and carpets, besides a case of tea, and I gave wine to those who would drink it; and I got the land for less than twopence an acre.* And he showed Pahom the title-deeds, saying:

'The land lies near a river, and the whole prairie is virgin soil.'

Pahom plied him with questions, and the tradesman said:

'There is more land there than you could cover if you walked a year, and it all belongs to the Bashkirs. They are as simple as sheep, and land can be got almost for nothing.'

'There now,' thought Pahom, 'with my one thousand rubles, why should I get only thirteen hundred acres, and saddle myself with a debt besides?. If I take it out there, I can get more than ten times as much for the money.'

V

PAHOM INQUIRED how to get to the place, and as soon as the tradesman had left him, he prepared to go there himself. He left his wife to look after the homestead, and started on his journey taking his man with him. They stopped at a town on their way, and bought a case of tea, some wine, and other presents, as the tradesman had advised. On and on they went until they had gone more than three hundred miles, and on the seventh day they came to a place where the Bashkirs had pitched their tents. It was all just as the tradesman had said. The people lived

---

* Five kopeks for a *desyatina*.

on the steppes, by a river, in *kibitkas*.* They neither tilled the ground, nor ate bread. Their cattle and horses grazed in herds on the steppe. The colts were tethered behind the tents, and the mares were driven to them twice a day. The mares were milked, and from the milk kumiss was made. It was the women who prepared kumiss, and they also made cheese. As far as the men were concerned, drinking kumiss and tea, eating mutton, and playing on their pipes, was all they cared about. They were all stout and merry, and all the summer long they never thought of doing any work. They were quite ignorant, and knew no Russian, but were good-natured enough.

As soon as they saw Pahom, they came out of their tents and gathered round their visitor. An interpreter was found, and Pahom told them he had come about some land. The Bashkirs seemed very glad; they took Pahom and led him into one of the best tents, where they made him sit on some down cushions placed on a carpet, while they sat round him. They gave him tea and kumiss, and had a sheep killed, and gave him mutton to eat. Pahom took presents out of his cart and distributed them among the Bashkirs, and divided amongst them the tea. The Bashkirs were delighted. They talked a great deal among themselves, and then told the interpreter to translate.

'They wish to tell you,' said the interpreter, 'that they like

---

* A *kibitka* is a movable dwelling made up of detachable wooden frames, forming a round, and covered over with felt.

you, and that it is our custom to do all we can to please a guest and to repay him for his gifts. You have given us presents, now tell us which of the things we possess please you best, that we may present them to you.'

'What pleases me best here,' answered Pahom, 'is your land. Our land is crowded, and the soil is exhausted; but you have plenty of land and it is good land. I never saw the like of it.'

The interpreter translated. The Bashkirs talked among themselves for a while. Pahom could not understand what they were saying, but saw that they were much amused, and that they shouted and laughed. Then they were silent and looked at Pahom while the interpreter said:

'They wish me to tell you that in return for your presents they will gladly give you as much land as you want. You have only to point it out with your hand and it is yours.'

The Bashkirs talked again for a while and began to dispute. Pahom asked what they were disputing about, and the interpreter told him that some of them thought they ought to ask their Chief about the land and not act in his absence, while others thought there was no need to wait for his return.

VI

WHILE THE Bashkirs were disputing, a man in a large fox-fur cap appeared on the scene. They all became silent and rose to their feet. The interpreter said, 'This is our Chief himself.'

Pahom immediately fetched the best dressing-gown and five pounds of tea, and offered these to the Chief. The Chief accepted them, and seated himself in the place of honour. The Bashkirs at once began telling him something. The Chief listened for a while, then made a sign with his head for them to be silent, and addressing himself to Pahom, said in Russian:

'Well, let it be so. Choose whatever piece of land you like; we have plenty of it.'

'How can I take as much as I like?' thought Pahom. 'I must get a deed to make it secure, or else they may say, "It is yours," and afterwards may take it away again.'

'Thank you for your kind words,' he said aloud. 'You have much land, and I only want a little. But I should like to be sure which bit is mine. Could it not be measured and made over to me? Life and death are in God's hands. You good people give it to me, but your children might wish to take it away again.'

'You are quite right,' said the Chief. 'We will make it over to you.'

'I heard that a dealer had been here,' continued Pahom, 'and that you gave him a little land, too, and signed title-deeds to that effect. I should like to have it done in the same way.'

The Chief understood.

'Yes,' replied he, 'that can be done quite easily. We have a scribe, and we will go to town with you and have the deed properly sealed.'

'And what will be the price?' asked Pahom.

'Our price is always the same: one thousand rubles a day.'

Pahom did not understand.

'A day? What measure is that? How many acres would that be?'

'We do not know how to reckon it out,' said the Chief. 'We sell it by the day. As much as you can go round on your feet in a day is yours, and the price is one thousand rubles a day.'

Pahom was surprised.

'But in a day you can get round a large tract of land,' he said.

The Chief laughed.

'It will all be yours!' said he. 'But there is one condition: If you don't return on the same day to the spot whence you started, your money is lost.'

'But how am I to mark the way that I have gone?'

'Why, we shall go to any spot you like, and stay there. You must start from that spot and make your round, taking a spade with you. Wherever you think necessary, make a mark. At every turning, dig a hole and pile up the turf; then afterwards we will go round with a plough from hole to hole. You may make as large a circuit as you please, but before the sun sets you must return to the place you started from. All the land you cover will be yours.'

Pahom was delighted. It was decided to start early next morning. They talked a while, and after drinking some more kumiss and eating some more mutton, they had tea again, and then the night came on. They gave Pahom a feather-bed to sleep on, and the Bashkirs dispersed for the night, promising to assemble the next morning at daybreak and ride out before sunrise to the appointed spot.

VII

PAHOM LAY on the feather-bed, but could not sleep. He kept thinking about the land.

'What a large tract I will mark off!' thought he. 'I can easily do thirty-five miles in a day. The days are long now, and within a circuit of thirty-five miles what a lot of land there will be! I will sell the poorer land, or let it to peasants, but I'll pick out the best and farm it. I will buy two ox-teams, and hire two more labourers. About a hundred and fifty acres shall be plough-land, and I will pasture cattle on the rest.'

Pahom lay awake all night, and dozed off only just before dawn. Hardly were his eyes closed when he had a dream. He thought he was lying in that same tent, and heard somebody chuckling outside. He wondered who it could be, and rose and went out, and he saw the Bashkir Chief sitting in front of the tent holding his sides and rolling about with laughter. Going nearer to the Chief, Pahom asked: 'What are you laughing at?' But he saw that it was no longer the Chief, but the dealer who had recently stopped at his house and had told him about the land. Just as Pahom was going to ask, 'Have you been here long?' he saw that it was not the dealer, but the peasant who had come up from the Volga, long ago, to Pahom's old home. Then he saw that it was not the peasant either, but the Devil himself with hoofs and horns, sitting there and chuckling, and before him lay a man barefoot, prostrate on the ground, with only trousers and a shirt on. And Pahom dreamt that he looked more attentively to see what sort of a man it was that was lying there, and he saw that the man was dead, and that it was himself! He awoke horror-struck.

'What things one does dream,' thought he.

Looking round he saw through the open door that the dawn was breaking.

'It's time to wake them up,' thought he. 'We ought to be starting.'

He got up, roused his man (who was sleeping in his cart), bade him harness; and went to call the Bashkirs.

'It's time to go to the steppe to measure the land,' he said.

The Bashkirs rose and assembled, and the Chief came too.

Then they began drinking kumiss again, and offered Pahom some tea, but he would not wait.

'If we are to go, let us go. It is high time,' said he.

VIII

THE BASHKIRS got ready and they all started: some mounted on horses, and some in carts. Pahom drove in his own small cart with his servant, and took a spade with him. When they reached the steppe, the morning red was beginning to kindle. They ascended a hillock (called by the Bashkirs a *shikhan*) and dismounting from their carts and their horses, gathered in one spot. The Chief came up to Pahom and stretching out his arm towards the plain:

'See,' said he, 'all this, as far as your eye can reach, is ours. You may have any part of it you like.'

Pahom's eyes glistened: it was all virgin soil, as flat as the palm of your hand, as black as the seed of a poppy, and in the hollows different kinds of grasses grew breast high.

The Chief took off his fox-fur cap, placed it on the ground and said:

'This will be the mark. Start from here, and return here again. All the land you go round shall be yours.'

Pahom took out his money and put it on the cap. Then he took off his outer coat, remaining in his sleeveless under-coat.

He unfastened his girdle and tied it tight below his stomach, put a little bag of bread into the breast of his coat, and tying a flask of water to his girdle, he drew up the tops of his boots, took the spade from his man, and stood ready to start. He considered for some moments which way he had better go – it was tempting everywhere.

'No matter,' he concluded, 'I will go towards the rising sun.'

He turned his face to the east, stretched himself, and waited for the sun to appear above the rim.

'I must lose no time,' he thought, 'and it is easier walking while it is still cool.'

The sun's rays had hardly flashed above the horizon, before Pahom, carrying the spade over his shoulder, went down into the steppe.

Pahom started walking neither slowly nor quickly. After having gone a thousand yards he stopped, dug a hole, and placed pieces of turf one on another to make it more visible. Then he went on; and now that he had walked off his stiffness he quickened his pace. After a while he dug another hole.

Pahom looked back. The hillock could be distinctly seen in the sunlight, with the people on it, and the glittering tyres of the cart-wheels. At a rough guess Pahom concluded that he had walked three miles. It was growing warmer; he took off his under-coat, flung it across his shoulder, and went on again. It had grown quite warm now; he looked at the sun, it was time to think of breakfast.

'The first shift is done, but there are four in a day, and it is too soon yet to turn. But I will just take off my boots,' said he to himself.

He sat down, took off his boots, stuck them into his girdle, and went on. It was easy walking now.

'I will go on for another three miles,' thought he, 'and then turn to the left. This spot is so fine, that it would be a pity to lose it. The further one goes, the better the land seems.'

He went straight on for a while, and when he looked round, the hillock was scarcely visible and the people on it looked like black ants, and he could just see something glistening there in the sun.

'Ah,' thought Pahom, 'I have gone far enough in this direction, it is time to turn. Besides I am in a regular sweat, and very thirsty.'

He stopped, dug a large hole, and heaped up pieces of turf. Next he untied his flask, had a drink, and then turned sharply to the left. He went on and on; the grass was high, and it was very hot.

Pahom began to grow tired: he looked at the sun and saw that it was noon.

'Well,' he thought, 'I must have a rest.'

He sat down, and ate some bread and drank some water; but he did not lie down, thinking that if he did he might fall asleep. After sitting a little while, he went on again. At first he walked easily: the food had strengthened him; but it had become terribly hot, and he felt sleepy; still he went on, thinking: 'An hour to suffer, a lifetime to live.'

He went a long way in this direction also, and was about to turn to the left again, when he perceived a damp hollow: 'It would be a pity to leave that out,' he thought. 'Flax would do well there.' So he went on past the hollow, and dug a hole on the other side of it before he turned the comer. Pahom looked towards the hillock. The heat made the air hazy: it seemed to be quivering, and through the haze the people on the hillock could scarcely be seen.

'Ah!' thought Pahom, 'I have made the sides too long; I must make this one shorter.' And he went along the third side, stepping faster. He looked at the sun: it was nearly halfway to the horizon, and he had not yet done two miles of the third side of the square. He was still ten miles from the goal.

'No,' he thought, 'though it will make my land lopsided, I must hurry back in a straight line now. I might go too far, and as it is I have a great deal of land.'

So Pahom hurriedly dug a hole, and turned straight towards the hillock.

IX

PAHOM WENT straight towards the hillock, but he now walked with difficulty. He was done up with the heat, his bare feet were cut and bruised, and his legs began to fail. He longed to rest, but it was impossible if he meant to get back before sunset. The sun waits for no man, and it was sinking lower and lower.

'Oh dear,' he thought, 'if only I have not blundered trying for too much! What if I am too late?'

He looked towards the hillock and at the sun. He was still far from his goal, and the sun was already near the rim.

Pahom walked on and on; it was very hard walking, but he went quicker and quicker. He pressed on, but was still far from the place. He began running, threw away his coat, his boots, his flask, and his cap, and kept only the spade which he used as a support.

'What shall I do?' he thought again. 'I have grasped too much, and ruined the whole affair. I can't get there before the sun sets.'

And this fear made him still more breathless. Pahom went on running, his soaking shirt and trousers stuck to him, and his mouth was parched. His breast was working like a blacksmith's bellows, his heart was beating like a hammer, and his legs were giving way as if they did not belong to him. Pahom was seized with terror lest he should die of the strain.

Though afraid of death, he could not stop. 'After having run all that way they will call me a fool if I stop now,' thought he. And he ran on and on, and drew near and heard the Bashkirs yelling and shouting to him, and their cries inflamed his heart still more. He gathered his last strength and ran on.

The sun was close to the rim, and cloaked in mist looked large, and red as blood. Now, yes now, it was about to set! The sun was quite low, but he was also quite near his aim. Pahom could already see the people on the hillock waving their arms to hurry him up. He could see the fox-fur cap on the ground, and the money on it, and the Chief sitting on the ground holding his sides. And Pahom remembered his dream.

'There is plenty of land,' thought he, 'but will God let me live on it? I have lost my life, I have lost my life! I shall never reach that spot!'

Pahom looked at the sun, which had reached the earth: one side of it had already disappeared. With all his remaining strength he rushed on, bending his body forward so that his legs could hardly follow fast enough to keep him from falling. Just as he reached the hillock it suddenly grew dark. He looked up – the sun had already set! He gave a cry: 'All my labour has been in vain,' thought he, and was about to stop, but he heard the Bash-kirs still shouting, and remembered that though to him, from below, the sun seemed to have set, they on the hillock could still see it. He took a long breath and ran up the hillock. It was still light there. He reached the top and saw the cap. Before it sat the Chief laughing and holding his sides. Again Pahom remembered his dream, and he uttered a cry: his legs gave way beneath him, he fell forward and reached the cap with his hands.

'Ah, that's a fine fellow!' exclaimed the Chief. 'He has gained much land!'

Pahom's servant came running up and tried to raise him, but he saw that blood was flowing from his mouth. Pahom was dead!

The Bashkirs clicked their tongues to show their pity.

His servant picked up the spade and dug a grave long enough for Pahom to lie in, and buried him in it. Six feet from his head to his heels was all he needed.